MW01135726

PRAISE FO

"Flynn is an excellent storyteller." — *Booklist*

"Flynn propels his plot with potent but flexible force."
— *Publishers Weekly*

The President's Henchman
"Marvelously entertaining." — *ForeWord Magazine*

Digger
"A mystery cloaked as cleverly as (and perhaps better than) any John Grisham work." — *Denver Post*

"Surefooted, suspenseful and in its breathless final moments unexpectedly heartbreaking." — *Booklist*

The Next President
"*The Next President* bears favorable comparison to such classics as *The Best Man, Advise and Consent* and *The Manchurian Candidate.*"
— *Booklist*

"A thriller fast enough to read in one sitting."
— *Rocky Mountain News*

The Big Fix

Joseph Flynn

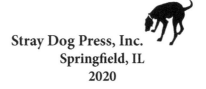

Stray Dog Press, Inc.
Springfield, IL
2020

BY JOSEPH FLYNN

The Jim McGill Series

The President's Henchman, A Jim McGill Novel [#1]
The Hangman's Companion, A JimMcGill Novel [#2]
The K Street Killer, A JimMcGill Novel [#3]
Part 1: The Last Ballot Cast, A JimMcGill Novel [#4 Part 1]
Part 2: The Last Ballot Cast, A JimMcGill Novel [#5 Part 2]
The Devil on the Doorstep, A Jim McGill Novel [#6]
The Good Guy with a Gun, A Jim McGill Novel [#7]
The Echo of the Whip, A Jim McGill Novel [#8]
The Daddy's Girl Decoy, A Jim McGill Novel [#9]
The Last Chopper Out, A Jim McGill Novel [#10]
The King of Mirth, A Jim McGill Novel [#11]
The Big Fix, A Jim McGill Novel [#12]

McGill's Short Cases 1-3

The Ron Ketchum Mystery Series

Nailed, A Ron Ketchum Mystery [#1]
Defiled, A Ron Ketchum Mystery Featuring John Tall Wolf [#2]
Impaled, A Ron Ketchum Mystery [#3]

The John Tall Wolf Series

Tall Man in Ray-Bans, A John Tall Wolf Novel [#1]
War Party, A John Tall Wolf Novel [#2]
Super Chief, A John Tall Wolf Novel [#3]
Smoke Signals, A John Tall Wolf Novel [#4]
Big Medicine, A John Tall Wolf Novel [#5]
Powwow in Paris, A John Tall Wolf Novel [#6]

The Zeke Edison Series

Kill Me Twice, A Zeke Edison Novel [#1]

Stand Alone Novels

The Concrete Inquisition
Digger
The Next President
Hot Type
Farewell Performance
Gasoline, Texas
Round Robin, A Love Story of Epic Proportions
One False Step
Blood Street Punx
Still Coming
Still Coming Expanded Edition
Hangman — A Western Novella
Pointy Teeth, Twelve Bite-Size Stories

DEDICATION

Mary Foy and all her clan.

Published by Stray Dog Press, Inc.
Springfield, IL 62704, U.S.A.

Visit the author's web site: *www.josephflynn.com*

Flynn, Joseph
The Big Fix / Joseph Flynn
397 p.
ISBN 978-0-9977506-1-4 trade paper
ISBN 978-0-9977506-0-7 eBook

Printed in the United States of America

PUBLISHER'S NOTE
This is a work of fiction. Names, characters, places, and incidents are either the product of the author's imagination or are used fictitiously; any resemblance to actual persons, living or dead, events, or locales is entirely coincidental.

Book design by Aha! Designs
Photo courtesy of istockphoto.com

ACKNOWLEDGEMENTS

Catherine, Cat, Anne, Susan and Meghan do their level best to catch all my typos and other mistakes, but I usually outwit them. For this book, I've added the efforts of my Advance Reading Team. I thank them for their input and interest. Please be kind, if one or two tiny errors remain.

AL
Reader Discretion Advised
Contains Adult Language

CHARACTER LIST

[in alphabetical order by last name]
Aidan Behan, Detective, MPD, Washington, D.C.
Abra Benjamin, FBI Director
Ellie Booker, freelance reporter/producer
Ibrahim Boutros, Major General in Jordanian Air Force
Rockelle Bullard, Washington D.C. Mayor
Edwina Byington, Patti's personal secretary
Hugh Collier, CEO of WWN
Celsus Crogher, CEO, Crogher Personal Protection
Byron DeWitt, former Deputy Director, FBI; now President Morrissey's husband
Carolyn [McGill] Enquist, first wife of Jim McGill; mother of Abbie, Kenny and Caitie
Lily Kealoha, Detective First Grade, NYPD
Donald "Deke" Ky, partner in McGill Investigations
Daphna Levy, Secret Service Special Agent
Leo Levy, Jim McGill's personal driver
Abbie McGill, oldest daughter of Jim McGill and his first wife
Caitie McGill, youngest daughter of Jim McGill and his first wife
Jim McGill, CEO, McGill Investigations
Kenny McGill, son of Jim McGill and his first wife
Patti [Grant] McGill, former President, head of Committed Capital
Marvin Meeker, principal in M&W Private Investigations
Galia Mindel, White House Chief of Staff for President Morrissey
Jean Morrissey, President
Constance Parker, lottery winner
Nelda Reed, parking enforcement officer
Dalton Rivers, Detective Sergeant, Maryland State Police
Putnam Shady, lawyer, husband of Margaret Sweeney
Margaret "Sweetie" Sweeney, McGill's longtime friend and conscience
Esme Thrice, administrative director, McGill Investigations
Lonnie Tompkins, member of the State Department's Diplomatic Security Service
Cale Tucker, employee of Committed Capital

Character List [continued]

Michael Walker [aka Beemer], principal in M&W Private Investigations
Aria and Callista Yates, Kira and Welborn's twin daughters
Kira Yates, wife of Welborn Yates
Welborn Yates, Lieutenant General, USAF

CHAPTER 1

Friday, February 1, 2019
McGill Investigations International — Washington, DC

Jim McGill and Margaret "Sweetie" Sweeney sat in the main conference room of their detective agency's headquarters building. McGill occupied the seat at the head of the table; Sweetie sat to his right. All the other chairs at the table were vacant at the moment. McGill had offered Sweetie the opportunity to take the top spot any time she wanted it, whether it was just the two of them in the room or the whole gang was there.

The gang being the partners from the offices around the country and the trio of partners from the Paris office: Yves Pruet, Gabbi Casale, and Odo Sacripant.

The only times Sweetie had accepted McGill's offer of taking the pride of place at the table was whenever there was a question of personal or professional conduct to discuss. She was the company's chief ethics officer. *The Washington Post* had heard of her job and asked Sweetie to do an interview on the subject of moral business conduct for its Labor Day 2018 edition. Her initial impulse had been to deny the request.

"Who am I to preach to anybody?" she'd asked McGill.

"You've already decided to spread the gospel right here," he'd replied.

"Sure, but that's just to a gaggle of gumshoes who sometimes need to be reminded of their manners and to make sure we don't have to settle a suit or put up bail money for an employee. Either of those things might embarrass both of us."

McGill had grinned. "You know better than most that I don't embarrass easily."

Besides having McGill's blessing on doing the Post interview, Sweetie's husband, Putnam Shady, and their daughter, Maxi, had urged her to share her thoughts on the subject with the public. Maxi had clinched the matter when she'd said, "Mama, you might make someone's life better."

Putnam had put the cherry on top. "Maybe even several someones."

To show that no good deed went unpunished, Sweetie's ideas on ethical business conduct had been a hit with the newspaper's readers, several of whom worked in television and wanted Sweetie to appear on their shows. Neither Putnam nor Maxi could persuade her to do that. McGill knew better than to even try.

The matter facing the two managing partners that morning, however, had nothing to do with honest business behavior. Their focus was monetary, i.e. was the company keeping its head above water? The answer to that was almost an embarrassment for both of them.

McGill grinned at Sweetie and said, "It's not quite like we can print our own money, but it's not far from that either. Unless we're interrupted by the Second Coming, this should be the eighth straight quarter with a double-digit increase in both revenue and profit over the previous quarter."

"Crime pays, huh?" Sweetie asked, uneasy about becoming affluent in her own right.

There had once been a time when she'd taken a vow of poverty.

McGill said, "I can't speak for the criminal element, but putting things right for people who've been wronged seems to be a paying proposition."

"People who can afford us," Sweetie replied.

"We're still taking *pro bono* cases. That number has gone up, too. It's right there on the spreadsheet with all the others, if you want to take a look."

"Yeah, okay," Sweetie said without enthusiasm.

McGill asked Sweetie a question that had never even occurred to him before. "You have the blues about something, Margaret?"

Without being specific, he'd just asked if everything was all right at home.

Sweetie understood. "Putnam's wonderful, as always."

"He used to be more than a little bit of a rascal," McGill said, "until someone came along and showed him the light, the truth, and the way."

"Yeah, that was me, spoilsport that I am. There are actually times when I miss some of his old mischief. He's improved himself so much that sometimes I think I've gone too far."

McGill said, "I could give him a good talking-to about all his high-gloss rectitude, but how far should *I* go?"

Sweetie smiled. "Tell him wearing a leather motorcycle jacket would be okay, but nothing with chains."

McGill grinned and nodded. "Maxi's okay?"

"I know it'll be years before she goes off to college, but I'm dreading it already."

"All I can say to that is if I have grandchildren by then, I'll put your name in to babysit."

Sweetie's expression became so sad McGill feared her eyes might fill with tears, showing him a side of her he'd never seen before. But Esme Thrice saved the day by buzzing them.

"Yes, Esme?" McGill asked.

"Boss, Marvin Meeker and Michael Walker are downstairs with Dikki. They don't have an appointment, but they'd like to have a word with you if you have the time."

Dikki Missirian managed McGill's headquarters building.

Former Metro PD detectives Marvin Meeker and Big Mike Walker, aka Beemer, had retired from the police department not long ago and had opened their own, much smaller, private investigations firm.

"Is Rockelle Bullard with them?" McGill asked.

Out of the corner of an eye, McGill saw that Sweetie was paying close attention, her unusual moodiness gone for the moment. Rockelle Bullard had been a Metro PD captain and Meeker and Beemer's boss. She'd hoped to go on to become the chief of police. When that hadn't happened, she'd upped the ante and her energy and won the mayor's office.

After a moment's silence, Esme came back and said, "Sorry, Boss, it's just the detectives, no mayor. They say they've come to see if you'd like to collaborate on a case with them."

McGill heard Beemer's voice through the intercom. "We can pay you, too."

Meeker added, "Just not as much as you're used to."

McGill grinned and looked at Sweetie. "Come on up, guys. We'll see what kind of bargain you can drive with Ms. Sweeney."

While they waited, Sweetie told McGill, "You handle the financial stuff around here."

"Except for how much the firm donates to charity," McGill reminded her.

"Yeah. Even so, if there's any bargaining to do with Meeker and Beemer, you handle it."

"Okay. I do need your opinion, though, about opening new offices in Europe. Did you get a chance to read the analyses Patti's guy did for us?"

When McGill Investigations needed business expertise beyond the means of its in-house staff, McGill turned to his wife's venture capital firm, Committed Capital, for help. He paid the going rate, of course.

Sweetie said, "I did my best not to let my eyes glaze over."

"And?" McGill asked.

"London looks like a good business proposition. I think we should wait on Berlin. The money in Germany would be good, but the politics there look a little touchy."

McGill nodded. "I feel the same way. Be a helluva thing if

Europe went crazy all over again in the early years of another century."

Before that dark possibility could be discussed, Esme buzzed them again.

"Mr. Meeker and Mr. Walker are here," she said.

"Please show them in, Esme," McGill said. "Did you ask if they need refreshments?"

"Maybe some champagne later," McGill heard Meeker say. "You know, if we all wrap up this case."

"It's that big a deal?" Sweetie asked.

Esme opened the conference room door so the conversation could continue face to face.

"Yeah, it is," Beemer, said. "What we're talking about here is $212 million."

"Gives you an idea of why we came knockin'," Meeker added.

Gangplank Marina, Washington, DC

Located in the Southwest Waterfront neighborhood of Washington, DC, the Gangplank Marina was home to the Atlantic Seaboard's largest number of live-aboard residents, people who made their homes year-round on their watercraft. The marina had docking space for so-called super-yachts with lengths overall — meaning the length of a vessel's hull measured parallel to the waterline — of 300 feet.

Of course, there was a docking fee of $4 per foot per day for all vessels over 80 feet, but if you had the money to own a yacht, you didn't worry about plugging the parking meter.

Ellie Booker, former producer and on-air reporter for World-Wide News and PBS, owned a Hatteras M75 Panacera that measured only 74 feet and six inches. So she might have had to pay just $3 per foot per day to dock her vessel, but she'd chosen a monthly fee with an option to extend to an annual charge. Taking a long-term point of view was an exercise in optimism for Ellie. Except for making a

TV cameo to help destroy the presidential hopes of former Senate Leader Oren Worth, she'd abandoned Washington, DC and on-air appearances two years earlier, certain that her life was in danger.

Now, Ellie's outlook on the future was secure enough that she only thought *maybe* somebody was still trying to kill her. The possibility that she might be a target, though, had been the impetus for her to sleep inside a hull rather than a house. The cruising range of her motor yacht was 542 miles. That was far from transoceanic — which was all right with her as she had neither the skill nor the nerve to attempt a solo ocean crossing — but it still could put a big stretch of water between her and any landlocked assassin.

At least, that was her hope.

The reason Ellie had to run in the first place was that her relentless pursuit of the next great news story had finally brought her up against someone who would not simply be satisfied to take her to court for exposing their alleged criminal activity. Ellie had cut her teeth in investigative journalism by exposing thieves, not killers. So it had come as a jolt to face mortal rather than financial jeopardy.

The possible need to flee was the consequence of Ellie's decision to find out who had killed Congressman Philip Brock. He'd been a one-man political wrecking crew. His seeming goal had been to bring down the federal government. His first step would have been the assassination of former President Patricia Grant. Then he'd have sent Congress into a fatal tailspin by calling a Constitutional Convention. The resulting political war between the two major parties would have taken a wrecking ball to centuries of familiar governance. The partisans on both ends of the political spectrum would have ultimately resorted to bloodshed and the result would have been anarchy.

At the start of Ellie's search for Brock's killer, she had thought that finding the guilty party might well cause her to be regarded as a national hero, both for bringing the assassin's name to light and helping to save the Republic from destruction. Her name might even become immortal in the ranks of American journalism.

What a chump notion that had been.

The killer hadn't turned out to be an aggrieved lunatic American but a female foreign assassin, Dr. Hasna Kalil. She had killed Brock in revenge for the murder of her brother. Bahir Ben Kalil had been Brock's accomplice in the plot to kill Patti Grant.

That still made for a damn great story, but only if Ellie could live long enough to write it and bask in the resulting fame and fortune. The way things had turned out, though, Ellie had to abandon all hope of banner headlines that had anything to do with the late Congressman Brock or the Kalil siblings.

What she had to concentrate on up to that very moment was making sure her precious pink backside didn't get shredded. She was going to turn to James J. McGill for help with that task. He'd promised to help her the last time they'd talked. Before leaving the marina, she made sure her vessel, *Dangerous Dame,* was locked and the security system was armed.

So was Ellie. She carried a licensed and concealed handgun.

She figured it would be best just to drop in on McGill.

That always made it harder for someone to brush you off.

The White House — Washington, DC

Lieutenant General Welborn Yates, USAF, received a call at his West Wing office. The first thing he took note of was that neither President Jean Morrissey nor Chief of Staff Galia Mindel was beckoning him. That meant there was little likelihood of a national crisis situation. The call also wasn't from his wife, Kira. So she and their daughters, Aria and Callista, were probably going through their days without any trouble.

The caller ID simply said: East Wing.

There was only one person in that part of the building who would call him: Byron DeWitt, President Morrissey's husband. Unlike James J. McGill, DeWitt hadn't given himself a nickname. He'd once jokingly suggested he could be called The President's

Squeeze, but that idea didn't fly. He did get away with being the second presidential male spouse to dodge the title of First Gentleman. By way of compromise, he was allowed to use his former FBI title: deputy director.

Welborn answered the call using that courtesy. "Good morning, Mr. Deputy Director."

"Good morning, General Yates. Would you have a few minutes to spare? I'd like to see you in my office."

Welborn felt his scalp tingle. Since the departure of Patricia Grant as president, he'd wondered on a daily basis how long he'd continue to hold a job at the White House. He'd done a few investigative chores for Jean Morrissey, mostly double-checking FBI security clearances of people being considered for presidential appointments to the executive branch. Each one of those efforts simply confirmed that the FBI had gotten things right the first time around.

That being the case, Welborn thought another posting might be a welcome change. Only he wondered how well he'd fit back into the regular chain-of-command after a decade of working in the White House and being answerable only to the Commander-in-Chief. Any new superior might be eager to let him know that he would follow *their* orders and no one else's from now on. Welborn could understand that reality, but he was hardly looking forward to it.

"I'll be right there, sir," Welborn told DeWitt.

Walking at a brisk pace to the office that had once belonged to several First Ladies took only a few minutes. Welborn knocked on the door as DeWitt had declined the use of a secretary. The voice from inside the office said, "Enter."

Welborn did as he was told and saw that DeWitt was on the phone.

He pointed Welborn to a guest chair, and the general took it.

Continuing his call, DeWitt said, "I'm so happy for you and Rebecca, John. The grandparents, too, of course. Thank you so much for calling. I'll tell Jean as soon as she has an open moment in her calendar … No, I'm sure your boy won't be in college by then," DeWitt said with a laugh. He told the caller goodbye and looked at Welborn.

"That was John Tall Wolf. Have you met him?" DeWitt asked.

"No, sir. I've heard stories, but I haven't had that pleasure."

"John and his wife, Rebecca, just became parents of a little boy they've named Alan Tall Wolf after his great-great-grandfather, Alan White River, the most famous train thief in American history."

Welborn nodded and smiled. "My family and I have seen that Super Chief on a trip to Chicago. It was a moving experience for all of us."

After taking a beat to enjoy the moment, DeWitt said, "You must have an idea why I called you out of the blue."

Welborn nodded. "The president is too busy to give me the news in person. I'm getting a new job in the Air Force."

"Not necessarily and not right away if you'd care to stay on here," DeWitt said.

That news brought Welborn up short. "I'm sorry, sir. I don't understand."

"General, I need your word to hold what I'm about to tell you in complete confidence for at least the remainder of this year. Well, you certainly can tell your wife, but only if she promises not to tell anyone else."

"State secret, Mr. Deputy Director?"

"Political top secret. How's that?"

Welborn nodded. "More than good enough for me."

"Okay, here's the deal. The president has decided not to run for a second term. After that, who knows what might happen? The country might elect a *man* as president. Might even be from one of those conservative parties whose names escape me at the moment."

Byron DeWitt made jokes about his memory after suffering a stroke that had almost killed him. Whenever the situation suited him, he pleaded a gap in his recall.

Welborn spent a moment in silent contemplation.

"My guess," he finally said, "is that any new president of any party might want fresh blood in the White House all the way around."

"Most likely, yes," DeWitt said.

"So what you're giving me here is a good deal of advance notice regarding my job prospects," Welborn said.

"More than that," DeWitt said. "I've reviewed your record with the Grant administration. You've come a long way during your years in the White House. Maybe you've had a little tutelage from James J. McGill on top of your Air Force training. In any case, you're one fine investigator. You've also been groomed by circumstance to know how to work at the highest level of our government. So, if you're interested in a lateral transfer, albeit in the civilian sector, FBI Director Abra Benjamin has a senior job opening at the Bureau. She's reviewed your file at my request and thinks you might be a good man for the job."

Welborn blinked twice at the thought of such a career change.

DeWitt saw his guest was processing the idea, but he gave Welborn something more to think about anyway.

He said, "The only thing is, Abra will need to know your decision on or before the end of March."

Now, Welborn leaned forward. "I don't even have to interview?"

"There would be an informal introductory lunch, just the two of you. But as long you don't dribble soup on your tie, it's a pretty sure thing."

Welborn thought, if he had things right, the presidential fix was in.

Still, he said, "I think I should meet with Director Benjamin before either of us makes a decision."

"That's fine. Would you like me to set up a day and a time?"

That seemed like too much of a rush to Welborn. "Is there anything you can tell me about Director Benjamin and what it would be like to work for her?"

There was plenty DeWitt might have told Welborn, but he limited himself to saying, "She can be as tough as a migraine and more aggressive than a bill collector, but what matters most to her is getting the job done and done right."

"I'd have no trouble with any of that but … I have some leave time accrued. If the president doesn't need me, I'd like a week or two to think about this. Talk to my wife about it."

"Entirely reasonable. I'll keep the door open for you for the rest of this month. By then, if you're interested, we should set up a date for you to speak with Director Benjamin."

Welborn got to his feet and shook DeWitt's hand. "Thank you, Mr. Deputy Director."

There was a handwritten note from the president on Welborn's desk when he got back to his office: *I'll back whatever you decide to do. Just let me know. Jean.*

The unconditional support from the Commander-in-Chief made Welborn's heart swell with both pride and gratitude.

Oddly enough, it also made him think: I wonder how I'd fit in at McGill Investigations.

He decided to drop in on his informal mentor and have a chat.

McGill Investigations International — Washington, DC

Beemer took a small glassine envelope from an inner pocket of his suit coat and slid it across the conference room table. McGill moved it another foot in Sweetie's direction so she could get a good look, too. They glanced at the contents and then at each other.

Turning to Meeker and Beemer, McGill said, "It's a lottery ticket for the Grand Slam game."

"Is this the big winner?" Sweetie asked. "The $212 million jackpot you mentioned earlier?"

"It's a color copy, but you check the winning numbers," Meeker said, "that's exactly what you'll find out."

"So which one of you is the lucky guy?" McGill inquired.

The two former cops shook their heads, denying the acquisition of sudden wealth.

Beemer said, "Was my brother-in-law, Samuel J. MacCray."

"Sammy to those of us who know him personal," Meeker added.

McGill nodded. "Okay, congratulations to Sammy, but I don't think the two of you are here to ask Margaret and me to sleuth out a crackerjack money manager for the lucky guy."

He slid the envelope back to Beemer.

"Was only one big winner in the whole drawing," Meeker informed his hosts.

Sweetie said, "That makes it an even bigger windfall for Mr. MacCray. I'd be happy to recommend some very worthwhile charities for his consideration, but that's still not the problem, is it?"

Beemer shook his head. "No, ma'am. See, what got reported online already is that the winner, the *only* winner, lives up in Maryland. Sammy lives right here in DC."

McGill and Sweetie turned to face each other, understanding the problem now.

Turning back to his guests, McGill suggested, "Might be a mistake, probably a matter for a lawyer or ten."

Beemer said, "That's exactly what Sammy did. He went to his uncle, Dexter Wiles, Esquire. Dexter was the one who got Sammy to put his ticket in his safe-deposit box. Didn't want it to get lost or anything."

"Good idea," Sweetie said.

McGill nodded. He pulled the glassine envelope back to where he and Sweetie could take another look. Closer this time. Checking both sides.

"Looks mint to me," McGill said. "Any chance Sammy has either computer or printing skills? Maybe both."

"This copy doesn't even show a crease in the original ticket," Sweetie added. "Sammy didn't even put it in his wallet? How'd he carry it home, if that's what he did?"

"That was exactly what he did," Beemer said. "He bought the ticket and put it in his shirt pocket, took it home and put it in his dresser drawer. Sammy wears his clothes loose, so the ticket didn't get wrinkled on the way home."

"Sammy's heavyset?" McGill asked.

Both of the visitors grinned.

Meeker said, "Yeah, he weighs in pretty good. Sorta like Schwarzenegger when he was young."

"So, he's a bodybuilder," Sweetie said. "World-class?"

Beemer replied, "Sammy doesn't compete. He just made himself strong when he was young so he wouldn't get beaten up or worse while he was incarcerated."

"What'd he do to get locked up?" McGill asked.

"Defended himself, only he got too enthusiastic about it," Beemer said. "A neighborhood guy about twice Sammy's original size ragged on him something fierce, calling him names, giving him pushes and shoves, little smacks upside the back of his head. Daring him to show he was a man and fight back."

"So he did," Sweetie said. "Let me guess how he started it: with a kick right where the bully wouldn't be able to raise any more jerks just like him."

The two former Metro cops looked at each other.

"Don't she talk nice?" Meeker asked his partner.

Beemer said, "Sure does."

"So Sammy did juvenile time?" McGill asked. "How much?"

"A year," Meeker said.

"Sounds light," Sweetie said.

Beemer smiled. "Dexter Wiles out-lawyered the State's Attorney. The prosecutor brought the former tough guy into court to show all the damage done to him, and it was considerable. But when Dexter asked the judge to have the two boys stand side by side, everybody saw who the heavyweight was. Some people in the court laughed out loud right then. One or two even cheered Sammy. The judge put a stop to all that, but even he was smiling a bit. Then Dexter took testimony from a dozen witnesses about how the bully had ragged on Sammy all the time. After that, things were pretty much settled."

Meeker continued the story. "The judge knocked the aggravated battery count down to simple battery. He said if Sammy had stopped after that first kick, he'd have let him go, but with all the other damage he did, that earned him a year at a youth facility."

"No legal trouble since then?" McGill asked.

Meeker and Beemer shook their heads.

Sweetie wondered about something else. "Does Sammy play the lottery regularly? He didn't just happen to feel lucky this one time?"

Beemer said, "He buys one ticket every week. Says he never really expects to win but he's willing to be pleasantly surprised."

"Let me guess," McGill said. "You two guys think you could find out what's going on here all on your own, don't you?"

The former Metro cops nodded in unison.

"But Mr. Wiles, being the shrewd attorney that he is, decided it wouldn't hurt to have someone with, let's say, a slightly higher public profile involved."

Beemer said, "Yeah, that's what Dexter said."

Meeker asked with a straight face, "Your rep *is* bigger than ours, right?"

"Only because I married well," McGill told them.

Sweetie rolled her eyes.

Before the conversation could go any further, Esme buzzed the conference room and said, "Boss, sorry to interrupt, but this must be a drop-in day. General Welborn Yates and Ms. Ellie Booker are here to see you."

Sweetie told Meeker and Beemer, "See, people are breaking down our doors to hire us."

"Who do you want first?" Esme asked.

"Who arrived first?" McGill parried.

"The same elevator brought them both."

"Do a coin flip," McGill told Esme.

Then he turned to Beemer. "What's your brother-in-law Sammy do for a living?"

Beemer said, "Sells Ford SUVs. Guy who owns the dealership spent some time inside a cell himself. So he's good on giving people second chances. Doesn't ever give anybody a third chance, though."

McGill nodded. "Reasonable. I have to think Sammy's also good to his wife or you guys wouldn't be here."

"Exactly," Meeker said.

McGill exchanged a look with Sweetie. That was all they needed.

"Okay," he said, "we'll take the case, but not as window dressing. We'll all share the actual investigative work; all of us will consult with each other as necessary."

Meeker turned to Beemer. "Told you he'd say that."

"And I told you," Beemer replied, "we'd do the same in his place." To McGill, Beemer added, "What kind of fees we talkin' here?"

"Is Mr. MacCray good at selling Fords?" McGill asked.

"Brings in a tick over six figures in a good year," Meeker said.

"Any kids?" McGill asked.

"One on the way," Beemer replied.

Sweetie slipped a Post-It Note to McGill with a per-day number on it.

He nodded and forwarded it to Beemer. The two visiting detectives took a look.

"That's *real* fair," Beemer said.

Meeker looked like he thought the fee was too good.

As if to prove him right, Sweetie said, "One more thing. If Mr. MacCray is held to be the legitimate winner of the lottery jackpot or even half of it, he'll make a donation equal to five percent of his gross winnings to a charity of McGill Investigations' choosing."

McGill hadn't thought of that, but he liked the idea and added, "That would reflect well on Mr. MacCray. Probably help him sell more Fords, should he continue in that line of work."

Meeker said, "We were thinking he might open his own dealership, but you make a smart point how the boy could generate some goodwill for himself."

Beemer added, "It's a deal."

***

Rather than keep anyone waiting, McGill asked Esme to send Ellie Booker in to see him while Sweetie spoke with Welborn Yates in her office. Ellie extended her hand to McGill, and he shook it, taking his time before letting it go.

Never one to be a shrinking violet, Ellie asked, "You checking me out, Mr. McGill?"

"Yeah, exactly," McGill said. "Please turn around."

"What?"

"Nothing personal, at least not in the way you might think."

Ellie grunted and did as she was asked.

While facing away from McGill, she asked, "Everything good? Buns firm, thighs toned?"

McGill ignored the questions, only saying, "Please take a seat."

Ellie took the chair that Sweetie had occupied, putting herself at McGill's right hand.

"What was *that* all about?" she asked.

McGill took his seat and said, "Without leaving any fingerprints, I was doing my best to see if you might be recording this conversation."

Ellie laughed. "Well, thanks for not groping me, but I'm not here to get a story."

"No?" Then it hit McGill. "You want to hire me?"

"Yeah, if that's okay. If you're not already tied up with something else."

"You saw the two men who left just before you came in here?"

Ellie nodded. "Looked like cops to me. Metro PD? I'll be good and not ask what they wanted. But I thought maybe they were here to see if you're hiring."

"You got the first part right," McGill said. "They *were* Metro PD, but now they're retired. Anything beyond that is confidential."

Ellie grinned. "Damn, I love secrets. Most of the time they're not worth going to the trouble of hiding whatever it is, but other times you can learn something really juicy or even crucial to the public interest."

"So how have *you* been, Ellie?" McGill asked.

"Cutting straight to the chase?" she asked. "As in what brings me here."

McGill nodded.

"Well, for one thing, a couple years back, you promised to help me with a certain matter. But you never got around to lending a hand."

McGill said, "Family comes first, and then you were gone. After several months, I figured you'd worked things out for yourself."

"That or maybe somebody planted me. You know, right next to Jimmy Hoffa."

A moment of pain flashed in McGill's eyes. It was barely a glimmer, but Ellie spotted it. "That idea did occur to you," she said. "And you didn't take it lightly."

McGill said, "You're not family, and any past relationship we had was more an exchange of favors than actual friendship. But I didn't like to think that ..."

"Somebody had croaked me?"

"Yeah."

"Would that have made you feel bad?"

"Bad but not guilty," McGill told her.

"How'd you deal with the bad part?"

"I told myself you could probably fall into a pit of vipers, and you'd knot them all together, make a rope ladder, and climb out of the hole."

Ellie grinned. "Yeah, but that'd just be professional courtesy on the snakes' part."

McGill smiled and asked, "What can I do for you, Ellie?"

"It's more than just a swap of favors this time. I want to hire you, pay the going rate. Be an actual client."

"What's the problem?" McGill asked again.

"I was overseas for a lot of the time I was away, and I got closer to a bad situation than I should have."

McGill nodded. "That can hardly be a first."

"Not even close. But all the other times the bad guys sent lawyers after me. This time I'm wondering if they might send shooters. And believe me, if that's the case, there'll be no professional courtesy."

McGill looked at Ellie closely. Two years away hadn't aged her noticeably, save for a slightly added depth to the crow's feet around her eyes. She still looked ready to take on the world if need be. That or make herself invisible.

If she were tired of living in the shadows though … maybe she'd finally admitted to herself she needed help getting out of a bad situation.

McGill asked, "What are the specifics of the problem, Ellie?"

"Tell you that only after you agree to take me on as a client."

"It usually works the other way around."

She nodded, put her hands on the arms of her chair and got to her feet.

"Okay, sorry I bothered you. It's just … well, actually this situation might bring up some bad old memories for you."

It didn't take McGill long to make the calculation. Nothing was worse than a loved one being in danger. Ellie had never had anything to do with McGill's kids or his ex-wife, Carolyn. That left only Patti, and Ellie had dropped out of sight right around the time of the foiled attempt on Patti's life by Representative Philip Brock.

"Okay, Ellie, you played the right card. I'll help you, but the courts don't recognize client-investigator privilege so if you want to keep things confidential, we'll have to work through a lawyer."

McGill had Putnam Shady in mind, but he'd need Sweetie's approval for that.

"Fine by me," Ellie said. "You'll let me know when you have the pieces in place?"

"Yes. If there's anything you can tell me now that won't harm you in court, if things ever get that far, I'm willing to listen now."

Ellie told him, "Like I said, I want to know if anyone is looking for me with bad intent. I especially need to know if someone's closing in on me."

"Things could really be that serious?" McGill asked.

Ellie nodded. "Oh, yeah. I wouldn't bother you about anything less."

"So how's the family, Welborn?" Sweetie asked, sitting behind her desk and looking at her guest.

Before going to see McGill, Welborn had changed into civilian clothes, a bomber jacket from Neiman Marcus, a Brioni black mock turtleneck, Wrangler jeans, and Asics running shoes.

He smiled and answered, "Great. Good health all around. Aria and Callista outwit me only half of the time these days, but Kira keeps giving them pointers. So it's only a matter of time before the patriarchy is overthrown."

Sweetie nodded. "That's the trend all right, but my guess is they'll all take good care of you in your old age."

"I hope so, but before then I need to make some plans."

Sweetie needed only a second to draw the correct inference. "The White House has given you notice? But that wouldn't affect the rest of your military career, would it?"

Welborn told her, "Not necessarily, no. I can't go into details, but I do have at least one other opportunity. The problem is, once you've spent a decade in the White House, any other kind of government work is bound to be a step-down. And if you can't put your heart into it, should you really be doing it?"

"That's easy," Sweetie said, "no, you shouldn't." Coming to the same conclusion Welborn had reached, she asked, "You're thinking of taking your investigative skills and experience into the private sector?"

He said, "I could live off of our savings, investments, and Kira's family money, only I'd like to keep my self-respect. Besides that, I think I'd be a more interesting husband and father if I found meaningful work to keep me busy."

"I'll go along with that, too," Sweetie said. "So … did you come to see Jim about a job?"

Keeping a straight face, Welborn replied, "I'd be willing to start in the mailroom. No, wait, that's what they do in Hollywood to find a job. Actually, I was given a lot of advance notice, and I won't lose my current post for quite a while. So, more than seeking immediate employment, I was wondering if there was anything I might do just to see if I'd fit well in the world of private investigation."

Sweetie laughed. "You want to be an intern?"

"Well, I don't know that I'd want to bring people their coffee, but if there were some way I might be of help while getting a feel for things, that would be great."

Sweetie thought about that while studying Welborn's face.

"You've got to be the most modest general in the U.S. military," she said.

"Just a part of my charm."

"You haven't told Kira yet about the news you received … what, just this morning?"

Welborn nodded. "Yes, this morning, and no, I haven't."

"Do you think you should?"

"I would have if she'd been home when I went to change clothes. I'll tell her this evening for sure."

Sweetie nodded. "How do you feel just being out of uniform? I know it felt strange to me when I first went from being a patrol cop to a plainclothes detail. I had to keep reminding myself I still had a badge. The jump from being a cop to a PI was even bigger."

Welborn bobbed his head. "I'm *still* a general officer in the Air Force, and just coming here in civvies feels funny, but I have a strong sense of who I am as a man, a husband, and a dad. I think I could make the adjustment without too much trouble."

"I can see that," Sweetie said. "We wouldn't take you on without paying you the going rate for an associate investigator, though. As chief ethics officer of this company, I won't allow anyone to work here without getting appropriate compensation."

"Would I get dental insurance?" Welborn asked with a grin.

Sweetie laughed. "Yeah, you would. But I'll have to talk this over with Jim. See if the overall workload calls for a new hire. You have time to come back after lunch?"

"Sure, I'm officially on leave right now. I don't have to go back to the White House for two weeks."

"Okay, then …" A thought popped into Sweetie's head. "You've always gotten along well with Patti, haven't you?"

Welborn needed a moment to process the question. He'd never thought of Patricia Grant McGill as anything but Madam President. "Yes, I have. President Morrissey also for that matter."

"Okay, good," Sweetie said. "The reason I asked is if we can't take you on right now, maybe Patti would have something in her security department. Seems to me any place dealing with billions of dollars going into high-tech investments might need someone on staff with sleuthing skills."

"Yes, it does," Welborn said.

Made him wonder why he hadn't thought of that.

Ellie Booker finished with McGill and headed toward the elevator bank thinking she'd played things just right. She'd gotten McGill interested in taking her on as a client by personalizing things. Implying that, who knew, maybe Ellie's possible continuing jeopardy might spill over onto someone else. Patricia Grant McGill for instance.

Ellie pushed the button to summon an elevator car.

It was unlikely, of course, that McGill's wife was in danger. Nobody had ever assassinated a *former* president of the United States. Still, it was undeniable, at least in Ellie's mind, that the world was getting crazier all the time, and there were more guns, bombs and other means of destruction falling into the wrong hands every day.

So who could say that some lunatic might not take it in mind to kill an historic figure despite her change in job status? A fine distinction like retirement from the Oval Office wouldn't necessarily stop a determined well-armed twitch from trying to make *his* mark on history. John Wilkes Booth, vindictive asshole that he'd been, had killed Abraham Lincoln *after* the rebel side had already lost the Civil War.

Ellie's musings were interrupted by the arrival of the guy with whom she'd shared the upward bound elevator. He gave her a polite smile and a nod. No come on, just a well-mannered acknowledgment of her presence.

Being the snoop that she was, she couldn't help but ask, "Your visit work out for you?"

He looked at her, weighed the appropriate response and said, "I think so."

The elevator car arrived and he courteously gestured her in first.

As the doors closed, she introduced herself: "Ellie Booker."

"Welborn Yates."

She grinned. "I know that name. You worked at the White House."

"Have we met?" Welborn asked.

"No. I haven't had the pleasure. Before now, I mean. I'm a reporter. I study lists of people's names, along with doing other snoopy things. You're an Air Force colonel, aren't you?"

"A general these days."

Ellie smiled. "Well, good for you. But you worked for Patti Grant, right?"

"I did work for President Grant, yes."

The elevator came to a stop at the ground floor and the doors opened.

Ellie and Welborn stepped out. She said, "Did I filch your time with Jim McGill?"

"I didn't have an appointment," Welborn said. "I just dropped in."

"Me, too. Sorry anyway if I cut in front."

"I spoke with Margaret Sweeney. So everything worked out."

Welborn opened the door of the M Street entrance to the building. That was when he saw a car make the sharp turn off Wisconsin Avenue and accelerate in their direction. Going the wrong way on the one-way street.

Ellie, looking over her shoulder at Welborn, about to thank him for holding the door open, hadn't noticed the car. Her face became a mask of shock as Welborn shoved her to the sidewalk.

He didn't stop there. He piled on top of her and began to roll with her along the pavement toward the shelter of a car parked at the curb. For a mind-freezing moment, Ellie thought she'd just become the victim of a lunatic assault. She was trying to reach for her gun when she heard the first rounds of gunfire.

Loud, close, and rapid-fire. Somebody emptying a clip of ammo.

She closed her eyes as pointed chunks of sundered pavement flew through the air. The deadly rounds of gunfire seemed to pursue them as they rolled together in a mad tumble doing their best to escape death. Ellie felt sure they weren't going to make it. She was going to die in the arms of the man she'd just met.

But then they slammed into the near side of the car at the curb, and it absorbed the punishment intended for them. No, *her,* Ellie thought. General Yates had just walked out of the building with the wrong woman.

And then there was a second volley of gunfire from a new direction.

Return fire? Someone from the McGill offices shooting back?

A chorus of shrieking sirens began to converge on their location.

If that wasn't enough, a storm cloud of helicopter blades rolled in close.

In the midst of this end-of-the-world scenario, General Yates decided now was the time to roll off of Ellie. That left her feeling exposed and naked to all the world's madmen. She wanted to grab him and pull him back on top of her.

Better he should —

He put his hands on her and rolled her onto her side, like maybe he was taking shelter behind her.

Only he rolled her back to look his way and said, "No blood on the front or back of you. I don't think either of us got hit."

Being both a reporter and a natural-born skeptic, Ellie had to make that determination for herself. She wasn't feeling any pain, but maybe that was just shock covering it up. She used both her eyes and her hands to examine her body. With a giddy sense of relief, she could find neither wounds nor flowing blood.

Her ears were ringing like crazy, yeah, but she'd still heard Yates when he'd spoken to her.

She said, "Let me take a look at you."

Ellie couldn't see any sign of damage. "Looks like you're good, too. How do you feel?"

"Bruised but not too bad, except for my right foot."

"You twist it rolling around with me?"

"Doesn't feel like a broken bone or a muscle strain. Feels like a burn. Maybe like stepping on a hot griddle."

"Let me take off your shoe," she said.

He nodded, and she untied the laces and slipped off the running shoe.

"Sonofabitch," Ellie said.

"What?" Welborn asked.

She showed him the sole of his shoe. There was a quarter-inch wide groove from toe to heel where a round had plowed clear through the Asics' understructure. You could see daylight through the opening. Ellie tossed the shoe to Welborn.

Then she took off his sock from the same foot. It had been shredded along the same line.

When Ellie showed Welborn that, he said, "What about my foot?"

She looked at it and said, "No bleeding, just a thin red line. I almost feel like kissing it. Only, with the mouth on me, that'd surely be the thing that kills you."

The next thing they knew, Jim McGill was standing over them with a gun in hand.

"Are you two okay?" he asked.

"Yes, sir," Welborn reported.

"Ellie?"

"Yeah. General Yates saved my backside. The guy should get a medal or something."

"What about the shooters, Mr. McGill?" Welborn asked.

"No official word, but from what I can see down the street, there's a car at the end of the block. Looks like a couple of male bodies inside, if I make things out correctly."

"Who put them down?" Welborn asked.

McGill said, "Metro PD, looks like."

Committed Capital — Washington, DC

Edwina Byington had been the personal secretary to President Patricia Grant through two terms in office. She'd kept her cool when the president had been impeached and when it looked like the country might soon be at war with China. The shooting kind, not some trade fuss.

The only times Edwina had been frightened was when the shadow of mortality had fallen directly over the president or someone close to her. There was the instance of Madam President's heart stopping in the midst of harvesting her bone-marrow for a transplant to young Kenneth McGill. That still gave her nightmares. Then there was the time Secret Service Special Agent Carrie Ramsey mistakenly had been kidnapped by villains who'd thought she was Caitie McGill.

Instances like those two had helped to turn Edwina's hair gray. Making the best of that situation, Edwina had cosmetically transformed the gray to silver and liked the result better than her original chestnut brown. In any case, she considered herself to be a tough, smart old bird who still had plenty of good years ahead of her.

That was why she kept her cool when Mr. McGill called that first day in February.

He didn't bother to say hello.

Just: "Edwina, I'm okay. I checked, and all the kids are all right, too."

"Very good, sir," Edwina replied. "You're going to let the other shoe drop now?"

"There's been another shooting outside my office building," McGill said.

"Other than yourself, Ms. Sweeney and other members of your staff, has anyone been … injured or worse?"

"There are two men down, the attackers. One's dead; the other is hanging by a thread."

Edwina focused on the most salient point. "Were these people attacking you, sir?"

"No. The target seemed to be … someone who came to see me, a prospective client."

"Seemingly someone with good reason, sir."

"Yes. Anyway, when Patti and I left home this morning, she told me she had a big meeting to start the day. She hoped to say hello at lunch time, but she wasn't sure she'd have the time. Using your best judgment, you should decide if there's any chance she'd hear the news and …"

Edwina looked up and saw the fear-taut face of Patricia Grant McGill in her doorway.

She told McGill. "Mrs. McGill has already been alerted, sir. She has an app on her phone. Anytime you make the news, she's informed."

Placing a hand over her phone, Edwina informed Patti, "All's well."

M Street Crime Scene — Washington, DC

Mayor Rockelle Bullard said, "Not that I'm any kind of expert, but the dead dude on the sidewalk looks like an Arab to me. Maybe Arab-American, but still. The nearly dead guy on his way to the hospital looked like he could be the dead guy's brother. Cousin at the very least."

The mayor sat in the back of her official ride, a Cadillac limo that she normally used only for visits to Capitol Hill or the White House. Occasions when she had to impress upon her city's federal overlords that they'd best take her seriously or she'd raise more hell than they'd ever thought possible. Make sure that the ones that heard *Hail to the Chief* when they entered a room got ticketed, and their personal cars got towed like those of any other citizen who didn't obey the rules of the road or parking restrictions. If they tried to mess with her on either of those counts, well, the police response time for, say, a break-in at a poobah's residence would strictly be a matter of where the call fell in the queue of local emergencies. Nobody would go to the head of the line just because he or she got voted into Congress or confirmed to a Cabinet post.

According to the Constitution, Congress had exclusive jurisdiction over the District of Columbia in "all cases whatsoever." Since 1973, however, Congress has allowed certain powers of government to be carried out by elected District officials. That situation was subject to revocation at any time, if it so pleased the Congress.

Rockelle's publicly stated position was that Congresspeople would be none too pleased if they had to work and live in what would become a virtual war zone, should they ever try to take her city and its residents back to the bad old days. In her most famous pre-election speech, Rockelle had said, "Nobody's going to whip us back onto the plantation. If Congress ever tries to rule us by command again, we'll all walk off our jobs, and I'll lead the way. This won't be just a headache for anyone who tries to step in and take over from our locally elected officials, it's going to be Code 3 for the nation's capital."

Code 3, Rockelle had explained to those unfamiliar with the term, meant a dire emergency situation, one that police should respond to with lights and sirens. For medical responders, Code 3 might also mean dead on arrival.

Congress hadn't been amused by Rockelle's none-too-subtle threat, but District residents of all stripes loved it. *There's no going back to the plantation* became a ubiquitous bumper sticker. Rockelle came to power in City Hall with a stunning 72% of the vote. Nobody in either the White House or Congress had ever won an election by such a margin. That made the power-brokers on Capitol Hill leery of challenging the new mayor.

"What about you, Mr. McGill?" the mayor asked. "You think these fellas are Arabs?"

McGill shared the backseat with Rockelle.

Ellie and Welborn sat on the facing jump-seat.

McGill said, "I think they are or were, depending on the individual. But I feel better thinking that they were brothers than making a hard guess about ethnicity."

The mayor turned to Welborn, someone she'd known for years.

"How about you, General? You got a look at the survivor before he was carted off, and you saw photos of the dead man."

"They're Jordanian," Welborn said.

The other three people in the back of the car all gave him inquisitive looks.

"You could tell these two guys' *nationality* just at a glance?" the mayor asked.

"Yeah, explain that one, Sherlock," Ellie added.

Welborn said, "I couldn't tell from their personal appearances. But the tattoos of their nation's flag were pretty clear giveaways."

"I didn't notice any obvious tattoos," McGill said.

"Neither did I," the mayor added.

Welborn told them, "They were small and fairly subtle. On each man's right hand, in the web of skin between his thumb and index finger was a small, circular tattoo, a roundel in four colors: red, black, white and green. The red is in a triangle at the apex of the circle. It has the shape of a slice of pie, and there's a white star on the red field. The other three colors, black, white and green are concentric circles. Each color stands for one of the country's ruling dynasties. The roundels are also markers on the aircraft of the Royal Jordanian Air Force."

Both Rockelle and Ellie started to speak; Ellie deferred to the mayor.

She asked, "How do you know all this?"

"I had occasion to meet a Jordanian military attaché at the White House. He was also a former fighter pilot. We got to talking shop. I learned a thing or two."

McGill asked, "That conversation was what led you to spot the tattoos in the first place?"

Welborn nodded. "My Jordanian friend said that the roundel was tattooed on the hand their pilots used to initiate their F-16s' weapons systems. It was a symbol that not only was the individual pilot bringing death to his enemies, so was their whole country. I kind of liked that. I might have done the same with the Stars and Stripes before I had my accident if I'd thought of it."

Ellie saw that McGill and the mayor knew about the accident Welborn meant.

She determined to find out for herself later.

"Well, you've still got your eagle-eyes, General," Mayor Bullard said, "And I'm happy you're here to give us a lead."

"Amen to that," McGill agreed.

Turning to Ellie, the mayor asked, "You'll be available to speak with my detectives, soon, Ms. Booker?"

"Absolutely, Madam Mayor. I didn't see much, thanks to General Yates saving my backside, but I'll be happy to answer the detectives' questions. Would it be all right if we do the interview on my boat? I'm at the Gangplank Marina."

The mayor said, "That'll be fine. You know I'm a former cop, right?"

"Yes, ma'am."

"So even if you didn't see too much, maybe you can explain why you're carrying a concealed weapon and how that might figure into a drive-by murder attempt today. You do have a concealed-carry permit for that weapon, I hope."

Ellie nodded. "Yes, ma'am, I do."

Turning to Welborn, the mayor asked, "You noticed her weapon, too, General?"

"I did, Madam Mayor."

"How about you, Mr. McGill?"

"Me, too," he said.

Turning back to Ellie, Rockelle Bullard advised. "You don't

need to get creative with your explanation about the gun. You didn't fire a shot today. Just might be the truth will set you free. And now I've got to go talk to the media."

Law Offices of Dexter Wiles — Washington, DC

"Turn on your television," Zala Wiles told her husband, Dexter, via the office intercom.

Mrs. Wiles was Ethiopian by birth, but she and her husband had met in Stockholm. A whirlwind romance had led to marriage, American citizenship, a new job, and night-time law school classes for Zala. That and getting away from Sweden's polar winters.

"Any particular TV channel, dear?" the lawyer asked his wife.

"Whichever you like that has local news, but do so quickly."

The lawyer took a remote control from a desk drawer and clicked on the office TV.

His colleagues of the moment, Meeker and Beemer, were present. They gave each other a look. Wondering what would come up on the screen.

Meeker said, "Super Bowl's not till Sunday."

"Baseball spring training's not for a couple weeks yet," Beemer added.

Wiles shushed them as the TV's picture and sound locked in. Mayor Rockelle Bullard was standing in front of James J. McGill's office building. A crowd of reporters hemmed her in, not that she couldn't have plowed through them with ease had she wished.

The mayor told the newsies and the city, "There was a shooting here this morning. You can see the damage the gunfire did to the building behind me. The likely target of the gunman was a member of the media whose name will be held in confidence for the time being."

"Why the secrecy?" a voice in the crowd called out.

"Because both the police and the individual involved requested confidentiality, and I don't want to do anything that might interfere with the investigation," the mayor said.

"Damn right," Meeker said, addressing the television.

Beemer nodded.

"One of the attackers was killed by a Metro PD officer," the mayor added. "The other was seriously wounded. It's not known whether he'll survive the day. Both police officers were unharmed, and the city is grateful for that."

"Was it a good shooting by the cops?" a reporter yelled.

Rockelle kept a straight face. "The entire incident will be investigated by the MPD. What I can tell you is I've seen a body-cam video that shows the deceased individual pointing a semi-automatic rifle at the patrol car in which the MPD officers were sitting. He pulled the trigger. The only reason the officers are still alive and unhurt was that the magazine and the chamber in the rifle were empty. Both officers yelled at the man to drop his rifle. When he didn't obey the order and attempted to seat a new magazine, the officer behind the wheel, who was closer to the man with the rifle, opened fire. In the heat of the moment, she emptied her weapon."

"She?" a reporter called out.

"Both officers are female. The second officer told her partner to duck when she saw a second man in the assailants' car lean forward with a gun in his hand. The second officer opened fire, grievously wounding the man. The investigation is proceeding as we speak. Traffic will be rerouted so as not to interfere with the detectives and technicians working in the crime scene. Members of the public attempting to get to and from their jobs on foot will need to use corridors established and enforced by MPD officers. I'd like to thank everyone in advance for cooperating with the police."

The expression on Rockelle Bullard's face told both the press and the public they'd damn well better play ball.

A newsie yelled out a final question: "Does any of this have anything to do with James J. McGill, as the shooting happened right outside his office building."

Rockelle couldn't quite repress a smile.

People, bless them, always wanted to know if a star personality was involved.

"Mr. McGill, being a civic-minded citizen," the mayor said, "stepped outside to see if he might be of help, but by that time the MPD had done its duty."

The mayor excused herself, got back into her car and left.

Most of the newsies clustered around the entrance to McGill's office building. In response to a persistent ringing of the doorbell, Dikki Missirian told them via an intercom that Mr. McGill would issue a public statement later in the day on his Twitter account. Other than that, he'd have no comment.

Dexter Wiles took Dikki at his word and turned off his television.

The lawyer looked at his guests and said, "Now, if I have things right, you two gentlemen spoke this morning with Mr. McGill, but you must have left just before all the excitement started."

"Probably didn't miss the shootout by more than the twenty minutes it took us to get here," Meeker said.

"Those two patrol cops did a helluva job," Beemer added. "Makes me proud."

Meeker nodded. "Facing off with a dude holding an assault rifle on 'em. Doesn't get any crazier than that."

"Highly courageous," Wiles agreed. "Might either of you know who that media person was, the one who came under fire."

"Yeah, we know her and the guy she was with," Meeker said. "We were leaving while they were waiting to see McGill."

Beemer elaborated, "Recognized the woman from TV. Know the guy because our paths as investigators have crossed with his now and then. Mayor knows him better'n we do."

"There's no chance either of these people would have interests that are at cross-purposes with our own?" Wiles asked, being cautious in a lawyerly way.

The two former cops looked at each other and grinned.

"What?" Wiles asked.

Meeker said, "Just appreciating your attention to detail, Dexter."

Beemer added, "The only thing those other two might have

in common with us is they have the same taste in big-name PIs."

"Unless one of them bought that other winning Grand Slam ticket up Maryland," Meeker suggested slyly.

It took the lawyer just a second to understand Meeker and Beemer were messing with him. "Not likely, as the Maryland winner has no reason to think there was another winning ticket sold here in DC."

"Right," Meeker said.

"So what have you gentlemen discovered so far?" Wiles asked.

"You mean before we even talked to Jim McGill?" Beemer asked.

Wiles nodded.

Meeker said, "Well, we found out there was a rigged lottery game in Iowa. Inside job. Guy who was the information security director for a number of multi-state games put in the fix. He rewrote the game's computer code so that on certain dates instead of millions of possible number combinations there were only a couple hundred. So if you covered all those combinations for a few hundred bucks, you'd make millions."

Beemer added, "Dude was smart enough at first to have family and friends in other states around the country make the buys. Then he got either lazy or stupid and bought a winning ticket himself in a convenience store right there in Iowa. The store not only had a video camera but sound recording, too. He'd shadowed his face with a hoodie, but a local investigator recognized his voice when he talked to the store clerk, and that was that."

Dexter Wiles steepled his hands.

"Man's thinking," Meeker said.

"Let's not interrupt," Beemer suggested.

"You have any other examples of lottery irregularities?" Wiles asked, ignoring the jests.

Meeker nodded. "Was this man and his wife in Michigan. They didn't do anything crooked, but the man spotted a wrinkle in the design of this one game, Winfall it was called, and by playing it a certain way at a certain point in the jackpot's progression, chances were real good you could win some nice money."

"Really?" Wiles asked. "What was he, a mathematician?"

"He was a convenience store owner," Beemer said, "but a real smart one. Figured things out all on his own."

"My, my, my," Wiles said with a look of concern crossing his face.

Both former MPD detectives noticed Wiles' displeasure.

Beemer pushed on with the story. "By and by, the Michigan lottery authorities woke up to what was happening and ended that game."

Wiles nodded. "Still, this fellow must have taken advantage of the situation for as long as he could, correct?"

Meeker and Beemer both laughed. Meeker added, "Who wouldn't?"

"Fact was," Beemer added, "Massachusetts had a game just like the one Michigan axed."

Meeker said, "So the man and his wife made regular trips east and cleaned up there, too."

Wiles said, "Then the Massachusetts lottery officials caught wise, too?"

"*Maybe* they did," Meeker replied. "But nobody got off his ass to change anything."

Beemer said, "Wasn't until some students at MIT figured out the same play the man from Michigan did, and then *The Boston Globe* newspaper discovered what the students were doing. The paper published a big headline story."

"*Then* the Massachusetts lottery people finally woke up from their nap and ruined things for everybody," Meeker said.

That summary made Dexter Wiles look even more worried.

"What's the matter, Dexter?" Beemer asked. "Meeker and I know how to both fly and drive up to Boston. We can find out if some of those smart-ass kids up there are messing with things again. Trying to keep Sammy from his rightful share of the jackpot, if not the whole thing."

The lawyer sighed, put the palms of both hands on his desk

and leaned forward.

He told the detectives, "There are many other institutions of higher mathematical learning, from Georgia Tech to Cal Tech. There are also, most likely, many gifted amateurs like the man from Michigan. Someone who might even own another convenience store. Say, up in Maryland."

Meeker and Beemer looked at each other and frowned.

"Can you buy lotto tickets online?" Meeker asked Wiles, as if the attorney might know. The detective never bought into any sucker plays himself.

Wiles didn't know the answer, but he Googled the question.

It turned out the answer was both yes and no. Some states allowed online lottery purchases; others didn't. A few states made all their games available; others picked and chose which games could be played online. There were questions of online age verification for those who played wherever the player lived. In most states, you had to be at least 18; in one 19; and in three 21.

Wiles asked Meeker, "Are you thinking that we might be working against someone who manipulated the Grand Slam game online?"

"Maybe," Meeker said. "Look at that guy back in Iowa, the one who got caught. If he'd played the game from home, or better yet used some third-party computer, he'd never have been spotted on that convenience store video. He'd still be robbing his employer most likely."

Beemer was now busy checking something on his phone, but he still chimed in, "No doubt about that. Now, looky here."

He turned his phone around and handed it to Meeker …

Who read aloud from the device: "'Ms. Joanne Gunther has to be the luckiest woman in the world or maybe just the smartest. She's won multi-million dollar jackpots in the Texas lottery *four* times.'"

Dexter Wiles was astounded. "How could that be?"

Meeker returned the phone to Beemer, and told Wiles, "The lady has herself a Ph.D. in statistics. When her Mama and Daddy told her to learn her numbers, she must've taken that as gospel."

Beemer told Wiles, "Marvin and me might have to check every math class across the country from the eighth grade on up. Doin' just the colleges might not be enough."

"We do have one thing going for us, other than getting James J. McGill to help us out," Meeker said.

"What's that?" Wiles asked.

Meeker turned to his partner and said, "Big Mike?"

Beemer knew where Meeker was going.

More often than not the two of them read from the same mental script.

Beemer told Wiles, "Genius or not, whoever's behind this scam got impatient and jumped the gun. He'd done it right, Sammy never would have had the chance to buy a winning ticket."

"But he did buy one," Meeker said. "He's right there doing it on another convenience store video. Of which we have a copy. You remember what else Sammy did, Dexter?"

The lawyer nodded. "He held the ticket up with himself and the store owner also in the frame and said, 'This is my ticket to riches.' He made that video with his phone."

"Doc-u-men-ta-tion," Beemer said. "Of which we now also have a copy."

"Did you tell Mr. McGill all this?" Wiles asked.

Meeker said, "Big Mike and I had a talk about that on our way to Mr. McGill's palace of private detection."

"It's really that nice?" Wiles asked.

Beemer said, "Oh, yeah. Anyway, we decided if we were going to involve the man, we'd have to play it straight with him. You know, in case we ever need a helping hand again."

"Hard as that might be to believe," Meeker added.

Committed Capital — Washington, DC

Both of McGill's thumbs and index fingers were on record as entry keys to Patti's place of business. As were retinal scans of both of his eyes. Seemed like overkill to McGill at first.

He'd told his wife, "If things get to the point where I lose more than one body part, I'll probably head to a hospital rather than stop in to chat with you."

"As well you should," Patti had replied.

Then she'd explained that the building's recognition algorithm had been refined to do more than just open the front door. Simply using his right thumbprint would provide admission to the building. Right thumb and index finger meant I'm here with good news. That would tell Patti to cut short any meeting or phone call to hear McGill's good news. Right thumb, finger and retinal scan meant *monumental* good news — like, "Honey, you just became a grandma." That would mean drop everything and pour champagne for everyone in the building.

Using physical keys from the left — sinister — side of the body was an escalating code of danger. Ranging from, "Call the cops," to "Lock and load," for the building's security people. At McGill's urging, Patti had hired a dozen skilled former law enforcement professionals to keep her workforce safe from both outside intruders and each other, e.g. an employee who might go off the rails for God only knew what reason.

McGill didn't want to see *any* kind of workplace tragedy occur at Committed Capital. Patti still had Secret Service Special Agent Daphna Levy hovering nearby for personal protection during working hours, of course. But as tough and inclined to self-sacrifice as Daphna was, even she had to go potty occasionally. When that happened, one of the private hires stepped in.

That day, McGill used just his right thumb to get into the building's underground parking area after Leo had stopped the Chevy at the gate. McGill knew his arrival would immediately be reported to Edwina Byington's desk. It was more than likely Edwina or someone else in the building had learned of the gunshots outside of McGill's headquarters by now. Passing the word to Patti would follow without delay.

By using just his right thumb, McGill would let Patti know that all was well. Relatively speaking anyway.

You could hardly blame your spouse for getting tense when someone fired a semi-automatic weapon in the direction of your offices. Even when only the shooter had bought the farm. McGill couldn't repress his own imagination from conjuring the real possibility that he might have gone downstairs to see Ellie Booker and Welborn Yates off.

What might have happened then with all those bullets flying?

McGill gave himself a shake as he and Leo got out of the Chevy.

"You want me to go get a cup of coffee, Boss?" Leo asked.

Committed Capital had its own dining facilities.

"Whatever you're in the mood for, Leo. Your credit's good here."

"Yeah, but yours is even better."

"Okay, the tab's on me."

The two of them parted ways, and when McGill reached the top floor, Patti came out of her office to hug her husband.

She stepped aside to let Edwina have a turn.

McGill appreciated both gestures of affection, but that didn't keep him from asking, "Anybody else want a hug?"

"That'll do for now," Patti said, leading him into her office, "but if anyone had embraced you on the way in I wouldn't have blamed her or him."

She closed the door behind them and delivered a passionate kiss to McGill.

He participated fully.

"I'm not sure I deserved all that," he said as Patti stepped back, "but I'll take it every time."

Holding McGill's hands in hers, Patti said, "What scared me about all this — other than the fact that you might have been killed — was the randomness of it all."

"It was kind of out of the blue," McGill agreed. Trying to lighten the mood, he said. "I could sit on that sofa over there, and you could sit on my lap."

"Don't think I wouldn't, but we might get distracted again."

"From?" McGill asked.

"Whatever you came to see me about. You might have just called and said. 'Hi, hon. Bad guys missed me again. What do you want to do for dinner?'"

McGill grinned. "That was a fairly good impression of me. Try to pitch your voice just a bit lower, though."

"Did you call the kids and Carolyn, Jim?"

"I did that on the way over here. They're all reassured, I hope."

Patti gave him a peck on the cheek and said, "Good."

She crossed the room and sat on the sofa McGill had mentioned. She patted the cushion next to her and said, "Sit."

McGill followed orders.

"All right," Patti said. "Tell me what I can do to help."

Dangerous Dame, Gangplank Marina — Washington, DC

Ellie Booker hadn't been back on her motor yacht for more than five minutes when the visitor's doorbell got pushed dockside. Ellie used her phone to cue the appropriate video cam and saw a white man and an Asian woman standing at the head of the ramp to her vessel. Each of them wore an off-the-rack suit and topcoat. She might have just stuck her head outside of the yacht's salon, but seeing who had come a-calling by opening the front door was so 20th century.

Also possibly a fatal mistake when you had assassins looking to gun you down.

The people who'd like to see her dead could afford to hire more than one hit team.

Hell, losing the first shooters might only motivate them to send a second, more skilled assault group to get her. That or one very patient all but invisible long-distance shooter who never missed his target. A ninja sniper or … even a man and a woman who could do credible impressions of MPD detectives? If that's who was out there.

The doorbell rang again.

Ellie pressed the intercom icon on her phone with her left thumb as she used her right hand to pick up her Beretta 93R, an easily concealed handgun that could fire three-round bursts. She responded to her visitors only by saying, "Yes?"

The woman replied, "Detectives Chen and Behan, MPD. If you are Ms. Ellie Booker, we need to talk with you about the shooting on M Street this morning."

Ellie said, "Each of you, please hold your badge and ID in front of you."

The cops looked mildly annoyed but did as they were requested. Ellie had her camera zoom in on the credentials. A DC cop's badge was a shield. The words Metropolitan Police formed an arc over the Capitol Building. A smaller arc at the bottom of the shield was marked Detective.

A photo of each cop, unsmiling, with name, rank, and number filled the other side of the badge wallet. Everything looked legit, but Ellie told the pair, "I've got image captures of your IDs. I'm comparing them with your department's personnel database right now and … okay, you're good. You may come aboard. I'll open the door to the salon, and you may step inside."

Chen replied, "You don't want to step out and meet us halfway?"

"No."

Ellie saw the two cops talking to each other, but their voices were too quiet for her to hear. Then they looked up, and Chen said in a clear voice, "Okay, Detective Behan just told me he considers himself expendable. I don't agree with that. If you do anything to harm him, God help you."

"He doesn't shoot at me, I won't shoot at him," Ellie said, "and if you think you can scare me, lady, get in line."

Detective Chen took a step to be the first visitor aboard, but

Behan put a hand on her arm and a word in her ear. After a moment, she nodded. Behan held his hands wide and smiled as he came aboard at the aft end of the vessel. He wasn't a bad looking guy at all, Ellie thought.

Probably had a fair line of Irish blarney in his repertoire, too, to calm down the Dragon Lady with just a bit of chat.

The craft had a sliding glass door as the entry to the salon. Well, not glass really. Clear polycarbonate resin. Bullet-resistant to anything less than a .50 caliber round. The extra protection was an option that Ellie had felt was a wise investment.

Behan had lowered his hands, but he didn't reach for a weapon, and he was still grinning as he stood outside the salon. Ellie pressed a button, and the door slid open. The detective asked, "May I step inside?"

Ellie nodded. As he approached, she looked to see if he carried his service weapon on his right or left side, but she didn't see any bulge under his suit coat. She'd heard of some cops keeping their duty weapon in a holster at the small of their backs, but that had always seemed to her like a long way to go if you needed to get off a quick shot.

Behan apparently understood her visual examination and brought his smile back for an encore. He said, "It's up my sleeve. Both sleeves, actually. I'm ambidextrous."

Ellie frowned. "Are you BS-ing me?"

"I'll show you if you promise not to shoot me. The hand you've got hidden behind your back? I have to think there's a gun in it."

Ellie let her right hand fall to her side, showing Behan he was right.

She said, "Your first name isn't Brendan, is it?"

He laughed and said, "No, it's Aidan."

"Which was one of Brendan's middle names," Ellie said.

"Oh, my," the detective said. "You have your own yacht, and you're well-read. So can you tell me, miss, who it is that would want to shoot you dead in our fair city?"

The guy had delivered his question using just the hint of a

brogue.

A charmer, no doubt about it, Ellie thought.

Then she noticed that Detective Chen had come aboard and had the smarts to stop outside of the salon.

"Is she your boss?" Ellie asked.

Behan didn't have to look behind himself to know whom Ellie meant.

He said, "We hold the same rank: Detective 1. We're colleagues."

"How's your memory, Aidan?"

"Crackerjack."

Ellie liked that answer. Old-fashioned, corny, and just what she wanted to hear.

"Good. Then how about we talk, and you can tell your colleague everything I said later?"

He thought about that for a beat. "I need to ask one more time: You promise not to shoot me?"

"I'll promise if you will."

"Deal." Ellie put her Beretta down on an end table.

Behan turned and gave Chen a shoreward tilt of his head.

She understood what he meant but didn't like it. She left the yacht grimacing.

Ellie said, "So go ahead and show me if you really have guns up your sleeves?"

Behan gave her proof positive. Quick as a wink, with the flick of his wrists, he had a small semi-auto in each hand. Then, like a magic trick, they were out of sight up his sleeves again

Ellie gave Behan a brief round of applause and gestured him to take a seat on the salon's sectional sofa. She brought him a cold Henry Weinhard's Root Beer and had one for herself. They clinked the bottles in a toast and Ellie sat opposite him.

"So, one more time, Ms. Booker, regarding the shooting on M Street this morning," Behan said, "who do you think it was trying to kill you?"

Ellie leaned forward and said, "Terrorists."

Committed Capitol — Washington, DC

McGill told Patti, "I need a computer whiz. Probably someone under 30 years old but with the maturity of someone older."

"Someone who can also pull rabbits out of his hat in his spare time?" Patti asked.

"Sure, but it doesn't have to be a guy. Could be a female. I'm an equal opportunity gumshoe."

"You've never worn gum-soled shoes in your life, I bet."

"Yeah, I think that sort of footwear went out of style before I took my first steps, but I still need tech help. Being in the innovation-funding biz, I thought you might be able to point me in the right direction."

"There are different types of computer wizardry, you know," Patti said.

"I do. I can explain in detail if you cross your heart and promise never to tell."

"I share confidences only with my dear husband."

"Okay, him I trust."

McGill told Patti about Meeker and Beemer's visit earlier that morning and the problem the two former MPD detectives were trying to solve for their client, the unrecognized co-winner of the Grand Slam game's big prize.

"Could be a bug in the lottery's computer system," Patti said after she'd heard McGill's story. "When was the drawing?"

"Wednesday night, not even 48 hours ago," McGill said.

Patti thought for a moment. "In people-time, that's not long. In computer-time, it's forever. Unless a flu bug or some other illness knocked all of the lottery's computer people and its public relations personnel on their backsides, there should have been a correction, a public announcement saying there were two big winners, not one."

McGill nodded. "I hadn't thought about an illness. This is flu season."

"Probably didn't happen that way, though," Patti said.

"Why not?" McGill asked.

"Well, the lottery never stops, does it? Not even after someone wins a big prize. The jackpot simply defaults to its starting point and then the prize-money starts to rebuild. If personnel critical to the operation of the game were unavailable and replacements couldn't be found immediately, a public announcement of a delay in the game would be unavoidable. More than that, the explanation for the game being stopped would have to be absolutely credible or the public would rightly think something was crooked."

"Meeker and Beemer didn't say anything about the game being stopped," McGill said.

He took out his phone and scrolled through the top stories on the websites of *The Washington Post* and *The New York Times.* Neither had any stories of the Grand Slam game going down or correcting the number of winners of the last big prize.

"Nothing online about the lottery," McGill said, "not even a mention that someone won a big jackpot."

Patti said, "The number has to be over $500 million these days to make headlines. A billion dollars, if you want saturation coverage."

McGill laughed. "That's an interesting bit of social commentary."

He lapsed into a silence long enough to realize he wasn't holding up his end of the conversation. He blinked and told Patti, "Sorry for drifting off."

"You were thinking of something," Patti said. "I didn't want to distract you."

McGill said, "I was. You made me wonder whether there would be another sweet-spot pot for someone who wanted to rip off a lottery drawing: big enough to make the risk worthwhile, not so big as to result in an unrelenting demand to publicize the winner."

Patti took a moment to consider that logic and said, "I can't fault that idea. So you think the situation here is a criminal one."

"Yeah. People used to rob banks because that was where the money was. Today, there's a whole lot more online."

"By far," Patti said. "So, returning to your request for help, I have someone who just came on staff here who might be able to help you."

"Can you spare him?" McGill asked.

"Not indefinitely or I wouldn't have taken him on, but for a reasonable time, and just for you, yes. He's in the middle of something right now. Should I ask him to meet with you tomorrow?"

"That'd be great. What's his name?"

"Cale Tucker. He used to work for the NSA, but don't tell anyone I told you that."

"My lips are sealed," McGill said. "What time can I meet with him tomorrow?"

"I'll talk with Cale and get back to you. Is that agreeable?"

"Absolutely."

"Now, let's move back to our earlier discussion."

"Why did someone try to kill Ellie Booker, almost killed both her and Welborn Yates, and why did she come to see me in the first place?" McGill asked.

"Right all three times. Also, why was Welborn on hand?"

"He's looking ahead and wanted to discuss job possibilities. That's what he told Sweetie."

"Would you take him on?"

"Sweetie told him if the work was there, yes. I agree with her. Welborn has come a long way as an investigator, and his actions this morning showed he has all the right physical moves for the job."

Patti nodded. "Which brings us to Ms. Booker. I assume you were the one speaking with her."

"I was," McGill said.

"And her problem is?"

"She wanted me to find out if she was in any danger."

Patti said, "It seems that question was clearly answered."

"No doubt about it," McGill agreed.

"But knowing you as well as anyone might —"

"Better than anyone else," McGill corrected. "Even Sweetie."

"Very well then. The first question having been answered — Ms. Booker is in danger — you'll want to find out who is behind it. Correct?"

McGill said, "That and a way to make them stop."

The White House/The Yates' Residence — Washington, DC

Before going home, Welborn Yates made a brief stop in the Oval Office at the request of President Jean Morrissey. He assured both the president and Byron DeWitt that he was well, and with the exception of a tear in the right leg of his pants, ready to go back to work, if that was what the president wanted.

DeWitt, a sharp observer, said, "Your knee was bleeding. Still is just a bit."

The White House physician, Dr. Artemus Nicolaides, was summoned. He made short work of cleaning and covering the abrasion, proclaimed recovery time would be minimal, and shook Welborn's hand before departing.

"Well done, General Yates," the president told him. "You saved a woman's life this morning. There will be a presidential commendation placed in your personnel file."

"Thank you, ma'am. It was more a matter of reflex than anything else."

One other woman was also present. FBI Director Abra Benjamin told Welborn, "It was the right reflex at the right moment. That's something you can't teach, and it can't be overvalued. I look forward to our meeting, General. I'll have my executive assistant call and see what time is convenient for you."

Welborn shook hands all around and then went home to the woman and the two girls who mattered most to him. With a daughter in each arm and his hands clasped behind his wife's back, there were several rounds of kisses and moments later, a bowl of fudge ripple ice cream for everyone. After the treat was consumed, his daughters gave Welborn cold-lipped kisses on his cheeks and left Mom and Dad to talk about grownup stuff.

The children were no sooner out of the kitchen than tears

appeared in Kira's eyes.

"How bad was it?" she asked. "How close did you come to ..."

She couldn't finish the question. Welborn didn't want to voice the word either.

He took his wife's hand and said, "I honestly don't know. I saw the barrel of the weapon poke out of the car window and after that everything was and remains a blur. I felt myself slamming into Ms. Booker and taking her down to the sidewalk. I know I rolled the two of us behind a parked car for shelter. But I didn't plan any of that. I just did it."

"You are a hero, Welborn," Kira said and gave him a kiss.

He had to laugh.

"What?" Kira asked. "You don't think so?"

Welborn shrugged. "If I had done nothing, I'm sure I would have been splattered right along with Ellie Booker. Maybe I was just saving myself reflexively. Could be, at some self-serving level of subconsciousness, I even thought it wouldn't look good to save myself and leave a woman behind to get gunned down. So I grabbed her as I ducked for cover."

Kira gave her husband a hard sock on the shoulder.

"Ow!" he said. "What was that for?"

"That was for pretending to think so little of yourself. The idea that you'd save someone's life only as a public relations consideration ..." Kira was at a loss for words.

Welborn kissed her before she began to sputter.

"You're right," he said. "My mother raised me better than that." With a deadpan expression, he added, "She told me to keep an eye out for book deals."

He had his hands up before she could punch him again. He grabbed Kira, spun her around, and sat her on his lap.

"See," Welborn said, "that was pure reflex, too."

Before she could get too angry and demand her freedom, Welborn told her about his meeting with Byron DeWitt that morning and learning that the president wouldn't be running for a second term. That and how he'd need to look for another job in two years or sooner.

Surprised on more than one count, Kira asked, "You'd leave the Air Force?"

He sighed and reluctantly nodded. "I think so, yes. I've grown accustomed to the rarefied air of the White House. You might even say I've been spoiled."

"Is that why you were at Mr. McGill's headquarters? To ask for a job?"

"More like to ask *about* a job. I didn't know if McGill Investigations had any openings. I talked with Margaret Sweeney. Mr. McGill was busy with two former MPD detectives and then with Ellie Booker."

"Were the former police detectives applying for work, too?"

"No. Margaret told me they were looking to collaborate with Mr. McGill on a case. She also told me that she and Mr. McGill would have to look at the company caseload to see if a new hire was needed."

"But they'd take you on if that was the case?" Kira asked.

"That's what I was told, and then there's another possible employment opportunity."

"My, my," Kira said. "You have had a busy day. Who would that job be with?"

"The FBI … as deputy director."

Kira's eyes got big, matching her smile. "Now, *that* sounds like a real opportunity."

"Yeah, and I briefly met Director Abra Benjamin in the Oval Office before coming home."

"The director was impressed by your heroics?" Kira asked.

"Yes. Very complimentary. Her assistant will be calling me to see when a convenient time for an interview might be."

That news earned Welborn another kiss, the passionate, lingering kind.

It was clear which job choice Kira favored.

The thing was, damnit, saving Ellie Booker's life just a few hours ago, besides being terrifying, was also the most fun he had since he had stopped flying fighter jets. The potentially deadly incident this morning had rekindled an appetite for thrills he thought he'd left behind years ago. Turned out his taste for adrenaline had only been snoozing.

He doubted he could feed that hunger working behind a desk at the FBI.

Rockville, Maryland

Constance Parker, as her father had told her from her very first days of being able to speak, was named after a virtue: the quality of always being faithful and dependable. Mama just called her Connie. That was a big relief because by the time Connie had turned ten years old, she'd decided it was impossible for anyone to be a good girl *all* of the time.

People just messed up every now and then. Sometimes without even trying. Other times because they were looking for a shortcut. An easy way out. But Connie quickly learned the hazards of rationalizing her misbehavior — without Daddy ever having to say a word.

A shortcut often turned out to be the longest way to get anywhere. That was because there were things called pitfalls. Unsuspected dangers and difficulties. If you were about to get into trouble by going down the wrong path, you'd have to back up and start all over again. Pitfalls could make shortcuts seem like the longest roads you ever walked.

Daddy hadn't told her about that. Neither had Mama. They just let Connie find out for herself. Experience being the best teacher of all. The same sense of caution applied to the idea of taking the easy way out. Sure, the closest door might be the *quickest* way out of a bad fix, but there was no saying you wouldn't step into an even worse set of circumstances.

After Connie had become an adult, these early tutorials on the realities of life ran through her mind like some old black-and-white film. She remembered watching a few of those old-time movies with her parents. They'd nod their heads when the script made some moral point that couldn't have been more obvious if it had been flashed on the screen in capital letters.

Back then, it had been all Connie could do not to groan.

Even so, she had liked the simplicity of the storylines in those films. Everything was so clear. Doing this was good; doing that was bad. Heroes and villains were plain for everybody to see. There was no mistaking one for the other. Good girls might face temptations, but they knew intuitively not to take up with bad boys or there would be awful consequences.

Shades of gray were for art films.

The clarity of the way a good life should be lived had fogged over for Connie on the day she came home from classes at Saint Wilhelmina, a Catholic girls' high school in Baltimore. Two police officers stood on the front porch of her home talking to each other. One of the cops was a young woman who was probably new to the job. She looked like she was on the verge of tears.

That scared Connie silly, but it didn't stop her from running up the front steps to see what had happened. In retrospect, she wished she hadn't been in such a hurry. She learned her mother had died in a terrible traffic accident.

As the male cop had explained it, Mama's car had stopped first in line at a red light. The driver of the city bus coming up behind her had a fatal heart attack. The bus slammed into the back of Mama's car pushing it into the intersection and moving traffic. Her car was hit by a truck heading one way and another bus going the other way.

In the softest voice he could manage, the male cop told Connie that her mother had died in that terrible accident. That dreadful news was shared just as Connie's father arrived. The young female cop hugged Connie as her partner repeated the story. He also said Daddy could go to the morgue if he wanted to do so, but the male cop added that he wouldn't recommend it.

Daddy said he'd go, but he refused to let Connie accompany him.

He told her, "You don't want to remember your mother the way she is now." That was the end of the discussion.

That was the only time Connie had ever seen her father cry. She didn't argue. She let her neighbor, Ms. McKinley, stay with her until Daddy got home looking 10 years older than when he'd left. That told her how awful the experience had been for him.

It also made Connie think she'd taken the easy way out.

At the very least, she should have argued with her father's decision.

She vowed to herself that she'd never give in so easily again. Five years later, when she was in grad school at Johns Hopkins, beginning the work that would lead to her doctorate in organic chemistry, Connie's resolve was put to the test.

Daddy was a pharmacist. He owned three drug stores right there in Baltimore where he and Connie lived. Two stores were in black neighborhoods; one was in a white neighborhood. He divided his workdays between all three stores. An armed robber wearing a Halloween monster mask shot him while he was in the store he usually closed. The gunman had wanted both cash and opioids.

Franklin Parker had two alarm triggers in the floor behind the counters of all three stores where he worked. One was a silent alarm and sent a signal to the security company to send the police immediately. The other alarm had the volume and sound characteristics of a 500-pound bomb exploding.

Parker was trying to decide which one to use when the robber told him, "Don't go hitting no alarm now."

The pharmacist had always made a point of being familiar with all of his customers. He certainly knew all of his regulars by both appearances and names. With most of them, he could also identify them by their voices alone. When the robber warned him not to trigger an alarm, he recognized the guy's voice.

It belonged to a young man who'd once tried unsuccessfully to court Constance.

Parker had been relieved that the boy's pursuit had proved

unsuccessful.

At that moment, though, all he said was, "Marcus?"

The robber momentarily went as rigid as if he'd been electrocuted.

Then he shot Franklin Parker. Fortunately for the pharmacist, the bullet hit him on the upper right side of his chest. No vital organs were damaged. The gunshot did knock him to the floor, but he was fortunate in that regard, too. Both alarm triggers were nearby. He used his left hand to slap them both.

The robber took the racket as his cue to flee. He didn't get a dime or a single tablet of drugs. Before Parker passed out from the pain, he wrote Marcus's name on his note pad. He recuperated quickly enough to testify against the boy at his trial.

Parker tried to keep Connie away from the courtroom, but as a young adult now she insisted on coming. She stared daggers at her one-time former suitor anytime he dared to look at her. Everyone present noted when the defendant quickly looked away. The appearance of guilt on his face was plain to all. He got the maximum sentences for the crimes of attempted second-degree murder and attempted armed robbery: 60 years.

Parker recovered physically, but he no longer had the will to keep his businesses going. He sold all three stores and got good prices for them. As he pointed out to prospective buyers, he'd been robbed only once, but the stores made money every day. Enough that an armed guard could be hired for each store and there'd be plenty left over for the proprietor.

Combining the money from the sales with the settlement from the city for the death of his wife, funds he'd invested conservatively, and the amount he received from the sale of the family home made Parker a millionaire thrice over.

He decided it was time to leave town and go live with extended family in Beaufort, South Carolina. He asked Connie to come with him, but he said he'd understand if she wanted to continue her education at Johns Hopkins. She did.

Parker bought a house for his daughter in Rockville; he didn't want her living in the city any longer. He also bought her a new Toyota Corolla, and put $250,000 into an index fund for her. Hugging his daughter before he headed South, Parker told Connie, "The bad luck your mama and I had in Baltimore, don't let it get you, too."

"I'll do my best, Daddy," she'd said.

Still, she thought bad luck might travel as easily as people did.

Maybe even more so. It could be waiting for you to show up somewhere.

That was certainly the way Constance Parker, Ph.D. felt these days ...

She'd agreed to be the front-woman for a lottery ticket winning $212 million. She had been promised $10 million for her participation. Despite her father's largesse, in recent times she'd needed money for both living expenses and her ongoing research project.

Work that might make life better for countless people.

That being said, she still couldn't fool herself.

She'd taken both a shortcut and the easy way out.

She had no doubt there would be pitfalls ahead.

McGill Investigations International — Washington, DC

Putnam Shady, attorney-at-law, was examining the damage done to the McGill Building by the automatic weapon's fire it had absorbed that morning. Dikki Missirian was with Putnam giving him a running estimate of the costs to repair the structure. The damage done to the building's nameplate alone would reach five figures to remedy.

The MPD cops standing guard and directing pedestrian traffic on the block had denied Putnam access to the crime scene until Dikki came out and vouched for him. Dikki had invoked both Jim McGill's and Margaret Sweeney's names. Saying they had summoned Putnam.

Putnam politely explained, "I'm married to one of the managing partners."

The cop on duty was smart enough to understand he hadn't meant McGill.

Putnam further clarified, "My wife asked if I'd take her to lunch today."

"You're not armed, are you?" the cop inquired.

"No, I don't have a permit for that sort of thing."

.Instead, he said, "Maybe you should be armed, I'm thinking. At least around this place."

Putnam waited for the cop to move away before he grinned.

Dikki asked, "What's funny?"

Putnam said, "The idea that there should be *geographical* gun permits. Places in a city where it would be a good idea to be armed and other places where it wouldn't be allowed. Depending on where you traveled, you might have a gun waiting for you when you arrived, but you'd have to leave it behind before you entered someplace deemed to be safe."

"That's crazy," Dikki said.

"And our current gun laws aren't?" Putnam asked.

Before a debate could begin, Sweetie stepped out of the building. She hugged Putnam and he returned the embrace. Before any greater affection could be displayed, Dikki said, "I'll be leaving now. The security people are the only ones left in the building?"

Sweetie dropped one arm and told Dikki, "Yeah, almost everybody else has gone home. See you tomorrow, Dikki."

He waved and headed off in the direction of Wisconsin Avenue.

"Everybody gets the remainder of the day off?" Putnam asked.

"It's a new policy I put into effect this morning," Sweetie said. "Anytime the building gets shot up everybody gets a paid vacation day. To get rid of the jitters. Maybe to decide if they really want to work in such a risky place."

Sweetie took a long look at the damage that had been done to the building.

She shook her head in dismay.

Putnam understood. He said, "I've never thought of it before, but for a new building, this place has begun to remind me of a historical site."

"Yeah?" Sweetie asked. "Which one?"

"The Alamo. Only the people here have managed to keep the opposition outside the walls."

"So far," Sweetie said.

Deke Ky, the reason Sweetie'd had to say *almost* everyone on staff had gone home, stepped out of the building. He greeted Sweetie and shook hands with Putnam.

"Do you have a concealed carry license?" Putnam asked Deke.

He got a smile in response. "After 20 years in the Secret Service, what do you think?"

"You wouldn't feel fully dressed without firepower?"

"Exactly. See you tomorrow, Margaret. See you around, Mr. Shady."

Deke also walked off toward Wisconsin Avenue.

Putnam asked, "Nobody drove to work today?"

Sweetie explained, "Besides the armed guards in the building, there are a few police techs looking at everyone's cars to make sure nobody stuck an explosive device in any of them. Leo apparently had anticipated such a thing, so he's got a gizmo that tells if anyone had monkeyed with Jim's car. Nobody had, but we're being careful with everyone else."

Sweetie took Putnam's arm and the two of them followed precedent and also headed off toward Wisconsin Avenue. It was Putnam's idea that they'd lunch at Martin's Tavern. That was the place where John F. Kennedy had proposed to Jacqueline Bouvier, and Putnam had done the same with Sweetie. Putnam hadn't gone so far as to ask for the same booth in which the future president had popped the question to his future first lady.

Putnam wanted a longer run than that star-crossed couple had managed.

As they strolled along, the sun broke through what had otherwise been an overcast sky. Putnam said to Sweetie, "If we spot a rainbow, we should start skipping and hum *Follow The Yellow Brick Road.*"

Sweetie said, "You're sweet, but I still have the sound of gunfire in my ears. Worse than that, I keep imagining how heartbroken I'd feel if things had gone the other way, if Welborn and Ellie Booker had been killed and the bad guys got away."

Putnam nodded. He'd have felt the pain, too.

Sweetie asked, "You called Maxi's school to make sure everything's okay there?"

"I did. The principal was quite understanding once I told her what happened at your workplace."

"Yeah. So you understand what Jim had in mind before all the shooting started, right?"

Putnam said, "He had it in mind for me to be the intermediary between Ellie Booker and your company so both parties would have the benefit of privileged conversations."

"Right. So how do you feel about that idea now?" Sweetie asked.

"In terms of protecting your business and Ms. Booker's privacy, and possibly her right not to incriminate herself, the idea is as sound as it was when it was first raised."

"You sound just like a lawyer," Sweetie said.

"Well, you knew what you were getting when you married me."

She leaned in and kissed Putnam, right there in public, something she never would have done to a man before meeting her husband.

"We could get a room," he said, "if you don't want to wait until we get home."

Now, she hip-bumped him.

Then in all seriousness, Sweetie asked, "Do you still want to play a part in all this, knowing now there are bad guys with orders to kill?"

Putnam said, "Your question implies that Jim McGill isn't just going to tell his prospective client to run and hide."

"No, he's not. We've already discussed that. He called Ellie, and now that she knows for sure that she's in danger, she wants to find out exactly who's behind it. Jim does, too."

"So, if Jim's involved, my guess is you are, too," Putnam said.

"Yeah."

Putnam sighed. "Well, whither thou goest."

"Only up to a point," Sweetie told him. "One of Maxi's parents has to remain at a safe distance."

Putnam fell silent long enough for Sweetie to ask, "No rebuttal?"

"The counter-argument is a young girl needs a mother more than a father."

"We both adopted Maxi, but you're a blood relation."

"Can't argue with that," Putnam said, "but I think the right example matters more than corpuscles. You'd be able to show Maxi how to grow up to be the kind of woman we both want her to be. I wouldn't."

Now, Sweetie fell silent.

They stopped walking as they reached Martin's Tavern.

"So, we'll both be careful, right?" Sweetie asked.

Putnam nodded. "If anybody comes to grief, it'll be the bad guys."

Just to be careful, though, they changed their minds about where they'd eat.

They'd go someplace that didn't have the slightest taint of tragedy.

Dangerous Dame — Gangplank Marina, Washington, DC

Ellie Booker looked out through the clear bulletproof door of her yacht's salon and saw two uniformed cops standing at the head of the gangplank leading to her vessel. Like they were bouncers at a hot new nightclub. Only these guys packed heat. There had been just one of them an hour ago. Playing the part of a friendly mariner with nothing to hide, she'd called out to the lone cop and asked if he'd like some coffee or a soft-drink. If he wasn't in the mood for either of those beverages, would he care for a beer?

The guy had enough of a sense of humor to laugh at the last

choice.

He'd said, "I'd love a beer, soon as I go off duty and give my girlfriend a call."

So he wasn't about to get himself into trouble with either his boss or his significant other.

Just what Ellie didn't want to hear from him. But his conscientious behavior became moot when the second cop showed up. Ellie had hoped if she'd given the first cop *anything* to drink he'd have to go find a place to pee, and she could sneak off. She hadn't exactly decided to leave her yacht unseen; she just wanted the option to do so.

The thought that had been preying on her mind the past several hours was that an anchored boat made a damn good target if the bad guys knew which marina it called home and the slip where it was tied up. Someone could come along with an automatic weapon or something even more destructive — a grenade-launcher, say — and wreak all sorts of hellacious damage.

Even if she wasn't killed in the first salvo, what could she do?

Dive overboard and swim for it underwater?

Ellie had never bought all that movie crapola about bullets whizzing through the water past the good guy without ever hitting him. To start with, she wasn't a guy. Nor was she particularly pure of heart. Either a bullet would find its target as a matter of her own bad luck or the bad guys would just toss an explosive charge into the water, and the shock-wave would turn her into jellyfish pudding.

While Ellie was entertaining those dark thoughts, she saw Detective Aidan Behan join the two uniformed cops on the dock. That made Ellie wonder where the Dragon Lady, Detective Chen, was. Outfitted with scuba gear, attaching a court-ordered tracking device to the hull of *Dangerous Dame?*

If that was the case, wouldn't it be funny if Ellie engaged the yacht's propeller? Suck Detective Chen right into its blades and make sushi out of the hostile harpy. No, sushi was Japanese, not Chinese. She couldn't think of an ethnically appropriate dish off the top of her head.

So, Ellie just slid the salon door open and called out to Detective Behan, "You guys forming a raiding party or what?"

Behan mimed the doffing of a cap and said, "Just the opposite, Ms. Booker. We're here to serve and protect with an emphasis on the latter."

The sonofagun had amped up his brogue, Ellie thought. The two uniforms laughed, and despite her best effort, Ellie couldn't help but feel charmed. She'd definitely have to watch out for that Behan guy.

She asked, "You've heard something about another threat?"

Staying in character, Behan said, "Perhaps we shouldn't converse at a shout."

Ellie gestured Behan forward and met him just as he stepped aboard.

No make yourself comfortable and have a root beer this time.

"So," she asked, "somebody still trying to do me in?"

The humor went out of the detective's eyes and he dropped the Irish accent. "Not that we know for certain, but as serious as the first attempt at killing you was, we decided to take no chances. With the permission of the White House itself, the MPD was given the unclassified parts of General Welborn Yates' military file. The man is clean as a whistle."

"Sure," Ellie said, "but maybe the pages you didn't see were the interesting parts."

Behan shrugged. "Could be, but the former deputy director of the FBI, Mr. Byron DeWitt, told our chief that he's seen the full document and General Yates really is the All-American Boy."

Ellie sighed. "He came through for me, that's for sure."

Behan said, "Eliminating the general as a target left you. As serious as the attempt on your life in Georgetown was, both the mayor and the chief decided it wouldn't look good for the city or the police department if we let you get killed."

"Yeah, you've got to watch out for bad PR," Ellie said. "It can be a career killer."

Behan grinned and slipped back into his brogue. "Sure and it is. Besides all that, I had the chance to read the entirety of *your* bio, as far as the printed word would have it. You're quite the investigative journalist and more than a bit of the hellion, aren't you?"

Ellie offered Behan a thin smile. "I just try not to take no for an answer."

"That's all well and good, but as this morning's ruckus showed, this crowd, the one that's so vexed with you, is no longer responding verbally."

That was a definite point, Ellie had to concede.

"So you and the guys on the dock are here to protect me?"

"They are. I'm here to see if I might charm a bit of helpful information out of you. Something that might keep you and any innocent police persons from harm."

"Are you really Irish?" Ellie asked. "And did you enter this country legally?"

Behan laughed. "I was born and raised in Dublin, but the building in which I debuted was the U.S. Embassy, American soil, and Mom and Dad, both born in Boston, were diplomats."

"And they let their son become a cop?"

"After the young scholar had graduated from Georgetown Law. But that's enough about me. Tell me about your *curriculum vitae*."

Ellie said, "Mom liked to drink; Dad liked drinking with Mom when he wasn't at sea with the Navy. I have a B.A. in Journalism from the University of Missouri. I tend to be feral in my approach to uncovering secrets. I've made some money, and I've pissed off quite a few people. Apparently, one or more of them want to kill me. Can't say I'm surprised."

Behan said, "All very interesting. Would you care to wax a bit more specific as to who it might have been looking down their gunsights at you this morning?"

Ellie thought about that for a moment. "You have a secure email address?"

He nodded. "Something my mother set up for me."

Ellie laughed.

Not embarrassed in the least, Behan told her. "She's very good at that sort of thing."

"Gimme," Ellie said.

She committed his email address to memory.

Then she told Behan, "Tell those two guys in uniform up on the dock to keep their eyes open, okay?"

"Oh, they know to do that," Behan said. "They're the only two brave enough to show themselves. Others are present, but they're very well hidden."

Damn, Ellie thought, if Detective Aidan Behan was trying to scare her, he was doing a damn good job.

Dumbarton Oaks — Washington, DC

"Well, I'll be darned," Patricia Grant McGill said after she opened the front door of the grand house she shared with Jim McGill. "The band is getting back together."

Her visitor, Deke Ky, repressed a sigh. Even former presidents demanded respect.

Well, some of them did.

"Yes, ma'am, that's one way to look at it," Deke said.

"Come in, Donald," she said, using her guest's formal name.

Something nobody but his mother ever did, and Mom was hiding out in Hanoi.

Hanging out with the Politburo there, anyway.

Deke stepped inside and glanced around. Most people would be sneaking peeks to see how members of the top one percent of the nation sheltered in place. Not Deke.

Patti saw that the former Secret Service special agent was actually doing a security assessment. She approved entirely. If Deke had any suggestion to make in the way of improvements, she'd pass it along to the powers that be of his former federal employer.

She'd guess that, at a minimum, he'd recommend that a former president of the United States not open her own front door. From a special agent's point of view, it would be better to let somebody more expendable handle that chore.

Even putting political standing aside, taking such a casual approach to life was a horrible idea for anyone possessing a massive fortune like Patricia Grant McGill's. Some kidnappers dreamed big. Why make things easy on them?

Hell, just the ensemble the former president was wearing had to be worth a small fortune. Deke could imagine some bandit with a gun and an eye for fashion saying, "Give me your purse, lady, and while you're at it, I'll take your frock, too."

Just the random thought of seeing the boss's wife disrobe might have been enough to make Deke blush, but the arrival of Jim McGill and Leo Levy saved him from embarrassment. McGill was dressed to the nines, too, in what had to be a bespoke suit. Leo didn't have his own tailor, but he was also sharply decked out.

Standing there in marked-down business attire from Men's Wearhouse, Deke felt like a poor relation.

McGill didn't seem to notice. He asked, "You find out where Fayez Mousa likes to dine?"

Compensating for his appearance with professional pride, Deke said, "I know where he's eating right now."

"Someplace not too far away?" McGill asked.

"Ten minutes with Leo behind the wheel," Deke said. "He'd just been served his appetizer when I headed here. He should be good for at least another hour."

McGill nodded in approval.

"And here I thought you boys got dressed up for me," Patti said to McGill and Leo.

McGill said, "Well, this is the anniversary of Leo getting his NASCAR certification."

"Yeah?" Deke asked Leo. "You didn't tell me that."

"I thought you and I'd step out for a sip or two after we got done with business," Leo told his friend. "You know, after Mom and Dad have turned in for the night."

Both McGill and Patti grinned.

Deke's spirits climbed.

But Patti said to McGill, "Why are you going to crash the Jordanian ambassador's dinner?"

He told her, "Those gunmen who shot up my shop this morning, the ones who almost killed Ellie and Welborn? They were Royal Jordanian Air Force at one time. Welborn spotted tattoos to that effect. I thought if I had a quiet chat with the ambassador, tell him I have the mayor's promise to keep the gunmen's nationalities secret, I might reasonably ask him for his government's help in finding out what the shooters' reason for going after Ellie is."

"Why you?" Patti asked.

McGill said, "Well, I have something of a social profile to talk with a big-time diplomat."

Patti replied, "And just in case you might have overrated your standing in DC society, you decided to take me out to dinner?"

McGill grinned. "*Exactement*, as the people in my Paris office might say. You said you wouldn't mind playing Nancy Drew just this once."

"Who knows?" Patti replied. "It might become a recurring role."

Marcel's — Washington, DC

The restaurant was labeled by one reviewer as "classic French with contemporary twists." Patti understood the seeming contradiction; McGill conceded he'd have to do a taste-test to find enlightenment. Most people would have had to wait weeks to get a table whatever their level of gustatory sophistication, but Patricia Grant McGill's former governmental occupation and her current private sector eminence made getting a last-minute table no problem.

Getting *exactly* the spot she and McGill wanted took only a slight personal nudge from Patti herself.

Ambassador Extraordinary and Plenipotentiary from the Hashemite Kingdom of Jordan to the United States of America, the honorable Fayez Mousa, was the sole occupant of a table in a corner nook of the restaurant that offered encircling drapery if one wished to dine privately in a public place. There were times when the ambassador availed himself of that amenity. Mostly, though, he preferred to be a people watcher.

It was politically useful for him to know who was dining where and with whom in Washington. His observations, at the very least, made for good gossip when he called home and spoke with his majesty. One never knew when the king might discern something important where the ambassador had seen only a reason to laugh. Though never aloud, of course.

Mousa wasn't sure, at first, what to make of the situation when former President Patricia Grant and her husband and henchman, James J. McGill, took the table adjacent to his. He was sincerely pleased when both eminent personages took notice of him, smiled, and gave him a discreet nod of acknowledgment.

The diplomat in Fayez Mousa admired the United States for producing two such able and beautiful women as Presidents Grant and Morrissey to lead the country. On a personal level, he envied both James J. McGill and Byron DeWitt for marrying such women. As a husband, however, he confessed solely to himself that he had a very hard time deferring to the judgment of his own wife.

Normally, he would think less of a man who would readily do so, but he was well aware of Mr. McGill's exploits facing down — and even beating down — villains of all stripes. Mousa knew to a certainty that he wouldn't have had the courage to attempt any such things.

He even sat back in his chair a bit when he saw McGill stand and approach him.

Had the man somehow intuited that he'd had improper thoughts about his wife?

The ambassador's nascent anxiety eased when he saw McGill

smile at him and extend a hand in cordial greeting.

"Good evening, Mr. Ambassador," McGill said. "Please forgive me for interrupting your meal. May I have a moment of your time?"

"Of course, Mr. McGill. Think nothing of it. Please take a seat."

The ambassador gestured to his guest to sit in one of the empty chairs at the table.

McGill had never met the man, but after eight years in the White House, he was far from surprised when total strangers recognized him and extended an unearned measure of courtesy. From a diplomat, though, civility was stock in trade. Well, from most foreign emissaries anyway; there were always exceptions.

"Would you mind if President Grant joined us?" McGill asked.

Mousa got to his feet. "I would be deeply honored, sir."

McGill stood and said, "I'll be right back."

Patti rose to meet her husband. She took McGill's arm and they stepped over to the diplomat's table. McGill made the introduction. "Ambassador Fayez Mousa, Patricia Grant McGill."

Mousa effected an elegant bow, gracious but not servile. "A great pleasure, ma'am."

"For me also, Mr. Ambassador." Patti said.

By now, the maitre d' was hovering nearby.

This was a confluence of power to be attended to at the restaurant's highest level.

McGill said to the ambassador, "Forgive my asking, sir, but do you drink champagne?"

"I do not imbibe alcohol, but thank you for inquiring. I wouldn't mind a glass of sparkling mineral water if we have something to celebrate. Do we?"

"Let's hope so. A matter of cooperation that might be helpful to all of us," McGill said.

Patti put in an order for the water, the wine, and the chef's vegetarian tasting menu.

McGill instructed the maitre d' that the table would like privacy after they were served. The curtain around the table would be drawn.

The Yates House — Washington, DC

With their twins, Aria and Callista, safely tucked in and fast asleep, Welborn and Kira Yates took to their bed. They went at each other like wild animals. Blood was not shed, but teeth marks were left on several points of anatomy. Keeping the resulting nerve signals from producing shouts of surprise and even pain became a part of the exercise.

They weren't so much trying to couple as to infuse each other with every cell of their respective bodies. It was only when Welborn almost propelled Kira off the bed and possibly out a second-floor window that their frenzy had to be curtailed. Welborn looped an arm around Kira's waist and saved her from a bone-breaking fall. He gently drew her close to lie on her side against him in a spoon fashion.

A minute passed before either of them had the lung capacity to speak again.

Then Kira said, "I think you might have kept me from sailing out into the backyard."

"That would have been hard to explain to the neighbors, wouldn't it?"

"The Goodmans are still in Curaçao; the Colbys are still in La Jolla."

Closing the last millimeter of space between himself and his wife, Welborn said, "Why don't we go somewhere warm in the winter? You've told me you come from a monied family."

"I do, but you've forbidden me from spoiling anyone who lives under our roof."

"What was I thinking?" Welborn asked.

"That our girls should have good character and we shouldn't be snoots."

"Well, three cheers for me then," Welborn said.

"I'd say you deserve a fourth cheer. You just saved a second damsel in distress in fewer than 24 hours."

"Laudable," Welborn said, "but I don't suppose you'd want me to make that my specialty."

After a beat of silence, Kira asked, "Are we going to discuss your job prospects?"

Welborn took a similar pause before saying, "Let's settle on the ground rules first."

"I believe that we've just displayed a certain amount of passion for one another."

"Indeed. I'd just like to make sure we don't do anything to preempt an encore."

"Well, you could take the side of the bed closer to the window."

Welborn laughed and started to nuzzle his wife's neck.

Kira lightly pressed her fingernails into her husband's thigh. "First ground rule: No distractions until we settle on the preservation of the only male member of this household."

Welborn sighed and let himself relax. "You're right. So, wasting no time, am I correct in thinking you'd prefer that I go to work for the FBI, assuming they'll have me, rather than become a McGill sleuth?"

"Yes."

"The reason being?" Welborn asked.

"Well, Flyboy, I haven't even begun to get bored by you. I'd like to keep you around and in working order for the foreseeable future."

"I'm just your plaything then?"

"Mine and the girls', in appropriate fashions."

Welborn said, "So if Aria and Callista were to come to me as young teens and say, 'Dad, we'd like you to teach us to fly so we can get a jump on being accepted by the Air Force Academy and become fighter jocks,' that would be okay by you?"

"I'd hate it," Kira said. "Maybe we should go our separate ways and see each other only on holidays."

"In that case, I'd die of heartbreak."

Kira shook her head. "Neither the girls nor I could have that."

"So … I'm leaning to the FBI job, if it's offered," Welborn said.

Kira rolled over to look at her husband. "Not just to please me, right?"

"Pleasing you is part of it," he admitted, "but another part is that I value serving my country. I'd likely be more able to do that in the FBI than working in the private sector."

Kira kissed him. "Hooray for public service."

Welborn held up a hand. "Try not to get ahead of things here. When I speak with Director Benjamin about the FBI job, I'm going to tell her that I wouldn't want to be stuck behind a desk full time. Every so often, I'll want to head an investigation or two in the field. Otherwise, I might become a potbellied bureaucrat, and my wife would lose interest and leave me."

Kira nodded. "A large part of your appeal is physical."

"Ditto," Welborn told her. "Beyond that, in what happened with Ms. Booker this morning, I rediscovered a part of myself."

"A death wish?" Kira asked, drawing back from her husband.

"I don't want to die," Welborn said, "but there is something viscerally satisfying for me in being willing to confront danger for a good cause. I felt that every time I took off in a fighter aircraft, and I felt it again this morning. It's a part of who I am."

Kira sighed and crossed herself.

"You're becoming religious?" Welborn asked.

"I might need to if things go the way you want."

Welborn added, "I'd also like to work just one case for Mr. McGill: help him find out who's threatening Ms. Booker."

Kira said, "I also might take to wearing a black shawl."

"I promise to duck if things get risky again," Welborn said. "I want all the time I can have with you and our two sweethearts."

Kira embraced Welborn and said, "You'd damn well better duck. I can tell you firsthand, as someone who lost her own dad, it's no picnic not having a father."

Marcel's — Washington, DC

Libations and food were served, and the curtain was drawn

around the table at which Jim McGill, Patti Grant McGill, and Fayez Mousa sat.

McGill said to the Jordanian ambassador, "In the interest of saving time, would it be acceptable if we speak as we dine?"

"Time is of the essence?" Mousa asked.

"At least one life is probably at risk, and two have already been lost," McGill said.

Mayor Rockelle Bullard had called McGill earlier that evening to let him know that the second shooter involved in the attempt on Ellie Booker's life had succumbed.

Without saying a word to anyone.

"American lives were lost?" Mousa asked, fearing the worst.

There was a note of uncertainty in the ambassador's voice, but he understood implicitly that if for some reason any American had died at the hands of a Jordanian, he or someone on his embassy staff would be speaking directly with the State Department and the FBI.

McGill made the reality of the situation plain. "The two fatalities are your country's nationals."

The ambassador grimaced but he also felt a measure of relief. He was now, possibly, free to feel aggrieved or even outraged. Depending on the circumstances, of course.

In any case, his appetite had been ruined. He looked at the bottle of champagne as if tempted by the thought of dulling the pain with alcohol. Good judgment, however, intervened on the side of keeping his head clear.

Still, he gestured toward the champagne bottle and said, "Forgive me, but I can't really see a cause for celebration. And how did you determine the nationality of those who died?"

McGill explained in detail what had happened outside his office building that morning. He was mildly surprised the diplomat hadn't heard the news through either mass or social media. He finished with the description of the tattoos on the hands of the two slain would-be assassins.

Mousa closed his eyes and uttered what might have been a

prayer in Arabic.

A prayer or a curse.

Opening his eyes, he looked at Patti first and then McGill.

"I am truly at a loss what we might have to celebrate tonight," Mousa said.

McGill said, "Let's start with the fact that two innocent civilians who were fired upon and the two police officers who tried to make an arrest didn't die. Then there's the fact that regrettable though their deaths may be, the two assassins will never again try to take anyone else's life. Finally, at least for the moment, your king and your country have been spared the embarrassment of a public revelation of the nationality of the two would-be killers."

That last point struck home for Mousa. He picked up his glass of sparkling water and took a drink. Then he asked, "How long can we keep that last point confidential?"

"Both President Morrissey and Mayor Bullard have agreed to withhold the shooters' identities for the time being," McGill said. "Maybe for a day or two. Certainly no longer than a week."

Patti added, "The United States and Jordan have a long and enduring friendship. The powers-that-be here in Washington, on both the federal and local levels, want to continue that relationship."

Fayez Mousa understood both intuitively and professionally what he was hearing. It would be helpful to both sides if the Hashemite Kingdom of Jordan aided its American friends in pursuing this investigation to find out who was behind this brazen murder attempt. Doing so would diminish the diplomatic downside of the shooting in Washington.

McGill echoed the ambassador's thoughts: "It's always better to be seen as part of the solution rather than part of the problem."

Patti added, "President Morrissey understands that if the FBI were to take over the investigation of the attempted shooting of two Americans in Washington by foreign nationals, there would be no way to keep the story from reaching the public."

"The Metropolitan Police will investigate?" Mousa asked. "Won't that be enough to draw media attention?"

"Yes," McGill said, "but not to the same degree as if the FBI were involved."

Patti told the ambassador, "An initial deal has been struck with the Metro Police. They will work with Jim and his people."

"The woman who was the target of the assassins had just become my client this morning," he explained to Mousa.

"You're sure the authorities will allow this?" the ambassador asked.

McGill said, "Mayor Bullard is an old friend, and it helps that I have my own police experience."

"Yes, of course." Mousa took a moment to absorb everything that he'd just heard. Then he asked, "How may His Majesty's government be of help?"

McGill said, "We have photos of the two shooters. We have photos of their tattoos. We have fingerprints, blood and tissue samples. We could send all of this information electronically to Amman, but with the whole world spying on the internet, President Grant suggested that sending the information the old-fashioned way, in a diplomatic pouch, might be safer."

Mousa nodded emphatically. "Yes, much safer and wiser. Thank you, ma'am." He thought for a moment. "Your governments, federal and local, must learn the identities of the assassins."

"That and the name of any organization for which they worked," McGill said. "Ideally, before the next team of shooters might arrive, if it hasn't already."

Patti said, "A second attempted assassination on American soil would certainly bring FBI participation into the investigation and global media exposure. That wouldn't be good for either of our countries."

"No, that would not be good at all," Mousa said.

"You have your car with you, Mr. Ambassador?" McGill asked.

"Yes, of course."

McGill said, "When we get up from the table, tell your driver to act as if your car is having engine trouble. Our car will be right behind yours. My driver will get out and look under the hood of your car with your driver to see what the trouble is. You'll stay in your car; we'll stay in ours. My driver will discreetly give the data on the would-be assassins to your driver. The engine trouble will be quickly resolved and we'll all be on our respective ways home."

Patti leaned forward and put a hand on Mousa's wrist. "Needless to say, we'll need the names of the dead men sooner rather than later. We'll need everything you can find out about them. The kingdom's swift cooperation will be its surest guarantee of continuing a strong alliance with the United States and a good reputation around the world."

"Yes, of course," Mousa said.

McGill poured champagne for himself and Patti.

Mousa picked up his glass of sparkling water once more.

"To successful cooperation and lasting goodwill," McGill said.

They all drank to that.

M &W Private Investigations — Washington, DC

Marvin Meeker stared at his desktop computer, refreshing the screen every ten seconds to see if the name of the Grand Slam lottery game winner — other than Beemer's brother-in-law, Samuel J. MacCray — had been publicly identified yet. The website for *The Baltimore Sun* popped up repeatedly like a nervous tic.

"You're gonna wear that damn thing out," Beemer said, "and it's the only computer we've got."

Beemer was lying on the office sofa. They'd bought one long and strong enough for Beemer to nap on. Meeker told him, "You'll wear out the furniture before I'm done with this machine."

The two of them had full pensions and reasonable amounts of savings that they could have lived on, but they both liked working cases. They especially enjoyed outsmarting bad guys who made the mistake of thinking they were smarter than two old former cops. More than that, it was a joy not to have to put up with the rules, regulations and superior officers of the police force.

Other than former Captain Bullard, now the mayor of the whole damn town.

She'd always leaned on them when she thought they were pushing their comedy routine too far, but she was fair and backed them up every damn time they'd stuck their necks out on some investigation. Of course, it didn't hurt that their batting average on closing cases was .995.

They'd kept count. Only five bad guys had either gotten away or been let go in court out of the 1,000 arrests they'd made in their careers together. Maybe Sherlock Holmes went them one better by never striking out on a case, but nobody else in town had topped them.

Not even James J. McGill. The man himself had told them once that his record didn't come close to theirs. But he'd spent more time on patrol and being a boss. Even with that disadvantage, though, he'd certainly made a go of it since turning P.I.

And he'd never let his good fortune, marrying a woman who got herself elected president, go to his head. He'd gone out and cracked some big cases.

Even so, Beemer asked Meeker, "You think we're really going to need Jim McGill's help?"

Getting no immediate reply, Beemer thought he might've drifted off for a moment and Meeker had stepped into the bathroom for a little relief. Just to be sure though, Beemer said, "You there, Marvin?"

"Damn right I'm here, and I just got us a news bulletin from Baltimore."

Beemer swung his feet to the floor and sat up.

"You got the name of the winner in Maryland?"

Meeker smiled at his friend and nodded. "Constance Parker. Lives in Rockville."

Stepping over to Meeker's desk, Beemer whistled. "You'd almost have to win the lottery to live up in that neck of the woods. Is Constance a well-turned-out white lady?"

Meeker's hands flew over the computer's keyboard and a

headshot of a woman appeared.

"Well, would you look at that?" Beemer said. "We have ourselves a rich sister. Not hard on the eyes either."

"Not at all," Meeker agreed. "You ready for a little road trip?"

Beemer said, "Man, Rockville is hardly more than motoring to the end of the block. Why don't we wait until morning?"

Meeker agreed up to a point. "Yeah, it's less than 20 miles. At this time of night, minding the speed limit, maybe take us half-an-hour from when we step out the door. In the morning, even in weekend traffic, who knows what happens? Maybe a semi-trailer carrying a load of Krazy Glue jackknifes and ain't nobody going nowhere. But it's your brother-in-law we're working for here, so you decide."

Beemer sighed. "Okay. Let's go."

"I'll drive and you can nap on the way," Meeker said, being gracious.

"You think we should let Jim McGill know what we're doing?"

Meeker laughed. "It's just the one woman we'll be dealing with."

"As far as we know," Beemer replied.

Dumbarton Oaks — Washington, DC

Leo stopped the car in front of the McGills' house.

"Not the usual weekend hours tomorrow, boss?" Leo asked.

Meaning did Leo have the day off.

McGill said, "I'll need you at eight a.m., Leo. I want to talk with Ellie Booker bright and early, but not at dawn. You pull someone out of bed, she's not as likely to confide her darkest secrets before she's had a cup of coffee."

"That was in your police manual back in Chicago?" Patti asked.

McGill grinned. "No, the good stuff never gets written down. A wise old detective, Dan Moretti, who worked violent crimes, told me even the worst offenders were a bit more civilized if they had a little something in their stomachs."

"Even if it's just caffeine?" Deke asked sounding dubious.

"Ideally, you'd hope they prefer decaf," McGill said, "but, yeah, even straight coffee. The idea is an empty stomach is a subconscious reminder that starvation might not be far away. Especially if someone else gets to decide when your next meal will be. That being the case, the mope will be more likely to resist if he's hungry. At least that's the way Dan explained it to me."

"You didn't follow his advice back then?" Patti asked.

McGill said, "In my patrol days, I'd just try to talk reasonably with the people I stopped. If a guy got combative, I'd give him a sharp kick on the ankle. That hurts like the dickens, and it made sure the guy wasn't going to outrun me. Also, the guy would look like a wimp if he started complaining about police brutality because of a boo-boo on his ankle."

"Probably be easy for you to claim it was all an accident, too," Deke said, nodding in approval.

"Yeah," McGill said.

Leo just grinned.

But Patti asked, "That kick was a part of Dark Alley?"

McGill nodded. "Even street brawlers rarely think about protecting their ankles, but most people can't fight worth a damn on only one good leg."

All three of McGill's companions in the car seemed to make a mental note of that point.

Then Deke changed the subject. "I'll call Lily Kealoha in the morning. See if any NYPD cops working the United Nations detail have heard anything about renegade Jordanians entering the country."

McGill said, "That'd be good. But we don't want the word to spread too widely and have it get back to the bad guys."

"Right," Deke said.

Patti added. "I can call Jean Morrissey in the morning and ask her to have the State Department's Bureau of Intelligence and Research start looking into this matter quietly."

"Okay, then," McGill said, "it will be a working weekend for all of us."

He and Patti got out of the car and watched Leo and Deke drive away.

Then McGill turned to Patti and asked, "You haven't caught the bug, have you?"

"What virus might that be?" she replied.

"You know what I mean."

"Work for you? I have my own business to run, remember?"

"I do. But you still haven't answered my question."

Patti grinned and said, "Please don't kick my ankle."

McGill embraced her. "Okay, I'll just put you in a bear hug."

"Mmm. I like that much better. Okay, I'll come clean, copper. I had fun tonight, negotiating with Ambassador Mousa, talking with the guys in the car, hearing something I hadn't known about your past as a cop. It was all a little … seductive."

"So I should counteract all that with stories about how frustrating and even aggravating the work can also be?" McGill asked.

"No, don't do that," Patti told him. "It would spoil the mood for when we go inside."

McGill had no trouble understanding that clue.

Dangerous Dame — Gangplank Marina, Washington, DC

Ellie Booker made what she thought might be a last chance phone call and was pleased when it was answered on the first ring.

"Ellie, my dear girl, I thought you might be calling soon."

She recognized Hugh Collier's voice but just barely. He sounded much older than she remembered and his voice was raspy. She couldn't hide her surprise or even get straight to the point about the help she wanted to request.

"Jesus, Hugh, what the hell happened to you?"

"Buggered the wrong bloke, I suspect."

Hugh was gay. He was also the chairman of the board and

managing director of WorldWide News. Hugh had transformed his late uncle's media empire from acting as a megaphone for right-wing politicians throughout the English-speaking world to being a news operation that actually played things straight. More or less.

He and Ellie had worked together off and on for years, but not for the past half-decade.

"AIDS?" Ellie asked.

"Nothing quite that simple. The medical wallahs are actually on the doorstep of solving that horrific problem. They're not quite so close to working out my situation."

"Goddamnit, Hugh, what's ailing you?"

"Ever the great reporter getting straight to the point," Hugh rasped. "My dear, I'm afraid I have bilateral testicular cancer."

Just hearing those words made Ellie feel sick.

Before she could even express her regret, Hugh continued, "My physician said my best chance was to be neutered."

"Oh, God, Hugh. I'm so sorry."

"You're not going to urge me to fight on?"

Ellie knew that before Hugh had arrived in the U.S., he'd been a top-level Australian rules football player. Footy, as they called it Down Under, had struck Ellie the few times she'd watched a match as a riot in which a ball occasionally changed hands. Even so, she recognized it was a bruising full-contact game in which the players used none of the protective gear American football teams donned.

Hugh had told Ellie more than once that it took "bloody great balls" to play the game.

"No, Hugh. Die with your balls on."

The afflicted man managed to laugh. "That's my girl. You know, of course, you're the only skirt I've ever wanted to shag."

Ellie replied, "You've never even seen me in a skirt, but thank you."

"Even in these sad days, my dear, I still have an imagination."

"You'd probably be disappointed."

"Well, there's always one way to tell for certain. Not that I'd be so heartless as to expect any actual physical contact in my condition.

But I wouldn't mind a peek before I take my final bow."

Ellie paused to think about that.

"I called to ask for a favor, Hugh."

"Yes, I thought you might. I know about your close call this morning. That American bloke who took you to the pavement was quick as a wink. My hat's off to him."

Ellie had spent hours watching television clips of the assassination attempt and aftermath in which she'd had the starring role. Well, co-starring anyway. Welborn Yates was the real headliner. Still, she hadn't seen a video that caught General Yates in action.

So …

"You bought the exclusive rights to that clip you just described," she told Hugh.

"I certainly did. That's why I thought I might hear from you."

Ellie asked, "Did you let the police see the video?"

"Sent a copy straight away to Mayor Rockelle Bullard. I rather like her. Told the good woman I'd embargo the video from use by WorldWide for 24 hours. Hoped that would give her people a good head-start. Most politicians, I suspect, would have huffed and said they'd set terms for the clip's release. The mayor only said, 'Thank you. I'll take that deal anytime.' I don't know that she's always so agreeable, but I like her grasp of reality."

"May I see the clip?" Ellie asked.

"Certainly. I'll screen it for you myself, and we'll discuss where we might hide you. That's the help you want, isn't it?"

"Yes, it is. Thank you, Hugh. If you really want to see me naked and promise not to laugh, I'll do that for you. You know, if you promise to drop dead immediately afterward."

Collier laughed again, this time almost sounding like his old self.

"You'll be flying into New York?" he asked.

"I'll be coming in on my boat."

"Very well. I'll find a nice spot at a yacht club and call you when I've made arrangements."

"Thank you. I'll check the marine weather forecast to make

sure I'm not heading into a storm and then up-anchor. If I don't hear from you first, I'll call you when I've made it halfway."

"Do hurry," Collier said. "I don't want to die before I see your pink bottom."

"Gay to the end," Ellie said.

"No question of that. I might also have a business proposition for you."

Despite likely facing another assassination attempt, that piqued Ellie's interest.

"I'll be there as soon as I can," she said.

"What the hell?" Detective Aidan Behan said. "Where could that woman be going after dark?"

Using binoculars, he had his eyes on the *Dangerous Dame.* He'd just seen Ellie Booker cast off the lines that secured her boat to its slip. Then she went to the helm and lit up the yacht. A moment later, the engine roared to life.

Ellie Booker was clearly heading out to … where?

Damned if he knew. Nobody on the MPD including Behan had thought she was going to make a run for it. No, that wasn't quite right. She wasn't a suspect in a crime; she was the intended victim of one. The police had no reason to restrain her freedom of movement.

For just a second Ellie's 74-foot vessel seemed to have a hiccup as it was clearing its slip. It resembled a car hitting a bump in the road. Only there was no road, so how could there be a bump? Maybe the vessel had hit a piece of floating debris in the water. That was the best guess Behan, a landlubber, could come up with.

Anyway, *Dangerous Dame* cleared the slip and maneuvered toward what Behan guessed was a passage to open water. He had a dozen special duty officers, the cops' answer to Delta Force soldiers, hiding out around the marina waiting to see if any bad guys came to visit Ms. Booker in the dead of night. They'd pounce if needed.

Behan would have been the guy to order the charge.

Watching Ellie Booker's yacht head out to open water, he wondered if he should request a helicopter to follow her. He was pretty sure the Metro PD didn't have its own PT boat to go after her. Though maybe Mayor Bullard could get the Navy to lend a hand. After all, she was the one who ordered up the special duty cops.

While still pondering his next move, Behan got a news alert through his earpiece.

The commander of the special duty guys was calling.

"We've got a floater."

"A what?" Behan asked.

"A body in the water. Wearing a diving mask, wet suit, and fins."

"Why the hell would anyone be doing that at night?" Behan asked.

"Looks like he's dead, been cut up pretty good."

"Jesus," Behan said.

"Thing is, the body surfaced right at the slip where the yacht just left."

"Oh, shit," Behan said, understanding what that might mean. "You think the guy was screwing with Ms. Booker's boat somehow?"

The commander said, "Yeah, that's just what I think, and he paid for it, too."

CHAPTER 2

Saturday, February 2, 2019, Rockville, Maryland

Meeker and Beemer arrived in Rockville just after midnight. Given the hour and exercising caution, they didn't go directly to Constance Parker's address, which Beemer had found online. They made their first stop the Maryland State Police building in Rockville. They asked to see the detective sergeant on duty. He was the guy who'd be in charge of any criminal investigations in the area that rose to a level above the resources possessed by the local cops.

The two retired MPD detectives decided to play everything straight — for their own good as well as in the interest of their client. Rockville was the type of well-heeled place where two black men couldn't loiter at night in a parked car outside a million-dollar home without arousing suspicion. Better to give the state police a heads-up beforehand than have to bail yourself out after being arrested.

It was a pain in the ass, but not nearly as big a one as playing things the wrong way. Maryland was thought of as a border state, just barely ascribed to the North, but Maryland had wanted to join the Confederacy during the Civil War and would have if the state's legislators hadn't been kidnapped by the Union Army.

Warfare then and now was always subject to unusual turns.

An ironic benefit of Maryland's forced loyalty to the Union

was that the state was not included as being under the writ of the Emancipation Proclamation. Only the slaves within the Confederacy were deemed to be freed by Abraham Lincoln's decree. Initially, anyway.

Meeker and Beemer didn't learn of these historical quirks at the police academy, but they were required reading at Howard University, from which the two men had graduated. It was the street smarts learned on the job, however, that informed them that there likely were plenty of crackers still living in Maryland, and more than a few of them wore police uniforms.

The visiting PIs even thought the detective sergeant in Rockville might be one of them.

Only he turned out to be African-American.

Nonetheless, Detective Sergeant Dalton Rivers turned out to be a pain in the ass.

He invited Meeker and Beemer into his office, but the moment their backsides hit the vinyl seats he'd offered them he asked, "You boys carrying?"

"Only the weight of the world," Meeker said.

Beemer kept a straight face.

Rivers frowned. He'd never cared for smart-asses.

Beemer told him. "We left our sidearms back home in DC."

"That's good, real good. Glad we got that cleared up." Rivers nodded in agreement with himself. Then he asked, "How about long-barrel weapons?"

Meeker didn't care if the Maryland statie liked him or not, and he said, "We're retired MPD detectives who set up our own business. We're not here on safari."

Rivers frowned and shook his head. He asked Beemer, "Is that man always like this?"

"Usually worse," Beemer said, "and if I wasn't so tired I'd be right there with him."

"Well, you two might've been hot stuff in Washington, but you're in a whole different world now," Rivers informed them.

"Which is why we dropped in," Meeker said, "hoping for a

little professional collegiality."

"Damn, you two know big words and everything," Rivers said mockingly.

Beemer, seeming to play the good cop, said, "Sure, you come to DC on business, we'll take you out for a dinner and drinks." Then he added, "We'll let you browse our dictionary while we're waiting for the food."

While the detective sergeant was working out a response, Meeker flipped a business card on the man's desk. Only this one wasn't from James J. McGill. It came from Washington, DC Mayor Rockelle Bullard.

Beemer, of course, was in on the plan on how they'd play this.

They'd discussed it on the drive to Maryland.

They'd thought they might have to use the ploy on some redneck, but it also applied to a guy like Rivers as well. Somebody in love with himself and his authority.

The detective sergeant glanced at the card and tried to act unimpressed. "That's supposed to mean something to me? An out-of-state mayor's business card. You might have just found it somewhere anyway."

"She was our captain when we handled all the biggest investigations in the city. You know, the *nation's* capital." Meeker said. "Give her a call."

Beemer added, "Another thing is your very own governor, right here in Maryland, is one of our mayor's big supporters. He did fundraisers for her, but maybe you didn't know that or it doesn't matter to you."

Both Meeker and Beemer leaned forward, awaiting a response, letting the guy know he wasn't going to win this spitting contest.

The combined weight of their stares forced Rivers to sit back in his chair.

"Y'all just mind your manners in this town and state," he said.

Meeker and Beemer got to their feet. Meeker picked up Rockelle's card.

Beemer started for the door.

Meeker saluted Rivers and said, “Yassuh, boss.”

Dumbarton Oaks — Washington, DC

More often than not, McGill and Patti no longer took business phone calls at home after 10:00 p.m. Eastern Time. Any call that came in after that was forwarded to an answering-service operator tasked with taking a message and delivering it the next morning during business hours. A phone might ring in the McGills’ home in the depths of the night only in the event of a serious injury or a demise suffered by someone on a short list of names.

That list also served as a directory of those whose calls should be forwarded at any hour.

It was a protocol McGill and Patti worked out to keep from having their sleep interrupted.

So when McGill’s phone rang at 1:44 a.m., a jolt of adrenaline brought him to complete and apprehensive consciousness. All he could think was, “Who died?” Somehow, it hadn’t occurred to him that someone he knew and held dear had merely suffered a grievous injury.

He answered the call by asking, “What’s happened?”

The ringing phone had also jarred Patti awake. “Who is it?”

The voice that would provide the answer to Patti’s question wasn’t one McGill had expected. It didn’t come from an employee of the call-service, someone who might remain phlegmatic about the demise of a stranger. Instead, he heard the tense tones of Mayor Rockelle Bullard.

She said, “Sorry about the damn time, but I got pulled out of bed, too.”

“Who is it?” Patti asked with a note of anxiety.

“Mayor Bullard,” McGill said, covering the phone with a hand.

Returning to the call, he asked, “What’s the problem, Madam Mayor? And how did you get through to me?”

The latter question provoked a harsh laugh. “Some answering

service guy took the call. He said I wasn't on the list of people to be put through to you. I *persuaded* him to add my name."

She laughed again.

"Scared him good, did you?" McGill asked.

"Only if he wanted to set foot in this town again. Seems he did. Anyway, the police in the person of Detective Behan called me just a short while ago. Behan tried the chief of police first, but her phone must turn off better than mine. I'm going to have a talk with her about that, but that's not your concern. What I thought you should know is Ms. Ellie Booker started up that fancy boat of hers and headed out to sea."

McGill thought he must still have some cobwebs in his mind. He asked, "Out to sea?"

The mayor said, "Yeah. Detective Behan is a resourceful type. I might make him chief of police later this morning. Anyway, he somehow managed to get a Coast Guard helicopter airborne and shadow Ms. Booker's yacht or whatever it is. Following Behan's suggestion, the chopper stayed within visual contact of the boat, but was far enough away not to be heard."

"That was good thinking," McGill said.

He momentarily covered the phone's mouthpiece again and whispered to Patti, "Nobody's hurt or dead."

She sighed in relief and let her head fall back on her pillow.

Her eyes closed, and McGill was glad she didn't want to play Nancy Drew right then.

"Yeah, well," Rockelle told McGill, "it was good thinking but there were limits to what the Coast Guard helicopter could do. It tracked Ms. Booker's boat down the Potomac to the Chesapeake Bay and heading toward the Atlantic Ocean, but the chopper had to turn back because of fuel concerns."

"So nobody knows where Ellie is?" McGill asked.

"She wasn't answering her phone and nobody else that I might bully answered either. But Detective Behan, bless him, made a note of what kind of boat Ms. Booker has. He's checking to see how far she can go before topping off her gas-tank again. Then he'll Google and see where she might either fill up or park her boat next."

McGill said, "That is good thinking. I'd like to speak with Detective Behan."

"You keep your hands off him, Mr. McGill. I need him on the MPD, even if I don't make him chief for a while."

McGill repressed a laugh. He had thought the detective might make a good hire, if not immediately then eventually.

"Noted, Madam Mayor," he said. Then he added, "Is this where the other shoe drops? You didn't call me at this late hour just to say Ellie's gone for a moonlight cruise, did you?"

Rockelle Bullard sighed. "No, I didn't. The police at the marina found a dead body in the water right in line with where Ms. Booker's boat left its slip or whatever you call it."

That put a knot in McGill's stomach.

"Was there any sign of foul play on the body?" he asked.

"No gunshots, no broken bones, but what I was told the man got cut up something awful."

McGill said, "Knifed?"

"No. The medical examiner at the scene said the damage was done by a propeller or two. You know, the kind on a boat. And Detective Behan said when Ms. Booker got underway, it looked like her yacht hit a bump, gave a kind of a jerk. He didn't know what might have caused that until he saw the body come to the surface. It was wearing a shredded wet-suit."

McGill squeezed his eyes closed for a moment.

"Someone was under Ellie's boat when she engaged the engine, and he was killed?"

"That's what the evidence suggests," the mayor replied.

"Ellie couldn't have seen him. She had no way of knowing what was about to happen."

Rockelle produced a mordant laugh. "Neither did the guy who got all cut up. But nobody's blaming her. Maybe she didn't even feel the bump in the road if you want to call it that. But the thing is, this dead man, he had a little round tattoo on his right hand. Sound familiar?"

"Another Jordanian flag?" McGill asked.

Patti opened her eyes a bit and began to listen, more intently apparently than when her peepers had been shut. Maybe Nancy Drew never slept.

Rockelle told McGill, "No, this one, I'm told, is a Lebanese flag. Getting another Middle Eastern country involved is not a good thing to my way of thinking."

"Not good at all," McGill agreed.

"You understand now what my main reason is for calling you this late, right?" the mayor asked.

McGill sighed. "The guy under the boat wasn't there to inspect the hull. He might have been there to put a hole in it. That or do something to … damage the propeller maybe. Leave the boat dead in the water to make a lovely target for some other vessel."

"Detective Behan also had another idea about those propellers. The boat, it seems, has two of them. If Ms. Booker is out on the ocean, like we think she is right now, and she loses the ability to point the boat in the direction she wants it to go, that wouldn't be a good thing if a storm came up. As I somewhat understand what was explained to me, you don't want a high wind hitting you directly sideways, or your boat can get tipped right over. Of course, if the guy who got killed did put a bomb on the hull, that'd sink your ship even in calm waters."

"Yes, it would," McGill agreed in a quiet voice.

"So, since we can't reach Ms. Booker, Detective Behan thought with her being your client, maybe she might call you. Could be a real good idea to put her on your list of acceptable late-night callers, too."

"I will," McGill said.

Hoping Ellie wasn't already dead.

The White House — Washington, DC

Chief of Staff Galia Mindel met Patti at the West Wing door to the White House. There had been a rift between the two women while Galia had been out of government work, after the Grant Administration had closed up shop. Then after a year in the wilderness, Jean Morrissey, the new president, had asked Galia to reclaim her old job as White House chief of staff.

Galia mistakenly thought Patti had made that happen.

She hadn't, but Galia apparently still labored under that misapprehension.

"Madam President, it's so good to see you," she said, extending a hand.

Patti shook it and said, "There's only one president around here, Galia, and it's not me."

"Yes, ma'am, but you still must have President Morrissey's ear because she cleared two appointments to speak with you. May I know what you have to tell her?"

The two women passed through the door held open for them by a Marine.

"You'll be in the meeting with us, won't you?" Patti asked.

"Yes."

"I know it's not easy to be patient in your job, Galia, but you'll hear the details in just a moment."

By denying the chief of staff advance knowledge of what she had to say, Patti guaranteed that she'd actually get to meet the president. If Patti had shared the information with Galia beforehand, there was a chance that the chief of staff might decide the president didn't need to bother with seeing her predecessor. Not about something Galia deemed to be unimportant.

Stranger things had happened than one president snubbing another.

Or even a chief of staff giving a former chief executive the cold shoulder.

Galia nodded and possibly even respected the countermove.

She opened the door to the Oval Office and the two women stepped inside.

Seated behind her desk when Patti and Galia entered, Jean

Morrissey got to her feet and crossed the room to greet the woman who'd broken the glass ceiling at the pinnacle of American politics. She embraced her friend, smiled, and said, "You just refuse to age, Patricia."

Patti grinned and said, "I sold my soul when I went into modeling. I think my reprieve from crow's feet is about to expire any day now. Then there will be hell to pay."

Jean laughed and said, "You'll just have to get that husband of yours to rub moisturizing cream into your face."

"Not a bad idea," Patti replied. "Is that what Byron does for you?"

"No, he just buffs my hockey scars." The president returned to the seat behind her desk and gestured to Patti and Galia to sit in the guest chairs. "You said you had important news, Patti. Not quite the same as saying bad news, but I've got a feeling that's what it is."

Galia leaned forward anticipating word of a problem.

"It's bad, yes, but on a small scale so far. Might be limited to one target. Then again, it could be the start of something bigger and more ominous."

Having set the stage, Patti told the president and Galia how the attempt on Ellie Booker's life had involved two pilots, former or current, in the Royal Jordanian Air Force, and how a possible effort to sabotage Ellie's yacht might have been carried out last night by another former or current military pilot, this one from Lebanon.

"I got the report about yesterday's attempted murder in my daily briefing," Jean said, "but I didn't hear anything about a yacht being sabotaged. And since when do newspeople make enough money to have their own yachts?"

Patti said, "I can't answer your second question, but Jim got a call from Mayor Bullard in the wee hours of this morning. I was too tired to listen closely, but he gave me the details when I woke up."

She filled in the president and the chief of staff.

"The MPD anticipated that there might be trouble at the

marina?" Jean asked. Off Patti's nod, she added, "That was good thinking."

"A detective named Aidan Behan felt it would be prudent."

"Good man," Galia said.

The president nodded.

Patti said, "Jim and I had an idea last night. We spoke with Fayez Mousa at Marcel's, one of those tables where you can draw a curtain for privacy."

"The Jordanian ambassador?" Galia asked. "You called him with a dinner invitation?"

"No, we barged in on the ambassador. Deke Ky located him for us. I called the restaurant and got a table next to his. So we dropped in on him and pulled the curtain. We told him about the shooters who tried to kill Ms. Booker and the tattoos on their hands. Jim asked for unofficial help in finding out who they were and what, if any, terrorist connections they might have had."

"What was Mr. McGill's interest in Ms. Booker in the first place?" Jean asked. "My briefing didn't mention his role."

Patti said, "She'd hired him just before the murder attempt — to see if she might be in danger."

Both Jean and Galia produced humorless laughs.

Then Galia told Patti, "Neither you nor Mr. McGill should have had unofficial contact with a foreign diplomat when the topic is criminal behavior by two of the diplomat's countrymen."

Patti looked at Galia and said, "You're right, but the murder attempt on Ms. Booker happened just as she stepped out of Jim's office building. He felt a responsibility to help her. I understood that. Now, with a possible second attempt on Ms. Booker's life, there is no longer any question of keeping the investigation in the private sector. Well, not solely in the private sector anyway."

Galia started to object again, but the president held up a hand.

"How did that second attempt turn out?" Jean asked.

"We don't know yet. Ms. Booker's yacht wasn't blown up at the marina, but she headed out to sea, possibly with an explosive attached to her yacht's hull. Detective Behan got a Coast Guard helicopter to track her as far as the Chesapeake and heading toward the Atlantic. Then the helicopter had to turn back because of limited fuel."

"Ms. Booker might be dead already," Galia said, "the victim of a terrorist killing."

Jean said, "I'll get back to the Coast Guard and have them start a search, assuming that the boat wasn't sunk. What's the name of the vessel?"

"*Dangerous Dame,*" Patti said.

Jean Morrissey smiled and shook her head. "Well, I like the woman's spunk. Let's hope she's still alive."

"Yes, let's," Galia said, "but, Madam President, neither Mr. McGill nor Mrs. McGill should have approached Ambassador Mousa directly, and this investigation has to be handed over to the FBI right now."

Jean Morrissey covered her eyes with one hand, as if feeling a head-of-state headache coming on, and sighed.

"Or it could be a combined effort," Patti said.

Galia frowned upon hearing that suggestion.

But the president lowered her hand, smiled, and said, "I have an idea."

Park Slope, Brooklyn — New York City

Detective First Grade Lily Kealoha was getting dressed for work when her phone rang. She was still walking on air from having her promotion announced yesterday. Getting bumped up to detective first grade meant she'd get more money in her paycheck — well, bank deposit actually — and her retirement payout would be bigger, too. Even if she left the department next year when that benefit became vested.

So she wore a smile even before she saw Deke Ky was calling.

They'd been seeing each other every month or so for the last year, one of them making the hop to DC or NYC. Lily was beginning to see the possibility of making their relationship more substantial if they could mutually decide on a place to live.

Lily answered the phone by saying, "Deke, I got it. I made detective first grade."

Stepping out of character from the way most people knew him, Deke replied, "I'd give you a kiss if I could."

Lily laughed. "Fake it. Just make the sound. But do it good so I'll believe you."

With only a slight hesitation, Deke followed her order. Putting his heart into it.

"Ooh, that was a good one, *kane!*" Man.

Being from Hawaii, she liked to throw a bit of her native tongue into their conversations.

Then she added, "I'm so glad I recorded that."

After a moment of silence, Deke said, "You're kidding. About the recording, I mean."

"Yeah, I am. I'd never do anything to embarrass you … without a righteous reason."

"I'll try to stay on your good side."

"So why'd you call?" Lily asked. "Are you coming to town?"

Deke said, "Maybe. I don't know yet. Did you hear about the murder attempt outside my office building yesterday?"

"What? No. Tell me."

Deke filled her in and gave her the news he'd just heard from Jim McGill about the incident at the Marina last night.

Lily said, "Damn, things are getting crazy down there."

"Yeah, so this next part isn't public knowledge yet. I know you won't blab, but I need to ask if you can pass it along to a few other NYPD cops you can trust to keep their eyes open and their mouths closed."

Lily said, "I know people like that. Good coppers, both male and female. What's the big secret?"

Deke told her about the three dead men with the tattoos: two Jordanian, one Lebanese.

"And these guys were all military pilots in their countries?" Lily asked.

"That's the working assumption," Deke told her.

Lily asked, "Aren't assassinations, especially one in the water, a bit out of a pilot's skill set?"

The question stumped Deke for a moment. Then he said, "You know what? One of the detectives in our Austin, Texas office was in the U.S. Air Force special forces."

"I didn't know the Air Force had special forces."

"Yeah, they do. I'll get my colleague's take on this."

"Good. So how can the NYPD help?" Lily asked.

Deke told her, "You've got a big diplomatic community up there. Talk to detectives who work the United Nations area. There or other places where the diplomatic crowd lives and shops. See if they can spot guys from Middle Eastern countries who have little circular tattoos of their countries' flags on the backs of their right hands between their index fingers and their thumbs."

"I can do that. I know some coppers I can trust."

"Good," Deke said. "If they can get names and photos of likely subjects, that would be even better. Some of these people might be honest military veterans, but others might be part of a band of assassins."

Lily said, "Right, and if they can try to kill someone, a famous reporter no less, in broad daylight down in DC, who knows what they might try here?"

"Exactly."

"You do some interesting work down there, *kane.*"

"And we have more warm weather, too," Deke said. "Something for a *wahine* to consider."

Rockville, Maryland

Meeker and Beemer had pulled more all-nighters during their years on the Metropolitan Police Department than they could remember. Had to be a thousand during their 25 years on the job. After leaving Detective Sergeant Dalton Rivers of the Maryland State Police, they thought it wouldn't hurt to do one more. Constance Parker's house occupied a large lot at the bottom of a street that ended in a cul-de-sac. At the beginning of February, the deciduous trees on the property, and there were many of them, had lost all their leaves.

That might have allowed the two big-city detectives to get a glimpse of Ms. Parker's house except her landscape artist — or maybe the lady herself — had a fondness for evergreens, too. The most Meeker and Beemer could see of the house from the street were bits of a roof line. The fact that the nearest neighbors to either side of the Parker property were a good bit distant suggested that the woman's lot and probably her dwelling were sizable.

A double-wide driveway, the kind that could easily accommodate oversized modern SUVs, was available for the two detectives to drive right in and get a good look at the house. Only they hadn't been invited to come a-callin'. The lady might tap 911 into her phone, and the local cops might roust Meeker and Beemer for trespassing if nothing else.

If that wasn't a strong enough deterrent, there were more officer-involved shootings than ever. Especially ones involving unarmed suspects, most of whom were black and running away from the police. Not that just about everyone in the USA, fleeing or not, *didn't* have a gun to call his or her own. It made for a very risky environment in which to be a cop.

Damned if you shot a civilian, maybe dead if you didn't.

"We agree it wouldn't be a good idea to go ring the lady's doorbell, right?" Meeker asked right after he'd parked their car just past the big driveway.

"Not until the sun comes up or maybe after someone delivers the morning newspaper," Beemer said.

"Right," Meeker agreed. "And how come no newspaper delivery people ever get clipped doing their jobs? Most of them work while it's still dark out. At least at this time of year."

Beemer consulted his iPad, focusing on crime statistics. "Nine newspaper fulfillment service people died on the job across the country last year. Six of them were women. Only one reckless homicide charge was filed."

"Damn," Meeker said. "Those people ought to get hazardous-duty pay."

"They ought to be allowed to shoot back, too," Beemer added.

"And get a bonus for being called newspaper fulfillment people instead of delivery folks."

That was as far as they could take that line of thought. Since there weren't any no-overnight-street-parking signs — the people in that Rockville neighborhood probably had never imagined such a thing — Meeker and Beemer had decided to sleep right where they'd stopped.

Actually, they were supposed to take shifts. Two hours awake, two asleep. But they hadn't done a stakeout like that in years. Meeker was supposed to take the first watchful shift. He made it fifteen minutes before falling asleep. Fourteen minutes longer than Beemer.

At 7:20 a.m., shortly after sunrise that morning, the sound of metal ringing against glass woke both Meeker and Beemer with a start. The two former cops reached for the guns they'd chosen to leave locked in their office safe the night before. Then they took note of the source of their wake-up alarm.

A 30-something woman was tapping a Beretta MP9 semi-automatic pistol against the window next to Meeker's head. The MP in the model designation stood for military and police. They were as common as bad attitudes and pension worries among big city cops, but you didn't see them all that much in the hands of female civilians.

Most ladies who owned guns wanted them for protection, sure, but lots of them also wanted weapons that were fashionable or fit neatly in their purses. Like a Glock 26 or a Model 642 Ladysmith revolver with finger grooves designed for smaller hands.

Meeker and Beemer did what they would have recommended to anyone in their situation. Be calm, stay quiet, and try not to wet yourself. Ever so slowly, they also raised their hands to show they were no threat.

"Who the hell are you two?" the woman shouted, clearly not impressed with their display of submission.

"Marvin Meeker and Michael Walker," Meeker said loudly enough to be heard through the raised window. "We're former police detectives with the Metropolitan Police Department in Washington, DC."

The woman, whom Meeker and Beemer clearly recognized from the photos they'd found online as Constance Parker, took a step back. Perhaps to get a better look at the two men parked outside her house. Or maybe to get a better angle on shooting the two of them.

In any case, she recognized a salient point: their ages.

"You two are *retired* from the police?"

"Yes, ma'am," Beemer said.

"Well, what are you doing here in Rockville, parked outside my house?"

"We came to see if you might talk to us," Meeker said.

"About what?" she asked.

"Your winning lottery ticket."

Constance Parker took another full step back and looked like she might indeed shoot.

Beemer, trying to keep his tone friendly, said, "My brother-in-law has a winning ticket, too. But his name never got any public mention."

That newsflash seemed to frighten Parker. "What's his name?"

"We'll tell you once you stop pointing that gun at us," Meeker said.

She didn't lower the Beretta. Taking a moment to think, she waved the gun to emphasize the point she was about to make. "You two better get out of here right now."

Meeker and Beemer didn't argue.

Meeker started the car and they drove off, ignoring the speed limit for the moment.

McGill Investigations International — Washington, DC

McGill had Ellie Booker's phone number and he'd called it a dozen times after arriving at his office. He wasn't quite as overwrought as if one of his children was in trouble, but he was still worried. Ellie had been the target of an attempted public murder the day before, and then she may have inadvertently caused the death of a diver who might have been trying to sabotage her yacht just as it left the Gangplank Marina.

Had the would-be saboteur affixed a time-bomb to the vessel before instant karma did him in? *Dangerous Dame* had still been underway when the Coast Guard helicopter saw it set out into Chesapeake Bay. But what had happened after that?

Trying to find the answer was making McGill more than a little anxious.

Every time he'd called Ellie's phone, it went straight to voicemail.

He heard a recording of her voice tell him: "This is Ellie. If you have something newsworthy to say, I'll get back to you."

The first time McGill had heard that message, he'd replied. "This is Jim McGill. There may be a bomb attached to your boat's hull. Is that newsworthy enough for you? This is no joke. If you have a raft or something on board, get into it now. Move as far away from your yacht as possible and radio for help. If you can call me, do that, too, but get off your boat now."

She didn't get back to him, and he didn't leave another message after any of his follow-up calls. McGill couldn't remember a time when he'd felt so frustrated. More than a little fearful, too. While Ellie wasn't a blood relative, he could imagine her in the role of the black sheep of his family. The kid who'd gone at least somewhat wrong.

He could have used some counseling from Sweetie, but she had a weekend outing that morning with Maxi's school band. McGill Investigations, as a business, was very broadminded about respecting the parental obligations of its employees. At that moment, however, McGill thought Sam Spade never had to worry about things like that.

Then again, Sam never needed a shoulder to cry on. McGill wasn't in tears either, but he was coming close to stomping his phone into many pieces for all the good it was doing him.

Esme Thrice interrupted his black mood, buzzing him. "Boss, Cale Tucker is here to see you."

It took McGill a moment to place the name. Then it clicked. The young guy Patti was lending to him. The one who'd worked for the NSA, though McGill wasn't supposed to know that. Maybe the kid would know how to make a phone call skip past the voicemail function and ring long enough to drive someone crazy and answer.

"Thank you, Esme. Please send him in."

She did better than that. She opened the door for Cale Tucker. He almost walked into one of McGill's guest chairs because he was busy looking over his shoulder at Esme until she closed the door behind her. Cale turned to look at McGill and pulled up short of colliding with the furniture.

"I'm Cale Tucker, sir," he said with a smile still lingering on his face.

McGill stood and extended a hand, which Cale shook.

"Esme is both married and gay," McGill told the young man.

Cale let go of McGill's hand and shrugged. "I saw the ring she's wearing, sir. I was just hoping there might be another like her back home. One who likes fellas now that I have a better understanding."

McGill grinned. The kid was honest and disarming. McGill gestured for him to sit and took his own seat. He asked, "How old are you, Cale?"

"Just turned 25 yesterday, sir. Is my age important to you?"

"I thought knowing it might come in handy if I think of a young lady who might enjoy your company."

The young man beamed. "That'd be some perk for a freelance assignment."

McGill liked the kid's spunk, too. "You mean Patti didn't make the same offer when you signed on at Committed Capital?"

"No, sir. I'll have to check the employee handbook again."

McGill laughed. "Okay, let's get down to business. How much do you know about mobile phones."

"More than most folks by a country mile."

McGill explained, "I've been trying to reach someone who was last seen on a boat heading into the Chesapeake Bay and turning toward the Atlantic. Each time I call, I get voice mail. I left one message and made several subsequent calls, but I haven't heard back. Does the fact that I keep getting voice mail mean that the phone is still activated?"

Cale shook his head. "What you're getting with voice mail is a connection to the phone's cellular network. If the phone's turned off or dysfunctional, the network doesn't know if it's in someone's pocket or on a rocket to Mars. Or in the case you mentioned, the phone might be lying on the ocean floor. "

That last possibility heightened McGill's anxiety.

"Regarding those last two probabilities, outer space and the ocean floor," he said, "is there any way for you to make a distinction?"

Cale smiled but didn't speak immediately. Then he said, "Without being specific, sir, I gave the last four years to serving my country. Not in the military but working in the same direction."

"Thank you for that," McGill said.

"You're welcome, sir. It was a chance meeting with your wife that led me to make a career change. She said helping the domestic economy grow and keeping the U.S. at the forefront of critical technology would be another way to show my patriotism, and it wouldn't hurt my bank account either."

"Patti can be very persuasive," McGill said.

Cale grinned. "Yes, sir. I imagine you'd know that better than anyone. So, I took a job with Mrs. McGill, and I agreed to come talk to you. I think I can help you with your problem. For one thing, it's fortunate you have satellite wi-fi here."

"I do?" McGill asked, genuinely puzzled.

"Yes, sir. There's a satellite dish, more than one actually, on the roof of this building. I asked Mrs. McGill what your tech capability is over here."

McGill had explored the interior of his headquarters top to bottom, but other than joking about installing anti-aircraft missiles on the roof, he had never given a thought to going up there. He told Cale, "Good to know. How does that help?"

"Well, you know that mobile phones depend on cell towers to make their calls, right?"

McGill was that informed. "Sure, I know that."

"Well then, how many cell towers would you guess there are out on the ocean?"

Feeling sheepish now, McGill guessed, "None?"

"Gold star," Cale said, smiling to soften the gibe. "So, without being able to use cell towers, your dish on the roof could send signals up to a satellite in earth orbit and bounce them down to a receptive dish at a distant point on the ocean."

"In that case," McGill said, "the other party would need up-to-date technology, too."

Cale gave a nod of approval to a student catching on quickly. "Yes. Mrs. McGill also told me the make and model of the boat in question — which I guess she got from you. So I did some quick research before coming here."

"That being?" McGill asked.

Cale continued, "What I found out was the Hatteras company, which built the yacht in question, makes satellite wi-fi an available option to its customers. It's one of the most popular add-ons. Even out on the ocean, people still want to make their phone calls."

"So I should be able to talk with the other party," McGill said.

"Yes, assuming both the wi-fi and the phone are functional."

McGill was about to ask why they wouldn't be. Then he remembered: If the yacht had been blown to bits, everything on it might be, too. Including Ellie.

Before McGill could dwell on that awful possibility, Cale said, "I have a few apps on my phone nobody else has yet. Because I'm the guy who wrote them. If you give me your friend's phone number, I can tell you if it went out of service in an anomalous way or if it's just been turned off in a normal fashion. That second possibility would also send all your calls to voice mail."

McGill gave Cale the ten-digit number for Ellie's phone.

He didn't need to repeat it after Cale took his own phone in hand. The young man tapped the number into his phone and then made an additional five taps. McGill kept count.

Cale stared at the phone's screen and then looked up. "The phone is still functional. The SIM card and battery are still in place. The battery is charged. Looks like the person you're calling just doesn't want to answer. That or somebody else has taken possession of her phone and is refusing to answer."

"Can you bypass the voice mail and make the phone ring?" McGill asked. "You know, to the point where the person just has to answer the damn thing."

McGill could see that he'd just given the young man a Eureka moment.

Another app would be written.

Cale said, "Not yet, but I can probably come up with something within a day or two."

McGill sighed inwardly and said, "You referred to my friend as her. How do you know my friend is female? Did Patti tell you that, too?"

Cale fought to keep a straight face but didn't quite succeed.

He said, "I used an app I already have on my phone. Just now, I turned your friend's phone on for a few seconds. I saw and recognized the name Ellie Booker. My app defeated her phone's security and transferred all the data stored on it to my phone," he said. "Without the benefit of a search warrant, what I did was illegal. If I immediately delete all that data, I might get a lighter sentence. I could also send it to your phone if you'd like. But then we'd both bear the criminal liability. You know, if we ever went to court."

McGill would bet his bottom dollar and all of Patti's wealth that the NSA didn't bother to get a warrant in a pressing situation.

Not that he could mention that to Cale. He only asked, "Can you retrieve all this same information later if you delete it now?"

Cale took a moment to ponder the question. He concluded, "Probably. If the phone is still functional. The other thing is I'm not the only one writing new software. Lots of very smart people are grinding around the clock. Somebody somewhere might already be beta-testing a way to thwart my app. A better idea would be to put the data from your friend's phone into a safe place where it can be retrieved — or deleted — as needed. That's what I'd do."

"Okay, let's do that," McGill said.

As long as he could determine whether Ellie was still alive and well, he didn't need to pry into ... well, whatever she might be storing on her phone. Or hiding there.

Cale told McGill he just stashed Ellie's data in a cirrostratus, the highest security cloud server yet devised. He gave McGill the URL and a 15-character password. Cale had provided both the physical location of the server and the key-code off the top of his head.

McGill's memory was still pretty sharp, but he committed this information to writing.

Cale looked like he thought that wasn't the best of ideas, but he didn't criticize.

He only said, "One thing I can tell you right now is where your friend's phone and, possibly, her boat are."

McGill's mood brightened. "Yes, I'd certainly like to know that."

Cale provided the latitude and longitude: 39° North, 75° West.

Then he added, "That's in the Atlantic Ocean all right, roughly at the mouth of the Delaware Bay." Cale looked back at his phone. He tapped the screen twice. "Assuming the phone is on the boat in question and not fastened to someone who's waterskiing, your friend is moving north at a pretty good clip. I can't tell yet if she's going to head up the bay. If so, she might be going to Wilmington, Delaware or Philadelphia."

McGill considered the two possibilities. "Philly, maybe.

Wilmington would be a surprise. What are the nearest big cities if she continues going up the East Coast?"

Cale looked at the map on his phone, but McGill had the feeling that the kid didn't really need a visual reference, could have told him off the top of his head.

He said, "I don't know if it truly qualifies as big, but there's Atlantic City. After that, there's New York City, of course. Then there's Providence and Boston. Beyond that, there's Canada and Greenland, if she's equipped to make it that far."

McGill grinned. "Canada, possibly. Greenland, I think we can rule out."

"Me, too," Cale agreed. "I don't see Ellie Booker hanging out there."

"Have you ever met her?"

Cale shook his head. "I've seen her on WorldWide News and PBS. I always thought she was pretty cool. Smart, tough, and willing to stick it to anyone who didn't give a straight answer to her questions."

"That's Ellie, all right."

"Do you know her personally?" Cale asked.

McGill said, "Yeah. You want me to ask for an autograph when I catch up with her?"

Cale smiled. "Sure, on a head-shot if you can manage that. But I was just thinking: Where would someone with a high media profile like hers most likely go?"

"New York," McGill said. "The city must have someplace Ellie can park her boat. It's also the only place on our list where you can get a same-day flight to anywhere in the world. Beyond that, you can lose yourself in the crowd if you choose to stay there."

Cale nodded, seeming to approve of McGill seeing all of those things on his own.

McGill recognized the game they were playing: see who could intuit the next move to make. He decided to push back. Find out how good the kid really was at his high-tech games.

He said, "I need a phone number in Manhattan. It's bound to

be unlisted. Maybe even camouflaged behind a false front. If you can get it for me, I'll ask Ellie if she'll talk to you personally."

Cale took a moment to think, and McGill could read his character if not his exact thoughts. The young man liked the ladies. Even though Ellie was too old for him to think of in romantic terms, most likely, he'd still get off just talking to her.

Cale nodded. The challenge was accepted, conditionally.

"Okay. I'll do it if you don't tell Mrs. McGill or any prosecutor who might talk to you."

McGill countered. "The prosecutor, okay. Patti only if you promise never to put her in a bad spot."

Cale needed only a moment to consider, and then he offered his hand. "Deal. Whose phone number do you want?"

"His name is Hugh Collier."

Cale nodded. "The CEO of WorldWide News. Sure, that's who Ms. Booker would go to see in New York … if she intends to see anyone at all."

McGill said, "Anyone at all would be much tougher to track down."

The kid ignored the verbal jab, consulted his phone, and provided McGill with three numbers for Hugh Collier. "One of those should work."

He shook McGill's hand and left, saying, "It was a pleasure meeting you."

McGill said, "Likewise."

He heard Cale politely start to chat up Esme before he closed his office door. Esme didn't have a sister, McGill knew, but he supposed a comely cousin was a possibility.

McGill called the first number he'd been given for Hugh Collier.

He got the man's voice mail. Collier sounded awful. His message explained why.

"This is Hugh. Please come straight to the point. I'm busy dying."

The White House — Washington, DC

When General Welborn Yates entered the Oval Office, after being summoned thirty minutes earlier, he saw four of the most powerful women in the world waiting for him: President Jean Morrissey, former President Patricia Grant McGill, Chief of Staff Galia Mindel and FBI Director Abra Benjamin.

The former president, the chief of staff and the FBI director occupied a sofa.

The president sat alone on a facing love-seat.

Welborn thought there was only one thing for him to do.

He raised his hands and said, "I surrender."

He got a laugh from everyone but only briefly. There was serious business to discuss.

The president told Welborn, "Please sit next to me, General, as I'll be the arbiter of your fate."

Welborn wasn't sure he'd like that, still hoping to chart his own path in life, but he followed the Commander-in-Chief's order. "Yes, ma'am."

"General Yates," the president said, "we'd all like to take the opportunity to commend you once again on your heroic and successful effort to save the life of Ellie Booker."

Welborn looked the president in the eye, trying to see what might come next. "Thank you, ma'am." Turning to the others, he added, "Thank you, all."

Director Benjamin spoke next. "General, have you gone to see Mr. McGill to ask about a job with his company?"

You didn't lie to the FBI, Welborn knew. Doing so was a federal crime.

"I went to see about the possibility of a job with his company, Madam Director. I didn't know of a specific opening to fill."

"How did your discussion go, General?" Galia asked.

"Mr. McGill chose to speak with Ms. Booker while I spoke with Margaret Sweeney. Regarding the possibility of going to work at McGill Investigations, she said it would depend on the existing workload and what future business demand might be. If another investigator was needed, Ms. Sweeney said that she'd recommend that I be hired."

"Have you considered staying in the Air Force, Welborn?" Patti asked.

"That was the first thing I did. But I came to realize it probably wouldn't work."

"Why not?" Patti asked.

Welborn allowed himself a small grin. "Because you spoiled me, ma'am, by installing me in the White House. Any other posting after that would feel like a step down even if it wasn't. Also, I felt sure some of my Air Force colleagues would feel I came by my current rank as a result of presidential favor rather than merit. Of course, if anyone said that to my face, I'd have to bust his nose for impugning your integrity and mine."

All the women in the room smiled.

Jean Morrissey smacked the palm of her left hand with her right fist.

Director Benjamin asked Welborn, "Have you decided, General, that you'd prefer to work in the private sector?"

"No, Madam Director, just the opposite. If you'll have me, I'd like to work for the FBI with one, no two, provisos."

Jean Morrissey beat Abra Benjamin to the obvious question. "What are the conditions, General?"

"I'd like to be in on the investigation of who's responsible for the attempt on Ms. Booker's life yesterday. Once that matter is resolved and, I hope, the people behind it are brought to justice, I'd like to go to work for the Bureau, and I'd like to do occasional fieldwork to keep my investigative skills sharp and my executive perspective realistic. In any case, continuing in service to my country would mean a great deal to me."

Jean Morrissey gave Welborn's hand a brief squeeze. All the other women nodded in approval. Patti asked, "Is this a decision you and Kira both agree upon?"

Just barely fighting off a blush as he remembered how that

discussion had gone, Welborn nodded. "Yes, ma'am."

The four women in the room consulted each other visually, and all of them came to the same conclusion. Director Benjamin said, "General Yates, please consider this as the employment interview I'd intended to have with you elsewhere." Turning to Jean Morrissey, Abra added, "Madam President, with your approval, I'd like to hire General Yates as the new Deputy Director of the Federal Bureau of Investigation. Furthermore, given his stipulation that he'd be allowed to investigate the matter of the attempt on Ellie Booker's life, I would assign him to work collegially with the personnel of McGill Investigations. Is that satisfactory to you, Madam President?"

Jean Morrissey nodded. "It is indeed."

She stood up, and Welborn also got to his feet. Shaking his hand, she said, "There are mounds of paperwork both for resigning from the Air Force and joining the Bureau, of course, and there's an oath for you to take to officially join the FBI. But Galia will see that all of that is expedited without delay. Congratulations on your new job, Mr. Acting Deputy Director."

Welborn shook hands all around and tried to keep his head from spinning.

Saving Patti for last, he whispered into her ear. "I'll try not to be too hard on Mr. McGill."

Aboard Dangerous Dame — Atlantic Ocean

Sitting in the captain's chair of her yacht, Ellie Booker saw she was making 20 knots, heading toward New York City on a blessedly calm sea. Ellie glanced at her phone. She half-expected it to ring despite being turned off. She knew, of course, that in any major city in the country, her location and movement could be tracked if she'd had the phone activated. She doubted the MPD could use her phone to track her on the ocean, but the feds had more money, technology, and mad scientists to use in their pursuit of snooping.

Hell, that was the National Security Agency's reason for being.

Who the hell knew what the geniuses working there might be able to do?

And speaking of government-funded tech wizards, there was also DARPA, the Defense Advanced Research Projects Agency. Their mission statement was "to make pivotal investments in breakthrough technology for national security." To kill even the slimmest chance of having personal privacy would be another way of putting it, Ellie thought.

So she viewed her best, if not foolproof, chance of pulling off undetected travel was to turn off her phone.

The problem with that was you never knew when you might get an unexpected call that was actually helpful or at least informative. Stranger things had happened. Then there was also the matter of connection addiction. Sure, it was a maddening and sometimes even fatal mistake to be plugged into the world at large, but when you isolated yourself you could truly feel withdrawal pain.

At least if you were a professional nosy-parker, a.k.a. an investigative reporter, you could. Something important might happen while you had your head buried in the sand. Not only would you want to know of that event in the moment, you'd also want to scream it to everyone else in the world so they could have their up-to-the-minute news fix, too.

Speaking of which, she was dead certain James J. McGill would like to know where she was and what she was doing. It had occurred to her that with his old-fashioned sense of gentility McGill might have walked her out of his front door yesterday. With General Yates there, too, that would have made a nice tight cluster of three targets for those homicidal pricks in the car to hose down.

Given her dark sense of humor, Ellie could imagine both Jim McGill and Welborn Yates trying to save her narrow backside at the same time. They might have hit heads, been staggered, but stayed upright. For her part, she might have just froze. The bastard with the automatic weapon might have mowed them all down if he wasn't laughing too hard.

All things considered, Ellie chose to turn her phone on for just a moment. She'd see who'd called and decide which messages, if any, to return. When she could do so as safely as possible. Of course, if there weren't any incoming calls ... maybe nobody really gave a damn about her.

Except for the bastards trying to kill her. They cared in the worst way.

She turned the phone on and was annoyed when it didn't instantly spring into action. She'd used the yacht's radio to make calls on the water before, but not her cell phone. She wondered if she needed to have the satellite wi-fi on to retrieve her messages. She brought that gizmo to life.

The phone rang so immediately that she dropped the damn thing.

Having quick reflexes, she snatched it out of the air. She saw it wasn't McGill calling, though she noted a dozen call-attempts queued up. She'd bet more than one of them was from him. Just then, however, Hugh Collier was calling. At least she hoped it was Hugh and not some flunky using his phone to tell her the boss was dead.

She accepted the call and said tentatively, "Hugh?"

He laughed like he was already gone and had just beaten the devil in a hand of gin.

"Still here, dear heart, though just barely. Where are you?"

"A bit south of Atlantic City. About 100 nautical miles from New York. Five hours out at my present rate."

"I'll never last that long, but I do so want to see you one last time. As I mentioned, I have a proposition for you, and you're going to disrobe for me."

Despite her genuine sorrow about Hugh's situation, Ellie responded with black humor, "You're really going to make me an offer I can't refuse?"

"Amusing, I know, but I hope that's it exactly," he said.

"So what is it?"

He hadn't told her of any offer the last time they'd spoken to each other.

"Oh, no," he said, "this proposition will be made in person or not at all."

Ellie replied, "You just told me you might not live long enough for me to arrive."

"By watercraft. I'll send a helo for you. You can be winched up from your boat. I'll have some chaps to bring it to New York for you. I'll also send a diver to take a quick look around."

"Look around for what?" Ellie asked, suspicious of ... she didn't know what.

"James J. McGill called one of my most closely guarded phone numbers moments ago. I didn't give him that phone number, and the few people who do know it swore to me that they didn't breach my trust."

Ellie said, "He must still be wired into the federal spook agencies."

"My assumption also," Hugh replied, "but I'm honestly grateful he reached me and I reached you."

A chill ran down Ellie's spine. "What did he tell you?"

"That you unwittingly foiled another attempt on your life."

Hugh gave Ellie the details on the diver she'd filleted. Including his tattoo. Her yacht had twin propellers with six blades each. She shuddered, thinking of the mess it must have made.

Hugh asked, "Didn't you feel the impact?"

"Yes, but I thought it was just a soggy old tree branch or something my boat shredded."

"Yes, I'm sure it did the job quickly. The question McGill raised, quite aptly, was did the bloke who gave his all have the time to fasten an explosive to your vessel. Something that might be ticking doggedly toward an explosion right now."

This time, Ellie's entire body went cold.

Hugh continued, "McGill told me he tried to reach you by phone several times but all he got was voice mail. He's properly frustrated and worried. I'm a bit concerned myself. I'm offering my chaps quite a bonus to risk going onto your yacht and looking under it."

Ellie had to clear her throat before she could say, "Fuck the boat, Hugh. Just get me out of here."

"The helo's already airborne," he answered. "Try not to die before I do."

McGill Investigations International — Washington, DC

MPD Detective Aidan Behan had just taken a chair in McGill's office when Esme buzzed him on the intercom. "Sorry to interrupt, boss, but Marvin Meeker and Michael Walker would like to speak with you, and General Yates just dropped in, too."

"Welborn's here?" McGill asked.

"Yes."

"Tell him just a minute. Then send him in. I'll take the call from Meeker and Beemer now."

"Right."

Detective Behan said, "You're busy. I'll come back later."

McGill picked up his phone but covered the speaker with his hand. "No, stay. I'll give you what little news I have in a minute."

Behan had come by to see if McGill had any word on Ellie's Booker's fate.

Answering the phone call, McGill said, "What's up, guys? Any new developments?" After listening just a moment, McGill echoed what he'd just heard. "Constance Parker pulled a gun on you?"

Hearing that tidbit Detective Behan leaned forward. The woman's name he'd heard was unfamiliar, but the implied threat to life was right up his alley. He also knew the names of two former colleagues. Meeker and Beemer were MPD legends.

Behan hadn't really expected that McGill had heard from Ellie Booker. He was just being diligent by checking with him. McGill said he hadn't heard from Ellie, but he thought he might learn something soon. He'd yet to explain his reason for feeling that way when he got busy in a hurry. Behan liked the sudden burst of activity. It jacked up his adrenaline.

"Okay, let's take it from the beginning," McGill said. "I'm going to put you on speaker. I happen to have an MPD detective with me right now. He's looking into details of the shooting that happened here yesterday, but it's always good to have another smart cop listening in."

Behan smiled upon hearing the compliment.

Meeker said over the speaker, "We drove up to Rockville, Maryland last night, right after Constance Parker's name hit the internet as the Grand Slam winner. We checked in with a state police detective sergeant who was a tight-ass but he didn't get in our way."

"Probably didn't want to cause trouble with the Metro PD, even though Marvin and I are retired," Beemer added.

Both McGill and Behan nodded.

"You had no need to mention my name?" McGill asked.

"Saved the big ammunition," Meeker told him.

McGill said, "Maryland would have more reason to be afraid of Mayor Bullard than me."

All three cops within the sound of McGill's voice laughed.

"Anyway," Meeker continued, "we parked legally on the street outside the lady's house. Dozed off. Come morning she's outside tapping on the window next to my head with a semi-auto. I might have a bad dream or two 'cause of that."

"Understandable. Did she make any direct threats?" McGill asked.

Beemer said, "No, but she got real nervous when I told her Sammy had a winning ticket, too. Like she knew something had gone wrong. Not thinking it was just a coincidence at all."

McGill said, "Is that your impression, too, Marvin?"

"Yeah, it is. But here's the thing. Big Mike and I checked out this lady's history pretty good. No criminal record whatsoever. Not even a traffic ticket. She's an academic. Got her doctorate with high honors."

"Where does she teach?" McGill asked.

Beemer told him, "She doesn't. She's the head of an organization called *Better Days.*"

"Self-help kind of place?" McGill asked.

Meeker replied, "We haven't got that far, but she didn't have a psychology background. Her schoolwork was in the area of biochemistry. We also found out her daddy was a pharmacist. So she's kind of working the same side of the street as him."

McGill took a beat to think. "Doesn't sound like someone who'd approach two guys in a car holding a gun. You have time to look into her father's background yet, see if he has any criminal record?"

Beemer said, "Haven't done that yet, but just looking at her my guess is she was raised right. I'm thinking her father's probably a legit guy."

"Well, something made her nervous," McGill said. "Is her neighborhood a place where people need to be careful about strangers?"

Both Meeker and Beemer laughed.

Meeker told McGill, "Rockville's a place where most people would want to live. Pretty and pricey. No riffraff allowed. Not unless they've got the cash anyway."

"Miz Parker's place is assessed for real estate tax purposes at $1.3 million," Beemer said. "We checked that, too."

Meeker said, "The feeling Big Mike and I have is the lady's anxiety is due to winning the lottery. Doesn't seem to fit with the way most folks feel when they come into a nine-figure fortune. Well, maybe eight figures after taxes, but still."

McGill asked, "Did she seem at all angry when she heard she might have to share the jackpot?"

There was a moment of silence before Beemer responded. "That was when she got really scared and told us to get on down the road."

"The way she was holding that gun, all nervous like, we didn't argue," Meeker said.

"You didn't mention Sammy's name as the other winner, did you?" McGill asked.

"No," Meeker and Beemer said in unison.

"Good. That leaves Ms. Parker with only one alternative," McGill said.

"You mean come to see us if we don't go back to see her," Meeker replied.

McGill said, "Yeah, stay out of Maryland for a while. If necessary, I can make a trip up there."

"You'd definitely blend in better," Beemer said.

"If you say so, but, guys, you know what else might happen, right?"

"Of course we do," Meeker said.

Beemer added, "Whoever has Ms. Parker so scared, *they're* gonna come see us."

"Right," McGill said. "Call if you need reinforcements or any other kind of help."

After McGill signed off, Detective Behan told him, "I never worked with those guys, but I saw them here and there and heard the stories. They've got reputations for wisecracking, but nobody in this town has closed more cases than they have."

McGill nodded. "They're good cops and good people. I'm going to bring in General Welborn Yates now. He's the guy who kept Ellie from getting killed yesterday."

"I'd be happy to meet him," Behan said.

McGill buzzed Esme and she sent Welborn in. Behan got to his feet, and McGill made the introductions. The two men shook hands and took their seats.

McGill told both of them, "I don't know exactly where Ellie is right now, but I have an approximate idea. She and her boat are on the Atlantic, maybe heading up the Delaware Bay to Philly or less likely Wilmington, Delaware. If she kept heading north, on the other hand, she might be near Atlantic City, New Jersey by now. Please don't ask how I know this because I've promised to keep my source confidential."

Behan didn't object, but Welborn said, "Really?"

"Truly," McGill replied. He added, "I think she's heading to New York City."

"Because?" Welborn asked.

McGill gave Welborn a look. The younger man sounded just a bit pushy to McGill. That wasn't at all like his normal demeanor.

Behan broke the tension by saying, "May I?"

McGill didn't know what permission the detective was seeking, but he nodded anyway.

Behan said, "Ms. Booker's a media figure, and New York is media central in the U.S. Maybe she sees what happened to her as a story to be …" He was going to say exploited but decided to go with a less loaded word. "… told."

McGill nodded. "That's what I had in mind, too. I contacted Hugh Collier, the chairman of WorldWide News."

Neither of McGill's guests commented on that, but both wished they could reach such an eminent figure on a moment's notice.

"I passed along the news of what happened at Gangplank Marina along with the speculation that Ellie's boat might have a time-bomb stuck to its hull. Collier didn't question the possibility. He said he'd do everything he could to reach Ellie."

"He can't do as much as the government can," Welborn said.

McGill heard a note of implied criticism in Welborn's voice. He wondered if the younger man was suffering some aftereffect of almost dying the day before. You didn't just shrug off an emotional trauma like that.

"That's true, Welborn," McGill said, "but neither you nor I have those resources at our beck and call."

Welborn said, "Actually, I do."

"You do? Since when?" McGill asked.

"Since about an hour ago. I was at the White House. I'm now the acting deputy director of the FBI. I'll be sworn in shortly."

Behan gave a short whistle to indicate his surprise.

The look on McGill's face said the same, but he managed to say, "Congratulations. Well, if you can get a helicopter and some bomb-squad people out to where Ellie's boat is, by all means, have at it."

"I will," Welborn said. "Now, how did you find out where Ellie is?"

McGill had told Welborn that he'd promised to keep his source's identity confidential, but you neither lied to nor stonewalled the FBI. Partial truths, though, seemed to be in bounds, McGill thought. At least he hoped so.

"I talked to Patti," he said, "and she helped me."

That newsflash sat Welborn back in his seat. The FBI could muscle a lot of people, but there were others, including a popular ex-president, who demanded and got kid-glove treatment.

Also, a conversation between spouses was held to be confidential by law.

Asking for details could be rebutted as a privileged conversation.

Welborn understood all that. He got to his feet. "Thank you for the help. I'll see what resources I can muster."

He started to leave when McGill asked, "Welborn, what was your reason for stopping by?"

The acting deputy director said, "I wanted to let you know that I wouldn't be applying for a job here after all."

He nodded to McGill and Behan and left.

"Okay, well, I'll be on my way, too," the detective said. "Thanks for your time, Mr. McGill." He got to his feet and asked, "You think that's what becoming an FBI big-shot does to a guy?"

McGill sighed. "At least some of the time apparently."

"Or maybe it's just an after-effect of almost getting killed," Behan said.

McGill's very thought. "Yeah, let's hope that's it."

"You'll let me know how Ms. Booker makes out?"

McGill said, "Sure."

***

While McGill was puzzling over what truly had made Welborn act out of character, Esme buzzed him again. "Boss, a gentleman from the Jordanian Embassy is on the line. He'd like to know if you're free to have lunch with Ambassador Fayez Mousa today."

"The guy is still on the line waiting for a response?"

"Yes."

"Did he say where the ambassador would like to eat?"

"The Jordanian embassy. At one p.m., if that's okay."

"Just the two of us or is Patti invited, too?"

"He didn't say. You want me to ask?"

"No, I'll just hope Patti's free for lunch. Tell him the two of us will be there. Oh, and I'll need the embassy's address."

"Got it. I'll be right back."

McGill hoped he'd just played things the right way. The protocols of international diplomacy were hardly required reading for a PI and former Chicago cop. Hadn't even come into play during his White House years. Patti had just nudged him in the right direction then. Still, it seemed to him if the ambassador had a staffer make the call, it wouldn't be impolite to have Esme speak for him.

Besides that, he wanted someone on hand with eminent political stature and a lot more international experience than he had when he talked with Mousa. Otherwise, who knew, Welborn might get snotty with him a second time.

And, once again, any conversation he and Patti shared would be privileged.

Esme came back on the line. "The ambassador would be delighted to see President Grant. When Ambassador Mousa's secretary asked whether you'd prefer to eat Jordanian, American or Italian cuisine for lunch, I said Italian. Is that all right? It seemed like a diplomatic choice. Should I have just asked you?"

McGill was pretty much an omnivore. There was precious little cooking at which he'd turn up his nose. "You did fine, Esme. Great choice, and I like the way you took the initiative."

"You're the best, boss."

"Tell me, Esme, do you have any female cousins?"

She laughed. "That's just what both Mr. Cale and Detective Behan asked me, after I told them I don't have a sister."

"So, do you?"

"I have three female cousins. All of them make me look plain."

"I doubt that," McGill said.

"Okay, there is a family resemblance."

"Did Welborn say anything to you?" McGill asked.

After a pause, Esme replied, "You mean other than, 'Have a nice day?'"

"Yeah, other than that."

"Oh, no. From what I understand, he's also very happily married."

Esme was including herself.

She told McGill, "That last question was kind of strange."

He replied, "Sorry, I'm just trying to sort something out. It was a bad guess."

"We all make those. Do you want me here all day?"

"No, you can take off at lunchtime."

"Thanks."

McGill sat back and wondered what Welborn's problem was, if he wasn't having trouble at home. He'd just gotten a plum job and … did he feel it was another gift? Like landing in the White House. Hell, McGill hadn't had anything to do with either of those events.

He'd have to ask Patti if she could think of an answer.

East 42nd Street — New York City

NYPD Detective Lily Kealoha stood on a street corner down the block from the United Nations building. With her was Diplomatic Security Service Special Agent Lonnie Tompkins, a son of the South. New Orleans, namely. In an after-hours bar conversation with Lily and a large gathering of other feds and municipal law officers, Tompkins had once claimed that Key West was the southernmost point in the U.S.

Lily told him he was wrong. Hawaii claimed that distinction. They made a bet: Whoever was wrong would buy a drink for everyone in the joint who had a badge. At the time, those people numbered close to a hundred. Being New York City, the average price per cocktail was sixteen dollars. Even allowing for beer drinkers, they were talking well over a grand.

Never mind the tip.

Turned out that Lily was right. Ka Lae, aka South Point, on the Big Island was the southernmost point in the U.S. Special Agent Tompkins didn't have the cash to pay for all those drinks just then, and his credit cards were maxed out at the moment. Lily let him get away with buying drinks for the twenty visiting law officers least likely to be back in the Big Apple anytime soon. After that, he'd have to make good for the others within the next year.

He did, but he always warned other agents and coppers not to make bar bets with Lily.

Even so, they formed a lasting friendship, though not one involving romance. Lonnie conceded that Lily was a joy to behold, but he said his tastes ever since he was a boy ran to blondes with Dixie accents. Lily hadn't taken offense.

"Whatever lights your lava lamp," she'd said.

He'd grinned and later gave her a lava lamp he'd found online.

Now, he was giving Lily the information she'd requested. "Just since you called me, I've spotted three guys with those little circular tattoos on their right hands, coming and going out of the building."

UN Headquarters, he meant.

"You were careful not to be obvious about it?" Lily asked.

"Nah. I just said, 'Yo, Omar. Get your ass over here and show me your hands.'"

"Subtle," Lily said, teasing him.

"Come on, Lily. You know I didn't just fall off the turnip truck. Of course, I was subtle. So slick, in fact, I set up a concealed vehicular perch where I could use a serious hi-res camera. I got headshots of all three and hand-shots of two of their tattoos. Even ran down the nations their tattoo flags represent. Then I sent all the images to my phone."

He took out his iPhone and showed Lily the faces and hands he'd captured.

She nodded in approval. "Nice work, Lonnie. Send those photos to my phone, will you?"

"Sure thing. You still have the same number?"

"Yeah."

The two of them kept in touch. They may not have been sweethearts, but each knew the value of having contacts in other large law enforcement entities. Lily looked at the photos as they arrived on her phone.

"Nice and sharp all right," she said. "These two flag tattoos, what countries do they represent?"

Lonnie told her, "Libya and Egypt. Neighbors, you know?"

Lily knew the two countries shared a border. "Yeah."

She examined the faces of all three men Lonnie had photographed.

"All these guys, they look like their next smiles will be their first ones," she said.

Lonnie shook his head, "If all of them are combat pilots and they've all seen action, you can bet they were smiling when it was mission-accomplished time."

"Yeah, you're right. The joy of the kill. Thanks for the help."

"Thanks for giving me the opportunity. If these dudes are all bad guys, I'm going to look good when I send their pictures to my boss."

Lily considered that observation. "How long before Diplomatic Security gets moving on this, you think?"

Lonnie sighed. "Hard to say, but when I point out the murder attempt in DC, and those guys having the same kind of tats, I hope that'll light some kind of fire under the great thinkers. You going to stress the urgency to the NYPD?"

"You bet," Lily said.

Even before she did that, though, she was going to call Deke Ky down in Washington.

She also wondered: If Lonnie had spotted three suspicious

guys in such a short time, how many others might there be?

She told him, "Remind me to buy you a drink soon."

Dangerous Dame — Atlantic Ocean Off the New Jersey Coast

After hearing from Hugh Collier that she'd killed a diver who might have stuck a time-bomb on the hull of her yacht, Ellie Booker looked around from her captain's chair using the Nikon Monarch waterproof binoculars she had onboard. She didn't see another vessel anywhere.

There'd be no help from a friendly boater anytime soon.

Ellie could use the yacht's radio to issue a distress call to the Coast Guard. Only she didn't know if their response time in a water-craft would beat Hugh's helicopter. Of course, the Coast Guard was famous for making rescues with their own choppers. Again, though, would one of their helicopters beat Hugh's air rescue?

Maybe but probably not by much. Of course, even a few minutes might mean the difference between life and death. Still, there were other problems about calling the Coast Guard. Involving them would lead to a federal inquiry about a bomb being placed on the yacht, and there would be a world of publicity if the *Dame* did get blown to bits.

Inevitably, the government would poke its nose into all the dark corners of her life, and every species of journalist known to man would do the same. She could see the headlines now: *Well-known media figure escapes bomb blast on boat — after almost being gunned down in Washington. What is she hiding?*

At least one of the investigative reporters would make it a personal quest to discover the truth behind the cover story: What really made Ellie Booker the target of repeated assassination attempts? Answering that question was where TV careers and book deals would be made.

And if one of her secrets was brought to light, all the others might be revealed.

Ellie couldn't afford that kind of exposure.

Not with either a death penalty or a life-sentence in prison being the consequences.

Better to take her chances now. She tapped the controls to shut down the engines and released the yacht's drogue. It provided a drag on the *Dame*, acting like the brake on a car, slowing her vessel's movement through the water. With her craft quiet and still no other boats in sight, Ellie went below into the engine compartment.

She strained to listen for any unusual sounds outside the hull. Despite the possibility of being caught in a fatal situation, she had to laugh. What was she hoping to hear? A ticking Timex alarm clock taped to a bundle of dynamite? That was ridiculous.

Wasn't it?

Only up to a point, she decided. If a bomb had been affixed to her yacht, it would most likely use up-to-date explosive materials and technology. Things that operated silently and provided a lot of bang for the buck. Most likely, there wouldn't even be a digital countdown screen.

After all, who would be in the ocean to see it?

Well, maybe Hugh's diver, if he got there in time. Still, if Ellie were going to build a time-bomb, she wouldn't give anyone a clue as to when it would detonate. Why provide the target any useful information? Let the poor sap guess when things would go boom. That'd make disarming the damn thing a lot more nerve-wracking and difficult.

Ellie went up to the galley, got herself a root beer, and tried to think rationally. If there were a bomb attached to the *Dame,* why wouldn't it have gone off already? Seemed to her like the big kaboom was overdue by now. Unless … what?

Maybe the bomb had been set to go off in the wee hours of tomorrow morning instead of early that day. Why would that be, though? Well, say, the bomb had been set to go off at two or three a.m. that morning. What if Ellie had decided to go out somewhere at midnight and didn't get back until dawn? Her boat would be a memory, but she'd still be alive and kicking.

Worse, from the bad guys' point of view, she'd know they were still hunting her, and she would do her best to disappear. Making their job a whole lot harder. So what would the advantage be of giving the bomb a longer fuse, metaphorically speaking?

Ellie took a hit of root beer to help her imagination work on that problem.

What came quickly to mind was a fail-safe assassin. Say, Ellie was to spend two consecutive nights away from the *Dame*. That would also foil a murder attempt using a bomb with a 48-hour trigger. But if she left the boat for a second consecutive night and there was a guy in position with a scoped rifle as a fall-back, he would eliminate her.

That would involve a higher risk for the killer but no more so than a drive-by shooting.

On the other hand, if she stayed aboard the second night and got blown up, the shooter wouldn't have to expose his presence.

Maybe the bad guys had needed an extra 24 hours to get their marksman in place.

That could be why the bomb, if there was one, hadn't gone off already.

Concluding that her analysis was at least possible, Ellie's gut twisted, and she could feel the root beer coming back up. She scrambled out of the salon and vomited over the side. Once purged, she looked up at an empty blue sky and said, "I hope you told your boys to go full throttle, Hugh."

Unknowingly, Ellie decided to take McGill's advice. She went to a storage locker and hauled out a Saturn inflatable dinghy. If she chose to abandon ship, and that time was fast approaching, she wanted to be ready. A 10-horsepower motor was available for the little vessel, but Ellie had opted for oars never thinking she'd really need the emergency craft.

Now she thought that had been a hell of a bad time to economize.

Zaatari Refugee Camp — Jordan

The largest detainment camp for Syrian refugees in Jordan had a population density of 62,710 persons per square mile. By comparison, that nearly matched the mass of humanity in Manhattan, which counted 66,940 people per square mile. The differences were Zaatari had no urban oasis like Central Park, no world-famous theater district, no choice of fine dining.

The biggest dissimilarity, though, was anyone who wanted to leave Manhattan was free to do so. Once inside Zaatari as a Syrian refugee, you were stuck. You were not able to move freely within Jordan, and unless you were very lucky, no other nation would legally admit you. You had only traded the hell at home in Syria for the one next door in Jordan.

Belaboring the obvious, living conditions in the camp strained to be even marginal. There were, however, several humanitarian organizations from countries around the world doing their best to make life in the camp livable. Working for one such charity, Physicians' Global Outreach or PGO, was Dr. Hasna Kalil, a surgeon who'd formerly worked under the aegis of Doctors Without Borders.

Dr. Kalil not only performed surgery under dauntingly primitive conditions, she also advocated for children in the camp whom she deemed to be intellectually worthy of being given a better education than a refugee camp could ever provide. It helped greatly that Dr. Kalil's family was well connected to prominent members of Jordan's power structure.

With letters of recommendation from people high in the government, Dr. Kalil had placed students from the camp in some of the best secondary schools in Germany, France, the United Kingdom and the United States. Their families went with them.

The students would matriculate at many of the world's best universities, mostly of the technical sort, and return to the Middle East to help change the balance of power in a newly evolving world. That was the plan.

Being selected by Dr. Kalil for an education abroad came to be regarded in the camp as the earthly equivalent of a trip to paradise. Not only did it mean liberation from squalid confinement, but it also provided a middle-class living by Western standards and an education only the elite and the very lucky from around the world enjoyed.

Given strict instructions by Dr. Kalil, the parents of the lucky young scholars were told to make sure their children lived up to their intellectual potential. Otherwise, if the schools they attended dismissed them for any reason, it would be back to the camp for everyone. That being the case, no further motivation was needed by anyone involved.

Not one of the students Dr. Kalil had placed over a three-year period had been singled out for anything except conspicuous and exceptional merit. The news media abroad loved to tell human interest stories about the scholars from the refugee camp. Newspaper readers and television viewers equally enjoyed seeing stories of the Zaatari scholars.

The children were so smart and polite, and the families all worked hard to blend in with the customs of their host countries, as they had been instructed. They were considered model immigrants. And for the time being they were. Things would change dramatically later.

Not that they really had to worry about being sent back to the camp.

Anyone who violated Dr. Kalil's rules would simply be killed, and their remains would disappear. Despite all her precautions, there was one thing Dr. Kalil had overlooked, possibly because she was a surgeon, not a psychologist. She hadn't counted on the power of seduction.

Social seduction for the most part, but the personal type also. The Zaatari scholars and their families weren't held in physical captivity. Their bondage was emotional and cognitive. They feared Dr. Kalil's wrath if they failed to follow her instructions. They'd intuited correctly that the penalty for failure would more likely be death rather than a return to the camp.

It would be far easier to dispose of the disobedient rather than bring them back.

Given that grim lever on their behavior and the appeal of their new lives in the West, a small but significant number of Zaatari families began to look for ways out of their predicaments. They started to see the important educational figures they had met in Europe and America as potential liberators.

None of them had dared to overtly cut ties with Dr. Kalil — say by applying for citizenship in their new environs — until one day an American newswoman named Ellie Booker talked to Latif Safar, age 16, a young man with a gift for the mastery of physics who was studying at the Winthrop Day School in Braintree, Massachusetts.

He confided to Ellie that while he was elated to be enrolled at such a fine school and living such a good life with his family in the United States, he also lived in fear every waking moment. In his sleep, nightmares made things even worse.

Ellie asked the obvious question: "What are you afraid of?"

Latif swore her to secrecy and then told her what Dr. Kalil had told him and the other Zaatari scholars. They would become the intellectual assault troops that would take over the world for their people, and the West would be the architect of its own demise. The scholars had pledged never to reveal this plan to anyone, not even their parents.

"So why are you telling me?" Ellie had asked.

"Because I *like* life here in America. I could never even imagine a place like this before I came here," Latif said. "I would *never* want to destroy this place. I hope one day to be a benefactor of the Winthrop Day School, not someone who destroys it."

On top of that, Latif confided that he had met a girl, Malika. "She is like nobody I have ever known. Her family is from Tunisia, but she is so … American. She will not let anyone tell her what to do. She says that her future is hers alone to decide. I feel as if I want to be with her no matter what she decides. I know I am smart. I can adjust to whatever she wants, and I will."

After expressing his love for both America and Malika, the

young Zaatari Scholar was willing to tell Ellie Booker everything he knew about Dr. Kalil.

The reason Ellie wanted to know about the revered doctor of the Zaatari Camp was simple. She wanted to find out who had killed Congressman Philip Brock, the presumed architect of the assassination attempt on former President Patricia Grant. Most of the lines of inquiry into the matter had to do with either partisan politics or lunatic misogyny.

Ellie, unlike most others, had long felt Brock's death had nothing to do with the assassination attempt. She saw it as an act of vengeance. A personal matter.

Wisconsin Avenue — Washington, DC

Nelda Reed, a parking enforcement officer, aka a meter maid, for the District of Columbia had the job of writing parking tickets that ranged in penalty amounts from $25-$200. In premium demand territory like Georgetown, fines skewed toward the high end of the scale. Nobody was ever pleased to see her work product regardless of the amount it would cost, but things could get really tense with a big number violation.

That was why Nelda preferred to hit and … well, not exactly run but to be at least a city block distant when the owner of a ticketed car saw the evidence that this wasn't his day. Or hers, to be fair. Women, in general, didn't tend to be as violent as men, but, oh Lord, could they screech. There had been times when Nelda thought she might lose her hearing. Or wish to. And you couldn't call in police help for a woman just getting loud and shrill.

Not unless she was also making a direct threat.

Anyway, Nelda's preferred method of carrying out her duty was to cite an empty vehicle and be on her merry way. Her least favorite obligation was to write a ticket for a car whose driver was sitting behind the steering wheel. If the knucklehead's meter was violated and he was just, say, talking on his phone to someone, Nelda would give a really loud sneeze, something she could summon on demand.

Then, if the driver saw her coming and pulled out into traffic without causing an accident, she'd just move on to her next violator, who, please God, would be nowhere near his car. But not everybody recognized Nelda's sneeze for a cue to get on down the road. She'd given the guy behind the wheel of the new Audi three of her best efforts, and he stayed right where he was. Staring off into space. She wondered if he was having some kind of seizure.

She'd never cited someone who was seriously ill.

Didn't like the idea of having to explain that one to Saint Peter if she ever made it as far as the Pearly Gates.

So she did something that violated only city regulations. She walked up to the driver's side of the car like she was a traffic cop and tapped on his window. That woke him right out of his trance or whatever the hell his problem was. The guy looked at her without malice and lowered his window.

In a polite tone, he said, "Yes?"

"Your parking meter is in violation," Nelda said. "You want to feed it, be on your way, or should I write you a ticket?"

The guy took a moment to think, like either options one and two weren't the right choices. He didn't look stupid. He was downright handsome in a white bread sort of way. In fact, Nelda thought, his grooming and bearing brought to mind a more specific characterization.

"Are you former military, sir?"

He nodded. "Air Force. You?"

"Army. You were an officer, weren't you?"

He smiled. "A general until this very morning."

"Oh, my," Nelda said. She gave a salute. "What I was just hinting at, sir, is you either have to move your car right away or I have to do my duty. You understand?"

"I do. Can you tell me something, soldier?"

Nelda said, "I will if I can."

"Did you have a hard time adjusting to civilian life?"

The question earned a dry laugh. "I hoped for a better career."

"What was your MOS?" Military occupational specialty.

Nelda hesitated before replying "Thirty-one Bravo, sir."

"Military police. What were your duties?"

Nelda's voice went flat. "Traffic control. I went in hoping I'd do crime prevention or even intelligence work, and what I got was making sure military vehicles didn't run into each other. Now, I watch out that cars don't overstay their parking time. How about you, sir? What were you doing in the Air Force?"

"I started out as a fighter pilot. Then I worked at the White House for Presidents Grant and Morrissey. Today, I took an important job with the FBI."

Nelda couldn't stop herself from laughing. She'd heard some whoppers from people trying to beat their parking tickets, but nothing came close to this one. Only ... just looking at the guy, him keeping a straight face, damn if she didn't come to believe what he'd just said.

"May I know your name, please," he asked.

"Nelda Reed, sir."

"Do you do good work, Ms. Reed?"

"Yes, sir, I surely do."

"You have an honorable discharge?"

"Of course."

"I asked that, Ms. Reed, because I didn't behave honorably today. I disrespected a man who always treated me well, who helped me to advance my career really. I don't know what got into me. All of a sudden, I thought I was somebody important, and I had to show him that. I was sitting here just now thinking of how I might make things right."

Nelda believed that, too.

She was about to cut him some slack when he added, "Please write that parking ticket for me, Ms. Reed. That will be a step in the right direction and, tell me, do you have a card?"

"What? Like a business card? No, sir, people in my job don't get those things."

"Very well. I'll give you one of mine. It's out of date now, but I'll put my cell number on it. I should be set up at the Bureau in a month. Give me a call, and I'll see what I can find for you in the way of an appropriate line of work."

"You're kidding, right?"

"I'm trying to make amends, soldier, starting with doing a good deed. If you want to stay in your present job, however …"

"And you want me to write you a parking ticket, not give you a pass?"

"Yes. As I said, please write the ticket and call me in a month."

"Yes, sir, General. Whatever you say."

She followed orders.

The man gave his card to her and saluted her as he drove off.

She returned the salute, and she liked being called soldier again.

Then Nelda Reed looked at the man's card. Sweet Jesus, the White House was embossed on it. So was the man's name: Lieutenant General Welborn Yates. She looked at the phone number on the back of the card and wrote down the date to make her call.

Aboard the Dangerous Dame — Atlantic Ocean

Ellie Booker knew that time never dragged more slowly than when you wanted something in a hurry. Of course, if what you wanted was to escape a situation that might take your life, time didn't just drag, it laughed at your expectation of deliverance. Mocked your attempts at escape.

She'd inflated the Saturn dinghy and had it ready to abandon ship. The oars were secured in their locks. Water and food sufficient for at least three days were aboard.

Looking westward, she estimated she was no more than five miles off the New Jersey shore. She shouldn't have any trouble rowing that far. Only who knew if contrary tides or currents might push her farther out to sea? She'd never taken such things into consideration before because her yacht didn't depend on sails to take her from Point A to Point B.

She expected the brute force of the vessel's engines to get her anywhere she wanted to go. The Twin Cat C-32A diesel engines each put out 1,600 horsepower. The *Dame* could bull her way through any weather short of a major hurricane. Hell, Ellie could probably beach her yacht in no more than 20 minutes, if that was what she chose to do.

Only superstitious dread kept her from attempting to do just that. If she tried to take the easy way out, she told herself, that was when fate surely would laugh and smack her upside the head. She could imagine getting the *Dame* to within a couple hundred yards of the coastline, able to ride up onto the beach using nothing more than accumulated momentum, but that would be when the bomb went off.

The longer she remained aboard, though, the more certain she became that there was a bomb stuck onto her hull somewhere. Hell, if the prick she'd shredded knew what he was doing, he'd have placed the bomb directly under the fuel tanks. Get the biggest bang for his buck.

The idea of burning to death even as she drowned was seriously challenging Ellie's bladder control. Every tick of the clock made her think the end was that much closer. She kept looking at the dinghy. Yeah, that'd be a way off the yacht, but by now she felt *certain* the same perverse gestures of fate that would keep her off the beach would also take her out to sea.

Then, of course, Hugh's guys would appear in the sky over the *Dame* only to find she was no longer there. Most likely the dudes in the helicopter would search for her, while their aircraft still had enough fuel to do so, but in a 12-foot dinghy she'd be easy to miss from even a couple hundred feet above the ocean. She'd seen lots of videos of the Coast Guard doing futile air searches over open water. She didn't like her chances in the dinghy, not at all.

All that left was to stay aboard the *Dame* and pray. Only Ellie hoped there was no God or she was bound for hell, no question. Given all the shit she'd pulled in her time she had no hope for a happy afterlife.

Having no other choice, Ellie tried distraction as her last chance of what … dying while she was still sane and above water. She tried to lift her spirits by thinking of her professional triumphs, the stories she'd broken that had made banner headlines, maybe even changed the course of the country's history. It wasn't just any woman who could make a claim like that.

Only the feats of which she'd once been so proud now seemed insignificant. What came to mind far more forcefully were the people who'd died at her hand. There were three of them now. The first, of course, had been Reverend Burke Godfrey.

He'd locked Ellie into his office while his church grounds were under siege by the U.S. military. Godfrey had wanted to relieve the pressure of the moment by having Ellie join him in his office shower stall and then in his adjacent bedroom. Instead, the bastard had gotten exactly what he'd deserved.

Ellie cracked his skull with a gun she'd liberated from the reverend's armory.

The medical diagnosis of what had killed Godfrey was a malignant cerebral infarction — a monster stroke — but would that have happened if she hadn't clobbered him with a gun first? She hadn't thought so at the time, but now she was inclined to think yeah, she'd killed him.

The coroner who examined Reverend Godfrey's remains would have argued that opinion. He'd ruled that the man might have died at any moment even without the trauma and even absent the injury, he'd had weeks to live at the most. Added to that declaration, the man's widow, Erna Godfrey, herself the killer of Andrew Hudson Grant, had asked that Ellie be shown mercy.

Given those circumstances, no prosecution was brought. Ellie had skated on what might have been an involuntary manslaughter charge that could have put her behind bars for years.

Ellie still had to tell herself that Godfrey's death was no great loss to anyone. That bastard had used the cloak of religion to advance his own extremist views and make his political endorsement a must-have requirement for any conservative office-seeker. It had been only recently, however, that Ellie had come to take comfort in the coroner's judgment.

The third person she'd killed, another man she supposed, was the guy who had her in such a sweat right now: the creep whom she felt certain now had stuck a bomb onto the hull of the *Dame.* She'd done that bastard in without even being aware of it. Given how badly his work was scaring her right now, she didn't feel a bit of regret that he'd died gruesomely.

If anything, she wished that she might have heard him scream. That would have been terrifying when it happened. Now, the memory would bring a measure of satisfaction if not comfort. She didn't worry about facing any legal or moral consequences for the SOB's death.

It was Ellie's second victim, a woman, who had landed Ellie in her current predicament. Yeah, well, fuck that evil bitch, too. Compared to her, Ellie was Mother Teresa and …

Ellie saw a dot appear in the sky. It grew larger with every beat of her heart, and each cardiac contraction brought a surge of hope. The sound of helicopter blades becoming audible produced a swirl in Ellie's heart, the chill of anxiety with a glowing expectation of deliverance. Would the rescuers reach her in time?

She saw two men open a hatch on one side of the quickly approaching aircraft. One man wearing a harness seated himself with his legs dangling outside the chopper. The other stood behind the first fellow.

"Hurry up!" Ellie yelled. "Hurry!"

The second man, the one who hadn't bothered with a harness, sat next to the first. Why wasn't he taking any safety measures, Ellie wondered. For that matter, would she need more than one guy to haul her up? Then she saw the second dude had a diving mask clinging to his forehead. He also had an air-tank on his back and swim fins tucked under an arm.

He was going to look for the bomb attached to the *Dame.*

Ellie didn't want to wait for him to get to work.

"Me first!" she yelled at the approaching helicopter. "Take me up first!"

That wasn't the way it worked. The chopper slowed and then hovered 20 feet above the ocean and 10 feet off the *Dame's* port side. The diver, now wearing his mask and fins and holding some kind of flashlight, pushed himself out of the aircraft and hit the water, disappearing below the surface. No doubt he was already on his way to find the bomb.

Good for him, Ellie thought, but meanwhile …

"Get me the hell out of here!" she yelled up at the guy in the harness who was already dropping down to the deck of her yacht.

Before she could repeat her demand, he had an arm around her waist, and they were being winched back into the chopper. Ellie wept in relief once she was aboard the aircraft … but then she thought they'd better back off a fair distance, so neither a shock wave nor any flying debris hit them and the chopper.

The pilot must have had the same idea in mind. Within the seeming blink of an eye, he'd moved the helicopter a half-mile away from the *Dame.* The guy who'd grabbed Ellie had planted her backside in the open doorway and secured her with a safety harness. The two of them stared out at the yacht.

That was when Ellie began to hope that the diver would be all right, too. Talk about a guy with big brass … She saw him break the surface of the ocean with something that looked to be about the size of a football in his right hand. He held it up to give those aloft a better look. Then he climbed the stern ladder onto the *Dame.*

He put the football thingy into the Saturn dinghy and pushed the little emergency boat into the water. He hauled in the drogue and quickly clambered up to the captain's controls. He put the *Dame* in motion, moving away from the dinghy at top speed.

Good God, Ellie thought, had the damn thing *really* been that close to detonating?

The helicopter mirrored the yacht's course, moving along

above it and a half-mile abeam the port side. Ellie and the rescue team Hugh Collier had sent to rescue her were the better part of a mile distant from the dinghy when the bomb exploded.

Everyone saw a geyser of ocean water shoot into the air. A moment later they heard the bang. Even at that distance, the sound was booming. After the roar faded, a radio call came into the helicopter.

A male voice said. "I'll find a nice berth for this vessel. Maybe help myself to a beer and a nap aboard once I get her tied up."

"Anything you want," Ellie called out to the man who helped to save both her and her boat. "A night on the town, my treat, for everyone on the team."

A hearty cheer passed through both crafts.

"Where was the bomb?" Ellie asked the man who'd found it.

"Well placed. Right under the fuel tank."

A tremor ran through Ellie. Her intuition had been accurate.

The guy seated next to her said, "Let's get you inside and I'll shut the hatch."

She nodded, and he facilitated moving her completely into the helicopter and sealed the door. With the return of relative quiet, he told her, "Mr. Collier was apprised of what just happened and that you're safe. He was glad to hear it, but he wants us to haul ass back to New York. He sounded pretty close to the end I was told."

"I want to say thank you to everyone, including Hugh," she said. "So, yes, let's make it damn fast."

The guy saluted.

"I'll talk to the pilot, see if there are any corners on the flight plan he can cut. For the moment, though, let's just say all's well that ends well."

Ellie nodded, but she knew things were far from being done.

M & W Private Investigations — LeDroit Park, Washington, DC

Meeker and Beemer had their offices in a late 19th-century

townhouse that stood almost in the shadow of Howard University, both men's alma mater. Each of them had homes within a five-minute walk of their place of business. The parabolic curve of the neighborhood's social status had gone from chic to shriek and back.

The fathers of the two former MPD detectives had both been patrol officers for the department back in the late 1970s. They'd bought their LeDroit Park homes at a time when the area and its characteristic Victorian townhouses had suffered from years of neglect, and some blocks had open-air drug markets. Housing prices in the bad old days had been affordable even for civil servants.

Them and canny, courageous young law school grads like Dexter Wiles.

His law offices were on the first floor of his LeDroit Park townhouse.

The lawyer and his wife, Zala, lived in the upper two floors. Made for an easy commute.

Meeker and Beemer had come to own their homes the old-fashioned way: They'd inherited them. When they saw the neighborhood was on the rebound, gentrifying as people said these days, they took a leaf from their fathers' books, pooled their money, and made a down-payment on their own Victorian townhome, regarding it as an investment. They rented it out until a year before they'd retired. By that time, the tenants had paid the mortgage down to a pittance.

They'd given their final renters 12 months notice that they'd have to leave because the detectives were going into the private investigations business, and they would need office space. Thus motivated to find new living quarters, the young couple who'd been living there had required only three months to take their computer engineering degrees up I-95 to Boston where their kind thrived.

Possessing no remodeling or rehabbing skills, the two detectives nonetheless supervised the conversion of the premises from residential to commercial. Each of them had an office that was roomy, comfortable, and welcoming. Just beyond their offices, lay a space with an entirely different feeling. It was cramped and drab and fell just short of duplicating the interrogation rooms they'd used as MPD detectives.

They'd debated whether to put an actual cell in the basement but decided not to do that after Dexter Wiles had advised them that one false imprisonment suit might bring damages large enough to seize all of their properties and bank accounts. Neither Meeker nor Beemer wanted any part of that scenario.

They held fast to keeping their interrogation room after forcing their lawyer to concede that there was no law against making either a suspicious character or even a deadbeat client sweat. Just so long as they didn't threaten illegal acts or no longer represented themselves as still being police officials, Wiles had said.

Meeker and Beemer didn't do either of those things, but they did hang a photo of a glowering Mayor Rockelle Bullard in the room. The shot had been taken back when she'd still been an MPD captain and had her gold badge pinned to her lapel.

Beemer had once suggested a copy of that photo should hang in every schoolroom, public and private, in the country. Meeker had added, "Every prison cell, too."

When Constance Parker unexpectedly showed up at M&W Private Investigations that day, the two detectives knew just where to sit her down: the interrogation room. The dreary, claustrophobic space took the woman by surprise after she'd complimented both men on what a nice office building they had.

She almost tried to back out of the room, probably would have done so if Beemer wasn't blocking her way. She didn't want to put her status as someone who might be free to go her own way to the test. Especially after Meeker told her, "Have a seat."

His words sounded much more like a demand than a request. She sat. Facing Rockelle's photo. She had to bite her bottom lip so it didn't quiver.

"You have your gun with you?" Beemer asked.

Connie Parker shook her head.

"Well, we've got ours," Meeker said.

Neither he nor Beemer displayed their weapons. Doing so wouldn't have fit with the strategy the two of them intuitively decided to employ. When the woman took the seat she'd been offered, the two investigators crowded her. They didn't make physical contact, but they severely limited her breathing room.

"Do you know what you did this morning was a crime?" Beemer asked.

"I didn't do anything wrong," Parker said.

Meeker said, "You pointed what we had every reason to believe was a loaded gun at us, and you ordered us to leave. Implying you'd shoot us if we didn't."

Beemer added, "Intentionally attempting to place another person in fear of imminent serious physical injury is a crime called menacing. That can get you a year in a jail cell. Some jurisdictions will even lock you up for two years."

Connie Parker's face sagged. Her chin even began to quiver.

"So what can we do for you, Ms. Parker?" Meeker asked.

He and Beemer leaned in, further reducing the woman's freedom of movement.

"I wouldn't shoot anyone," she said. "I was just scared, trying to defend my home."

The two former MPD detectives laughed, going into one of their favorite interrogation routines. Beemer said, "Yeah, playing things that way might work if you were a white lady in Mississippi. 'Lordy me, those two black men put me in fear for my life.' But being an African-American woman yourself and living in Maryland, I don't think that'd win a lot of hearts and minds."

"I gotta agree with you there, Big Mike," Meeker told Beemer.

Being mocked made Connie angry. "But I was afraid."

"Of what?" Meeker asked. "My friend and I were asleep until you woke us. What kind of threat were we to a woman armed with a gun?"

Connie started to speak but caught herself. "I don't have to explain myself to the two of you."

Beemer replied, "You didn't have to come see us either, but you did. Why was that?"

She looked at both of them, but turned quickly away from Meeker when she took notice of the photo of Rockelle Bullard glaring at her over Meeker's shoulder. To Beemer, she said, "I came here to make a business proposition, one I'd like you to take to your brother-in-law. I would have gone straight to him, but you never told me his name."

Beemer said, "I think we'll still keep that to ourselves for now."

"What's the proposition?" Meeker asked.

Connie gathered herself, squared her shoulders. "I'd like to offer him a million dollars not to contest my sole claim to the Grand Slam lottery prize."

Keeping a straight face, Beemer said, "One million instead of half of $212 million? Doesn't seem like an irresistible deal to me."

"You don't get the whole amount if you take the lump sum," Connie told him.

"How much do you get?" Meeker asked.

Connie frowned. "After taxes, $64 million. That's what I was told."

Meeker, who was good at math, said, "So you'd be offering my partner's brother-in-law less than two pennies on your dollar. Hallelujah! He'll go for that for sure."

Connie Parker's jaw firmed. "You don't have to mock me. A million dollars is nothing to dismiss out of hand. If my offer is not accepted within 24 hours, it will be withdrawn, and I will have my lawyers fight you in court and countersue your claimant, and the two of you as well if you persist."

She gave them her phone number and got to her feet. "I trust I am free to leave."

Beemer made room for her to open the door and step out. "You always were free to go."

Meeker added, "Don't slip on the stairs as you leave. Wouldn't want you to have to file two suits."

McGill Investigations International — Washington, DC

Deke Ky was in his first-floor office when his phone chimed. He wondered, as he did most times he got a call, if it would be his mother, Musette Ky, reaching out to contact him. He hadn't heard from her in years and was beginning to think he never would. Their relationship never had been an easy one. When he'd first gone to work as Jim McGill's personal Secret Service bullet-catcher, Deke's mother had told her son to be ready to die for McGill.

Sure, that also had been part of his job description, but it was one thing to hear it from your boss and another to hear it from your mother. That still rankled Deke. Maybe it would be better if they never spoke again.

On the other hand, Musette had kept him from bleeding to death after he'd been shot on Thanksgiving night many years ago. That had to be taken into account, too. Maybe they would be able to make peace again someday.

In any case, he saw it wasn't Mom calling. Far better, it was Lily Kealoha.

"Aloha, *wahine,*" he said, taking the call.

She replied, "Aloha, *kane*. Got some news for you. Maybe it's good news, but it should be interesting at the very least."

"Great. What is it?"

She told him about the three headshots and two hand photographs Diplomatic Security Special Agent Lonnie Tompkins had taken outside of the United Nations building.

Deke was pleased but also puzzled about one thing. "How come your friend got three face photos but only two hands?"

"You know, I never thought to ask," Lily said. "I thought he did real well as it was."

Deke said, "You're right, he did. I was just wondering. Please give him my thanks, if that's appropriate."

Lily laughed. "Lonnie's the kind of guy who'd be happy to have a former Secret Service special agent buy him a drink. So any chance you might be coming this way soon?"

Deke was glad to hear Lily ask that question. He was beginning to think she might be getting too close to this State Department guy for his liking. Deke said, "At the first opportunity, professional or personal."

"Glad to hear it, *kane*. Oh, one thing you might tell Mr. McGill. Lonnie's going to tell his boss about these characters and how they might be related to the shootout in DC, and I'll be telling my boss right after we're done talking. So a bunch of us professional law enforcement types will be looking into this matter, too."

Deke said, "That's as it should be. I'll let Mr. McGill know, too, of course."

"Yeah, sure. I was wondering how things stand with him these days, his status with us official cops now that his wife is out of the White House."

"You mean does he still have enough pull that people with badges shouldn't ever think of stepping on his toes?" Deke asked.

"Yeah, that."

"Well … I heard through the Secret Service grapevine that President Grant went to see President Morrissey this morning. People will have to read into that whatever they want."

"Mr. McGill's still seriously connected is how I'd read it," Lily said.

"Me, too, but unless someone goes out of his way to be a jerk, there's no worry."

Lily said, "Right. I really liked him when we met, and I'm still thinking I wouldn't mind working with you down in DC once my pension is locked in."

Deke said, "If he doesn't hire you, I'll start my own private detective agency."

Embassy of the Hashemite Kingdom of Jordan — Washington, DC

Ambassador Fayez Mousa met Patti and McGill at the embassy's front door. They didn't even have to ring the doorbell.

The diplomat's extraordinary deference was no doubt due to Patti's presence, McGill knew. Had he appeared without his better half, he might have been greeted by a Third Secretary who'd arrived in the U.S. within the previous 24 hours.

Mousa gently took Patti's hand as if he meant to kiss it, but he didn't. He only inclined his head and said, "Madam President, a pleasure to see you as always."

He shook McGill's hand with an agreeably firm grip. With some of the foreign diplomats McGill had met, he'd felt as if he'd grasped a damp sponge.

Mousa showed his guests into his office, got them seated, and inquired if they'd care for something to drink. Alas, he didn't have anything with an alcohol content on the premises. Other than that he could provide a wide variety of coffees, teas, and soft drinks.

Patti graciously declined, and McGill did likewise.

The social graces having been observed, the ambassador got down to business. "I must admit, Madam President, I find myself in something of a confusing situation. Prior to the arrival of you and Mr. McGill, I was contacted by the White House chief of staff, Ms. Mindel. She said the United States was always grateful to see that a former American president was treated with the highest regard by foreign envoys, but I should bear in mind that you no longer speak for your government."

Patti nodded and said, "That's correct, Mr. Ambassador. President Morrissey speaks *officially* for the United States on matters of policy."

Mousa caught the point of emphasis. "And unofficially? I would still be puzzled if President Morrissey, herself, hadn't also called me this morning. She asked me to listen carefully to what you and Mr. McGill had to say. She added that your country and mine would likely be able to help one another. She also said some matters are best handled quietly."

McGill couldn't keep himself from smiling.

Both Patti and Mousa didn't miss that.

The ambassador asked McGill, "You disagree, sir?"

"Not with President Morrissey's desire to keep things quiet, but when the bad guys attempt an assassination in broad daylight in Georgetown it's going to make news. We can do our best to keep a low profile but that doesn't mean the gunmen will go along."

The ambassador nodded. "You are right, of course, and we must all defend ourselves. Within the present realities, I think the president and His Majesty simply mean we must do our best to go about our end of things as subtly as possible."

Hearing mention of Jordan's king, Patti asked, "How did His Majesty take the news you gave him, Mr. Ambassador?"

Mousa took a moment to consider his reply. "He was deeply concerned. As you might know, His Majesty flew an attack helicopter for Jordan's army. The idea that two of our military aviators have become assassins was hard for him to hear."

McGill and Patti had no trouble understanding that, but they both sensed that Mousa was holding something back. So they waited. Let the silence build.

"May I ask that you not repeat to anyone what I am about to say?" the ambassador asked.

McGill let Patti handle that one. She said, "Assuming it won't hinder stopping a further attack, yes."

Nailed it, McGill thought.

Mousa nodded. "This is a personal matter for His Majesty, this situation with the pilots and their tattoos. You know of Muath Al-Kasasbeh, of course."

Patti nodded. It took McGill a moment to summon the memory, but he nodded, too.

The Jordanian air force pilot had been captured by ISIS after his F-16 crashed in Syria in December of 2014. A month later, the jihadis put the man in a cage on public display, set him ablaze, and burned him to death. For those not on hand, a video was made available globally.

Mousa continued, "It was after that young man's terrible death that other pilots in my country's military began to wear the tattoo you mentioned: my country's flag on their right hands. They wanted our enemies to know that not just our military but all of Jordan would be coming to avenge our fallen hero and show them no mercy."

Patti nodded.

McGill said, "Perfectly understandable."

"Yes, but what very few know is His Majesty was going to wear one, too. The queen talked him out of it. She said to him he was perfect just the way he was, and no one would ever doubt either his courage or his love of our country."

McGill could imagine Patti doing the same sort of thing for him. Not that he was a king.

Patti told Mousa, "So his Majesty must have felt he'd been betrayed when he heard about the would-be assassins here in Washington."

Mousa only nodded.

"Could be the tattoos were just misdirection," McGill said.

That notion startled the ambassador. "What do you mean, sir?"

"Well," McGill said, "the shooters here in Washington no doubt hoped they'd get away unharmed, but they must have taken into account the possibility they might be killed or captured. If either of those things happened and people saw the tattoos of Jordan's flag, well then, by using *misleading* tattoos the larger portion of the blame would be directed at their enemies. They'd be wounding Jordan's heart again."

Through clenched teeth, Mousa muttered something, a curse possibly, in Arabic.

Then he said, "I will share your idea with His Majesty. Thank you, Mr. McGill."

"There's one more thing," McGill said.

He told the ambassador about the diver who may have sabotaged Ellie Booker's yacht.

"That guy had a Lebanese flag tattooed on his hand," McGill said.

"Which also might be a point of deception," Patti suggested.

"Yes," McGill added.

"How are we to see through this veil of evil?" Mousa asked.

McGill had a suggestion. "When you talk to His Majesty ask him to have the pilots he most trusts to look for either phonies or the traitors in their ranks. Also, start a search for the tattoo artist, probably just one guy —"

"Or woman," Patti added.

"Okay, or woman," McGill added, "whoever did the bad guys' tattoos. Knowing who that person is would be a good start to an investigation."

A grim smile formed on Mousa's face, and he nodded.

McGill felt he might have just sentenced someone to death.

But after the murder attempt in front of his workplace, he didn't feel too bad about it.

Mousa stood up and extended his hand to Patti and McGill. "I am most grateful to both of you. Now, will you please join me in the embassy dining room for lunch. "

McGill and Patti were happy to accept. Patti said she hoped the ambassador would pass along any useful information he might come to possess.

He said he would, of course.

Unless the king decided otherwise, the two Americans knew.

After dining and getting back into the Chevy with Leo at the wheel, McGill told him they'd drop Patti off at Committed Capital before heading back to his office building. The former first couple was silent on the drive.

Patti felt a sense of satisfaction in meeting with the foreign diplomat, a feeling that she'd sworn to herself she would never need again. Well, there was no question that she could never be president again, but maybe she could be some kind of unofficial adviser to the high and mighty.

McGill's thinking was far more focused: Was Ellie Booker still alive?

Hugh Collier's Townhouse — Manhattan

Ellie Booker's heart rose into her throat, almost choking her, when she saw the CEO of WorldWide News in his final moments. Rather than surrender to emotion, she fought back her grief and tried to bring a final smile to her old friend, rival, and sometimes nemesis.

She asked him, "You want to see me nude just the way I am or is there time for me to take a quick shower? After a night on the ocean, I'm not as fresh as a daisy."

The doctor, the nurse, and the guy in a three-piece suit who were in attendance all frowned.

Hugh, bless him, smiled to the extent that he could.

"Sit next to me," he said. "The rest of you can leave with my thanks. George, leave your briefcase with us."

The guy in the suit nodded. He and the others left, the nurse giving Hugh's hand a gentle squeeze before departing. She was also the only one with tears in her eyes.

Ellie sat on the bed next to Hugh, and she also took his hand.

"Goddamnit, Hugh, who am I going to fight with once you leave?"

The question evoked a brief laugh. Hugh said, "Knowing you, you'll always find someone. James J. McGill perhaps. If he won't take the role, maybe my ghost will haunt you."

"Fine by me. An ectoplasmic you is better than none at all."

"My, my," Hugh said. "Ellie Booker is about to shed a tear or two. Now, I've seen it all. I can depart in peace."

Ellie tightened her grip. "Wait a minute. You said you have an offer for me. What is it?"

The hint of another smile appeared on Hugh's face. "That's my girl, showing me your naked ambition if nothing else. Look in the briefcase George left behind. You'll find a job offer for you in there. I've signed the contract. So has George as the witness. All it needs is your signature to go into effect on this very day."

Ellie's core sense of ambition forced her to release Hugh's hand

and dig the contract out of the briefcase. Her eyes widened as she saw the legacy she was being handed. Hugh was leaving her all his personal wealth, a sum expressed in nine figures. Beyond that were more millions connected to a five-year contract to act as World-Wide News' chief executive officer and managing editor.

Nearly dumbfounded, she looked at Hugh and asked, "Why me?"

"Who better?" he replied.

She didn't have an answer for that and only asked, "You have a pen?"

Hugh responded with the closest he could come to a wicked smile.

He said quietly, "Not on me."

"And of course you can't get up to find one," she said.

"No," he answered even more softly, as if he was starting his final journey.

"And if I leave the room to get one, that would void this agreement, wouldn't it?" she asked.

Hugh only smiled ever so slightly.

Ellie said, "You set things up this way because I once told you that a great reporter should never be caught without a pen. So she could write something down on the palm of her hand if need be. Well, buddy, I asked for a pen as a matter of courtesy. I still practice what I preach."

She reached into the gap above the top button on her shirt and took out the pen clipped to her bra. "That's why you didn't want me to strip," she said. "It wasn't because of the other people in the room. It would have spoiled your fun if you had seen the pen before you offered me the job."

Hugh gave her one last smile and closed his eyes, but he wasn't gone yet.

With a gesture of his right hand, he beckoned to her to come closer.

Ellie signed the contract first, and then she leaned in next to him.

Hugh made a confession: "I killed Uncle Edbert."

Sir Edbert Bickford. The prior lord and master of WWN.

Someone known by all and mourned by none.

"Why?" Ellie asked, not terribly surprised by the admission.

In a thready whisper, Hugh said, "The old sod intended to shoot me on his yacht. I took his gun away and tossed him into the Potomac. He'd never learnt to swim … and I dived in and held him under."

Those were Hugh Collier's final words. He was gone.

Nonetheless, Ellie whispered in his ear, "If you ever do come to haunt me, I'll tell you about the people I've killed. All three of them. Of course, that number might grow."

As Hugh's body started to cool next to her, Ellie read through her new contract and smiled.

Then she called McGill.

Committed Capital — Washington, DC

Patti gave McGill a smile and a kiss goodbye as Leo brought the Chevy to a stop in front of her office building.

McGill said, "I thought I'd seen your entire repertoire of smiles by now, but that last one just now took me by surprise. It's almost as if you had a mischievous thought."

"You've certainly seen *that* one before."

"I was thinking of another kind of merriment," McGill replied.

She said, "Well, this is different. I was thinking I might become your official entrée when you need to speak with someone who'd otherwise put you off. I enjoyed our little discussion with Ambassador Mousa. I felt helpful."

"So you have gotten the Nancy Drew bug," McGill said.

"Maybe a little, an impulse to indulge every now and then. I'm certainly not ready to abandon the business I've started. We have important work to do, and as I've mentioned there are a few things almost ready to knock the world on its keister."

"In a good way, I hope," McGill said.

"We are definitely on the side of the angels," Patti told him.

After another quick kiss, she stepped out of the car.

Per McGill's habit and his instructions to Leo, they waited until they saw Patti safely enter the building. She was assisted in that effort by Cale Tucker, who arrived on foot just in time to open the door for the boss. The two of them smiled upon meeting and went inside where they were joined by Special Agent Daphna Levy who safeguarded the former president when she wasn't with her husband.

And sometimes when she was.

"Where to, Boss?" Leo asked.

"Let's go talk with private detectives Meeker and Beemer."

Leo tapped the names into his mapping program, looked at the route the computer suggested and made only two changes in his mind. He told McGill, "On our way. Software says it's a twelve-minute trip."

"And what do you say?" McGill asked.

"Eight minutes unless you want me to get fancy. Then it's six."

"How about if we take it easy?"

"Ten minutes."

Even with Leo whistling *The Tennessee Waltz* as he drove, they made it in nine.

McGill, who'd been timing the trip, said, "Show off."

Leo just grinned as McGill got out of the car and went up the steps to Meeker and Beemer's offices. It was the first time he'd visited, and the two new PIs took him on a tour. Including the interrogation room.

McGill was impressed, especially by the room where suspects could be sweated with the photo of Mayor Bullard back in her cop days glaring down at them.

"You guys are giving me some ideas about re-doing a corner of my own building," he said. "Maybe I'll throw in a couple of ne'er-do-wells in a cell subsisting on bread and water."

Beemer said, "We thought of having a cell."

Meeker added, "Our lawyer talked us out of it."

"Probably for the best," McGill conceded.

They went to Meeker's office to continue their discussion. Taking turns in narrating their story, as was their custom, the two men told McGill of Constance Parker's visit and her million-dollar offer to Beemer's brother-in-law, Sammy.

McGill thought about that for a moment. Then he asked, "She didn't put a sweetener on top of the million for the two of you?"

Meeker and Beemer shook their heads and then looked at each other.

Turning back to McGill, Meeker said, "That offer was … what would you call it?"

"Cheap," Beemer said. "What with all the money she's got coming."

"Maybe just looking at you gents she could tell you weren't for sale," McGill suggested. "By the way, Sammy would be willing to settle for half of the jackpot, wouldn't he? Making a separate arrangement with Sammy and his lawyer, about how much you will get for your efforts?"

Beemer said, "Marvin, Dexter, and I have already worked out our cuts." Meeker added, "You still good with the number you gave us, Mr. McGill?"

He told them, "Sweetie now thinks we should work *gratis.* Bump the amount you give to charity. Let's say we ask for a dollar as a special introductory offer. How's that?"

"We can afford to pay the amount we agreed to," Beemer said. "Well, actually, once we get paid we can do that and add to the charity pot."

McGill said, "I like to see a new business get a running start. So don't think I regard you guys as a charity case, too. I appreciate how hard it can be to get rolling, and having been a cop myself, I value the work you did for this city."

Meeker and Beemer looked at each other. They both nodded.

"Okay," Meeker said. "So where do you see things going from here, Mr. McGill?"

"First, I think it's time you start calling me Jim. May I call you Marvin and Big Mike?"

They nodded.

"So, Marvin and Big Mike, I hate to be critical, but there are differences between a cop asking questions and a PI doing the same thing. I've learned that the hard way. I think you guys have made a mistake, but if you're careful, maybe we can use it to our advantage. Do you know what I'm talking about?" McGill asked.

Meeker and Beemer looked at each other, and then Beemer responded.

"I've been feeling lately it wasn't a good idea to mention our client was my brother-in-law. I should have left him anonymous."

Meeker nodded. "Yeah. Ms. Parker must've found us by taking down our car's license plate numbers. We didn't give her our names."

Beemer followed. "As little privacy as there's left in the world, if she knows my name, she can find out my family connections. She might go straight to Sammy and offer him that million."

"We better call him right now," Meeker said. "Dexter, too. So he knows where things stand and might have something smart to tell Sammy."

McGill said, "That's what I was thinking among other things. When you're a cop and have thousands of brothers and sisters in blue looking out for you and your family, you've got good reason to think your back will be covered. When you're two guys out on your own …"

He shrugged and waited to see if they saw the further implications.

"You think that woman might try to steal Sammy's winning ticket?" Beemer asked McGill.

Before he could answer, Meeker took the next step. "Hell, she might even go to Sammy's house and case it for some creeps to break in later."

"Or?" McGill asked. "You know, if someone really goes off the deep end."

Meeker and Beemer looked at each other, using one another as a source of inspiration.

Beemer spoke first, “You think if that Parker lady brings other people in on this they might kidnap Sammy’s wife or something?”

“The ransom being his winning ticket,” Meeker said.

“I didn’t see the woman,” McGill said, “didn’t have a chance to judge her character. But you have to plan for whatever is possible. If she was willing to pay a million dollars to buy off Sammy, well, you can hire some truly evil thugs for a lot less than that.”

Meeker and Beemer looked at each other. With all their combined years as cops in Washington, they could fill a phone book with the names of offenders they’d heard of or even personally arrested.

“We can hire guys and women still on the job to look out for Sammy and his family,” Beemer said.

Moonlighting cops, he meant.

Meeker nodded. “We’d better start making calls right away.”

“Don’t forget Lawyer Dexter Wiles,” McGill said. “He needs at least a heads-up. There’s also one more thing the two of you should look into.”

“What’s that?” Beemer asked.

“Well,” McGill said, “maybe Ms. Parker is trying to buy off Sammy on the cheap because she doesn’t really expect to see the full prize money.”

“Why wouldn’t she?” Meeker asked.

McGill said, “Well, this is just my guess, but I agree with Big Mike. A million dollars was too low-ball an offer for someone expecting, what, maybe a hundred million dollars after taxes to come her way. Five million would have been a much more reasonable and appealing offer.”

“So why didn’t she do that?” Beemer asked.

McGill turned to Meeker. “Marvin?”

Meeker intuited where McGill was going. “Because the lady might be fronting for someone else and giving us a million would be a good chunk of what she’s really getting.”

McGill nodded. “Start looking at Ms. Parker.”

Both Meeker and Beemer said, “Yeah.”

"But guys, one more thing," McGill added. "Besides the idea of Ms. Parker hiring thugs to come down this way, she might also be spreading some money around up in Maryland to protect herself."

Meeker and Beemer looked at each other, both of them wondering whether Maryland State Police Detective Sergeant Dalton Rivers might be up for sale. Or, who knew, maybe he could just be a sucker for a sweet-talking, good-looking woman.

"Yeah," Beemer said, "you never know when trouble's right around the corner."

"Amen to that, brother," Meeker added.

Rolling with Leo — Washington, DC

McGill was riding with Leo, who was now listening to music through his earbuds, making good time as always in getting McGill through DC traffic, when Ellie Booker's phone call came through. McGill answered immediately.

"Hi, it's me," Ellie said. "Sorry for not getting back to you sooner."

McGill heaved a sigh of relief. "I'm glad you're able to call anyone. Did you get my message or did you hear from Hugh Collier, and where are you now?"

She said, "I had my phone turned off, and the moment I turned it on Hugh was in my ear. More than that, he sent a helicopter out to take me off my yacht."

The perks of the ruling class, McGill thought.

It still caught him by surprise that he was tangentially one of the privileged few.

"Collier told me he was dying," McGill said, "and he did sound almost spectral."

Ellie told him, "He wasn't kidding. Hugh died holding my hand."

McGill sighed. "That was comforting for him, I hope."

Ellie laughed without humor. "Yeah, we were antagonists more often than not, but in our own strange way, we loved one another. I think it meant a lot for him to see and speak to me one last time. At least, that's what the evidence suggests."

"What evidence?" McGill asked.

"He left me a huge pile of money and a high-paying job."

McGill wasn't gauche enough to ask how much money, and he had a good guess about the job. "You inherited the CEO-ship of WorldWide News?"

"Sure did. That and managing editor of all news content."

McGill whistled. "I'm impressed."

"Me, too. This is not the way my luck usually runs. In fact, if I didn't have a signed and witnessed will-slash-contract in hand, I might think I was delusional."

"You might be imagining the whole thing if you had some kind of shock out on your boat," McGill told her.

"Then I'd also have to be kidding myself that Hugh isn't lying dead right next to me at this very minute. I really should call the hired help to come and take him away pretty soon."

"That would be the decent thing to do," McGill agreed. "So, let me guess, your boat didn't blow up after all."

"My dinghy did," Ellie told him.

She explained what had happened.

"Damn," McGill said, "that was close."

"Yeah, teach me to turn my phone off."

"Where do we go from here, Ellie? You now know people are making a determined effort to kill you. It's time for the cops and the feds to step in."

"Yeah, I suppose there's no getting around that, but I still want you to work the case, too."

"The guys with badges probably won't like that."

Ellie said, "Detective Behan strikes me as a reasonable guy, and you must know some feds who'll cut you slack from your White House days."

"One or two," McGill conceded, "but both the MPD cops and the FBI agents are really good at what they do."

"More often than not, I'll concede that much," she said, "but I've got information I'll share with you, but not them."

"What kind of information?"

"Actually, I won't share it with you directly. Remember how you said we'd need to use a lawyer to keep things confidential? You didn't mention any names, but how about Ms. Sweeney's husband, Putnam Shady? I've heard about him and did a little checking online just now. I think he'd be a smart choice for both of us."

"Putnam is very good at what he does, and I've come to trust him completely."

"Good enough for me."

"And the reason you want to use a cut-out is confidentiality, right?"

Ellie said, "My protection and yours. Of course, you could say no, but from all those phone calls you made to me, I think for some unguessable reason you have a small measure of affection for me."

McGill went silent for a moment.

"Or not," Ellie said. "If you can't do it, I'll look for someone else."

"I won't be involved in any criminal act," McGill said.

Now, Ellie was slow to respond. When she did, she said, "I'll end the professional relationship if I see that point approaching."

"Okay," McGill agreed, "I'll help you."

"Thank you. I'll call Mr. Shady so you won't have to."

McGill heard a knock on his office door, something that happened only occasionally. Most times, if people wanted to visit his office, they checked in with Esme and she informed McGill. Sweetie was an exception. She had no-knock privilege and could walk right in. Same with Patti and the kids, only they liked to chat with Esme, and the offspring got a kick out of having their arrivals announced.

Made them feel like big-shots, they'd told him.

Still, on edge from yesterday's attempted double-murder and hearing just a moment ago that a bomb *had* been placed on Ellie's boat, McGill took a flat-nose Colt .32 caliber revolver, a six-shot cop gun, out of a desk drawer. It wasn't the kind of weapon that would put a round through a targeted individual and also take out two innocent bystanders behind the bad guy.

Before anything overly dramatic could occur, McGill remembered that he'd given Esme the afternoon off, and Dikki had assured him that all of the alarms that would signal an intruder breaking into the building were in perfect working order. McGill returned the Colt to its drawer.

"Who is it?" he asked.

"You taking a nap in there?"

It was Deke, twitting him for being so slow to answer.

"No, just trying to adjust to the new environment. Come on in."

Deke opened the door, left it that way, and took a seat. He looked at McGill and said, "Yeah, this Georgetown area's going downhill fast. Maybe you better put up another building somewhere safe."

"Sweden?" McGill asked. "Only I hear even the Swedes have their problems these days."

Deke nodded. "You're right. There's no place safe."

"You didn't visit just to spread a little cheer, did you, Deke?"

He shook his head. "I talked to Lily Kealoha this morning. She got in touch with Diplomatic Security Service Special Agent Lonnie Tompkins, a friend of hers. Acting on Lily's request, he spotted three men of Arabic appearance with flag tattoos on their right hands. They were seen entering or exiting the United Nations main building. He even got photos of the guys' faces and the relevant hands of two of them. I'll send the pictures to your phone now."

Deke effected the transfer.

McGill looked at the men's faces first, impressing their likenesses deeply enough to know who they were if he ever had occasion to see them in person. Then he studied the images of the flags and asked,

"Which countries' flags am I seeing here?"

Deke pointed them out using his own phone. "Egypt and Libya."

McGill said, "Add those to Jordan and Lebanon and we're talking four different countries so far."

"Yeah," Deke agreed. "Special Agent Tompkins only caught a glimpse of the third guy's tattoo. Didn't have time to photograph it. He's reviewing the flags of the countries in the region to see if one jumps out at him."

McGill thought for a second. "Maybe ask him to take a look at flags for countries in Southeast Asia, too. I remember reading that ISIS is in the Philippines now."

"Good point," Deke said. "I'll pass the word along to Lily. She raised another question I hadn't thought about. She said she hadn't known that Air Force personnel included special ops guys. That made me think of Gene Beck down in Austin. Didn't he serve in Air Force special ops?"

McGill nodded. "The official job he trained for was called combat controller. Among other things, they specialize in airfield seizures, airstrike controls, and communication matters. They train in free-fall parachuting and … damn," McGill said.

"What?" Deke asked.

"I just remembered: Gene told me he was also trained in underwater and maritime operations."

Deke whistled. "That sure fits in with someone messing under Ellie Booker's yacht."

"More than messing," McGill said. He told Deke about Ellie's narrow escape.

"Damn," Deke said.

McGill said, "More than that, Gene also told me Air Force special ops guys also call in air strikes."

Deke thought about that for a moment. "Yeah, of course, that's what the Air Force would do, but the bad guys can't possibly have …"

His mind caught up with his vocalization, and that stopped

him cold.

McGill knew just what he was thinking. “They don’t have their own stealth bombers? Right, but if you want personalized air destruction, what do we know is all the current rage?”

“Drones,” Deke said.

McGill sighed. “Right. Just like the Secret Service used to worry about a drone doing in Patti and me. So far, the bad guys have tried to kill Ellie on the ground and in the water. That pretty much leaves an air assault as the next step. And now she’s in New York City where Special Agent Tompkins spotted three guys with tattoos.”

“Let’s hope she’ll take your next call promptly,” Deke said.

“Yeah,” McGill agreed, “but I’d feel better having you on hand in New York.”

There was no way Deke was going to argue with that.

McGill’s phone rang not ten seconds after Deke left to make arrangements for getting to New York. He and McGill agreed that flying made more sense than driving. They both had the feeling that time was of the essence.

McGill sent a text to Ellie informing her that Deke would arrive in NYC as soon as possible. She should remember that Deke was deeply experienced in personal protection and not give him a hard time about doing whatever was necessary to keep her safe. To emphasize the point, he added the news about possible bad guys doing business at the United Nations.

He’d just sent the text when his phone chirped. Patti was calling. McGill said a quick, silent prayer that all was well on his wife’s front. He said, “Hello, my dear.”

“Greetings to you, my henchman.”

Patti’s use of his nickname put McGill on alert.

Her tone of voice, though, didn’t carry a tone of alarm. Maybe just a little wariness.

"What's up?" McGill asked.

"Abbie called me. No special reason. She said she was in the neighborhood and wondered if she might take me to a late lunch, as we haven't had an occasion to talk in person lately."

"She's a sweetheart, that child. Young woman, I suppose, would be more apt."

"Yes, it would, but I understand what you mean on both counts. As it turned out, I have some things to do that will keep me busy the rest of the afternoon, but I said I'd love to have her drop by for a hug and a quick catch-up."

McGill said, "And now you're taking the time to fill me in, but being the suspicious type, I feel there's more to this story."

"There is. I was getting Cale Tucker's evaluation on a new business proposition. The idea is exciting, but I'm not sure how long it would be exclusive to our investment group. Elements could be patented, but overall there'd likely be other ways to reach the same end. Resulting in fierce competition."

McGill was genuinely interested in Patti's new line of work, but at that moment paternal instinct and investigative experience took him in another direction.

"Abbie was introduced to Cale Tucker?" he asked.

"Yes."

"And since you have a time commitment of your own here?"

"You're on the right track," Patti told him.

"Abbie went out with Cale."

"She did. They did. An early dinner and then a foreign film that interests both of them." Patti waited for McGill's response and when it didn't come quickly she asked, "Does any of this bother you?"

McGill told her of Cale asking Esme if she had any sisters or cousins.

"Maybe he's just a bit lonely," Patti said.

"Or he's a hound."

Patti chuckled, and McGill asked, "Something's funny?"

His wife told him, "You weren't around when I was in modeling and the movies but, believe me, I know all about hounds. I've also had appropriate discussions on the subject with all three of our children."

McGill had long ago told Patti to think of his children as hers, too. With great gratitude, and deference to Carolyn, the children's birth mother, she did. Patti felt free to discuss any topic with them.

"And how did they react to this tutorial?" McGill asked.

"Abbie took written notes; Ken nodded frequently when instructed in how not to behave with females; Caitie laughed pretty much throughout and reminded me of how good she'd become at Dark Alley."

"Yeah, ironically, I'd worry less about Caitie in this regard than Abbie," McGill said.

"Me, too, but Abbie's also strong in many ways. She'll be all right with Cale. I just thought you should be aware of a new development."

"Thank you. I appreciate the heads-up. You think you'll be free in time for me to take you to dinner?"

"Of course, I'm the boss."

"Me, too," McGill said, "not that I always feel like it."

Florida Avenue — Washington, DC

Putnam Shady, at home alone while Margaret and Maxi were on a school outing, was waiting for a call from Darren Drucker, the third wealthiest man in the country. Drucker had provided the seed money to start Share America, the country's first mutual lobbying fund. Just as a mutual insurance company was owned by its policyholders, Share America's lobbying firm was owned by and devoted to the interests of its stake-holders, average Americans.

At first, it cost $100 per year to buy into Share America and obtain a voting right as to which political policies the firm should advocate. When it became clear that millions of Americans couldn't afford even that modest amount to have their voices heard in Congress, Putnam had suggested that groups of five be allowed to pool $20 each to buy a share.

Drucker had agreed with Putnam's idea, but he'd said the holders of pooled shares would have to agree unanimously on how they wanted their votes to be cast. Putnam liked that, and pooled votes were made available. People flocked to the offering. The idea that you could persuade — or muscle — Congress into voting for the interests of the average American for just $20 was highly appealing.

The mutual lobbying fund had $200 million to work with at that moment in 2019. Drucker was also covering the relatively modest overhead expenses of office space and staff salary.

Special interest lobbying firms fought back, of course. They also raised enormous sums of lobbying money. Where they couldn't match Share America, though, was in the number of voters each side could drive to the polls when it was time for the next election.

The masses of people who wanted to increase taxes on the wealthy was simply far greater than those who wanted to cut Social Security and Medicare benefits. A social and political upheaval was in the making, and to his delight, Putnam Shady was in the thick of the disruption. It made him feel even better when Margaret had told him he was doing the moral thing.

Putnam couldn't guarantee that everything would work out the way he hoped, of course. He had to plan and scheme as hard as he could. The questions he most frequently asked himself always started with the words, "What if …"

At the moment, he was applying that formula to a specific point of politics: *What if Jean Morrissey decides not to run for a second term as president?* He didn't think she'd bow out. Very few presidents had: only Polk, Coolidge and Johnson, sort of. LBJ had served less than two years as president after John F. Kennedy had been assassinated and one term of his own, but he declined to run for his own second term.

George Washington had declined to run for a third term, saying two were enough.

So history said that Jean Morrissey likely would run for a second term but, who knew, maybe she wouldn't. Putnam wanted to be sure Share America wasn't caught napping either way. His phone rang but it wasn't Darren Drucker.

Ellie Booker was on the line. He knew, of course, she was a media person. One lucky to be alive at the moment.

Putnam answered by saying, "I'm sorry, Ms. Booker, I don't do interviews."

"That's okay. I'm looking for a lawyer, not a talking head. I need someone to act as a privileged intermediary between Jim McGill and me."

Putnam asked the obvious question. "Is Mr. McGill aware of your interest?"

"He is. We just talked and he said okay. If you're not interested, I'll try to find some other attorney we can both trust."

"How do you know you can trust me? We've never met."

"I've done extensive research on Mr. McGill, including who his closest friends and colleagues are."

Putnam grunted. "So you know my wife qualifies on both counts."

"I do. I even took a hard look at you."

"I hope you didn't intrude on my daughter's privacy or we can end this conversation right now."

"I'm aggressive when it comes to doing my job, and other times, too, but kids are off-limits. Unless, of course, they've emancipated themselves, adopted a public persona, and are acting like real shits. That being the case, your daughter is safe from me."

"Reassuring," Putnam said coolly. "You expect me to take your word that Jim McGill has agreed to the relationship you've proposed?"

"I wouldn't want you to represent me in any way if you agreed to what I propose without checking with Mr. McGill first. At the moment, I'm simply starting a conversation that I hope will work out to everyone's benefit."

"I really don't take on private clients anymore, Ms. Booker. I'm quite busy."

"With Share America, I know. It would be contrary to the nature of your organization if I offered you a huge sum of money. So I'd like to suggest providing you with something else that might benefit your work."

"What's that?" Putnam asked.

"A large amount of TV time so you reach far more people than you already have, a chance to truly tip the political balance in your favor."

Putnam said, "And how can you do that?"

"I was at Hugh Collier's bedside when he died less than an hour ago. He made me the boss of WorldWide News before he went. I have a five-year iron-clad contract. It's a happy coincidence I also believe in what you and Darren Drucker are doing. I'll give you a big stage on which to persuade as much of the country as you can."

Putnam couldn't help himself. He had to laugh. "You didn't study under the devil when it comes to purchasing souls, did you, Ms. Booker? You're awfully good."

Ellie told him, "I'm sure Ms. Sweeney can advise you on the matter of moral peril better than I can. Anyway, that's what I can offer, and I've told you what I want: a privileged conduit to Mr. McGill, and soon. I imagine your wife has already told you about my near-miss with mortality."

"She has told me. I walked over to the McGill Building shortly after all the excitement."

"*Terror,* if you were in the gunsight," Ellie corrected.

"You're right, and I'm sorry. I shouldn't have belittled your situation."

"Yeah, and my yacht was almost blown up with me aboard earlier today."

"Jesus. So you want me to —"

"Listen to why I'm on a hit list, pass the word on to Mr. McGill in confidence, and hope he can find a way out for me. Especially since I'm about to step into a very big spotlight."

"I'll call Jim," Putnam said. "But first you need to do an electronic funds transfer to my account. Paying my fee before we get into a professional discussion will establish privilege."

M & W Investigations — Le Droit Park, Washington, DC

"A million dollars?" Sammy MacCray asked with a mixture of incredulity and disdain in his voice. "Hell, no. I'm not accepting that."

His wife, Beemer's sister Francine, nodded in agreement, her arms crossed in front of her.

The two of them sat in Beemer's office along with Dexter Wiles. Beemer sat behind his desk; Meeker stood next to him.

"Didn't expect you to," Beemer told Sammy. "I just had to put the offer out there so you'd know we weren't holding anything back on you."

Wiles nodded and told his clients. "That was the ethical thing to do."

"Okay," Sammy said, "that takes care of the ethics. Where do we go from here?"

"And did you get Mr. McGill to work with you?" Francine asked. "You know, in case any big-shots get involved on the other side."

Meeker told her, "Yeah, we've consulted with the man. He's willing to help."

"Already made a good suggestion or two," Beemer added.

"How much money does he want for his time?" Sammy asked. "He's not asking for a slice of the pie, is he?"

Dexter Wiles was curious, too, but he waited for an answer in silence.

Beemer said, "All he asked for was a dollar."

The clients and their lawyer looked suspicious.

"I doubt that's his customary rate," Wiles said.

Sammy and Francine nodded in agreement.

Beemer told them, "He said it was an introductory offer, but if that hurt anybody's feelings, he and his partner want five percent to go to charities they name."

Sammy nodded. "Charities? I can live with that. How about you, Francie?"

Francine was mulling the proposition, looking for tricks.

"Yeah, okay," she finally said. "As long as our names are on the donations, too."

With that settled, Meeker voiced something that McGill hadn't considered. "Big Mike and I gave y'all a family discount on our services, and we'll stick with that, but my guess is Dexter, who's also kin to Sammy, is in for a percentage of the recovery. Isn't that right, Dexter?"

"Well, yes, that's customary," the lawyer said, doing his best not to sound greedy.

Beemer told his sister and her husband, "We surely don't want to argue with customs, now do we? Still, what we should consider here is you would have had to take Mr. McGill's usual fee off the top of what you get before Dexter gets his share."

"Yes, of course," Wiles said.

Meeker picked up the thread. "But since Mr. McGill is asking only a dollar for himself, the percentage he wants given to charity, that should come off the top before you figure out what Dexter's cut is."

"You also take off how much you're paying Marvin and me, too," Beemer added.

The couple nodded and both of them looked at their lawyer.

He kept a straight face and nodded wordlessly.

"Glad to see we all understand each other," Beemer said. "Now, I have to tell you about a mistake I made and how that's gonna be an expense, too."

"What'd you do, Michael?" Francine asked.

"I mentioned to Constance Parker that my brother-in-law bought the other winning ticket."

"So?" Sammy asked. "Why's that a big deal?"

Beemer said, "Ms. Parker came to us with her million-dollar

offer. We never mentioned our names to her. We didn't tell her where we live or work, but she still found us."

Meeker continued, "The lady must've written down the license plate number of our car. She used that to track us down. She's either resourceful or she knows people who are. What worries us is someone might be coming to visit Sammy and Francine next. Maybe to make you a slightly better offer, maybe to stick a gun in your face."

"Take your winning ticket right away from you," Beemer said. "Make their problem disappear."

Meeker added, "Saving them tens of millions of dollars. People have killed for a lot less than that."

Sammy frowned and said, "They'd better be damn good shots, if they try any shit like that. It'd take more than one shot to put me down. And besides that, the ticket's in my safe deposit box. Nobody but me and Francie can get into that."

Meeker and Beemer looked at each other. With a nod, Beemer passed the baton to Meeker.

He told Sammy, "Simple fact is, it doesn't matter how big and strong you are if someone shoots you in the head. You're either dead or so messed up you'd wish you were." He turned to his partner, "Big Mike."

"He's right," Beemer said. "We've seen both things. But, Sammy, you've got to ask yourself what you'd do if someone grabbed Francie, her being pregnant and all. They say to you, 'Mr. MacCray, you go get that ticket for us or say goodbye to your wife and unborn baby.'"

"Then they probably kill everybody anyway, once they do have the ticket," Meeker added.

Beemer said, "That's why we're going to have off-duty cops watching you all. You too, Dexter, you and Zala. Anybody tries to get at you then, the officers will use deadly force to see only the right people survive."

After hearing all that, Sammy and Francine hugged each other.

It was their lawyer, Dexter Wiles, who asked the practical question, "You two can get all the cops you'll need?"

"Yeah, we think so," Meeker said. "We got a call into our old boss, Mayor Bullard."

"How much will all that protection cost?" Wiles asked.

Meeker laughed. "Well, it's a good thing Sammy won the lottery."

Beemer added, "That or Marvin and me flip a coin, and one of us sells his house."

Dumbarton Oaks — Washington, DC

McGill couldn't restrain himself. While Patti was showering before they went out to dinner, and he had the rest of the house to himself, he made a phone call. He peeked out a living room window while the call was going through. He saw Leo and Daphna leaning against McGill's Chevy. Leo had told him once they liked to talk about having the Levy surname in common. They'd discussed having their ancestries traced and see if there was either a recent or distant intersection of their families.

McGill had thought of doing that for them and presenting the results as a gift.

He'd probably have to act soon or it would be a nice idea not acted upon in a timely fashion. That was, they'd beat him to the punch. Then he'd scold himself without telling anybody. Except Sweetie. She'd find an appropriate penance for him to do.

McGill's call went through, and Cale Tucker answered.

The younger man had a note of amusement in his voice as he said, "Mr. McGill, nice to hear from you."

"Just wanted to let you know that Ellie Booker is okay, although there was a bomb on her yacht's hull."

"Wow. So you got through to her, and she abandoned ship in time."

"No." McGill gave him the details. "So your finding Hugh Collier's private number for me was what saved the day."

Cale was savvy enough to reflect the credit for a happy outcome.

"I only did the grunt work," he said. "It was your idea to call the man. Sorry to hear he's gone. He really turned WorldWide News around. Now, that was a big job."

McGill said, "Speaking of which, do you know someone who's really good with big numbers?"

"That would be me, sir."

"Great. Saves time looking for someone else."

"What can I do for you, national security permitting?" Cale asked.

McGill explained the problem Meeker and Beemer faced and his role in assisting them. The young man was silent for a long enough time that he thought the connection might have been lost. He turned to look at the stairway to the second floor and see whether Patti might be on the way down. She wasn't. McGill asked, "You still there, Cale?"

"Yes, sir. Just thinking about the problem you and your colleagues are looking at."

"Too difficult to address without a supercomputer?" McGill asked.

Cale said, "I'll definitely need some data crunching help, but I was looking at a preliminary step before we get to that point."

"What's that?"

"Defining motive," the younger man said. "Why are the perpetrators messing with a lottery operation?"

"Money," McGill suggested.

"Sure, but what else?"

"Why would there need to be anything else?"

"There wouldn't if simple profit was the only impetus. But what if there was a national security aspect?"

McGill was about to suggest that Cale was still thinking like an NSA employee, but then he caught up with what Patti's new employee was considering. "It could be a cyber-attack," McGill said, "with a two-fold purpose. Provide the thieves with the world's international currency, the dollar, and if somebody finally catches on, the United States will be humiliated. The chumps can't even protect a game of chance that keeps the common man pacified by dreaming of riches."

"Right," Cale agreed. "It'd be a twofer benefit. What game are we looking at here?"

"The Grand Slam. Last Wednesday's jackpot."

"I wonder how long they've been working this scam, whoever they are?" Cale said.

That idea surprised McGill. "You don't think this is the first time?"

Cale said, "Doesn't have to be. Might be the first time this particular game was hacked. The hackers might have used software that worked on other games but wasn't a perfect fit for the Grand Slam until they tweaked it."

McGill gave a soft whistle. "That would be a national shaming."

"Can't have that," Cale said. "We've got to smack these people upside the head."

"No argument here," McGill said, "but let's work from small to big. Get Samuel J. MacCray his money and go from there. You know, in case the great curtain of national interest descends on us."

"Agreed. Only now I have a problem."

"What's that?" McGill asked.

"I'd have to delay work on a project for Mrs. McGill to take on your job."

McGill said, "I'll talk to her."

"I won't ask what you'll say," Cale told him. After a beat, he asked, "Aren't you going to instruct me on how to behave with your daughter?"

That had been McGill's original reason for calling.

He said, "I was, but now I think you already know how I deal with adversity."

"I do."

"Good. But you might not have looked into something else."

"What's that?" Cale asked.

"What Abbie's brother and younger sister would do to anyone who caused their big sister any distress."

Cale said, "And what might that be?"

"Better that you should never find out," McGill told him.

WorldWide News Headquarters — Midtown Manhattan

The news crawl on the front of the WWN Building spread the word of Hugh Collier's passing to the city and the world: *WWN CEO Hugh Collier died this afternoon at 4:53 Eastern Standard Time. Please raise a glass to Hugh's memory. That was all he asked.*

In addition to the other responsibilities Hugh had left to Ellie Booker, he'd also asked her to vet the guest list for his funeral service at St. George's Episcopal Church. Scratch the name of anyone she didn't think belonged. Oh, and write his eulogy, something crisp and funny, not necessarily to be entirely in good taste, and not to exceed five minutes in length.

Standing in front of the building alongside Deke Ky and Lily Kealoha, Ellie watched the second part of the newsflash glide by: *WWN'S new CEO is esteemed news producer and reporter Eleanor Booker.*

Deke looked at Ellie and said, "I wish you hadn't included that part."

"It was part of the deal," she replied.

"I never knew your full name was Eleanor," Lily said.

Ellie said, "Just one of my dirty little secrets."

Deke said, "The news that you're alive and prospering only increases your risk quotient. It really would have been better to let the bad guys think you went down with the ship. At least for a little while anyway."

Deke's words drew no rebuke; they only made Ellie grin. "That might have been exactly the way Sir Edbert would have played it. Announce a lie and then celebrate a miraculous resurrection. Show biz. Gay as Hugh was, though, he liked to play the news straight."

"Good for Mr. Collier," Lily said. "Shows he trusted you to take care of yourself."

"That or he didn't mind if I join him in hell soon," Ellie said.

Deke told her, "We'll do our best not to let that happen."

Ellie gave him a look. "I know you've already been shot once, and I don't doubt you'd take a bullet for James J. McGill, but you'll understand if I'm skeptical that you'd sacrifice yourself for me."

"Okay," Deke said, "you've got a point. If I see someone point a gun at you, I'll just push you out of harm's way and then return fire."

Lily looked shocked.

Ellie only laughed. "The pushing part worked last time for General Yates."

They headed off to make the rounds of Manhattan nightspots where the resident UN diplomatic community liked to wet their beaks.

A moving cordon of Joint Terrorist Task Force plainclothes cops and federal agents, including Lily's friend Special Agent Lonnie Tompkins, encircled Ellie, Lily, and Deke at a distance of 20 feet. While that might have provided some measure of comfort to Ellie, she remembered what the FBI agent in charge of the assignment had said to his men and women before they'd all set out into the chill New York night.

"We take down any would-be assailant without a shot, if we can. If discharging a weapon can't be avoided, we damn sure hit the right target, not any innocent bystander or, God help us, one of our own people. Not to mention one of the people we're shielding, former Special Agent Ky, or Ms. Booker."

Lily wasn't mentioned by name because she was a cop, *one of our own people.*

Ellie had kept a straight face upon hearing the official pecking order.

She'd finished in last place.

Then the FBI agent-in-charge added, half-jokingly, "Remember, let's all be aware of the inherent danger of circular firing squads."

The guy made Ellie think that searching for guys with a particular sort of hand tattoo among the city's millions was a task that called for a lot of drinking. But she'd wait until she made it home alive before getting a buzz on.

Still, assuming she did survive, being part of the hunt at the start of her new job gave her one great story to tell.

The Yates House — Washington, DC

After coming home, Welborn played with his daughters for hours. He got down on the carpet and wrestled with them. Played hide-and-seek. Laughed when they intuitively got the gag and played along when he put a lampshade over his head and pretended to be a piece of furniture.

Aria said, "That sure is a funny-looking lamp."

Callista added, "I think Mommy should take it back to the store."

After that, going out into the backyard, he gave each girl what he said was the sensation of a fighter-jet taking off. Seating one daughter at a time on his shoulders, telling them to hang on tight to his jacket collar, he'd go from a standstill into a full sprint. He'd make quick turns, crouch and jump to change altitude. And all the while he'd make a rumbling sound to emulate the roar of a jet engine.

Both daughters laughed continuously and demanded several turns.

Kira watched the whole time, sharing the enjoyment, worrying that her children's career paths were being carved in stone. Finally, after making sure that each child had received the same number of rides, but with each of them still demanding more, Welborn made coughing and wheezing sounds, giving his wife a momentary chill. Then he winked at her, let his legs go wobbly which wasn't entirely an act, and collapsed to the scruffy wintertime grass.

Aria and Callista both leaped on their father, trying to tickle him into further adventures. He kissed each of them on a cheek and said, "Ladies, even the best fighter-jet in the world needs to be refueled every so often."

"How long does that take?" Aria asked.

"At least overnight. Sometimes maybe a month."

"That's *too* long," Callista protested.

"Maybe a week then?" Welborn counter-offered.

The two sisters whispered in each other's ears, and then they turned to their father.

"Okay," they said in unison.

Still supine, resting on his elbows, Welborn asked, "Can I tell you a secret?"

The girls nodded.

"I have just enough fuel left for one more ride. I can't give it to one of you because that would be unfair to the other. But how about I give a ride to Mom?"

Kira snorted. "Not outside and not while there's still light in the sky."

The light was fading fast, and the air was getting colder. Everyone went inside. Welborn and the girls went to their respective bathrooms to clean up. Kira took four burger patties out of the fridge, three of them plant-based, one from a critter who'd given its all, and began to grill them.

Kira was the holdout who insisted on real meat.

Everyone agreed that Mom's choice smelled better, but the girls were sold on the idea that theirs and Dad's provided better jet fuel. By the time dinner was over, Aria and Callista were ready for bed, hours before their usual time. Welborn told them any kind of pilot had to be well rested before he or she sat down at the controls in the cockpit. That was the rule. You can't fly if you can't keep your eyes open.

The twins were asleep the moment after receiving their parental goodnight kisses.

Kira closed the kids' bedroom door and put her hands on Welborn's shoulders.

"You wore them out on purpose," she said.

"I did, but I thought my way was more fun than taking them on a 20-mile forced march with full packs."

"Okay, I'll go along with that, but what was your reason? I'd like to think it's just so you can get your hands on me sooner rather than later, but I bet there's more to it than that."

"Yeah, there is. Let's go downstairs, and I'll pour a couple of drinks."

"My, my this is serious."

Kira lit a gas-fueled fire in the living room fireplace, and Welborn joined her on the sofa with two glasses of deep red liquid. "Plant-based drinks," he told his wife.

"What a charming idea."

"Mine is Cabernet Sauvignon," he said. "To make up for your real burger, yours is beet juice."

"So I shouldn't spill it on your shirt? Because the stain would never come out."

"Oh, all right, I don't need to make any more mistakes. You've got wine, too."

He raised his glass and Kira touched hers to it.

After taking a sip, she asked, "What's the mistake you've already made? I get the feeling it's a big one. Also something that doesn't involve the girls or me directly."

Welborn told his wife of his rude, even condescending, behavior with James J. McGill. She listened closely and made sure she understood all the details. Then she shook her head.

"You demanded to know Mr. McGill's source of information even after he told you it was confidential?" Kira asked. "I just want to make sure I have that right."

"You do."

"And you tried to … what's the word? Bigfoot?"

Welborn nodded.

"You tried to big-foot an investigation Mr. McGill was working."

"I did."

"Then, as a parting gesture, you said you wouldn't be taking a job he hadn't formally offered?"

"That, too," Welborn admitted.

Kira gently touched her husband's forehead with the back of her hand.

"You don't seem feverish," she told him. "So I'm glad you didn't pass whatever got into you on to the girls."

"Yeah, me, too, but I do feel somewhat sick about how I behaved. I was trying for hours to figure out just what got into me."

Kira took another sip of wine. "You think it could be some kind of reaction to the shock of saving Ellie Booker and almost getting shot yesterday? I still get chills if I picture you almost dying, and when I imagine the girls losing their dad, even now, it almost makes me cry."

In fact, Kira's eyes were filming over.

Welborn leaned forward and kissed her.

"I do think I experienced something of a post-trauma emotional spasm, but it's not just that. After a while, I finally got a hook into my feelings. I started to wonder why I was able to save Ellie Booker when I hadn't saved Keith Quinn, Joe Eddy, and Tommy Bauer."

Welborn's Air Force friends, fellow fighter jocks, who died in the car crash he alone survived.

Now, his eyes began to fill with tears.

"Oh, honey," Kira said. "How could you have saved them?"

He told her, "I could have demanded that I take the wheel. I'd had the fewest drinks and the fastest reflexes. At the very least, I should have insisted they all wear their seatbelts. I did neither of those things. I did nothing but plop my backside down and make sure I had my three-point safety belt buckled.

"All that must have been going through my mind subconsciously, but what really outraged me in Mr. McGill's office was that I *had* managed to save Ellie Booker. I'd succeeded, but now some bastards are *still* trying to kill her."

Kira said, "Think of how you'd feel if you hadn't saved her at all."

Welborn nodded. "I did just that. It'd be Keith, Joe, and Tommy all over again. I think that's why I felt I had to save Ellie again. Me, not anyone else. But how was I going to do that? Well, hey, I'd just been made acting deputy director of the FBI. I was now one of the most powerful law enforcement officials in the country. I had amazing people and resources at my beck and call. I would save Ellie Booker again and as many times as it took for her to stay safe."

Kira put her glass on an end table and relieved Welborn of his.

She held both of his hands and said, "If I didn't know you as well as I do, I'd explain to Mr. McGill what you're going through. But you're going to do that and tell him you're sorry."

Welborn sighed. "I will. I'll call him first thing tomorrow."

"As for Ellie Booker, saving a person's life once is as much as anyone can ask. Keep any future heroics in reserve for me and our two little sweethearts. Okay?"

"Yes."

"And internalize whatever your apology to Mr. McGill costs you. You know, so you won't go off on your new boss, the director of the FBI."

Welborn couldn't help but laugh.

Piss off Abra Benjamin? Heaven forbid.

"You're really too good for me," Welborn told his wife.

Kira kissed him and replied, "We've both known that all along."

CHAPTER 3

Sunday, February 3, 2019
En route to Beaufort, South Carolina

Big Mike Walker, aka Beemer, got to spend a whole 45 minutes alone at home with his wife before heading out to Dulles Airport to catch a red-eye flight to Charleston, South Carolina. Mayline volunteered to drive him to the airport, though they didn't have as much time to talk on the way as she'd have liked because Beemer, or Michael as she addressed him, spent some of that time on the phone speaking to Mayor Rockelle Bullard.

The call was routed through the car's speakers so Mayline could listen to both ends of the conversation.

"Has Jim McGill been of any help?" the mayor asked.

Beemer knew you didn't lie to Rockelle Bullard any more than you would to your mama. Assuming your mother was close to knowing just about every last secret in the world and was only checking to see if you were playing things straight with her. That and having the power to make your life miserable if you didn't tell the truth.

Beemer replied, "He made a point of explaining to Marvin and me that there are differences between having a badge and a PI license. Got us to thinking in a new frame of mind."

Mayline mmm-hmmed in favor of that notion.

"Glad to hear it," the mayor said. "As much as I like Mayline … you in the car there, girl?"

"Yes, ma'am. Got my eyes on the road, my hands on the wheel, and my ears on every word you and Michael say."

The mayor said, "Good. Then you can remind your husband of anything he might forget that I said."

Beemer couldn't keep himself from laughing. "The next time that happens will be the first time."

"Good," the mayor said. "Now, Jim McGill could afford to make a mistake or two as he got started in his new career because he had a Secret Service special agent looking out for him at all times. He also had a wife who could call out the Marines for him if he ever got in big trouble. You and Marvin don't have any of that. So I'm actually glad you called me to see about hiring off-the-clock cops to look after those you hold dear. You okay with that, Mayline?"

"Yes, ma'am, but you know I can put up a fight if I have to."

"I certainly do," Rockelle said, "but the best fight is always the one that never gets started."

"Amen," both Beemer and his wife said.

The mayor continued, "That being the case, I'm going to talk to our chief of police and have her increase patrol activity in Le Droit Park, paying particular attention to the Walker, Meeker, MacCray, and Wiles' houses. M&W Private Investigations being a commercial enterprise, that's where you and Marvin should have your off-duty hires concentrate, Big Mike."

"Yes, ma'am. Thank you for your help. Makes me glad I voted for you."

Rockelle laughed. "Yeah, I bet. Marvin did, too, I hope."

"I'll be sure to ask him," Beemer said.

"I voted for you, too. I'll tell you that right now," Mayline said.

"Thank you," the mayor told her. "If you can take your eyes off the road for just a second, Mayline, tell me what you see behind you."

Mayline had a good interval with the car ahead of her and nobody was signaling a merge into her lane so she glanced at her rearview mirror. Beemer looked over his left shoulder. They both saw the same thing, an unmarked police car with two plainclothes cops inside, tailing them by three car lengths. Cops and their wives recognized other cops even when they weren't in uniform.

"Friendly faces," Mayline said.

Beemer only smiled.

"Those officers will see you safely home, Mayline. Big Mike, you make sure you watch yourself down in South Carolina and let me know what you found out when you get home."

"Yes, ma'am."

The mayor finished with a promise any politician would love to make.

"One of my constituents hits the jackpot," she said, "I'm going to make damn sure he gets to keep it."

Several hours later, Beemer pulled up to the house in Beaufort, South Carolina that his research had provided. The sun had just crested the eastern horizon. He thought the Parker residence was pretty impressive. Not so much for size, but for being oh so pretty and well-tended. Wasn't quite a gingerbread place, but it made Beemer remember a French term he'd learned in college: *bourgeois.* Meaning somebody with the cultural, social, and financial capital to belong to the middle class. In this case, maybe even upper-middle class.

Small business owners and entrepreneurs were often lodged in that stratum, Beemer had been taught. With a jolt, Beemer realized that *bourgeois* also described him and Marvin these days. The former public servants had become capitalists. How about that? Social mobility.

Franklin Parker still had them beat. The research he and Marvin had done online regarding Constance Parker had revealed that her daddy once had three drugstores up in Baltimore. *Haut bourgeois*, if Beemer remembered his sociology class right. Definitely upper-middle class.

The man had even managed to send his daughter, Constance, the grand prize lottery winner in Maryland, to college at Johns

Hopkins, all the way to getting her Ph.D. Now, that must've taken a sizable chunk of money. He'd have to ask Marvin to look up just how much tuition they were talking here.

Constance Parker's top-of-the-line academic status brought a new question to Beemer's mind: How many people with doctorates played the lottery? He'd bet serious money that the percentage wasn't even half of that for high school graduates. Unless, of course, as he and Marvin had already thought, you were talking about math whizzes. Those kids looked at beating the odds as playtime. One that could pay big money.

Putting aside the analyses of higher education, Beemer turned to considering practical matters. How was he going to present himself to Franklin Parker? Ringing his doorbell first thing in the morning and asking the man if his daughter was involved in something shady didn't seem like a productive approach.

Beemer was still working on that problem when a neatly dressed man who looked to be maybe 70 or so, wearing gold wire-rim glasses and a white goatee, opened the front door of the house. He held a double-barreled shotgun in the crook of his left arm.

Beemer, who'd seen bad guys use every sort of firearm short of heavy artillery during his days as a cop in DC, pegged the weapon as a Mossberg Maverick. Wasn't a doctor in the world could put someone back together who got hit by two rounds from that weapon.

That being the case, Beemer got out of his rental Chrysler 200, closed the driver's door and stayed on the far side of the car. He didn't know for sure how well the sheet metal of the car would stop the shotgun pellets if the man started firing. He could take shelter on his side of the engine block, but some of the load was likely to ricochet under the car and impact him.

It was one of those times when being a big man was a disadvantage.

Someone shorter and lean like Marvin might scrunch down behind the wheel.

Beemer tried something like that, he just knew he'd get his ass shot off.

The man with the shotgun called out, "Who are you, and what do you want?"

Beemer answered truthfully. "My name is Michael Walker, sir. I'm a former detective with the Metropolitan Police Department in Washington, DC. If you're Franklin Parker, I'd like to talk with you."

"Regarding what?"

Okay, Beemer thought, here's where things could get touchy.

Still, he figured the truth was his best choice. "Your daughter, sir."

"Constance?"

"Yes, sir."

"Are you saying she did something wrong? I wouldn't believe that. And how do I know you're who you say you are?"

Beemer saw a light go on in the house next door, and a face appeared at an upstairs window.

"You've heard of Mayor Rockelle Bullard in DC?" Beemer asked.

The man nodded.

"I can give you her home phone number. She'll tell you who I am."

"You know her number at home?" he asked.

Beemer called it out from memory. The man took a phone out of a pocket, and Beemer repeated the number slowly for him. He made the call, said hello, and apparently didn't get much further. Not only had he been cut off, he seemed to be getting an earful.

His only spoken communication was, "Yes, ma'am. Sorry I disturbed you."

The man put his phone away and told Beemer. "The mayor seemed to know I was calling about you. She asked me to extend you every courtesy — in a loud, angry voice."

"She can get like that," Beemer told him. "Are you Franklin Parker?"

The front door of the neighboring house opened, and a middle-aged man with a pistol in hand stepped out to see what was happening. He looked at his neighbor first and then Beemer.

"Everything okay, Mr. Parker?" he called out.

The older man held up a hand, asking a moment's patience from the neighbor.

"Why are you here, Mr. Walker?"

"I'd like to speak with you about your daughter, Constance, winning the lottery."

Beemer saw the old man blink twice behind his spectacles.

"Connie won a lottery? How big was the prize?"

"Two hundred and twelve million dollars."

"Hey, hey, Frank, way to go," the neighbor said. Then his mood changed. "You think this guy is going after your daughter's money?"

"Are you, Mr. Walker?" Parker asked.

"Yes, sir, I am. In a strictly legal way. I represent another person who also has a winning ticket but hasn't been recognized publicly as of yet."

"Sounds like a con man to me, Frank," the neighbor said. "I should call the police."

"I'm perfectly agreeable to that," Beemer said.

"Why did you come calling so early, Mr. Walker?"

"I just flew in from Washington."

Keeping his eyes on Beemer, Franklin Parker asked his neighbor, "You have your phone on you, Billy?"

"You bet."

"Google something for me, will you? This man's name is Michael Walker. Says he was with the Metropolitan Police Department in Washington, DC. Claims to know the mayor up there. Even had me speak to a woman he says is the mayor. See if there's anything online about him. A photo would be good, too."

"Right, right," Billy said.

He set to work and shortly thereafter let out a soft whistle. He looked up at Beemer and then back at his phone. He took what he'd found over to Franklin Parker. The old man took a glance and then opened his hand. Billy put his phone in it.

A minute later, Parker returned his neighbor's phone and let his shotgun's barrel point at the ground.

"You think my daughter might be in trouble, Mr. Walker?"

"That's one possibility, sir."

Parker gave Billy a pat on the shoulder and thanked him.

Then he invited Beemer to enter his house.

McGill Investigations International — Washington, DC

McGill and Leo Levy got to the office early, before everyone but Dikki Missirian. Although Dikki now owned and operated three rental properties of his own in town, and didn't really need the salary McGill paid him, he spent most of his waking/working hours at McGill's new building. There were more than a few times McGill had suspected Dikki slept overnight in his office. He had a sleeper-sofa there. Said he used it for naps.

Not that McGill had ever seen him nod off during work hours.

Asked why he put in more than the 35 hours per week that he and McGill had bargained for, Dikki had told McGill, "My other holdings are business investments, though I do have a fondness for the building we first shared. This new place I am still getting used to, but it's where my extended family and new friends work. So this is where I will be, too."

Upon hearing that he was "extended family" McGill decided that he'd have to invite Dikki and his blood relatives over to the Dumbarton Oaks house to have dinner with Patti and him — but he hadn't gotten around to it as of yet.

Instead of going to his office by using either the elevator or the stairs from the underground parking structure, McGill and Leo went back out to the sidewalk and looked at the exterior of the building, still bearing the fresh scars from the gunman who'd tried to gun down Ellie Booker and Welborn Yates.

Within a minute of their arrival, Dikki stepped out of the front door and joined them. He shook hands with the other two men. All of them understood the sentiment. Their workplace had been attacked, but it was still standing. Business would quickly return to normal and not be interrupted for any significant amount of time.

Dikki said, "I have arranged for contractors to come out and provide estimates on repairing the damage that was done. All three companies have very, very good reputations. I will speak with Ms. Sweeney about having the building's insurance company confer with the contractor we choose. Is that all right with you, Jim?"

McGill had no idea whether his business liability insurance covered terrorist attacks.

Maybe Sweetie knew. He should have her, Putnam and Maxi over to dinner soon, too. Make it a combined affair with the Missirian family.

Just then, though, McGill had another idea.

He told Leo and Dikki, "When Patti and I visited Munich last year, after we stopped off in Paris, we saw this civil service building on … *Ludwigstrasse,* I think the street was. The whole ground floor of the building was pockmarked by bullet holes. A hellacious battle must have been fought there, the Germans holding the fort from inside and the Americans attacking from the outside. I felt sure it was no oversight that the damage hadn't been repaired. The place had become a memorial, a reminder of the ways things could go terribly wrong. A lesson, too, that you have to be ready for whatever comes down the road."

"Why did you go to Munich?" Dikki asked.

"I wanted to put some flowers on the grave of a client we failed to serve in a timely manner," McGill said. "Patti was generous enough to humor me."

"So now you are thinking maybe we don't repair our building?" Dikki asked.

"Considering the idea," McGill told him.

Leo said, "The Alamo's still dimpled by bullet-holes from that dustup with the Mexicans."

Dikki missed the reference, but McGill smiled and said, "Yeah?"

"Well, they fixed up a lot of the damage from the battle, but they left a few bullet holes, I think, for historical reference and atmosphere," Leo replied.

McGill smiled, "Yeah. Maybe that's the way to handle things. Take the scars on the building and reconfigure them into something artful and thoughtful, a reminder of looking the Grim Reaper in the eye and saying, 'Not this time, buddy.'"

"Except for those two dudes with their tattoos," Leo reminded him.

McGill was about to say, "That works for me, too," but a Cadillac limousine flying Jordanian flags pulled up at the curb. A tinted rear window glided down, and the face of Ambassador Fayez Mousa came into view.

He asked, "May I have a moment of your time, Mr. McGill?"

McGill had enough Washington savvy by that time to recognize a DC chat-and-run moment. He nodded and went around to the other side of the car. Former president's henchman or not, you didn't ask a top-end diplomat to scoot over.

Once he was seated, the driver put the car in motion.

"We're going somewhere?" McGill asked.

He noticed the partition between the front and back seats was raised.

"Only around the block, sir. A moving car is a more difficult target for eavesdropping than a stationary one."

"Okay," McGill said, thinking: Learn a new thing every day.

"I have news from his majesty," Mousa said. "Thanks to your inspired suggestion we have found the tattoo artists."

"There was more than one?" McGill asked.

"A couple, a man and his wife."

McGill frowned. "Pardon my lack of awareness, and forgive me if I misspeak, but a woman tattooing a man in your culture, well, I have a hard time seeing that."

Possessing diplomatic patience, Mousa replied, "There are

more social variations than one might think. Most of these are quite recent, and there is pressure to prevent their spread."

"So your security forces arrested both of these people? To question them, at least."

"Only one of them, the man, survives."

"The woman resisted being taken into custody?" McGill asked.

Mousa shook his head. "Her husband slit her throat before our men could stop him."

McGill was shocked. "Why would he do that?"

"The husband was knocked unconscious with a rifle butt before that question could be asked. We are waiting for him to regain his wits. We have speculated why he killed his wife, but before I tell you what we think, I would like to ask you what you think."

McGill didn't take long to answer. "She knew something he feared she would reveal."

"Yes, exactly, but what?"

That took McGill a bit longer, but he answered without worrying about being culturally insensitive. "He tattooed men; she tattooed women. There are women involved in this plot, too."

Mousa nodded. "This is the conclusion we have also reached: female assassins."

Having dealt with one who'd tried to kill him, Loris Springstone, aka Taps, he had no trouble believing that being an assassin had become an equal opportunity occupation.

A role he'd yet to see on the world's stage was a female Arab combat pilot.

The ambassador seemed to read McGill's mind and told him, "Yes, there are a precious few female combat pilots in our part of the world. Major Mariam al-Mansouri of the United Arab Emirates was the first. Still, with the cooperation of friendly neighboring states, we have managed to check them all. None had a flag tattoo on her hand."

Just as the limo completed circling the block and pulled to a stop in front of the entrance to McGill Investigations International, the man with his name on the building threw a curveball to the ambassador.

He said, "Maybe the female members of this group are a bit more discreet about where their tattoos get placed. Say somewhere the public at large would never see. Maybe only their husbands could tell you the location. Try to keep the male tattooist alive long enough to tell you if that's the case."

McGill's suggestion to Mousa both surprised and troubled the diplomat.

When McGill got out of the car, he was the one jolted by the unexpected.

Welborn Yates, all by his lonesome, stood in front of McGill's front door.

As McGill drew closer to Welborn, he saw the younger man's right hand tap his chest three times, and he said, *"Mea culpa, mea culpa, mea maxima culpa."*

Through my fault, through my fault, through my most grievous fault.

Franklin Parker's House — Beaufort, South Carolina

The former pharmacist and the former police detective sat in facing armchairs.

"My daughter really won the lottery?" Franklin Parker asked, looking as if the idea still lay beyond the boundaries of belief.

Beemer said, "She did. The Grand Slam lottery game, sir."

"And you said the amount of money was $200 million."

Beemer leaned forward and told him, "Well, the gross figure is actually $212 million. That's if you take payments spread out over 20 years. If you ask for a lump sum right away, which is what most people take, and then you deduct the tax bite, which gets taken up front, you're still looking at probably a bit north of $100 million."

The older man sat back in his chair and his mouth fell open

just a bit. He shook his head, and tears came to his eyes. "I so wish my wife could hear this. Our little girl coming into all that money." He went from weeping to laughter. "Who am I trying to kid? I wish my wife was with me just so I could tell her my arthritis is acting up. I'd take her company as my lottery prize any day. You could keep the money. Are you married, young man?"

"I am, sir. Twenty-two years."

"Then you know what I mean."

"I do. What I'm trying to understand now, though, is why your daughter didn't call you with the good news. Is your relationship … do you speak regularly?"

Franklin Parker nodded. "Of course, we do. At least once a week. Usually on Sundays."

"So you might expect her to call today."

"That's right. Not this early, though. After all these years of being retired, I still get up like I need to be at work first thing." He shook his head. "That's just more wishful thinking. The idea of having something meaningful to do. You said you're a private investigator, and you were a police officer. Do I have that right?"

"I worked patrol and then I became a detective," Beemer said. "My partner and I each worked 25 years with the Metropolitan Police Department, and now we have our own business. Forgive me for saying so, but don't you think with this kind of news, your daughter might have called earlier? The winner was publicly announced this past Friday. Of course, most players check their lotto tickets the night of the drawing. That was this past Wednesday."

Parker sat back in his chair, an arm extended on each armrest. It didn't take him long to say, "Now that you bring that up, she should've called with the news. Just so I could be happy for her. It's not like I might meet my Maker at any moment, but at my age you never know when that final day might come."

"Are you in any need of financial help, sir?" Beemer asked.

The question made the old guy laugh and even slap a knee. "Me, need money? No, no. I don't have the kind of money we've been talking about, but I don't want for anything."

"And you made sure your daughter got a running start, too?"

"Of course, I did. That girl's the only person I ever loved as much as I did my wife. Where is all this going, young man?"

Beemer played it straight with Franklin Parker — up to a point.

"There's another player with a winning ticket, sir. He hired my partner and me to find out why he wasn't publicly named as a co-winner."

"You're trying to take some of Constance's winnings?" The old man sat taller in his chair as if he'd just straightened his spine.

"No, sir. Our client only wants what's rightfully his, an equal share of the jackpot."

"Maybe he falsified his ticket," Parker said.

Beemer told his host, "There's a video of the ticket being printed by a certified lottery outlet, and my client immediately showed it to the camera, exposing the winning numbers. Those are the facts. The mystery is why the lottery didn't identify two winners."

Growing still more defensive, Parker said, "Well, that's something you should ask the people running the lottery, isn't it?"

Beemer nodded. "Yes, sir. We intend to do that. Only we want to have as many facts in hand as we can before we go to them. Do you know, sir, that your daughter has a gun?"

"A pistol, yes. She keeps it at home for protection."

"My partner and I parked on the street outside her house. We arrived late and didn't want to disturb her. We wound up falling asleep in our car. Your daughter came out early the next morning and woke us up by tapping her gun on a window. She had the gun pointed at my partner's head."

Franklin Parker frowned deeply. "Weren't you armed, too?"

"No, sir. We left our weapons in DC. Just like I did coming here to talk with you."

An element of stubbornness attached itself to the older man's expression. "She couldn't have known that."

"We told her. She still waved her weapon around in a manner that might have caused an accidental discharge. My partner and I have been in a lot of dangerous situations, but I was never more scared than I was at that moment."

Parker got to his feet. Beemer followed suit.

"I think you'd better leave my house, Mr. Walker."

Beemer got to his feet. "Yes, sir. There's just one more thing I have to tell you. Your daughter found her way to our business office. We didn't give her our names or the location of where we work. We think she memorized our license plate number and worked things out from there. She offered my client a million dollars to drop any claim to the lottery prize."

The old man's face sagged. He understood the implication.

"Yes, sir," Beemer told him. "That's what someone who has something to hide would do. Buy her troubles off cheaply. We'd appreciate it if you'd tell your daughter that things would work out better for everyone if we were all on the same side."

Beemer gave Parker one of his business cards.

"If there's someone back home in Maryland," Beemer added, "someone giving Constance trouble or bad advice, I have to tell you that Mayor Bullard isn't our only friend. James J. McGill is also working this case with us. We'd all like to settle this matter fairly. Thank you for taking the time to speak with me, sir."

Beemer left without looking back.

He didn't see the old man plop down on his chair holding his head in his hands.

Hugh Collier's Townhouse — Midtown Manhattan

In addition to his other largesse, Hugh Collier had ceded to Ellie Booker a year's free residence in his home. That way, as Hugh's will explained, she could get straight to work in her new job and not mess about with a search for new lodgings. In Manhattan, that was no small consideration. Given the competition for a decent, never mind comfortable, place to live, an apartment hunt could be a grinding, dispiriting exercise.

Of course, if you were rich, things were much easier.

Make that *really* rich. Even people pulling down a mid-six-figure salary could be left gasping at what a place with elbow room in a hot Manhattan neighborhood would set them back, and that was just *rent*. None of the money you spent on putting a decent roof overhead bought you a bit of equity.

In a moment of black humor, Ellie's favorite kind, she thought maybe she'd move WWN's headquarters somewhere more affordable. There was no law that said every big news source had to be in New York City. Hell, CNN had its center of operations in Atlanta.

Maybe that's what she should do, take WWN south. Not compete directly with CNN by going to Atlanta, but what about, say, the Research Triangle in North Carolina? They had some fine universities down there. A good talent pool to draw on. That was one idea.

Or she could start a nationwide competition for the right to be WWN's new HQ. She wouldn't get all the perks and subsidies Amazon had been offered, but she'd bet she could swing a sweet deal. Maybe good enough to build her own mansion somewhere.

Austin, Boston or Chicago to cover just the first three letters of the alphabet.

Those were the exciting thoughts Ellie carried with her to bed that night.

In the early darkness of the following morning hours, all of Ellie's ideas for a bright future morphed into nightmares of mortality. Everywhere she looked people were trying to kill her, and nobody would lend a hand to help her.

She saw herself once again coming out of James J. McGill's new office building with General Welborn Yates. The car with the killers in it came roaring up. Only this time the general didn't save her, he pushed her out into the open while he ducked for cover.

Somehow she didn't get killed when they fired, but she found herself at the Gangplank Marina, starting to cast off and make her run out to sea in the *Dame*. Detective Aidan Behan was watching her. He just shook his head and said in a sad tone, "Not a good move."

What the hell did he know? It was only when she looked back while sitting in the captain's chair that she saw something floating in the water behind her. Looked like a body that had gotten all chewed up. Had she done that? She'd felt some kind of bump as she'd pulled out of her slip.

Before that question could be answered, she was out on the deep blue ocean. The sun pushed its way through a thin overcast. Hugh had just called and told her there was a bomb on her boat. So she'd gotten into her inflatable dinghy and rowed for her life. The *Dame* receded into a mist, and she finally felt safe, until she noticed an unfamiliar metal box at the front of the dinghy.

It didn't help that the box didn't have a digital countdown timer. The damn thing still ticked loudly enough for her to hear. Wouldn't that be great? Some terrorist asshole had wired sticks of dynamite to an old Timex alarm clock and that would be the device that would kill her.

Ellie had just started to reach for the metal box when she woke up.

She made a quick trip to the bathroom, putting physical distance between her and the nightmare. After finishing that chore, she slid back into bed and pulled the covers up. Not wanting to go right back to sleep in case her subconscious had another horror show waiting, she stared up at the ceiling and reviewed the real life events that led her to the present moment.

Ellie had joined a group of war correspondents. She was doing front-line reporting on the fighting in Iraq and Syria. She and other newsies were embedded with U.S. special forces operators and Kurdish troops, male and female.

As far as Ellie knew, she was the only reporter who carried a concealed weapon, a Beretta 93R, which could fire three-round bursts. She'd had no call to use it up to that point.

Wanting to conceal her true identity for fear that the military would turn down her application to visit the war zone, knowing what a trouble-maker she could be, Ellie had given her hair an amateurish bleach job, wore contact lenses that turned her brown eyes green, and had stained her teeth to a betel juice brown. She wore khaki shirts and pants a size too large to hide her lean muscular physique and her compact firearm.

She'd used her own passport, but the army wasn't looking over her shoulder when she presented it to get on her flight. To establish her bona fides to the military, she'd also fabricated an ID card from a news-gathering organization that she had gone to the trouble of actually incorporating: New World Digital, aka NWD.

The way new journalistic websites cropped up like weeds in the spring, none of the other newsies she traveled with in the war zone took her as anything less than legitimate. For one thing, her toughness when hostiles started shooting in their direction was more like that of the military personnel than a graduate of a journalism school.

She ran toward the trouble, not away from it. Had a damn nice sprinter's kick, too.

Some of the big news organization reporters started to call her a hot dog just waiting to be grilled. They made jokes about what kind of death benefits a start-up like NWD might pay to her beneficiaries. Maybe a bouquet of lilies for the funeral.

Ellie welcomed the isolation, pleased that *none* of the ace reporters who accompanied her recognized who she really was. At least two of them should have. Those clowns had actually been introduced to her at an awards event, but in a war zone things could be powerfully distracting, sometimes in the blink of an eye.

A local with bad intent might pop out of an alley or from behind a rock formation with his finger on the trigger and a burst of automatic weapon's fire as a way of saying hello. Then there were the roads paved with artillery shells to be used as improvised explosives. For the personal touch, there was nothing like a suicide bomber, either automotive or pedestrian.

The U.S. military had informed the newsies of all the dangers they might face before they were allowed to venture into potentially hostile areas. Most of the journalists took the warnings seriously, and responded appropriately, agreeing to follow whatever orders their military escorts gave them. They didn't want their own families back home to cash in on life insurance policies anytime soon.

Ellie used Taylor Woolworth as her *nom de guerre* and was the only reporter who'd thought to crack wise about any of the possible dangers she and her colleagues might face.

"You think the bad guys weed out their sad-sacks?" she'd asked the Delta Force captain who'd been giving the newsies fair warning about what might be in store for them.

A sergeant stood stoically silent beside the officer.

"What do you mean, Ms. Woolworth?" the captain asked.

"Well, you know, we've all seen those training videos of the other side's fighters swinging rung to rung on monkey bars and crawling under barbed wire and whatnot."

"Yeah," the captain said, waiting for whatever came next.

"All those guys look real tough and strong," Ellie said, "but what about the washouts?"

"I don't know what you mean," the captain said in a flat voice.

"I was just thinking that outside of special forces like you guys, nobody's army has only natural athletes and crack shots in their ranks. It seems to me like at least some of the bad guys have to be fuck-ups. You know, suicide bombers who trip halfway to their targets and, oops, blow up only themselves. Or maybe the auto mechanic for a vehicle-bomb isn't top-notch and the damn thing breaks down in the middle of nowhere, but the bomb goes off anyway because the timer malfunctions, too."

The captain didn't think Ellie was funny at all.

The sergeant standing next to him had a hard time keeping a straight face.

"Ms. Woolworth," the captain said, "if you think any part of what we're about to do is fun and games, you should turn around right now and go home."

Ellie's face fell and she looked properly chastened.

Even so, she asked, "So I got things wrong then?"

The captain was clearly disappointed that Ellie hadn't taken the hint and departed.

So he did what anyone who didn't want a screw-up to be blamed on himself would do.

He passed the buck.

"Sergeant, I want you to take very good care of Ms. Woolworth."

"Yes, sir," the sergeant said.

"Try not to let her trip. She might fall on a functional improvised explosive."

"Yes, sir."

The captain departed, followed by the other newsies, many of whom shook their heads as they passed Ellie, as if she were a blight on their profession.

When all of the others were out of earshot, the sergeant asked Ellie, "Are you gonna be a true pain in the ass? Because if you do something stupid, I'd rather lose my job than my life."

Ellie shook her head. "I was just fucking with your boss. I knew from the moment I saw the two of you, I'd rather work with you than him."

That took a moment for the sergeant to process. He smiled and shook his head.

"Okay. Just don't put me or any of my people in danger."

"I won't."

"If you get your ass shot off by disobeying one of my orders, let your last thought be: 'It was my own damn fault.'"

"Will do."

"And if you like the next soldier you see better'n me, just say so."

"I will," Ellie said.

Knowing if she did that it would become someone else's responsibility to keep her alive.

Turned out she saved Sergeant Desmond Jones' life and screwed up her own future. Several days later, the group of newsies and their military escort stopped for lunch in a flyspeck town in Syria that had been taken by the good guys three days earlier and was judged to be asshole-free, i.e. no hostile forces in the vicinity.

Per usual, Ellie ate lunch by herself.

Sergeant Jones was on a satellite phone call home. It was a special allowance call as the sergeant's wife had just given birth to a son back in Michigan, and his father was calling with the good news. The captain didn't want the sergeant to hold up the rest of the unit babysitting the other newsies and urged him to cut the call short.

Didn't make it an outright order because he wasn't that big a jerk.

Ellie spoke up and said she'd rent a motorcycle to catch up with them.

By that time, the captain had seen that Ellie was the most courageous civilian he'd ever met. So even if he didn't like her, he had a measure of respect for her. He said okay and made sure she knew where they were going and how to get there.

Ellie did.

The captain said, "Let the sergeant drive the motorcycle."

"Sure," Ellie replied, "assuming he knows how."

Having no intention to rush Sergeant Jones' call, Ellie tapped him on the shoulder and pointed to a medical aid tent operated by Physicians' Global Outreach. Their mission was to treat the incidental civilian casualties of war, of which there was an endless supply. Ellie thought there might be a human interest story to be had inside the PGO tent even if that wasn't her first choice of story material.

It turned out there was a *great* story inside that aid station.

That was where Dr. Hasna Kalil was hanging her shingle at the moment.

Miz Smith's Convenience Corner — Washington, DC

After hearing from Beemer in South Carolina that Franklin Parker wasn't likely to be any help in getting things right for Sammy MacCray, Marvin Meeker recruited two off-duty MPD cops to accompany him to the convenience store where Sammy had bought his winning ticket. It was one of a half-dozen stores in an embryonic chain that had started right there in the Le Droit Park neighborhood.

The idea behind the stores' growth was based on a number of selling points. They'd all be located on corners where there was a goodly amount of both pedestrian and vehicular traffic so people could see a shopping opportunity from four directions. The prices for impulse grocery items beat the other nearby convenience outlets. The staff was all smart, friendly, and honest, showing what a $15 per hour starting wage could buy. There were no alcohol, tobacco or vaping sales, helping to create a family-friendly environment and keep troublesome people away. There were, however, lottery ticket sales to anyone 18 or older.

After all, everyone deserved some chance of getting rich.

In the store's first hour of business, Meeker approached a smiling woman standing behind a counter whose name tag read: Yasmin. Sammy had bought his ticket from a guy named Dwight. Meeker's guess was Dwight wasn't anywhere near as attractive as Yasmin, a mature lady whose pert look was doing a fine job of defying the calendar.

"Good day, officers," Yasmin said. "May I get you gentlemen something to drink?"

The store had a small selection of fountain drinks. Provided by the staff. You didn't have to tap your own glass. Another appealing feature of the store.

Meeker turned to his companions, Richie and Simon, and said, "She made us as cops, guys, and I think she's just being polite pretending she doesn't know I'm retired. Well, no longer working for the MPD anyway."

With a look of mischief in her eyes, Yasmin said, "Come on now, fellas, tell me if any of you looks like he's ready for an old-folks home."

Meeker laughed. Richie and Simon grinned.

Meeker said, "We'll get to our drink order in a minute. By any chance, is Dwight here?"

Yasmin shook her head. "Sorry."

"Did you hear about the man who bought a winning lotto ticket here?"

The smile left Yasmin's face.

"Something wrong?" Meeker asked.

"I heard a story about that."

"A story, huh?"

Yasmin looked around. There were only two other people in the store at the moment, but they were young, had their fountain drinks already, were sitting at a table in a far corner, and had eyes only for each other.

"The boss said not to talk about it," Yasmin said. "Sammy MacCray told us he won, but the lottery hasn't said nothing. They're supposed to pay retailers like us $5,000 for selling a winning ticket. This being a good place to work, the boss says he's ready to take $1,000 off the top and split the rest evenly among us employees."

"Sounds fair," Meeker said. "So why shouldn't you talk about it?"

"That was the word from the lawyer."

The two cops standing behind Meeker chuckled.

Meeker dropped his voice to a near whisper. "Listen, I've got something else that needs to be kept close to the vest."

Yasmin nodded. "Okay."

"I'm working for Sammy as a private detective. That's what I do now that I'm retired from the police."

"Them, too?" She nodded at Richie and Simon.

Meeker said, "I hired them on for this job."

"What job?"

"You heard that a lady up in Maryland was named as the only winner."

She nodded. "That's what has us all so upset. It's like we're getting cheated here."

Meeker made a guess. "You're the manager on duty, aren't you?"

Yasmin nodded.

"If you don't mind, I'd like to ask you to call your boss to come in."

"Why?"

"Because I think there could be some bad people behind that winner in Maryland, and I'm afraid those people might come here. Maybe right before the store closes, if my feeling is right."

Yasmin needed a moment to find her voice, and there was fear in her eyes now. "Why would they do that? All we did was sell the ticket."

"Sammy said he showed the ticket to Dwight and held it up in front of that security camera behind you. The people I'm thinking about might want to see if you have a hard copy of the video. If you don't, they might want help accessing the server where that video is stored."

A bolt of anger displaced the fear Yasmin had felt.

"What if we don't want to tell them *any* of those things?" she asked.

Meeker said, "These might be the kind of people who won't take no for an answer. That's why I brought my friends. Anyone tries to give you trouble, well, they know how to deal with all kinds of that stuff. And they're being paid by me. Won't cost this store one cent."

Yasmin looked at Richie and Simon. They nodded their heads.

"So if your boss is in town, Miss Yasmin, why don't you give him a call?"

"Her," Yasmin said. "My boss is a woman."

She took out her phone.

Hugh Collier's Townhouse — Midtown Manhattan

It turned out Sergeant Desmond Jones did know how to drive a motorcycle. As he confessed to Ellie — or Taylor Woolworth as he knew her — his father had been an outlaw biker until he'd met Desmond's mother. Dad fell hard for her and learned immediately that following the path of the Lord was the only way to win her heart.

That being the case, he gave up alcohol, drugs, and a life of crime. Her demands had been palatable to him because she'd told him Jesus didn't have anything against riding a motorcycle with your wife holding on tight behind you. As was often said, it was a match made in heaven.

Having been the baddest badass in his gang, Darius Jones used his lion's share of the bikers' most recent drug sales to open a garage in which he repaired cars and motorcycles, those of the brethren and straight customers, too. He did the first-class work of a natural mechanic and charged fair prices. Without his ever having imagined the possibility, he became a pillar of his small-town community.

Even more surprising than that, Darius discovered that he liked his new role in society. It was no less than his wife and son deserved. Only young Desmond seemed disinclined from the start to follow in his father's new footsteps. By the time Desmond reached his late teens, he was only a hop, skip and a jump from doing a long stretch in a penitentiary. The prospect of which was breaking his mother's heart.

So Darius, threatening to break several of his son's bones if he argued the point, took Desmond down to the nearest army recruiting office and told the recruiting sergeant, "This boy thinks he's tougher than nails and more dangerous than a house on fire. I've brought him down here to see if he's right."

The recruiter looked at father and son, and he asked Desmond, "Is that right?"

Desmond nodded.

"Do you have any criminal record?"

Desmond shook his head.

"How old are you?"

"Seventeen."

The recruiter was pleased to hear that the kid wasn't nonverbal. He asked Darius, "You'll provide parental consent? That's required for someone your son's age."

"Yeah," Darius said.

Looking back at Desmond, the recruiter asked, "What kind of military specialty might interest you?"

"Special forces," Desmond said. It was the only one he'd ever seen on TV.

The recruiter told him, "You have to be 20 years old to join a special forces unit. If you join the army now, you'll have to earn the equivalent of a high school diploma while assigned to another military unit. You'll also have to score 110 or higher on a General Technical Test, and earn a combat operations score of 98 or higher on the Armed Services Vocational Aptitude Battery. You think you can do all that?"

Desmond had the smarts to ask, "Will I have the time to do the studying while I'm working another job?"

That made the recruiter smile. "Sure, you will, and maybe even get four-to-six hours a night sleep, too."

Desmond looked at his father.

Darius only asked, "How bad do you want to find out just how tough you are, boy?"

That was the only prompting Desmond needed. He asked the recruiting sergeant, "Where do I sign?"

Sergeant Desmond Jones had told Ellie Booker that much of his life's story — plus he was naming his son Darius after his father — as he was working on the motorcycle she'd bought for $300 while he was talking to his family back home.

The motorcycle was a 1961 Triumph TR6 Trophy model. The grinning local who sold the machine told Ellie and Sergeant Jones that the bike had belonged to an Englishman who'd "fallen ill" in the village many years ago. Before passing on, the foreigner had said it was the kind of bike, disguised as a German BMW R75, that Steve McQueen had ridden in The Great Escape.

Sergeant Jones had said, "Yeah, right."

Still, as he tightened this and that, applied oil here and there, filled the gas tank, and used a manual pump to inflate the tires, he made an offer to buy it from Ellie for $1,000 and pay to have it shipped back home, too, just as soon as he got his next pay.

Ellie told him, "You get us caught up with the captain and the other newsies, and I'll give the damn thing to you."

She'd been hoping for a more up-to-date machine in good working order.

Sergeant Jones gladly accepted Ellie's offer. Then the two of them were on their way, zipping down a dirt road, Ellie holding on tight as the sergeant swerved left and right to avoid the larger holes in the road. It looked like the tired asphalt had been heavily shelled and not all that long ago.

The ISIS straggler or advance scout, take your pick, was lying in wait for the pair of infidels on the motorcycle behind a dumpy little knoll several meters off the road to their right. The bastard would have had to be deaf not to hear them coming. He opened up with some kind of assault rifle. The curved magazine on the weapon made Ellie think it was a Kalashnikov AK-47. Not that she'd gotten more than a glimpse. Then Sergeant Jones screamed in pain, leaned to his left and took her and the cycle down into a skid and off the opposite side of the road.

Their momentum didn't take them far before the loose gray-brown soil acted as a brake. Sergeant Jones, somehow had mastered his pain by the time they stopped, even though Ellie could see he was bleeding out of a hole in his back.

In a quiet, agonized voice, he told Ellie, "Unsling my weapon and put it in my right hand. Whoever shot me is gonna be coming in for the kill."

In fact, Ellie could hear footsteps approaching at a quick pace.

There was no time to get Sergeant Jones' M4A1 carbine off his back and into firing position for him. Instead, Ellie slapped her Beretta 93R into the sergeant's hand. She whispered directly into his ear, "Safety's off, ready to fire a three-round burst."

Seconds later, that was just what the sergeant did, caught the grinning jihadi square in his face as he made the mistake of thinking he'd already taken care of the American man and would have a few moments of pleasure with the woman before he killed her.

With the immediate threat disposed of, Sergeant Jones told Ellie, "Hope you meant what you said about knowing how to ride this machine. Go get help before I bleed out."

Ellie said, "Yeah, bullshit. We're not going to look for some GI medic who could be God knows where. We're heading back to that PGO aid station."

She got out from under the bike, helped the sergeant get to his feet, and righted the motorcycle.

"Those docs don't help military personnel," Jones said through clenched teeth.

Ellie took her pistol back and slung Sergeant Jones' carbine over her shoulder.

"Wanna bet?" she said. "You just hang on, and don't lose that satellite phone."

McGill Investigations International — Washington, DC

McGill sat in his office with Welborn Yates. Sweetie joined them. Welborn explained his misplaced anger. He'd thought he was past blaming himself for the deaths of his three Air Force friends, and then he'd heard that someone whose life he had managed to save was still being threatened. Without realizing the connection at first, the situation had set him off. He'd taken out his anger on someone he had no reason to blame.

"So it was nothing personal, not against me anyway?" McGill asked.

"No. I'm ashamed of the way I behaved," Welborn said.

"You've had professional counseling on survivor's guilt?" Sweetie asked.

"Yes. I also had the satisfaction of knowing Linley Boland had died."

Sweetie said, "He was the guy who killed your friends?"

Welborn nodded. "I thought that was all I needed to help me heal. Saving Ms. Booker's life seemed like icing on a redemption cake … until I learned that someone is still trying to kill her. Then it was like everything had come undone. I was almost waiting for the ghosts of Keith, Joe, and Tommy to tell me I still had more work to do."

A tremor passed through Welborn.

"I certainly don't want another spirit to haunt me."

McGill told Welborn, "I heard from Ellie yesterday. She's alive and well."

Hugh Collier's Townhouse — Midtown Manhattan

Ellie's reminiscence of events in Syria made her wonder how best to tell it, in print or film?

She thought the best way to decide was to keep unspooling it in her head.

Dr. Hasna Kalil told Ellie Booker, "I don't treat American soldiers."

Ellie Booker had made the trip back to the no-name speck of a Syrian village on the $300 motorcycle with Sergeant Desmond Jones slumped against her back. She had her left hand behind her straining to hold onto the man's shirt so he wouldn't fall off the motorcycle. Her right hand was on the side of the handlebar with the throttle that controlled the machine's speed. She slowed to swerve around deep potholes and gunned the old machine in stretches where the poor excuse for pavement was relatively straight and undamaged.

All the while, she could feel the heat of the sergeant's exhalations against the back of her neck. In any other situation that would have been creepy in the extreme. During that seemingly interminable ride, though, Ellie took comfort in the tangible knowledge that he was still alive.

For the first time in more years than she could remember, Ellie wanted to pray. Ask God — whose very existence she usually denied — to spare the sergeant. The man had just become a father, damnit. He deserved to live to see and hold his son. Show him how to be a man. Straighten him out, if that was what the kid needed someday. Let him discover what he could be. Only, for the life of her, Ellie couldn't remember a single prayer to say.

Her own father had never been around long enough to teach her one.

Her mother was in the bottle too often to bother.

All Ellie could do was say, "Please, please, please."

If God did exist and was omniscient, her meaning would be clear.

Her prayer was answered to the extent that Sergeant Jones was still breathing and bleeding when they reached the Physicians' Global Outreach tent. Using strength Ellie had never guessed she possessed, she pulled the sergeant upright and dragged him into the tent. She managed to get him up and onto an open surgery table. That was a blessing in itself.

Then a clearly angry Dr. Hasna Kalil stormed into the tent, up to Ellie, and told her, "I do *not* treat American soldiers."

That handful of words was enough to stun Ellie momentarily. She looked around and saw three other men resting on other operating tables. None of them was conscious, but neither were they visibly bleeding. All of them, going by the rise and fall of their chests, were breathing. More than that, none of them seemed to be in pain. Meaning, most likely, they'd all been anesthetized. They'd been given treatment Dr. Kalil intended to deny Sergeant

Jones.

Ellie took a step back from the doctor, unslung the sergeant's M-4 carbine from her shoulder, and pointed it at the doctor, the only other conscious person in the tent, and said, "You'll do your damnedest to save Sergeant Jones, or I'll kill you right now."

She clicked off the carbine's safety, and her eyes showed no sign of a bluff.

Even so, Dr. Kalil only shook her head.

So Ellie upped the ante. She nodded at the three unconscious men.

"After I kill you, I'll kill all of them, too."

Ellie saw alarm in the doctor's eyes now and knew just how to play her next card.

She said, "You don't believe me, I'll shoot one of them right now."

"No, no," Dr. Kalil said, "I will work on your soldier. I will do my best, but I can make no promises."

"I can," Ellie told her. "If my guy dies, so do you and your guys."

Thus motivated, the doctor set to work, which included the use of a scalpel.

Ellie stood close enough to watch the procedure — she'd never been upset by the sight of blood — but far enough away not to be slashed by a quick swipe of the doctor's surgical blade. The whole procedure took less time than Ellie would have expected. She thought it might have taken hours even if someone else had stepped into the tent to assist the surgeon. But nobody did, and Dr. Kalil was sewing up the sergeant in just short of an hour. Maybe his wound hadn't been as bad as Ellie had thought or that was the way field surgery went. No time wasted.

You just put the equivalent of a patch on a problem so the patient could be shipped to a real hospital where the serious repairs would be made.

Ellie had been dividing her time between four points of focus: that Dr. Kalil made no sudden attack on her; that she didn't purposely sabotage Sergeant Jones' chances to survive, say by slicing through a major blood vessel; that help from a PGO colleague didn't arrive unexpectedly; and that one of the three anesthetized guys didn't wake up and become hostile.

No adverse event occurred, and Ellie was sure she'd sorted out a major part of the situation: Dr. Kalil was willing to sacrifice her own life if need be, but one or more of the guys she'd already attended to was someone she considered indispensable. That would also make one or more of those guys people the U.S. Army would like to question or see dead.

Taking all that into account, Ellie had thought the doctor might have repaired Sergeant Jones' damaged innards as best she could. That would be easier for her to do than trying to fake a surgical fix. Then when the doctor presented Ellie with her best effort, she'd expect her captor to relax, at least a little bit.

After all, Ellie was an American woman. She might have her moments of courage, but at heart she would be as soft as most of her kind were thought to be. Ellie would relax, and the woman who truly knew the horrors of war and was a warrior herself would strike.

That was the way Ellie read the situation, and she was pretty damn close.

Dr. Kalil finished suturing the incisions she had made and turned to look at Ellie, having picked up her scalpel once more, even though she no longer needed it for any medical purpose. Ellie kept the M-4 carbine pointed at Dr. Kalil and took a step back.

She didn't want the surgeon either to lunge at her with the blade or to slice Sergeant Jones' throat with it. Dr. Kalil seemed to understand her enemy's reasoning and hesitated for a moment as if the two of them were playing something of a chess game with neither of them having a full understanding how either of the queens on the board might move.

The doctor kept her weapon in hand and stepped between two of the recumbent men on their surgical tables.

"What more do you want of me?" she asked Ellie.

"Tell me which of those guys is the big deal for you," Ellie said.

"Or are they all important?"

The doctor didn't so much as glance at any of the men as Ellie had hoped she would do.

So Ellie said, "If you're going to be coy, I'll have to assume they're all important. Shoot them all and you, too."

Ellie flicked a lever on her weapon. She'd seen the special ops guys do it several times.

"Okay," she told Dr. Kalil, "my weapon's on full rock 'n' roll. I can get all of you in a heartbeat. Or you can tell who the big prize is. You try to fake me out, though, I'll know if you're lying. I've dealt with liars my whole life."

The doctor only shrugged as if she cared not at all who lived and who died.

"Yeah," Ellie said, "that's not a bad play. So tell me this: Did you really think I'd believe that asshole popping up out of nowhere and trying to kill the sergeant and me was just one big coincidence? Well, maybe I did for about two seconds. But on the way back here I was absolutely certain you talked to somebody, maybe someone here in this mud-hole town, even the guy who sold us his motorcycle, or you made a call. 'Hey, two Americans are coming your way. Give them an appropriate welcome.' You did that, right?"

The doctor didn't say a word, but the defiant look in her eyes gave her away. She'd set up the ambush all right.

Ellie said, "You don't want to admit that? Okay, tell me just one other thing: Did you enjoy cutting off Representative Philip Brock's head? You know, for killing your brother."

That made Hasna Kalil's face go slack with surprise, but the memory of what she'd done also filled her with glee. She twirled the scalpel in her hand and held it as if she thought she might drive it through one of Ellie's eyes, and then she charged.

Ellie was ready for her. She didn't fire the carbine. She sidestepped, leaving her opponent to pierce only air, and swung the butt of the rifle, slamming it into the near side of the doctor's skull. The sounds of bones cracking were twofold: the first one sickening, the second worse.

Hasna Kalil fell to the ground as if she had been shot. There were no spasms. Not even a twitch. The doctor's cervical spine, the connection between mind and body, had been severed. Her eyelids didn't even have time to close.

Having underestimated the force of the blow, Ellie murmured to herself, "Holy shit, I did it again."

Then she used Sergeant Jones' satellite phone to call for help.

It seemed within minutes the sky was filled with military helicopters rushing to help.

The first group of good guys was about to run into the tent and Ellie decided the story should be recreated visually. She'd pay good money to watch it on high-definition TV.

McGill Investigations International — Washington, DC

Welborn Yates was still in McGill's office with Sweetie when the phone rang.

McGill answered by giving his full name: "James J. McGill."

"It's me, boss," Deke Ky said.

McGill put the call on speaker. "Sweetie and General Yates are here with me."

A moment of silence followed, and then Deke asked, "Is Yates there in his new job capacity?"

A good question, McGill thought. Yes, Welborn had apologized and given a seemingly sincere and plausible explanation for his rude behavior, but that didn't mean he wasn't also on the clock working for the FBI. "Welborn?"

He said, "Still Air Force at the moment. Haven't signed the separation papers from my old job much less signed on for my new one."

McGill exchanged a brief look with Sweetie. Each gave the other a small nod.

"Go ahead, Deke," McGill said. "Speak freely."

"Right. Last night and early this morning, Detective Kealoha, a

Joint Terrorist Task Force composed of plainclothes cops and federal agents, and I went nightclubbing in all the Manhattan hotspots that cater to New York's diplomatic community. We were looking for gents, and being fair-minded, ladies who might be sporting tattoos akin to the ones found on the corpses of the guys who tried to do in Ms. Booker."

"And?" McGill said.

"Well, we had different people involved in doing the count, and we had to make some allowances for overlaps, but we came up with what we think is a reasonable estimate: 83 men and three women."

McGill responded with a soft whistle. "Makes me wonder how many more we might find on Embassy Row here in DC, and in consulates general around the country."

"We should find out," Deke said. "Leave no stone unturned and all that."

"Right," McGill agreed.

Then he explained how some of the individuals bearing the tattoos were legitimate patriots of their homelands, and how the king of Jordan almost became one of them.

Deke said, "I can see that. You know who we should call in on this? Elspeth Kendry. She grew up in Lebanon and speaks fluent Arabic. She has an understanding of the culture, too. Hey, maybe she should even be in on the interrogation of that tattoo artist the Jordanians caught. You know, if they'd go along with the idea."

"Good thinking, Deke," McGill told him. "I'll call Patti and ask her to call Jean."

That notion produced a laugh from Deke, who wasn't known for merriment.

"What's funny?" McGill asked.

"Just the idea that you can call the present and former presidents by their first names, and they'll pick up the phone when you call," Deke said.

McGill agreed. "Yeah, that does have its advantages. I probably won't be that lucky with the next administration."

Deke laughed again, though more briefly. "With your luck, I wouldn't be surprised if the next person to sit in the Oval Office is your long-lost best friend."

That got laughs from everyone in McGill's office.

"We can always hope," he said.

Deke said, "I called Gene Beck to ask if Air Force special ops guys ever do things like attach bombs to boats and ships. He said there's a program called Advanced Skills Training that includes a phase broadly known as water. It stresses the development of maximum underwater mobility. He said the only reason he told me that is because I served in the Secret Service. So I didn't ask if he personally knew how to attach a bomb to a boat. If I had to bet, though, I'd say yeah, he does."

"Okay, then," McGill said. "Everybody who gathered all this information was teetotaling last night, right?"

"I certainly was, but the volume of the music in some of those places still has my head throbbing. Didn't get much sleep at all."

"Stay in New York," McGill said. "Get some sleep in a quiet place and call me back when you're rested."

"Absolutely."

McGill clicked off his phone.

He told Welborn, "You might want to share Deke's news with Director Benjamin if it hasn't made its way to the FBI yet."

Welborn said, "My guess is it's in-house but making its way through channels. Won't look bad for me if I get it to her before anyone else. Thanks for understanding I have no intention of ever being a full-time jerk."

"Things like bad moments are best kept to a minimum," McGill agreed. "Something I know from personal experience."

Welborn stood, saluted McGill and Sweetie, and left.

Sweetie told McGill, "If his FBI job doesn't work out, I still wouldn't mind having Welborn working here. Doing penance graciously is a virtue."

"I'll be sure to remember that the next time I screw up," McGill said.

"And if you don't, I'll remind you," Sweetie told him.

She left to take care of a task on her own desk.

No sooner had McGill been left to his own devices than his phone rang again.

His daughter Abbie was calling. Not bothering with a hello and almost bubbling with delight, she said, "Dad, I spent the night with Cale Tucker, and it was wonderful."

Mayor Rockelle Bullard's Limousine — Washington, DC

Very little in the way of city government operations escaped the notice of the mayor. The two murder attempts on media figure Ellie Booker were on the top of her list, at least for the moment. But knowing that Marvin Meeker and Big Mike Walker had hired off-duty cops to act as bodyguards was also a large blip on her radar screen.

She knew both of her former detectives down to the first words they'd ever spoken, literally. She'd talked with both of their mamas about that. She knew that both of them had graduated *magna cum laude* from Howard University, though Meeker had been known to gripe he should have been *summa cum laude.* So when she heard from Meeker and Beemer that they needed help, Rockelle wanted to know what that was all about.

In fact, she wanted regular briefings.

So she decided to take a Sunday drive to Le Droit Park and the offices of M&W Private Investigations. If her former minions weren't at their place of business, she'd summon them.

She had Detective Aidan Behan with her. He had phoned the mayor earlier that day to say he'd received a short phone call from Ellie Booker.

"So she's alive," the mayor said after Behan had joined her in the mayoral limo.

"And prospering," Behan added. "She's taken over WorldWide News, what with Hugh Collier having expired yesterday. I suppose we'd both know that if we followed stories about big media more closely."

"I do keep an eye on that subject," Rockelle said.

Giving it just a moment's thought, Behan felt that was a smart thing for a politician to do. He said, "I went online and pulled up *The New York Times* site. They had both the death announcement and the new high-poobah-in-chief story on their homepage."

"I didn't see that in the *Post*," Rockelle said.

Behan made a guess. "You're talking the hard copy edition, right?"

"Yes."

"Ah, well, that's old news, got printed last night. The front page might've been set yesterday afternoon."

The mayor said, "I like to hold an actual newspaper in my hands."

"Tradeoffs for everything, ma'am."

That reality often irked the mayor. "So why did Ms. Booker call you in particular."

Behan said by way of demonstration, "She likes it when I put a bit of the Irish lilt in me voice."

Rockelle replied, "And I like the recordings of Nat King Cole, especially when they dub in Natalie doing a duet with him, but give me the real reason."

Behan replied, "Well, Ms. Booker heard from a source she didn't reveal that I was responsible for keeping an eye on her boat, and my guys and I found the body she ran over with said craft. She thanked me for my efforts, told me she wouldn't be alive if I'd slacked off. A bomb was found on the underside of the vessel. Some character who knew what he was doing removed the bomb from the *Dangerous Dame*, put it on a handy dinghy and hit the gas in the yacht. The bomb detonated shortly thereafter."

"So she was onboard her boat moving away when the explosion happened?" Rockelle asked.

"No, she was on a helicopter the late Mr. Collier had sent to pick her up."

"My, oh, my," Rockelle said, "that woman has the luck—"

"Of the Irish?" Behan asked. "That might be my doing, too."

The mayor rolled her eyes. "I was going to say the luck of a lottery winner. Which brings us to my former colleagues and their latest investigation."

She gave Behan the gist: two jackpot winners, only one officially announced, bystanders in possible jeopardy.

A pensive look formed on Behan's face, something a former police captain couldn't miss.

"What?" Rockelle asked. "What're you thinking?"

Behan said, "More remembering than thinking. I recall my father telling me a story about the Irish Sweepstakes."

"That's a lottery over there?" Rockelle asked.

"Yeah, it was. Tickets were sold internationally. The money was used to finance hospitals."

"Well, that sounds like a worthwhile idea."

Behan nodded. "To be sure, but what I'm trying to remember was some sort of scam where someone was trying to involve the Sweepstakes in some way. But that was a long time ago, and I was just a kid, a lad as we used to say over there. I'll have to give my father a call. I'm sure he'll remember."

The limo came to a stop, and the driver said, "Ma'am."

He inclined his head, and the two passengers saw what he was pointing out.

Beemer was sitting slumped over on the front steps of his place of work sound asleep.

They might've thought he was dead if they hadn't heard him snoring.

McGill Investigations International — Washington, DC

McGill asked his eldest child, "Abbie, isn't this subject something better discussed with your mother, either one of them?"

In the silence that followed, McGill thought he almost heard his daughter laugh, and then in a tone that fell just short of indignation she said, "*Dad,* it wasn't like *that.*"

Which was a relief for McGill to hear, but also a bit of a puzzle. Abbie was a looker by almost anyone's standards, and he'd already witnessed the eye Cale Tucker had for the ladies. So where was the disconnect?

Not daring to ask, he said, "Well, I'm glad you had a good time nonetheless."

"What I meant to say was we *talked* all night, covered subjects from A to Z. We didn't agree on everything, of course, but we found room to disagree without a bit of rancor."

That last bit led McGill to do a bit of arithmetic. Cale had told him he was 25. Legal voting age for presidential elections started at 18. So he said, "Don't tell me Cale voted against Patti in her second run for the presidency."

The silence at the other end of the call, McGill estimated, lasted a good 10 seconds. Then Abbie said, "He voted for Mather Wyman."

"He might need to go to work for him then," McGill opined.

"Dad, you're not going to tell, are you?" Abbie asked in a stressed tone.

"You've put me in an awkward spot, sweetheart. I don't like to keep secrets from Patti."

Sweetie poked her head into McGill's office. She whispered, "Bad time?"

McGill waved her in and saw she had a sheet of paper in her hand.

Abbie seemed to have fallen silent again, but McGill thought he heard two muffled voices speaking in the background. If she returned to the conversation without having come up with a solution to the problem she'd raised —

His daughter was back, speaking clearly and with a tone of relief in her voice. "Dad, it's all right. Cale just told me that during his job interview he told Patti how he had voted. He said Patti could understand his voting for a man she'd chosen to be her vice president. So Patti knows, and it's not a problem."

McGill asked, "Why didn't he just say that in the first place?"

"Probably should have," Cale said audibly in the background.

Which might be either the admission of an honest mistake or a glib evasion, McGill thought.

Then McGill took things one step further. Could the kid just be *testing* him? Seeing how sharp the old man might be. At first, McGill's temper started to spike. Then he thought, if Cale just had a challenging sense of humor, driving him away would be a mistake.

Battles of wit with Cale might be fun.

Abbie must've put her hand over the speaker, he thought, because he didn't hear a peep out of the other end of the conversation.

Sweetie filled in the gap. "Anybody in your family ever play the Irish Sweepstakes when you were a kid, Jim?"

McGill shook his head. "The only wagering that went on in my family was when one of my extended relatives was foolish enough to challenge my dad at darts. Dad would spot most of the relatives 100 points and let them stand a foot inside the toe-line, and nobody ever beat him."

"Did he ever hustle anyone?" Sweetie asked.

McGill laughed. "Never. He only played family members, and he used the money he won to buy the wives drinks. So there were never any hard feelings."

·Abbie came back on the phone all cheer and glee. "Dad, you just won 20 bucks for me."

"Cale was trying to put one over on me, huh?"

"Yeah, I said it would never work. You losing your cool. "

"Looks like it didn't," McGill said.

Not that Cale wouldn't be sly enough to throw a bet to impress a girl.

"Have him come into the office if he'll work on a Sunday," Sweetie said. "I've got something an egghead might enjoy looking into."

McGill passed along the request.

Cale said he'd be happy to help.

Just the right way to play things, McGill thought.

Either to win Abbie's heart or to beguile her for his own pleasure.

Not that the two couldn't go hand in hand.

M & W Private Investigations — Le Droit Park

Rockelle put a hand on Beemer's shoulder and asked in a loud, gruff voice, "Are you sleeping on duty, Detective?"

Beemer sprang to his feet like a jack-in-the-box popping up. "Not me, Captain."

Then he rubbed his eyes and remembered he was no longer a cop. He saw Mayor Bullard grinning at him and a detective he thought was named Behan standing next to her. The detective had the smarts to keep a straight face. He also had a phone pressed to his ear and looked like he was listening to someone.

"Yes, Da," Behan said. "Thanks for explaining things. Yes, I imagine there was quite the uproar until things were cleared up. Ta."

Behan put the phone back in the inside pocket of his suit coat.

Beemer took his eyes off the detective and put them on Rockelle. "That wasn't funny at all. You mighta given me a heart attack. You run for mayor again, you're gonna have to *win* my vote back."

Rockelle told Beemer, "I kind of doubt the winning margin is going to rest on one vote, but let's remember I'm allowing you to hire moonlighting cops to keep clients and families safe. That and provide extra patrols in your neighborhood."

Beemer sighed. "Okay, you've still got my vote."

"Warms my heart," the mayor said.

"Y'all want to go inside?" Beemer asked.

"We do," Rockelle said, "but why didn't *you* go inside and sleep on a sofa. It's not cold enough today to die of exposure, but you might've come down with some ailment."

Beemer said, "I can't sleep on airplanes; I hadn't slept in more than a day. I was so tired when I got to the front steps here I couldn't remember which key opened the door. I thought I'd just sit down for a minute until it came to me. Next thing I know, you're yelling in my ear."

Rockelle sighed. "I'm sorry, Michael. I was just trying to have a little fun. I wouldn't blame you if you vote for someone else."

Beemer said, "Yeah, you would."

He found the right key and let his visitors step inside.

Behan extended his hand. "Detective Aidan Behan."

Beemer shook his hand. "Michael Walker, also known as Big Mike and Beemer."

"Will Michael do until we know each other better?"

"Sure." Turning to Rockelle, he said, "I'll call Marvin."

"Already here," Meeker said, bounding up the steps. "Got the mayor's call a few minutes ago."

"Yeah?" Beemer asked. "She wake you up out of a sound sleep, too?"

"Nah, it's almost lunchtime. I've been up quite a while."

"Everything good around here?" Beemer asked.

"Mayline's fine. So's everyone else." Meeker told him. "And I've set up a trap."

Rockelle said, "Why don't we pick someone's office and talk there unless you want to go to that interrogation room I've heard you got here."

They went to Beemer's office. He stretched out on the sofa there. Meeker took the seat behind Beemer's desk. Rockelle and Behan sat in the guest chairs, the mayor introducing the police detective to Meeker.

"I'm here," the mayor said, "because knowing you two private citizens have hired off-duty police officers to protect a client, his wife, their unborn child, a lawyer, his wife, and Michael's wife, I wanted to make sure nothing's gone wrong so far." Addressing Meeker specifically, she added, "I'm surprised you didn't want protection for your sister and your niece."

"They're out in California," Meeker said.

Rockelle nodded. "Okay, then, where do things stand so far?"

Meeker said, "As I said, I've set up what I think could be a nice little trap."

"Where," Rockelle asked, "and who's catching who?"

"Sammy bought his lottery ticket at a place called Miz Smith's Convenience Corner," Meeker said.

"Which one?" Rockelle asked.

Meeker provided the location only a few blocks away.

"How will any bad guys know where he got his lotto ticket?" Rockelle asked.

Beemer answered from his recumbent position with his eyes closed. "I made the mistake of mentioning my brother-in-law was the winner. Then Constance Parker found out this is our work address. So she knows our names. That ought to be enough for anybody with a bit of computer know-how to find Sammy's name. You find that, you'll get his address. You know where he lives, you draw a tight circle on a map, find all the places inside that circle that sell lottery tickets. Then you go out and ask people is this where Sammy plays his numbers or whatever. If that doesn't work right off, you draw a bigger circle and keep asking."

Meeker added, "Only Sammy lives maybe a block-and-a-half from the *Miz Smith's* where he bought his ticket. Probably wouldn't take a half-hour to find it."

"And then?" Rockelle asked.

Everybody in the room, including Behan, knew she was just testing, not contesting, Meeker's logic.

Meeker said, "Then the bad guys, if they're smart, just say, 'Hey, so is this the place where Sammy MacCray bought that winning lotto ticket?' If they get some gullible clerk to say yes, and they're smart they say, 'Hey, that's great. Let me buy a ticket, too.' Then they leave peacefully and have someone who knows how to hack the store's video log, copy the video of Sammy buying the winning ticket and delete the original. Take things from there."

Beemer added, “If they’ve got more muscle than brains, then they just follow somebody else’s direction and use an armed robbery as a cover for taking the video.”

Meeker and Beemer turned their gazes on Behan.

He only nodded his agreement.

Rockelle took it from there. “I can buy all that, and I’ll have additional cops backing up the officers you’ve already hired, and I’ll put plainclothes cops in the store in case the bad guys are inclined to get violent. I don’t want anyone on our team, and that includes civilians, getting shot.”

Both Meeker and Beemer gave her a salute.

She turned to Detective Behan. “Did you get some relevant information from your father, Detective?”

That question threw Meeker and Beemer. Behan explained the earlier discussion of the Irish Sweepstakes he’d had with the mayor and then what he’d heard from his father.

“The way the Sweepstakes worked,” he told the others, “there was a multi-step process. You bought your tickets, which were available internationally, and if your ticket had an initial winning number, of which there were many, its stub was returned to Ireland. All the ticket stubs with winning numbers were put into a barrel and later a certain number of them were blindly withdrawn. Each of the chosen stubs was randomly matched with the number of a horse running in a major race in either Ireland or England. Ticket holders whose stubs matched the horses that won, placed, or showed got cash prizes.”

Meeker said, “Damn, that’s a long way to go.”

Beemer added, “Must’ve been a lot of people you had to trust, too.”

Behan smiled. “My father told me that thousands of counterfeit tickets were sold here in the U.S. and most likely in many other countries. There weren’t many complaints because relatively speaking there were only a very few winning numbers … and then there was the time when the draw of numbers from the barrel didn’t quite go according to plan.”

The smile on Behan's face made Meeker, Beemer, and Rockelle all demand to hear the story's payoff.

McGill Investigations International — Washington, DC

Sweetie was finishing the same story Detective Behan was telling at Meeker and Beemer's shop. She told McGill, "It was a relatively competitive horse race that year. There were favorites, of course, mounts that were reasonably expected to win, place, and show but not by more than a neck or maybe even a nose."

McGill had never played the horses, but he had heard of races that were fixed. Stories had it that fixing such competitions went back to the days of Julius Caesar. In modern times, crooks were known to have paid jockeys many thousands of dollars to fix a race.

What Sweetie told McGill that day had the irony of using the word fix in its original meaning: repairing something that was out of order.

Sweetie continued, "The chief steward at the track in Ireland didn't like the order of the post positions assigned to the horses in the race. The positions were supposed to be assigned by a blind drawing, but the favorite horse and its two closest competitors had been given post positions two, three, and four. Literally the inside tracks."

Sweetie added, "Post position number one wasn't favored by most horses and jockeys because many horses shied from running so close to the rail, and jockeys didn't like starting in a spot where they and their mounts might be pinned against the rail by other riders.

"The chief steward didn't know for sure that the three slim favorites had deliberately been given the inside tracks for competitive purposes and to make the race more exciting or if bettors somehow had suborned the assignments of post positions. In any case, without either official permission or knowledge, the man had his six-year-old son do a second blind drawing, and the positions the boy drew were the order in which the horses ran.

"The favorite and the two closest competitors now had positions on the far outside of a 15-horse race. None of them finished in the money. At first, the track officials held their tongues on the repositioned horses to save themselves any embarrassment. Any bettors who thought the fix was in had to keep quiet or admit their complicity in an illegal scheme."

McGill asked, "So how'd the truth come out?"

Sweetie said, "Time passed, and so did the chief steward. At his funeral, his now-adult son told the story."

"I love it," McGill said. "What those results also mean is that some people who weren't ever intended to win the Irish Sweepstakes got the prize money."

"Now who does that remind you of?" Sweetie asked.

M & W Private Investigations — Le Droit Park

"Sammy MacCray," Mayor Rockelle Bullard said when Detective Behan asked who his story reminded the others of. "The fix was in for Constance Parker, but somebody added another fix."

Meeker and Beemer looked at each other; Beemer was sitting up by now.

"Okay," Meeker said, "I can buy that, but who made the second fix, the righteous one?"

Beemer said, "Can't know that until we find out who made the first fix."

"Maybe we can draw some inferences from the horse-race story," Behan said. "It likely had to be an insider, probably someone with advanced computer skills. We don't know who that is, but we might have some new strings to pull on."

Rockelle asked, "Like what?"

Behan said, "Well, let's assume the bad guys want to make sure their lottery results look as legit as possible."

Meeker smiled and said, "I'm with you now. So what the crooks do is make sure one or two other players get five of the winning numbers right and pick up those prizes that pay one or two million bucks. Scatter a bunch of other smaller-time winners around, too."

Rockelle agreed, but only up to a point. "Okay, I can see the small-fry collecting their money, but the scammers running this operation, they're not going to let even a few million dollars get away from them."

"The mayor's right," Beemer said, "letting nickels and dimes slide is okay, but not millions of dollars. The question now is do they use a front person like Constance Parker for those six-zeros prizes, too, or do they pick up those checks themselves?"

Behan consulted his phone. "You can ask one of them. Guy named Ed Kingsley, qualified to win a million dollars, only he paid extra for the multiplier and won two million. It's on the lottery website." Behan showed them with a smile. "He lives right here in DC, too."

Mayor Bullard said, "Detective Behan, you work with my friends Marvin and Big Mike on this. If Mr. Kingsley looks wrong to *all* of you, Detective Behan will make an arrest."

Then the mayor took out her phone and called James J. McGill.

McGill Investigations International — Washington, DC

"Jim McGill, may I help you?" The caller ID on McGill's phone said: *Mayor WDC.* But he'd been around the block often enough to know that phone numbers and the names of callers could be spoofed. Things had gotten to the point where people had been advised not to use the word yes in a phone conversation with a stranger.

That simple three-letter affirmation might be recorded and used in a con game against the unwitting person who'd uttered it.

McGill didn't have to worry about that. The unmistakable voice of Rockelle Bullard replied, "I'm hoping I can help you."

McGill put the call on speaker.

Rockelle started to recount the conversation she and Detective Behan had had with Meeker and Beemer. McGill grinned and at an opportune moment told the mayor he and Sweetie had the same chat, giving credit to Sweetie and her dad for telling him of the Sweepstakes saga.

Rockelle laughed. "Great minds think alike and all that. I just called to ask if you'd like to bring all your experience as both a cop and a P.I. to the group going to talk with this guy, Ed Kingsley."

Before McGill could answer, there was a soft knock at his office door. Esme opened it, having come in on a Sunday at her own volition. Putnam Shady stood next to her. Sweetie saw him and her face immediately filled with concern. He shook off her worry and pointed at McGill.

"You still there, Mr. McGill?" Mayor Bullard asked.

"Sorry, Madam Mayor. An unexpected visitor just showed up. Someone I probably need to give some time to."

Having been reassured that her daughter, Maxi, was okay, Sweetie piped up, "Madam Mayor, this is Margaret Sweeney. I wouldn't mind speaking to Mr. Kingsley. I have the same police and P.I. experience Jim does, and it might not hurt to have a woman's point of view."

Rockelle laughed again. "Ms. Sweeney, in my experience, that *never* hurts."

The mayor gave Sweetie a time and a place to rendezvous with the others and said goodbye. Sweetie gave Putnam a kiss on her way out, a gesture of affection both McGill and Esme saw. Something Sweetie never would have done even a year or two ago.

Putnam closed the door behind his wife and took the seat in which she'd sat.

He asked McGill, "Will anyone be able to overhear us in here?"

McGill said, "No."

"Are you recording this conversation?"

"Unh-uh."

"I'd like you to write a check to me for $1,000, drawn on a

business account."

McGill understood implicitly that Putnam was establishing a lawyer-client relationship with him, an idea he'd raised earlier. McGill wrote and signed the check. He also put his signature on a contract Putnam presented to him. He didn't bother to read the agreement. Putnam wouldn't think of doing anything sneaky that Sweetie might find out about later.

Putnam put the paperwork into his briefcase and slumped in his chair.

"It's as bad as all that?" McGill asked.

"I got very little sleep last night thinking about this situation. In my bad old days, when my conscience could swim in a thimble of someone else's blood and not worry about the taint, I would have turned down this request to get involved. Having been instructed in moral behavior by my wife and trying to set a good example for my daughter, I didn't think I could just cut the connection when Ellie Booker called me."

McGill sighed. "That was my idea originally."

Putnam forced out a dry laugh. "If you were my only source of concern, I would have said sorry, no can do. But I knew I'd have to share that news with Margaret, and I don't want her to think less of me."

"One of the great rewards of loving your wife," McGill said.

That was the best he could do to provide comfort to Putnam. "So what did Ellie have to tell you?"

The lawyer took a deep breath and exhaled by saying quietly, "She killed someone."

McGill took a moment before asking for clarification. "Accidentally?"

"We're not talking about the guy who tried to blow her boat out of the water," Putnam said. "She told me about that, too. In fact, she said a camera aboard the helicopter that rescued her recorded the dinghy where the bomb had been placed going boom. That was Hugh Collier's doing, not hers, but she has plans to use it."

"How?" McGill asked.

"I'll answer that in just a minute. Ellie also suspects and would like to know if you have security video-cams on this building. I thought I saw some the other day when I picked up Margaret after the murder attempt on Ellie and again when I came in today. Some places, though, just use facsimiles of cameras to scare off thieves."

"Ours work," McGill said.

"Thought so. Did you give a copy of the murder attempt to the cops?"

"Yes."

"Yeah, I thought that would be the case, too."

"So who did she kill?" McGill asked.

Putnam told him what he'd heard from Ellie about the events in Syria.

McGill listened closely without interrupting. When Putnam finished, he said, "So according to Ellie, she acted in self-defense."

"Doing so after threatening to kill Dr. Kalil and three unconscious men," Putnam reminded him.

"Maybe she meant that, maybe she didn't," McGill said.

Putnam smiled broadly. "If I didn't know better, I'd think you went to law school."

"What's indisputable," McGill said, "is she saved Sergeant Jones' life. He's still alive, isn't he?"

Putnam nodded. "Thank God for that. In that way, she's an all-American hero. We probably couldn't seat a jury anywhere in the country where at least one person wouldn't vote to acquit her on that basis alone. I know I would."

"Me, too," McGill said.

"Then there's Ellie's suspicion that at least one of the late Dr. Kalil's three unconscious patients was a big fish among the bad guys. Playing a big part in nabbing him will also go a long way in making sure she doesn't go to prison."

"Assuming the military brass or the national security people would be willing to testify," McGill said.

Putnam agreed. "They might be reticent, but I think Sergeant Jones, his family, and the other special forces people in his unit might sway things in her direction."

McGill took that under consideration and nodded. "Might even get Jean Morrissey's backing, in which case any other objections would be moot. So, if there's no real legal jeopardy, then ..." McGill worked through the rest of the equation quickly. "Ellie's more worried than ever that the bad guys will keep trying to kill her."

"Yeah, so she's hoping with you working one side of the street and the FBI working the other, she'll at least get some breathing space. You know, until someone can invent a cloak of invisibility."

McGill said, "That would be a very good trick, especially working the new job she's just inherited."

"There's more to that than you know," Putnam replied.

"What?"

"Something I strongly advised against. Hell, I begged her to forget about the crazy idea."

McGill waited in silence to hear the rest.

"Jim," Putnam said, "she's going to ask for a copy of the tape of the shooting outside your building here. She's already got the video of the explosion at sea. She's going to request police photos of the guy her boat chopped up, the one who placed the bomb intended to kill her."

McGill understood now.

He said, "Ellie's going to confess to the killing in Syria. She's going to show the whole country — hell, the whole world — all the gut-churning images. Show the whole thing on TV."

Putnam nodded.

"She'll become the biggest terrorist target in the world."

"That's why she'd like the field cleared up just a bit before she goes public," Putnam said. "But that's not all."

McGill's jaw dropped. "What else could there be?"

"Ellie says Dr. Hasna Kalil was the one who took Representative Philip Brock's head off of his body. She did that because she blamed him for killing her twin brother Bahir Ben Kalil. And you know who Brock was trying to kill in the name of all-out anarchy."

In a quiet voice, McGill said, "Patti."

Putnam told him. "Ellie says that point will be in the documentary, too."

Now, McGill no longer felt he had to help Ellie.

He *wanted* to help her.

Miz Smith's Convenience Corner
Le Droit Park, Washington, DC

Meeker and Beemer sat in a 10-year-old tan Toyota Camry down the block from the convenience store. The car ran great, didn't have a scratch anywhere on its polished cream-colored body, and most importantly it didn't have the license plates that Constance Parker had seen on Marvin Meeker's BMW 330i. Beemer thought it would have been too on-the-nose for him to own that brand of car. So he went with a Volvo XC60 SUV. But the two P.I.s decided not to go with that car either. They didn't want a vehicle that could be traced back to either of them.

The Toyota had dealer plates on it and came off the used car lot of the dealership where Sammy worked. It would be returned the next morning and the plates would come off it.

"Got an idea," Beemer told Meeker as they watched for anyone with a suspicious appearance or manner entering the store.

Yasmin, the shop's manager, was in the store with Simon and Richie, the undercover cops, for company and protection.

Meeker said, "What's your idea?"

"It's about who's probably in on this scam with Constance Parker."

"I'm just reading the woman's university bio at Johns Hopkins," Meeker said. He had an iPad on his lap. "She got top grades in college just like you and me. Now, she's a researcher there. So how do we know anybody's in on the lottery prize with her?"

"You're just raising a debating point now," Beemer said. "The woman waved a gun at us, tracked us down, offered us a million-dollar payoff. She isn't your run-of-the-mill ivory tower intellectual, now is she?"

Meeker said, "Got me there, so, yeah, she's not alone in whatever's going on."

Beemer replied, "What's going on is how a great big pile of lottery money gets stolen and divided. For the first ten minutes or so, after Sammy came to us, we both thought this was some kind of an honest screwup, right?"

"Pretty much," Meeker conceded. "There's still a chance of that. Just about everyone under the sun hates to admit publicly that he or she messed up. It'd be hard for the lottery people to keep their game up and running if they say, 'Oops, we made a boo-boo. That last drawing we had? There were two big winners, not one.' They do that, all sorts of suspicion falls on them and maybe Sammy too."

Beemer frowned. "I hadn't gone that far in my thinking, but you could be right. But we know — or I do, anyway — that Sammy isn't a hustler here."

"I'll take your word on that," Meeker said.

"Good. We also both agree that Ms. Parker's afraid of something, right? And it's more than just her own guilty conscience."

"Somebody's either working with her or working her over," Meeker said. "My feeling is someone has a hook into her."

Beemer agreed. "Mine, too. But she's still looking to make out somehow. We can work on what that is next. But what I'm thinking is, somebody bigger than Ms. Parker has a plan here. She's just the public face, being cut in for a nice piece of money, but nothing like what the guys who came up with the idea will be getting."

"Right," Meeker said. "Too bad we couldn't find that Ed Kingsley dude who won the two million. Having him to talk to might have given us a lead."

Meeker, Beemer, Detective Behan, and Sweetie had checked out the thirteen people named Ed Kingsley in the District of Columbia who were 18 and older, age-eligible to buy lottery tickets, and found twelve of them at home. None of them admitted to buying a winning lottery ticket, and all of them passed the smell test administered by three former cops and one current investigator.

The thirteenth Ed Kingsley wasn't home, the top floor apartment of a three-story walkup that had so far avoided the city's tide of gentrification. A tipsy neighbor who was sitting on the front stoop drinking from a bottle wrapped in a brown bag told the investigative crew, "Saw the dude just the one time. Well, maybe twice. But the second time I might've been imagining things. Anyway, the guy never said a word to me. You know, after I asked if he might help me buy a bottle. Not talking would've been okay if he'd come across with some cash, but he didn't."

Asked for a description of the mute neighbor, the drinker had thought for a moment and said, "White skinny dude in tight clothes. Kinda tall, but not NBA or anything."

"Carrying a gun, you think?" Sweetie had asked.

Always an important point to consider when you went looking for someone.

Just the idea, though, sent a tremor through the drinker. "He looked mean enough to shoot someone. Has this face like a hawk and dark hair that came to a point in front. Shit, you think things have got to the point around here where a little panhandling might get you killed?"

"Maybe, maybe not" Behan said.

But conditions had reached the juncture where neither past nor present cops would buy a drunk a drink. The SOB might stumble into traffic and go out with a bang. Ruin some old lady's otherwise perfect driving record.

Sweetie said she had other obligations and had to be on her way.

The guys all thanked her for helping out, and Behan said he had a few other things to take care of himself but give him a call if they needed someone with current police powers.

Putting aside the day's futile Ed Kingsley hunt, Meeker asked, "So, what're you thinking, Big Mike? Some kind of organized crime types are using Constance Parker as their public face?"

Beemer said, "Wouldn't be the first time it happened, somebody who should know better thinks she can make a deal with the devil and get away with it."

Meeker's eyes suddenly got big. He smiled and he said, "And maybe, in the end, hard work does get rewarded. Would you look at that?"

Beemer was already doing so. Two guys were crossing the intersection ahead, against a red light, and heading toward Miz Smith's Convenience Corner. One of them looked like he'd been built from spare tank parts. The other dude was skinny, kinda tall but not NBA, wore tight clothes and had dark hair that came to a point on his forehead.

Meeker and Beemer looked at each other and said, "Ed Kingsley."

As soon as the two men entered Miz Smith's, Meeker and Beemer got out of Sammy's car.

Glad to be at home in DC and packing their sidearms.

To be extra careful, they put in a quick call to Detective Aidan Behan.

Welborn Yates' House — Washington, DC

The Yates twins, Aria and Callista, had a question for their mother that evening: "Why isn't Daddy helping you put us to bed?"

Not infrequently, the two girls would speak as one, seemingly reading from a script invisible to everyone else. Kira sometimes wondered if they could converse without bothering with the spoken word. That thought was both eerie and somewhat comforting. Scary if they were plotting some mischief behind Mom's back; reassuring that one of them would never be lonely as long as the other was on the same wavelength.

Able to say without the need of any phone: *Hang on, Sis, I'm coming.*

She told the twins, "Your father thinks he might be coming down with a cold. If he's right, he doesn't want you catching it. That's why he only gave you a hug and not a kiss goodnight."

"Oh," they said in unison. Apparently buying Mom's improvised explanation.

Or letting their mother think she'd gotten away with something.

In any case, they were tucked in and had their eyes closed by the time Kira got to their bedroom door. She smiled and told her girls, "You're just pretending to be asleep."

The two pairs of young eyes popped open. Aria only frowned, but Callista explained, "We're *trying* to go to sleep so we can talk with Grandpa."

Kira asked, "You mean Grandpa Robert?" Welborn's father.

The girls shook their heads and said in one voice, "No, Grandpa Edward."

Kira's father, who'd died in a hotel fire when she was six. His name had been mentioned to the children, and they'd even seen his photo in a family album. But the only description of the man they'd been given was that he'd gone to heaven a long time ago.

"You talk to my father?" Kira asked, her eyes moistening.

The two young heads bobbed in reply. Aria added, "He's really nice."

Kira was unsure of what to tell her girls. All she could come up with was, "Please tell Grandpa Edward that I said hello."

Going downstairs, she wanted to tell Welborn what she'd just heard from their daughters, but he beat her to the conversational punch.

"I apologized to Jim McGill for acting like a jerk. I realized my reaction was tied to Keith, Joe and Tommy's deaths. I think I might need some psychiatric help."

Kira told him, "Me, too."

Miz Smith's Corner Convenience — Washington, DC

The guy who looked like he ate anabolic steroids at all three meals had Yasmin in a choke-hold when Meeker and Beemer entered the store. He wasn't exerting sufficient pressure to hurt her, just enough to keep her up on her toes. The dude the two former MPD detectives thought of as Ed Kingsley turned to see who'd entered the store behind him and his massive friend.

Ed saw two black men with guns in their hands, weapons pointed directly at him.

He told Meeker and Beemer, "We will kill the woman if you do not surrender your weapons. We have already told these others the same thing, and now we are losing patience. Especially my large friend who has little self-restraint in any case."

The others Ed had mentioned were Simon and Richie, the undercover cops working their side-job. They also had their weapons out and pointing at the two thugs.

Meeker asked Ed, "Is that some kind of Polish accent you got there, Ed?"

"Sounds like it to me," Beemer said.

Ed gave the newcomers a dirty look. The hulk also looked at Meeker and Beemer with displeasure. Richie might've popped the big guy in the head right then, but Meeker and Beemer were directly on the other side of him. The round in Richie's Glock might go straight through the thug's skull and do considerable damage to the next guy in line. So what Richie did was scoot to his right. Got a nice angle on Goliath's right ear. In one side of his skull and out the other with nobody else hurt would be acceptable shooting.

No friendlies in the way on that angle.

"We are not Polish," Ed said with a sneer in his voice.

Beemer said, "I guess not, you say it like that. Hey, Marvin, didn't we read somewhere it's the Russians who don't have any use for the Poles?"

"Yeah, I think you're right about that," Meeker said, "but you know what I can't figure out about Ed over there. Why're he and the gorilla robbing a convenience store when he just won two million bucks in the lottery?"

The putative Ed Kingsley's mouth dropped open, a silent

confession.

Then he regrouped and in a desperate voice shouted. "We will kill her. We will kill the woman."

Detective Aidan Behan stepped through the door, gun in hand, just in time to hear the second half of that threat. He assessed the situation and took the shot within a heartbeat. His round cleaved the crown of the big thug's skull.

Fortunately for Yasmin, as the mug's knees buckled, he fell backward, and she landed atop him. Beemer, Richie, and Simon converged on Ed Kingsley like an NFL defensive line sacking a hapless quarterback. They didn't kill him, but they left him so bruised and battered he probably thought his friend had gotten off easier with a quick death.

Meeker pried the monster's dead hands off Yasmin and helped her up. He held her close as her shaking diminished. After a moment, she asked Meeker, "Aren't you supposed to tell me I'll be all right now?"

Beemer laughed and said, "I like that lady's style. Maybe she should come work for us, Marvin."

To which, Detective Behan added, "I hope this store's video shows a righteous shoot or I might need a new job, too."

McGill Investigations International — Washington, DC

McGill and Cale Tucker were alone in the building when the call from Mayor Rockelle Bullard came through. McGill put it on speaker. The mayor recognized the bottom-of-a-well vocal quality that produced.

"You got someone listening in with you?" the mayor asked. "Ms. Sweeney maybe?"

McGill said, "Sweetie's at home with her family, Madam Mayor. I have a young fellow with me. I'm asking him for a bit of freelance help."

"You don't mind him hearing your business?" Rockelle asked.

"He was out all last night with my daughter," McGill replied.

"Oh, my. I guess you'll be talking about his business, too, then. All right, just a few minutes ago, two men tried to rob a Miz Smith's in Le Droit Park. One of them is a man named Ed Kingsley. The man just won a $2 million lottery prize. He had a big ugly friend with him. They were threatening the life of a female store employee when Detective Aidan Behan entered the store and killed the man who represented the immediate threat to the woman."

"Behan seems to have a knack for being in the right place at the right time," McGill said.

"He surely does, and once again I'll say don't even think of poaching him from me."

"Now, Madam Mayor, would I ever do such a thing? I don't think we even have an opening at the moment."

"You're saying all the right things, Mr. McGill, and I still feel uneasy."

"Well, maybe you'll have to find a little extra money in the city budget for civil service workers."

"We are *not* going to talk about raising the taxes required to do that."

"Right. So are Marvin and Big Mike going to be in on questioning Ed Kingsley, who, I assume, is the surviving bad guy?"

"He is, and no, we can't take any chances with that, as I'm sure you know even if you're pretending not to."

"Some jurisdictions are more flexible than others. For instance, if your two former colleagues were to provide a few notes, say, questions worth asking, to people still on the force, that would probably pass muster. Especially if the interrogators memorized the questions. Didn't have to read from a visible script."

Rockelle laughed. "Is that how you did things back in Chicago?"

"We got inventive at times."

"I bet. Anyway, I wanted to ask if you might know anyone with the right kind of high-tech background who might know how to rig a lottery drawing so you get a big winner and a $2 million winner."

"And someone who throws in a monkey-wrench and produces

a second, unwanted big winner."

"Yeah, that, too," Rockelle said. "Seems to me you'd need a second computer genius for that, someone who wants to mess with his boss."

"A disgruntled worker would be one possibility," McGill said, "but I can think of others."

"Yeah? Like who for instance?"

"An angry spouse, an alienated child, a hostile professional rival."

Rockelle had to laugh. "Yeah, grievances make the world go 'round, don't they? Anyway, if you know anyone who might consult on this situation, I'd be happy to hear from him or her."

"I'm sitting here with him right now," McGill said. "I asked him to stop by to discuss this very issue. Well, that and one or two other things."

"You're doing this to help Meeker and Beemer?"

"Well, they are paying me a dollar and have promised to make a charitable donation to the benevolent organization of Sweetie's choice."

"Good for all of you then. Let me know if you get somewhere with this."

"Will do, Madam Mayor."

McGill ended the call and looked at Cale. "You think you're up to this?"

The young man said, "Let me make sure I've got the parameters right: How does someone fix a supposedly random and televised drawing so that one predetermined person wins the big prize?"

"That and a smaller but still substantial prize of $2 million," McGill said.

Cale told him, "If you can fix six numbers, fixing five is just a subset of the first problem. Then there's the matter of directing the winning ticket to a specific individual, but that's no big deal."

"It isn't?" McGill asked.

Cale shrugged. "You print the winning ticket first. Then you rig the drawing to match it."

McGill was tempted to say, "Duh!" Maintaining a more sophisticated image, he went with, "Of course."

Cale continued, "The other part of rigging the game is preventing a randomly sold ticket from also being imprinted with the winning numbers. After all, you've gone to a lot of trouble to hit the jackpot. You don't want some schmo to share your loot just because he plunked down two bucks."

McGill said, "So it had to be somebody inside the scheme who messed with the computer code or whatever that supposedly assigns numbers at random to a given ticket."

Cale paused to consider that assumption, and said, "Probably. I don't play any lottery games, but I think a player can still choose his numbers manually. If that's the case, there would have to be a line of code in the altered software that would refuse to print out the predetermined winning numbers. You'd need to substitute another number for a personally chosen one. But it couldn't be a visually obvious substitution: You couldn't swap a 7 for a 6. Maybe you could get away with substituting a 3 for an 8."

McGill said, "I wonder how many people who choose their own numbers even bother to check their tickets. I'd think many of them would just assume the machine printed it correctly."

Cale added a thought. "Another thing to consider is whether the player keeps the slip with his favorite numbers on it or it's disposed of by the player or the vendor. Even if a person kept the slip with his own numbers, though, how could he prove he'd picked those numbers *before* the drawing was held."

After lapsing into silence for a moment, Cale smiled.

"You've got something?" McGill asked.

"Nothing in the way of an immediate solution, but it's an idea nonetheless. It goes back to your suggestion of an inside saboteur."

"And that led you where?"

Cale said, "You've heard of the Dark Web?"

McGill nodded. "Heard but never visited."

"That's wise. Well, there's a place in cyberspace called the Black Hole after the region of spacetime with gravity so strong that not even light can escape it. The name alone is supposed to scare away most people, and it does. But among those who do travel there, you'll find some of the biggest braggarts ever born."

"Guys who might laugh about re-rigging a multi-million dollar lottery?" McGill asked.

Cale nodded.

McGill asked Cale, "You can go there without causing yourself any lasting problems?"

"I can," he replied.

"You'd never tell Abbie about this?"

Cale shook his head and said, "I was wondering when we'd get around to that subject: the idea that I'd better not mess around with your daughter."

McGill grinned. "I'm glad you can help me, but that wasn't the worry I had in mind."

"No? What was?"

"Your safety. Did Abbie ever mention to you something called Dark Alley?"

"No. Is that on the Web, too?"

McGill shook his head. "It's very much a part of the physical world. The way I describe it is organized street fighting. Vicious and entirely without mercy. My uncle taught it to me. I taught it to all of my kids."

"So you're saying it's possible Abbie might hurt me?"

McGill said, "I thought you should know."

Dumbarton Oaks — Washington, DC

McGill and Patti lay on their backs in bed, holding hands, staring up at the ceiling, waiting for their heartbeats to return to a normal pace before attempting to go to sleep.

Patti told McGill, "If it's all right with you, I'd like to have my employee back tomorrow."

"You mean Cale?"

"Yes."

"Okay, but he might need to use his coffee break or his lunchtime to look for a braggart I need to find."

"A braggart?" Patti asked.

"Someone who's smart enough to pull off a sophisticated computer stunt and dumb enough to cross people who'd probably kill him if they knew what he'd done."

Patti turned her head toward McGill. "What kind of person would be foolish enough to do something like that?"

McGill looked at his wife, something of which he never tired. "Probably someone male who thinks he's the smartest guy in the building but needs to prove it to other guys by boasting."

"I think Cale might be the smartest person at my company," Patti said.

"In terms of technical gifts, I might agree. When it comes to understanding people and how to get them to work toward your goals, I don't think anyone in town comes close to you."

Patti scooted next to McGill, turned on her side, and laid an arm across her husband's chest. "I love it when you talk dirty to me."

McGill laughed. "On top of being persuasive, you also have beautiful penmanship."

Patti eased herself atop McGill. She could hear the pulse in his throat accelerate.

"Did you warn Cale not to go too far too fast with Abbie?" she asked.

"I told him I'd trained her in Dark Alley."

Patti chuckled and no further words were exchanged that night.

CHAPTER 4

Monday, February 4, 2019, Dumbarton Oaks
Washington, DC

The gleaming black Mercedes limo flying the flag of the Hashemite Kingdom of Jordan with Ambassador Fayez Mousa inside arrived at the McGill house early enough that the overnight Secret Service detachment felt it necessary to call the house to see if the former First Couple were of a mind to receive a visitor, foreign dignitary or not.

McGill had just finished getting dressed. Patti was still enjoying a long shower.

"Ambassador Mousa of Jordan would like to see you and Mrs. McGill, sir," the senior special agent on duty told McGill. "Should I let him in?"

"Yes, please. Ask him if he'd like to have coffee with us in the kitchen or if he'd care to speak with us in my office. Let him know I'll be down in five minutes. Mrs. McGill will be with us in ten."

"Yes, sir," the agent said.

McGill hadn't expected to have 24-hour protection for his and Patti's home this long after they'd left the White House. President Jean Morrissey had insisted, however, that it would continue as long as she was in office. McGill hadn't checked but he assumed that having a security detail would lower the cost of his homeowner's insurance, what with armed guards keeping burglars at bay and ready to call the fire department at a moment's notice.

He informed Patti about their visitor's arrival. She cut her shower short and said she'd be downstairs soon. McGill found Ambassador Mousa in his office, not the kitchen. That might've suggested a diplomatic sensibility about visiting a former president's residence without advance notice. Then again, the office might be seen as a more appropriate setting to deliver news of considerable gravity.

McGill shook hands with the senior Secret Service agent on duty who had kept the diplomat company. "Thanks, Jeremy. I assume we had a quiet night."

"All's well, sir."

"My regards to you and the detail," McGill said.

The senior special agent saluted and departed. McGill left the door to the room open.

He said, "The Secret Service offered you coffee or tea, Mr. Ambassador?"

"Yes, thank you, sir. I declined."

"Would you care to wait until my wife joins us before we start our discussion?"

"I would, please." Mousa glanced at his watch.

"She won't be long," McGill told him.

The diplomat managed a pro forma smile. "If I seem to be in a bit of a rush, I do not mean to be impolite, but my next stop is the White House."

McGill raised an eyebrow. "You came here first?"

"As I was directed by Chief of Staff Mindel. It was suggested, though, that I do not tarry."

Knowing Galia as he did, McGill understood. She'd defer having the ambassador speak to President Morrissey first in favor of making the man hurry with Patti, maybe give her and McGill a thumbnail version of events while Jean Morrissey got the full picture.

Oh, well, that was still Galia's job.

But McGill couldn't help but wonder what the White House chief of staff would do after Jean Morrissey left office. The voting public rarely — at least since FDR died — elected a president of the same political point of view for four terms in a row. Maybe Galia could get a job as a TV talking head.

Who knew, maybe even Ellie Booker would hire her.

Patti entered McGill's office while he was still pondering alternate realities. She shook Ambassador Mousa's hand and said good morning. McGill offered her his chair behind the desk. She shook her head. It was his office, after all.

McGill sat and Patti stood to his right.

Ambassador Mousa took an Apple laptop computer out of his attaché case.

He said, "Your security people did a check of this machine, but agreed not to review the video recording I've brought to show you and President Morrissey."

McGill asked, "You got the tattoo artist to talk?"

"I must ask you, please, to hold as confidential this information and some of the other details I'm about to share with you. I'm sure you'll understand which ones when you see them."

Both McGill and Patti nodded.

Mousa said, "We were about to start, shall we say, the more traditional methods of inquiry when Ms. Elspeth Kendry of your Secret Service offered to join us."

"She made it to Jordan that quickly?" McGill asked.

The ambassador shook his head. "She participated via Skype. The tattoo artist who killed his wife is named Samir. He expected pain to be our main tool of persuasion. He was startled to see a striking woman wearing Western garb on a computer screen confronting him."

Mousa elaborated, "He actually had the nerve to say, 'Torture me if you wish, but do not shame me in front of a female infidel.'"

Patti only smiled thinly, but McGill said, "I'll bet that didn't go over well with Elspeth."

"Not at all," Mousa said. "Speaking in British accented but

otherwise perfect Arabic, she told him to sit up straight in his chair. Like a mother addressing a misbehaving child."

"And he did, didn't he?" Patti said.

Mousa nodded. "I will show you now, and pause the video to translate for you."

He clicked on the recording of the interrogation.

"Your wife would have given her own life if you hadn't taken it from her, wouldn't she?" Elspeth asked.

Samir lowered his head and didn't answer.

"Look at me, you dog!" Elspeth ordered.

The man obeyed, both fear and hatred burned in his eyes, and tears ran down his face.

Continuing in a harsh tone, Elspeth said, "You knew she was strong; that was the problem you had with her. But did you ever really love her?"

"Yes, you demon, I did!"

"All right, I believe you," Elspeth said, easing her tone. "I know of your customs. Each party to a marriage must give consent. As pathetic as you are, your family must have searched far and wide to find a suitable bride: one you'd favor and one who would also be willing to accept you."

Samir glared at Elspeth with raw hatred. She'd nailed the situation.

Elspeth continued unabashed: "I'm told many marriages in Jordan are of the same blood. Your wife was most likely also your cousin in some measure."

Samir averted his eyes, possibly to hide his shame.

"Is that it?" Elspeth continued. "Oh, the poor woman."

For just a moment, Ambassador Mousa closed his eyes.

Looking up, Samir spat at the camera. He yelled and cursed at Elspeth's image.

A man's open hand entered the video frame and slapped Samir's face hard. The prisoner's rant ended and his tears began. He looked in the direction from which the blow had come and fear filled his newly bruised face.

Once more, Elspeth told Samir, "Look at me."

Perhaps fearing another blow, he did.

Elspeth told him, "You didn't kill your wife because you were afraid she'd reveal all your secrets. You killed her because you feared letting her see you betray your own cause."

Wounded by the truth, the flow of Samir's tears increased.

He hung his head and refused to look up at anyone.

An unmoved Elspeth spoke in English to someone offscreen: "He's ready to talk. He'll tell you everything you want to know. At worst, a few minor body blows will be all you'll need to prompt him. He's that weak."

The video ended, and Ambassador Mousa closed the lid of the laptop computer.

McGill asked the diplomat, "Was Elspeth right? Did he talk?"

"He did," the diplomat said. "Our interrogators feel confident they got everything he knew. Unfortunately, that was not as much as we all had hoped."

Patti said, "He was able to tell you his contacts in Jordan, but not other neighboring countries?"

Mousa responded, "He has a male cousin who lives in Lebanon and is in the same line of work. He also does the same type of tattoos. My government is considering the most productive way of approaching this fellow. We are reaching out to friends in the region. We hope the cousin will be able to provide further leads. I'm afraid, though, that from this point forward His Majesty's government will have to work solely with President Morrissey and the United States' intelligence agencies. We do, however, appreciate your assistance in these matters."

Both Patti and McGill said they understood.

They shook Ambassador Mousa's hand and saw him to his car.

Constance Parker's House — Rockville, Maryland

Franklin Parker and his daughter sat across the kitchen table from one another. Each had a cup of black coffee. A plate of wheat toast sat between them. Parker added strawberry jam to his slice; Connie took hers dry.

She watched as her father cleaned his Sig P226 semi-automatic handgun between bites of toast and sips of coffee. He'd offered to do the same for her Beretta. She'd told him she maintained her weapon at all times.

Franklin Parker had driven 565 miles from his home in South Carolina to his daughter's place in Maryland because he didn't want to take any chance of either losing his weapon to the TSA or being hassled about having an unloaded gun in his checked luggage. There shouldn't have been any problems if he followed all the rules, which he always did, but you never knew how people with badges might react to a black man in possession of a gun.

Actually, he did know. Things could get out of control in a hurry. Driving to Maryland, he not only made sure his gun was in the trunk and unloaded, it was also disassembled. Moreover, there wasn't a round of ammunition in the vehicle.

All that didn't mean he wouldn't be hassled if he was stopped by the wrong kind of cop, but it would make difficulties at least somewhat less likely. He also made sure he didn't exceed the speed limit. That meant the trip had been eight-and-a-half hours long, including bathroom and coffee breaks. Not too bad for a young or even early middle-aged person, but once you had passed 70 years old it was a long hike.

He knew something was wrong with Connie the minute he saw her. She'd been surprised by having him turn up on her doorstep, sure, but he'd seen more than that on her face. His little girl was scared. He'd seen such alarm in her eyes only a few times when she was growing up, but he remembered each instance as if they'd all occurred in the past week.

So he'd simply put his arms around her and said, "I am so happy to see you."

For her part, Connie didn't ask why her father had made the long drive. Starting that conversation in any fashion would lead to only one thing: the truth. She wasn't ready to share that news, not yet, and with any luck at all, never.

So when her father had announced he was sore and tired and would love nothing more than a warm bath and a good night's sleep, Connie had been only too happy to oblige. Her own sleep had been scarce and troubled since finding the two former cops from DC parked outside her house. After talking with the two of them, both in Rockville and Washington, she knew she was in trouble. The plan she'd been assured would work flawlessly had blown up in her face, and things weren't likely to get any better.

She hadn't slept more than 15 minutes at a time for almost two days now.

Crazy as the situation was, though, having her father under the same roof with her made her feel somewhat better, almost safe. Yes, he was an old man, but he'd kept himself in good shape, and his love for her was absolute. So last night she'd slept soundly if not peacefully.

When she woke up that morning, she even had something of an appetite.

Until she saw her father sitting at the breakfast table cleaning his handgun.

So, after sipping her coffee and finishing a piece of toast, she asked the inevitable question, "How much do you know, Daddy?"

He'd finished his chore by then and put his Sig P226 semi-auto off to one side.

"I know only what Mr. Michael Walker told me. He came to see me bright and early yesterday morning. He said my daughter had won hundreds of millions of dollars in the middle of last week. He asked me if I'd heard the news from you. I had to admit I hadn't."

Parker gave his daughter time to respond, and when she didn't, he continued.

"Mr. Walker told me there was a second lottery winner who'd yet to be publicly acknowledged. Then, he said, you offered to pay that other person a million dollars to drop his claim and go away. It was right about then I asked Mr. Walker to leave my house."

"Did he?" Connie asked.

"Yes, and he was quite polite about it. I spent the better part of an hour trying to think of a good reason why you'd keep your news secret from me and why you'd try to buy off someone else who also got lucky. I couldn't think of a single one. So I had to admit to myself that if there wasn't a good reason, there had to be a bad one. That hurt me in my heart, but I still felt I had to come up here and hear you out. Try to decide what it is a good father should do."

Connie was about to speak when Parker held up a hand.

"Please don't tell me to go back home. It still hurts me how I lost your mother. There's no way in the world I'm going to lose you, too. Not while I'm still drawing a breath."

Connie Parker began to cry. She didn't dab her face with a napkin. She simply sat in her place at the table and let the tears stream down her cheeks and fall where they may. Parker couldn't abide that for more than a heartbeat. He got up, wedged the Sig P226 into the waistband at the back of his pants and helped his daughter to her feet.

He led her into the living room and sat her on the sofa. He went to the windows looking out on the front yard. He closed the drapes Connie had opened when she'd come down for breakfast. He didn't see anyone, but he still checked that every door to the outside world was locked. Old Baltimore instincts for safety had come back reflexively. He never bothered about locking his doors in Beaufort. His neighbor, Billy, had good instincts about looking for anyone who didn't belong in the neighborhood. Also, Parker kept his shotgun next to his bed.

You got shot once in an armed robbery, as he had, that could incline you to the idea of being ready to shoot first.

He walked back to his daughter and asked, "Where do you keep your ammunition, child? Still down in the basement?"

She nodded.

Parker went downstairs and loaded two magazines, one he put in his weapon, the other he dropped into a shirt pocket. Then he returned to the living room, sat next to his daughter, and said,

"Talk to me."

"I came up with a big idea, Daddy."

"I'm not surprised. Can you share some details with me?"

Connie said, "I've developed a new drug. I thought I was working on a sedative, but it turned out to be more than that."

Parker sat back and smiled, his pharmacological interest piqued. "A non-habit-forming sedative, I hope."

"Yes, but then there's the unexpected part."

"You're speaking speculatively, I assume, going by your lab work. You haven't yet reached the point of clinical trials."

"No *official* trials," Connie said.

Worry clouded Parker's face. He said, "You've experimented on yourself?"

Connie nodded. "Myself and a few friends, all of whom had the risks explained to them."

Parker asked, "These are people in the health sciences field, individuals who understood what you told them and might even have insights you lack?"

"Two of them are colleagues, one is a lawyer, and another is in investment banking. I was just looking to come up with something that would let high-stress professionals get a good night's sleep without any of the downsides of the present generation meds."

Parker winced at his daughter's unorthodox and possibly illegal approach to a clinical trial and said, "You've recorded the results of your ad-hoc approach?"

"I have."

"And?" her father asked.

"My friends, the ones who've taken the drug, all of them want more. Like right now and as much as they can get."

Parker both shook his head and laughed. "And you think those aren't signs of addiction?"

"Daddy, I've been off the drug for a month now. So have my test subjects. None of us has suffered any withdrawal symptoms. It's just that we all like to feel —"

"Great after a good night's sleep?"

"There's more to it than that," Connie said, "there are unintended beneficial qualities. You not only sleep well, you wake up with this amazing sense of serenity. You see all of your obligations and anxieties with this amazing sense of proportion. You know exactly how to go about your life in the most effective way possible. I'm calling the drug *Clarity*."

Parker sat back and asked the obvious question: "If this pharmaceutical works all those wonders, how come you're in such a fix right now?"

Connie summoned a sad smile. "Like I said, Daddy, I haven't taken any Clarity for a month. Insights don't last unless they're reinforced. More than that, it's going to take some really serious money to get my drug both developed the right way and to preserve my position as the major stakeholder."

Parker understood: You took your bright idea to a Big Pharma company, your drug became their drug lickety-split. He also implicitly understood that the few million dollars he might have given his daughter wouldn't be nearly enough to fund her new enterprise.

He also recalled that one of Connie's test subjects was in investment banking.

"Your banking friend, he was the one who hooked you up with this lottery scam?"

Connie shook her head. "It was the lawyer. He told me he knows someone who's a math whiz. He'd figured out a way to increase his chances for a big payoff. I did some research and I found out there were such people. One woman in Texas who has a Ph.D. in statistics has won big payoffs *four* times."

Parker thought about that. "So why didn't this math genius just take all the money for himself?"

"Because he thought he might be banned from playing if he won big jackpots more than a few times. Or the lottery people might come up with a counter-measure even he couldn't beat. Using front people, giving them a cut, he could win big jackpots indefinitely."

"So how much money were you offered?" Parker asked.

"Ten million dollars. That's still not enough to get Clarity to the point of government approval and sales to the public, but it is enough to get investor interest on terms favorable to me."

Parker sighed. There was a certain, if risky, logic to what his daughter had done. "Then this other fellow in Washington came along with the same winning numbers."

"Yes. I was very disappointed. I tried to buy him off, as Mr. Walker told you."

"Must've been a real long-shot, two winning tickets sold on the same date."

"That area of study is outside my field," Connie said.

"Yeah, mine, too," Parker said. "The other thing I don't understand is why neither the lottery people nor anyone else identified this fellow Samuel J. MacCray as the other winner."

Connie was about to say she didn't know the reason for that either.

Only she was interrupted by someone pounding on the front door of her house.

And yelling, "Constance Parker, open this door right now!"

McGill Investigations International — Washington, DC

McGill sat in his office that morning with Sweetie. He'd left instructions with Esme that there were to be no interruptions except for family emergencies or notice that the building was on fire.

"How about an armed attack by hostile forces?" Esme had asked.

Most times, McGill would have considered that a joke, but after the recent shooting outside his enterprise's front door, he had to take the inquiry seriously.

"Yeah, that, too, but nothing else," he replied.

Nonetheless, while he was in the midst of sharing with Sweetie the news he'd heard from Putnam Shady that Ellie Booker had killed a woman she suspected of being a terrorist and the killer of Representative Philip Brock and was going to confess to it publicly, his intercom buzzed.

McGill looked at the gizmo like he couldn't believe what he'd just heard.

Sweetie responded for him. "What's up, Esme?"

"Cale Tucker is on the line. He says this is the only time he'll have to speak with Mr. McGill before this evening, and he's pretty sure Mr. McGill would like to hear what he has to say. So I took the chance, despite knowing I might get chewed out."

"Is Esme going to get scolded, Jim?"

McGill shook his head. He said, "Good judgment call, Esme. Thank you. Please put Cale through."

"Yes, sir. You're welcome." She made the connection.

"What's the word, Cale? You have something from the Black Hole?"

That query produced a questioning look from Sweetie. McGill held up a hand. He'd explain later.

Cale said, "I do. It wasn't a boast; it was a complaint and a warning to others."

"But we are talking about some computer whiz who put in a fix on the lottery, right?"

"Exactly. This hacker, who I feel sure is a guy, comes right out and says that he fixed the lottery the way he was asked to do. When it came time for him to be paid, though, he said he got only half of what he'd been promised. He was told to take it or leave it."

McGill said, "So he took the half-payment and griped to an audience of other black-hat hackers who might be the next to be hired by the guys who stiffed him."

"Right," Cale said.

Sweetie announced herself and asked, "Cale, how do you know the hacker was male?"

After a short pause, he replied, "I can tell you this only because an academic paper on the subject is about to be published to the general public soon. There have been studies done on the relationships between profanity, syntax and testosterone levels."

McGill laughed. "You mean guys curse more?"

"It goes beyond the frequency of vulgarities. In that regard, women have been rapidly catching up to men in recent years. It has more to do with sentence structure, where obscenities are placed for emphasis. A linguistics Ph.D. did the study, and the gender differences are clear. We're dealing with a guy here, and when he wasn't paid in full, he inserted a second winner into the lottery game. Just the thing to give the welshers a headache."

McGill said. "Do you think you can pin down who this guy is, Cale?"

After a brief silence, he said, "Yeah, probably, but I've got this day job now, about to start in three minutes, and I promised the boss I'd give her my undivided attention."

McGill said, "I gave her the same promise. I appreciate your calling before you hit business hours. Let me know what I can do for you."

"I was thinking I might like some Dark Alley lessons," he said.

"Sure, why not?" McGill said.

"Not from you, sir. I thought Abbie might be my instructor. Bye."

The damn kid was gone before McGill could respond.

Sweetie laughed. "You've got your hands full with that guy, Jim."

"Don't I know it? Oh, well, I have great faith in Abbie's good judgment." McGill crossed himself for extra reassurance.

"Meanwhile, what did you mean about Ellie Booker killing someone?" Sweetie asked. "I didn't ask Putnam because I wasn't sure I wanted to know."

McGill told her the story he'd heard from Putnam, after he'd presented Sweetie's husband a check for one thousand dollars to act as his lawyer. He outlined the story of Ellie saving the life of Delta Force Sergeant Desmond Jones, and how she took the life of Dr. Hasna Kalil.

Sweetie absorbed all that while maintaining a stoic appearance.

McGill gave her time to sift through the implications of Putnam acting as Ellie's lawyer and what the consequences might be not only for her husband but also for Maxi and herself. It was possible the whole family might be targeted if the people hoping to avenge Dr. Kalil's death decided to cast a wide net of retaliation.

There was also nothing to say another attack on anyone entering or leaving the building in which they sat was out of the question. Sweetie was about to share that thought when McGill read her mind and nodded.

"I know," he said. "Our business has already been connected to Ellie Booker. She was attacked right out front. Neither she nor we have to acknowledge our connection. It's already a matter of public record."

Sweetie sighed and shook her head. "Why would she want to go public with this?"

McGill coughed up a humorless laugh. "She's now the head of a media empire. Having the boss assert that she acted in self-defense to kill a terrorist-doctor who decapitated a U.S. congressman is what you might call a big story."

Sweetie put a hand over her eyes as if she felt a headache coming on.

"I know," McGill said. "It's a lot to think about. If it's any consolation, Putnam also told me he's already looking to find a criminal defense lawyer for Ellie. That might deflect hostile interest away from us. Events have proved twice that attacking this building is no easy task. We know how to defend ourselves against the bad guys."

Sweetie said, "Yeah, but do we want to keep on doing it? And what criminal defense lawyer in his right mind would take on Ellie Booker as a client?"

McGill replied, "Margaret, there are lawyers who'd defend the Roman soldiers who nailed Christ to his cross. As for me, I'm going to New York and have a chat with Ms. Booker."

"And I get to hold down the fort?" Sweetie asked.

McGill nodded.

Sweetie sighed and accepted the task. She went to her office. Maybe to make sure Maxi was safe in her schoolroom. Possibly to urge Putnam to hurry up with finding Ellie a new lawyer.

McGill picked up his phone and called Patti.

She said, "It's too early for us to plan a dinner date. So what is it you have in mind, James J. McGill? If it's borrowing Cale again today, the answer is no."

"He wants Abbie to teach him Dark Alley," McGill said.

Patti laughed. "Having a young woman kick your heinie is a novel approach to romance."

"I hadn't thought of it that way," McGill said. "You've made me feel better already."

"Just one of my many talents. So what favor would you like this time, Jim?"

"May I borrow your company plane? You know, if it's freshly washed, gassed up, and ready to fly."

"You may, provided, of course, that you tell me where you want to go."

"I'm going to Manhattan to see Ellie Booker. Not that I expect to succeed, but I want to ask her to kill a big story that might only endanger a lot of people needlessly."

"She is the head of WorldWide News now," Patti reminded him.

"I'm well aware."

"What you might not have considered is that the acquisition of power can have profound effects on a woman."

"Said the woman who knows that better than anyone except Elizabeth I, Catherine the Great, and Cleopatra," McGill said.

Patti laughed once more. "None of those ladies had a nuclear arsenal at her disposal."

"A very good point, and the subtext I'm missing here is?"

"Jim, if you want to get anywhere with Ellie Booker, you'd better come up with a damn good *business* reason to change her mind."

"Oh," McGill said.

Constance Parker's House — Rockville, Maryland

Franklin Parker all but shoved his daughter, Connie, into the stairwell to the basement. "Stay there. Call the police. Tell them it's a life-and-death emergency."

"But, Daddy, my gun's up in my bedroom."

The pounding on the front door resumed. So did the shouting.

"Open the damn door. I'm getting mighty angry out here."

Connie was about to speak when Parker held up a hand to silence her. He called out, "Who the hell are you? You better tell me before I start shooting."

In a different tone entirely, the door-banger called out, "Oh, shit no. Don't do that. I'm the police."

Parker wasn't about to take that as gospel. He said, "Hold your badge out in front of the window to your left."

After a moment of silence, the man outside called out. "I'm gonna show you my badge. You shoot my hand, I promise I'll kill you."

Parker replied, "You keep on being nasty, I'll shoot through the door right now."

The man outside said, "Shit, shit, shit! Okay, let's dial it back. No more threats from either of us. I'll just show you my badge."

Parker gestured to Connie to step out of the stairway. She did just as a hand holding a shiny object appeared on the outside of the living room window adjacent to the front door. Parker's vision wasn't bad, but he couldn't read what appeared to be lettering on the object.

Connie had the eyesight to accomplish the task. She whispered, "Daddy, it says Detective Sergeant, Maryland State Police."

"You're State Police?" Parker yelled.

"Yes, damnit!"

"Why didn't you just say so right off?"

After a pause, the man replied in a sullen tone, "Because I was angry … and the last time I worked the street I was on the fugitive apprehension squad. We just kicked in doors and made arrests."

"So you're here to make an arrest?" Connie yelled.

"No, ma'am. I'm here to protect you."

Parker said, "Who asked you to do that?"

"The goddamn mayor of Washington, DC and her friend the goddamn governor of Maryland."

"What's your name?" Connie asked.

"Detective Sergeant Dalton Rivers."

"Why're you in such a bad mood?" Parker asked.

"I worked all night, and I got this assignment right before I was going home."

Opening her front door, Connie asked, "Would you like some coffee and a sweet roll?"

Sounding less than hostile for the first time, Rivers said, "Yes, ma'am. I'd appreciate that."

Traveling to WorldWide News Headquarters
Midtown Manhattan

As McGill boarded the Committed Capital Gulfstream G6, he wondered if he'd ever again travel anywhere all by himself. That'd have to be a car trip, of course. Even if he flew commercial, he'd have a hundred-plus other passengers and the flight crew with him. He supposed he could take flying lessons and get a little airplane of his own in which he could make short hops hither and thither. Only he didn't trust aircraft that used propellers to get airborne.

Besides all that, he usually found good reasons to bring companions along when he went out into the world. On this trip, there was no question he'd bring Leo. If there was anyone who could bob and weave through big city traffic like he was navigating a slalom course, it was Leo. McGill had also invited Welborn Yates and MPD Detective Aidan Behan to accompany him.

His motive in doing so was to gang up on Ellie Booker psychologically. Welborn had directly saved Ellie's life by knocking her down before a hail of bullets could do the same, only fatally.

Detective Behan had indirectly saved Ellie's life by keeping watch on her boat and alerting everyone to the possibility of the *Dangerous Dame* being sabotaged, leading to the discovery of a bomb attached to the yacht's hull.

Welborn had been free to make his own choice to accompany McGill.

Detective Behan had been put on detached duty by Mayor Rockelle Bullard.

The two men who'd come to Ellie's aid hit it off immediately, and Behan didn't even look askance when Welborn told him he was going to become a big-shot with the FBI. Leo sat next to McGill on the jet and read a copy of *Road & Track* while humming *Folsom Prison Blues.*

McGill looked out a window enjoying the shades of blue in a crystal clear sky while thinking, as he often did, that he had to be the luckiest former Chicago cop ever. More so than even Dennis Farina.

As if he needed further proof of that, a gleaming new Mercedes-Benz S Class sedan was waiting for them. Behan sat up front with Leo. Welborn sat in back with McGill. The 11:00 a.m. traffic wasn't half-bad for Manhattan. For most other places, it was a stock-car race that allowed all sorts of trucks into the competition.

Leo now changed his humming tune to *De Camptown Races.*

Behan joined in by providing the "doo-dahs" as called for.

Leo seemed to cruise where other vehicles crawled. Not once did a red light interrupt their progress. The only times they stopped were when emergency vehicles claimed the exclusive right of way, a not infrequent occurrence. Even then, they were always the first back in motion.

Leo gave McGill a heads-up: "Five minutes out, boss."

McGill turned up the volume on the phone so the others could listen in and called Ellie Booker's private line. She'd given him the number when she'd come to ask for his help. He wondered if Cale Tucker could have found it for him if he'd needed that. Yes, he decided, the young man could. That was when a surprising thought popped into McGill's head: Was there any chance Cale might become his first son-in-law?

Possibly. Which led him to think that Caitie, over in Paris, would simply cohabitate with her first serious boyfriend. Before he could get too deeply into that disturbing idea, the call he'd made to Ellie Booker went through.

She answered by saying, "Putnam Shady ratted me out, told you what I intend to do, didn't he?"

"He did," McGill said, not wanting to argue a secondary point.

"And you're here in town, aren't you?"

"Quite close by, in fact. Please call down to your building's parking structure and have them provide a space for us."

"Us?"

"My driver Leo and me."

McGill didn't want to give away the presence of either Welborn or Behan.

"And what if I said I was busy?" Ellie asked.

"Is that what I said when you came to me unannounced? Is that what you'd want me to say to you from now on?" McGill asked.

He was ready to play hardball if necessary.

Sounding as if she were speaking through a locked jaw, Ellie said, "Okay, you've got your parking slot. How much time will you need?"

"I don't know. Depends on how the conversation goes."

"I'm famous for being stubborn, you know."

McGill replied, "And I'm renowned for being persistent."

"I can hardly wait." Ellie broke the connection.

Leo and Behan remained mum.

Welborn said, "That went well."

McGill told them all, "See if any of you can think of a good business reason why Ellie Booker shouldn't paint a bull's-eye on herself."

Welborn had a reply for that, too. "Use the reason Kira gave me why she'd never look for another husband: It'd take too long to find an adequate replacement."

"Good one," Behan said with a smile.

McGill didn't say so just then, but he, too, thought that idea had merit.

Constance Parker's House — Rockville, Maryland

Meeker and Beemer arrived at Constance Parker's house ten minutes after Detective Sergeant Rivers did. They used a single ring of the doorbell to announce their arrival rather than beat furiously on the door. Franklin Parker still looked through the peephole before admitting them.

Remembering that Beemer had said he'd been an MPD cop, Parker asked him, "Your mayor sent you and your friend, too?"

Beemer nodded. "May we come in?"

Acting on his own initiative, Parker said, "It'd be rude to leave you standing outside."

He let them in and closed the door. Beemer introduced Meeker. Neither of the two private investigators nor Rivers looked happy to see each other. Even so, the glummest person in the house was Connie Parker.

She asked Meeker and Beemer, "Are there any more of you coming?"

Meeker shook his head. "Not that I've heard."

"The mayor used to be our captain on the MPD," Beemer said.

Meeker continued, "She had the idea that you're stuck in the middle of a very bad and undoubtedly criminal situation that's about to fall apart."

Beemer added, "Mainly because it's already crumbling down in DC."

Connie's brow knitted with apprehension. "What do you mean?"

In their usual two-part dialogue, Meeker and Beemer told her of Ed Kingsley winning $2 million in the lottery, his subsequent attempt to rob a DC convenience store of its video files, and the demise of his large partner in attempted crime. Questions about the narrative came from two directions.

Parker asked, “This big fella, he had the storekeeper in a bad way?”

The situation reminded him of when he'd been in mortal jeopardy in his own shop.

Rivers wanted to know, “One of you two put the guy down?”

Meeker answered the first question: “The guy looked strong enough to snap the lady's neck with just one little squeeze.”

Beemer told Rivers, “Detective Aidan Behan of the MPD shot the assailant, one round straight to the brainpan.”

The Maryland cop nodded in approval. “Glad it wasn't one of you two.”

“So are we,” Meeker said.

“Either doing the shooting or getting shot,” Beemer added.

Meeker continued, “But the situation being what it was, the mayor thought Ms. Parker might be the next in line for misfortune.”

“So she called this fine state's governor, worked out a mutual assistance agreement, and here we are,” Beemer said.

“Carrying our weapons with official permission,” Meeker added.

Rivers didn't like that one bit, but he knew better than to start a fight he couldn't win.

Didn't want to get shot in his brainpan either, if that was the way even retired Washington cops did business.

Beemer stepped close, but not too close, to Connie. “So, Miz Parker, would you like to tell us what's going on with all this lottery business? You know, before someone asks you to steal a convenience store's camera, too.”

“Which is now in police custody anyway,” Meeker said. He moved to his partner's side and played the bad cop. “So maybe whoever's behind this whole thing just decides it's too risky to let you stay alive.”

Detective Sergeant Rivers joined them. “Much as I hate agreeing with these two, ma'am, I can't argue with them on this.”

Franklin Parker made it unanimous among the men in the room. "This has all gone too far, Constance. I don't want anyone else to die, especially you. So you tell them or I will."

That made Meeker, Beemer, and Rivers turn their heads to look at him.

But only until Connie, tears now streaming down her cheeks, said, "All right, Daddy. I will."

Ellie Booker's Office — Midtown Manhattan

Ellie said, "Hell, if I'd known we were going to have a party, I'd have hired a band."

The office she'd inherited from Hugh Collier was large enough for a tennis court. A bank of windows provided a panoramic view of Lower Manhattan. McGill thought he could just make out the Statue of Liberty in the distance, but maybe he was just imagining that. What was plain, in the first few hours since she'd claimed the space as her own, Ellie Booker had cleared it of all her predecessor's furnishings.

The walls were bare except for shadowy outlines of the paintings, photos, and professional awards that Hugh Collier had hung there. Indentations of furnishings, a huge desk, a conference table, accompanying chairs, facing sofas, and a few massive flower pots left the carpet looking old and tired.

In place of all the former space fillers, Ellie had brought in a simple four-legged maple table which gave the impression that anything beyond right angles was frivolous. The chair behind it, in which Ellie sat, also lacked the grandeur that most big-time CEOs would require.

McGill thought that last point was a good move.

No boss should ever sit on a throne that made him or her look small.

An Apple MacBook computer and a cell phone were the only business tools visible.

A single folding chair had been brought in for a visitor.

Or possibly a suspect, McGill thought. Ellie might have a high-intensity lamp on order. Something she could shine into the eyes of whomever she wanted to give the third degree.

"Love what you've done with the place," McGill said.

"Yeah, but getting back to my point, you said you were here with Leo."

McGill nodded. "He stayed with our rental car. He likes to make sure nobody messes with any vehicle he drives."

Ellie wasn't buying any distractions. She told McGill, "You didn't tell me that General Yates, Detective Behan, and former Special Agent Ky were with you."

McGill took the only seat available. His companions stood behind him.

"Deke met us in the lobby. He got to New York before we did and has done a bit of investigating. I asked Welborn and Aidan to come along for moral support. I thought you'd be glad to see them."

"Moral support, huh? Emotional leverage is more like it," Ellie said.

"We'll see if that's even possible," McGill said.

"However you put it, Putnam Shady told you about the story I plan to break, and you want me to shit-can it."

"Basically, yeah."

"Because you care so much about me, right?"

"Well, you did come to see me about finding out if you were in trouble. I thought helping with that was a worthwhile use of my time."

Ellie said, "I was going to pay you for that once we hired Putnam Shady. I can make an electronic funds transfer right now. Just give me an amount and an account number."

McGill leaned forward. "Don't you even want to know what I've found out about the people who have it in for you?"

Now, they were talking about trading information, Ellie's preferred currency.

She also realized McGill was trying to scare her. Make her do the sensible thing. Save her own sweet backside. As if reading her mind, McGill played his next card.

"Being tough is a good thing," he said. "Playing General Custer at the Little Big Horn, not so much."

Picking a nit to buy time, Ellie said, "Custer was a brevet general during the Civil War. By the time he fought the Lakota Sioux, he was back to lieutenant colonel."

McGill smiled. "See, you do appreciate the value of information. Whatever his rank, you think Custer would have gone through with his plan if he'd had advance warning of what was waiting for him?"

Ellie frowned. "The man was a barbarian. He got exactly what he deserved."

"You feel the same way about yourself?"

"No."

"So, let me share something that might be helpful. Keep you from charging up the wrong hill."

Ellie gritted her teeth and nodded.

McGill nodded to Deke. He took an iPad out of a coat pocket, stepped around to Ellie's side of the desk and brought up an image of a roundel tattoo. He said, "This is the kind of tattoo worn by each of the men who tried to shoot you in Washington. It's based on the flag of Jordan. But it's not just a terrorist symbol."

"What is it then?" Ellie asked.

"It's a symbol that originated, as far as we've learned, with the Royal Jordanian Air Force. It's a sign of the Jordanian kingdom defending itself and striking out against its enemies. Variations of this tattoo are now used by the military forces of other countries. It means the whole nation, not just one soldier, sailor, or airman is coming after you."

Ellie understood the permutation that came next. "Or the terrorists of that country."

McGill nodded. "Yeah."

Deke resumed from there. "Federal agents and NYPD officers

of the Joint Terrorist Task Force have done discreet observations of persons wearing such tattoos among the various diplomatic personnel based in Manhattan. The current count as of …" Deke looked at the time display of his iPad, "thirty-eight minutes ago was 114. Following up on the first 30 persons we spotted wearing these tattoos, 11 have been graded as needing further investigation as potential terrorist actors or enablers.

"There are 117 diplomatic missions in New York City. There are 195 members and observer states at the United Nations. In total, we're talking about several thousand people, many of whom travel home and back here at irregular intervals. Then, of course, there are rotations of foreign diplomats from another country to the United States.

"Many of the countries in the UN are not friends of the U.S.A. So the American intelligence community has to keep track of many thousands of individuals who freely come and go at irregular intervals. All of this is common knowledge, no big news story at all."

McGill picked up the thread. "Now, in addition to all the other things our national security people have to watch for, they also have to be on the lookout for people with little flag tattoos on their right hands. Then they have to determine which ones are homeland patriots and which are the terrorists. It's a good bet, though, that at a minimum there are dozens of bad guys here, and we've already seen three of them go after you."

Ellie said, "So you're telling me there are plenty more awaiting their chance?"

"Maybe," McGill said. "Bad guys, the ones who aren't totally nuts, have to do a cost-benefit analysis like anyone else. My take is going after you has already cost them three of their front-line men. If you keep a low profile, maybe they'll think you're not worth the trouble of losing any more of their people."

Ellie shook her head. "Drive-by shooters aren't rational people. Neither are bombers. You never hear of anyone in those lines of work being given retirement dinners."

McGill had to agree. "No, you don't. Still, you don't have to energize them. You don't want to put yourself at the top of their to-do lists."

Behan spoke up for the first time, using a soft brogue and telling Ellie, "You can't imagine what a pity it would be seeing someone whose life you saved get killed anyway."

Welborn added, "I came up with a glib reason why you shouldn't do anything foolish, but the truth is I'm just being selfish. Your death would wound me. I've been through that kind of pain before. I don't want to go through it again."

Ellie looked at both Behan and Welborn.

"Would you do it again?" she asked. "Try to save me. I mean, it's not like either of you is hot for my bod or longing for my undying affection."

Behan raised a hand. "I might have been."

"Conditional tense?" Ellie asked.

"Well, I thought a cop and a reporter might make an interesting couple. Almost sounds like a high concept for a Netflix show. But I can't see myself with a media mogul."

That drew a laugh from the men in the room. Well, Deke smiled anyway.

Ellie sighed and told Behan, "You and I should have a drink in any case."

"Getting back to the point," McGill said. "I've done the job you hired me to do: tell you who's after you and the degree of danger I think you face: foreign terrorists and imminent peril."

Suspicion in her voice, Ellie said, "That's it? You're not going to try to push any harder."

McGill said, "Well, sitting here discussing the matter and listening to the other guys speak, I did come up with an idea that might let you live a little longer."

"Just a little, huh?" Ellie asked.

"You do make things difficult, Ellie," McGill replied. "At the very least, however, there is a story in it for you."

"Tell me," Ellie said.

McGill said, "Well, the first thing you do is hire Celsus Crogher."

Constance Parker's House — Rockville, Maryland

Before Connie sat down to tell her story to Meeker, Beemer, and Detective Sergeant Dalton Rivers, the Maryland State Policeman put in a call to Rockville headquarters. He requested and received six state cops in three patrol cars to guard Connie's house, front, back, and in a four-block orbit. It had been Franklin Parker's idea that the police should establish a security perimeter.

None of the cops on hand in the house, active duty or retired, chose to argue with the suggestion. Once everybody felt well-protected, Rivers said to Connie, "Okay, Ms. Parker, let's hear what you have to say."

She gave them the same story she'd told her father: She'd developed a new wonder drug, one that could alleviate both anxiety and depression while also providing intellectual and emotional direction that would best serve to insure a happy life.

That notion made Rivers grin. "All that in one little pill? I believe I'd stock my whole medicine cabinet with it."

"I'd buy stock in the company," Meeker said, "but it does sound TGTBT."

"What's that?" Connie asked.

Beemer translated, "Too good to be true."

Pushing aside the cop cynicism, Connie turned to look at her father. "Is that the way you feel, too, Daddy?"

He said, "I would never doubt your scholarship, Constance, nor your work ethic, but think of how you might feel if someone else had done your work and told you what it could do."

"You have a point, Daddy. I'll be right back, if you gentlemen will excuse me for a minute."

"You don't intend to leave your house?" Rivers asked.

Connie shook her head. "Just going down to my basement lair

where all us mad scientists do our best work."

She did exactly that and returned within 90 seconds, holding a small brown glass bottle.

Connie told the others, "It should have occurred to me shortly after my father arrived last night that I had emotional help nearby. For that matter, I might have availed myself of it before I went to Washington to see Mr. Meeker and Mr. Walker."

She uncapped the bottle and poured five small blue tablets out of the bottle. She held out her hand displaying them to the others.

"You going to take all those?" Meeker asked.

Connie put the bottle down on a living room end table and shook her head.

"One will do the trick. There's one each for you four gentleman, if you're in the mood to see whether I'm playing some sort of game here. And one for me."

The four men looked at one another with varying degrees of reluctance clear on their faces.

Then Parker said, "It will be my pleasure."

He started to extend a hand and then withdrew it. He looked at Meeker, Beemer, and Rivers. "Would one of you gentlemen be so kind as to make a selection for me? You know, to show you I haven't been coached as to which pill to select."

The other three men looked at each other, and then Meeker stepped forward.

He looked at Connie and said, "How about I pick one for both you and your father? And you take yours first."

She nodded. "That's fine." She extended her hand to him.

To guarantee a random selection, he put his left hand over his eyes, and moving his right hand slowly he found Connie's extended arm and slowly worked his way to her palm. He found the tablets with his fingertips and picked out two from opposite sides of the grouping.

Meeker opened his eyes and gave one tablet each to Parker and Connie.

Father and daughter looked at each other, love and trust clear in their eyes, and popped the tablets into their mouths and swallowed.

"You don't need a drink of something to wash the pills down?" Meeker asked.

Parker shook his head.

Connie said, "I wouldn't recommend anything but clean water. No tests have been done with anything else, but instinctively I'd recommend against alcohol."

"So are you feeling anything yet?" Beemer asked.

"It takes just a minute or so to metabolize," Connie told him.

"And then you feel better?" Detective Sergeant Rivers asked.

Connie told him, "You feel peaceful, completely at ease. Like a good massage or a warm bath might make you feel. Only it's even more complete than that, and as you relax, any mental fuzziness you have about personal problems disappears. You can see and understand your life much more clearly."

Meeker, Beemer, and Rivers all looked at one another.

Beemer stepped forward and said, "I'll try one."

He took a tablet from Connie's hand and popped it.

Rivers went next.

Meeker said, "You don't mind, Big Mike, I'll be the designated driver."

Ellie Booker's Office — Midtown Manhattan

"So rather than spike my story and do an impression of Howard Hughes, living like a hermit, I should go forward with the story and expose myself to all these foreign killers you claim are here in town. Do I have that right?" Ellie Booker asked McGill and the others.

McGill replied, "Well, as I mentioned, the first thing you do is hire Celsus Crogher and his executive protection company. Thanks in no small part to myself, Celsus knows how to deal with difficult clients, people who refuse to follow all the usual protocols."

Deke Ky rolled his eyes, a silent comment Ellie caught.

That made Ellie smile and tell McGill. "You and I are more alike than either of us would ever admit."

McGill said, "You write better, but I'm more charming."

That got a laugh from everyone in the room, even Ellie.

"I'll give you that, on both counts," she conceded. "So other than hiring a bodyguard and his men, all of whom I will undoubtedly piss off, what do I do next? I'm assuming now that you and your friends will be watching from the sidelines."

Welborn and Deke nodded, each having his own reasons.

Aidan Behan was clearly still mulling things over.

"You should bow out, too," Ellie told him. "I'm not worth the trouble."

Behan said, "I'll be the judge of that if you please. In any case, I'll still want that drink you mentioned. It might become a story I tell the children of my future wife, whoever she might be."

That scenario made Ellie frown.

Before things could go too far off the track, McGill added, "I'll likely also be an observer, someone to help coach Celsus Crogher on what he might expect from said difficult client."

The look Ellie directed at him was skeptical. "Why don't I ever see you as someone content to sit on the sidelines and kibitz?"

McGill smiled. "I might be preparing for the time when I become a gray eminence."

"Yeah, right," Ellie said.

"In any case," McGill said, "the crux of the plan is to identify and enlist the help of the good guys with the roundel tattoos and get them to point out the bad guys infringing on their idea and design. I have to think the honorable fellows would be resentful."

Every head in the room nodded.

But Ellie asked, "How are you going to identify the good guys and get their cooperation?"

McGill said, "I've been talking with the Kingdom of Jordan's ambassador to the United States. He was dismayed, to put it lightly, that his country's national emblem is being disgraced by murderous fanatics. The last time we spoke, he informed me that in the future he'd be able to speak of the matter only with U.S. national security agencies."

McGill turned to look at Welborn. "Fortunately, we have someone in the room who will soon qualify for that description."

Welborn said, "I'll speak with Director Benjamin as soon as we leave here."

Ellie asked him, "You're FBI?"

"Soon," he said.

Behan added, "Don't hold that against him. He's a good guy."

"Yeah," Ellie conceded. "Someone saves your life, you have to cut him some slack."

McGill added, "Of course, if there's any bureaucratic delay, I'll speak with my better half. President Morrissey still takes her calls. My thinking is to find trustworthy people, ideally someone of high military rank, in each of the countries whose armed forces personnel use the tattoo, and have him or her start the hunt for the bad guys who are infringing on their copyright, so to speak."

"And there's the first part of the story right there," Ellie said. "WorldWide News covers an attempt to corrupt a symbol that had been conceived as a noble gesture. The heroes of the region have been ripped off by the killers."

McGill told Welborn, "The Bureau should advise the State Department to watch for members of foreign diplomatic delegations who leave the country in a hurry without any credible explanation. Those people will bear further scrutiny."

"Absolutely," Welborn agreed.

"I like what I've heard so far," Ellie said, "but then what?"

McGill said, "Then we do A-B tests on the threat levels directed at you."

Ellie understood. "I make public appearances, first after the story about the tattoos runs and then after the story of what I did in Syria."

"Right," McGill said. "Of course, Test B will depend on you surviving Test A."

"Isn't that what Celsus Crogher and his people are for?" she asked.

McGill nodded. “Yes, they are, and they’re the closest thing you’ll find to a presidential security detail, but as Celsus has told me *ad infinitum*, no defensive plan is ever perfect. So if you don’t have a guardian angel, you’d better hope one happens to be passing by in a moment of need.”

Ellie produced a joyless laugh. “With me, the only angel nearby would be one of the fallen kind.”

McGill didn’t want to argue the possibility of personal redemption at that moment.

Instead, he asked, “Why don’t you tell us what happened over there in Syria, at least to the extent you plan to reveal on WWN?”

Ellie did. She provided the kind of specific detail that comes from a memory that would never fade. She gave a clear outline of going to Syria allegedly to report on the fighting there. In truth, she’d gone to the war zone to find Dr. Hasna Kalil. Ellie felt certain the doctor had killed Representative Philip Brock.

She’d done so to avenge the murder of her brother Bahir Ben Kalil. Brock and Ben Kalil had been fast friends. They spent most of their free hours together, Ellie’s investigation had revealed. Brock would have been indicted and imprisoned for the attempted assassination of President Patricia Grant, if he hadn’t fled to South America.

There was no tangible proof that Ben Kalil was part of Brock’s murder plan, but with all the time the two men spent together, it seemed unlikely he would have been ignorant of it. Add in the fact that Ben Kalil’s murder occurred just before Brock left the country and it surely seemed Brock was eliminating a witness who could incriminate him.

Having seen a photo of Brock’s decapitated head, how its severing had been done with seeming surgical precision, Ellie had come to feel sure the executioner wielding the blade had been none other than the sister of Bahir Ben Kalil, Dr. Hasna Kalil. That and Brock’s death hadn’t been swift but hideously protracted.

Upon hearing all that, McGill leaned forward wanting to ask a dozen questions, but he'd been involved in enough interrogations to know you didn't interrupt someone who was speaking freely.

Ellie continued her narrative, telling the men in her office of spotting Dr. Hasna Kalil in a no-name excuse for a village in Syria. She said she and Sergeant Desmond Jones were the last Americans to leave the town that day. They departed on a motorcycle she'd purchased locally.

The two of them had lingered behind after most of the special forces unit and the rest of the newsies had departed because the sergeant had received a satellite phone call from back home telling him he'd just become a father. When the happy conversation ended, the two of them hit the road to catch up to the others.

She told the visitors to her office, "We were ambushed by a guy with an AK-47. The sergeant got hit by a round and both of us went down under the motorcycle. I gave the sergeant a handgun I was carrying. He killed the bad guy who was coming to finish us off, and I managed to get Sergeant Jones back to the PGO medical tent in that dump of a town."

"That's when you confronted the doctor?" McGill asked.

Ellie said, "Yeah, that was when she said she didn't treat American soldiers. So I threatened to kill her if she didn't."

"You popped her?" Behan asked.

"No," Ellie said. "She pretty much dared me to kill her, but there were these three guys who looked like they had surgery themselves that morning and were still unconscious. When I threatened to kill them, too, the doc got to work. I told her if the sergeant died on the operating table she and the other three were toast."

"Would you really have done that?" Welborn asked.

Ellie gave him a look. "Absolutely."

McGill asked, "What happened next?"

"Dr. Kalil finished working on the sergeant, sewed him up, and scalpel in hand decided to stand guard over one or more of those other three guys. Then she lunged at me."

"And you shot her," Behan said.

"No, I actually tried to keep her alive. I sidestepped the scalpel and clocked her with the butt of the sergeant's M-4. I put a little too much muscle into it. Probably from the adrenaline rush. I fractured her skull and severed her cervical spine. That's what I was told later.

"I used a satellite phone to call in the good guys. The army doc who choppered in to attend to Sergeant Desmond took a quick look at Dr. Kalil and said she was probably dead before she hit the ground."

"Her body was taken away, along with the unconscious men on the tables?" Welborn asked.

"Yeah," Ellie said. "The army never told me who they were. Maybe I'll try to find out sometime."

McGill brought up another point. "Nobody in the U.S. military mentioned the possibility of any charges being filed against you?"

Ellie shook her head. "No. They were pretty ticked-off that I'd been traveling under an assumed identity. I think they were as angry at themselves as me about that, the way I'd been able to fool them. But their gratitude for saving Sergeant Desmond's life outweighed any hard feelings. Some of the guys from his unit said I should get a medal, but I'm not holding my breath about that. Even if it would be awarded secretly."

"So as far as Uncle Sam is concerned all is forgiven?" McGill asked.

"I haven't heard otherwise, and they've had time to arrest me if they wanted to."

McGill said, "And when you first came to see me last week, you honestly hoped that the bad guys might have forgotten about you?"

"Not forgotten so much as having other things to do closer to home."

"Well, now we know that's not the case," Behan said.

Ellie nodded. "Yeah. I like the idea of sorting out the good guys with tattoos from the guys with the bad ink, and I like the idea of having good bodyguards for the time being, but going back over things again just now something new came to mind."

"What's that?" McGill asked.

"I'd dyed my hair blonde and was wearing green contact lenses when I was over in Syria. How would anyone in the boonies of a foreign country recognize me for who I really am?"

"And your answer is?" McGill said.

"The guy who sold me that old motorcycle, he said it was just like the one Steve McQueen used in *The Great Escape.* That movie was made well over 50 years ago, and it was shot in Europe. All that makes me think the motorcycle guy, despite all of us American devils being bound for hell, has a fascination with Western culture. He was the only local I came in contact with over there who might be able to make the connection if he saw a photo of how I really look. Plus, I feel pretty sure he was in on setting up the ambush on Sergeant Desmond and me."

Nobody quibbled with Ellie's conjecture.

McGill said, "So he fingered you when he saw a photo some hostile party's intelligence unit over in the Middle East provided to him. Since you were posing as someone with your actual occupation, maybe it didn't even take that long."

"Yeah, the little shit," Ellie said. "Too bad I didn't have the opportunity to pop him while I was locked and loaded. There is one good thing about his being alive, though."

"What's that?" Behan asked.

"I have a very clear memory of what the motorcycle guy looks like. I can describe him to a sketch artist. If he's in town helping the bastards look for me, our guys can look for him."

"Maybe follow him right back to his boss," McGill said.

Rockville, Maryland

Connie Parker rode with Meeker and Beemer to the police facility in Rockville. Detective Sergeant Dalton Rivers preceded them in an unmarked official vehicle. Franklin Parker decided to stay at his daughter's house. He was excited by the work Connie had done in developing a new drug, but he felt a moment of unease that she'd experimented with it on herself and her friends before animal studies had been done.

Now, he'd tried it, too, and all in all, he felt pretty good. He felt more *settled,* he'd guess you'd call it. Maybe animal studies weren't a requirement with this particular drug.

With that concern tabled, his mind turned to the problem of having his daughter's work funded by some seriously dubious characters. Big Pharma wasn't the only outfit that could muscle in on a young woman's ingenuity. Organized crime could be quick to recognize a golden opportunity when it saw one … if that was who had really promised to give his daughter $10 million.

If that were the case, not only might Connie's drug make billions in sales for someone who'd somehow rigged a lottery game, those people might also launder rivers of dirty money through the new drug company they formed.

Or maybe a crime syndicate wouldn't bother getting legal approval and just sell Connie's brainchild as a street drug. Then again, why break laws when you could make piles of money legally? Well … it might be a simple matter of impatience. Why waste time and lose sales going through a lengthy approval process when you could begin sales immediately? On the internet as well as the corner sidewalk.

More than that, some people just enjoyed flaunting the law and getting away with it.

Sheer perversity might be a reason for selling a drug outside the law.

This last misgiving made Franklin want to speak with his long-departed wife, seek her counsel and comfort on this matter. Then the drug he'd taken reoriented his thinking again. He now felt glad Mahalia wouldn't be burdened by the problem. Connie was on her way to the state police station — with those two detectives from Washington — to help the local authorities look into the situation. That was the way things should be handled.

Franklin had decided to stay put. That was the right thing for him to do just then.

Detective Sergeant Rivers had left a patrol car with two state policemen out front.

Franklin found that a comfort, too.

Connie sat in the backseat of Meeker's BMW 330i. Meeker, as he'd said, was the designated driver. Beemer sat shotgun.

"How you doing, Big Mike?" Meeker asked.

"Fine, just fine," Beemer said.

"You're not seeing any golden lights or hearing angels playing their harps?"

Beemer smiled. "It's not like that. You know how weed can make you mellow and silly?

Keeping his eyes on the road, Meeker said, "Yeah, I do know that."

"Well, the mellow part's the same, only I also feel more alert, not silly at all."

"You think you could drive if you needed to?" Meeker asked. "You wouldn't be distracted working out all the mysteries of the universe or anything?"

"I'm happy working on the mystery we got right here."

"Well, that's good. You think I should try this stuff?"

Beemer told his friend, "Marvin, you try it when I'm the designated driver."

"Glad to hear you can still make sense."

Beemer grinned. "I wasn't so mellow, I'd smack you upside the head."

The two men laughed, and Connie asked Beemer from the backseat, "Would you really hit him?"

"Heck no," Beemer said. "You hear that? I'm so mellow I didn't even say, 'hell no.'"

"That tells me something right there," Meeker said. He looked at Connie in the rear-view mirror. "There are times in police work when you *want* to have an edge. Mellow won't cut it."

Beemer replied, "I don't know, Marvin. You spread this stuff around wide enough there might not be any more crime or wars even."

Meeker wasn't having any of that. "Okay, you just lost me. I'm not going anywhere near this drug." He took another look at Connie in his rear-view mirror. "What's the name of this lawyer who put you on to the people running this lottery scam?"

"Jiminy Johnson," Connie said.

Meeker laughed. Even Beemer, mellow though he was, smiled.

"Jiminy as in cricket?" Meeker asked.

Even Connie couldn't deny the humor now. Merriment filled her eyes. "Yes, that's who he reminded his parents of when he was born. That's what he told me."

"And Jiminy is what you call him?" Meeker asked.

"I call him J.J. That's what most people do. You wouldn't want to get him upset. He's of a size with Mr. Walker."

"You hear that, Big Mike?"

"I did, and you're right, Marvin. There are times when you need an edge."

Meeker pulled into the State Police parking lot behind Detective Sergeant Dalton Rivers' car. The state cop got out of his car and walked over to where the others were standing. He looked at Beemer and asked, "You doing okay? I mean with taking that drug and all."

Beemer said, "Yeah, I'm all right."

"Not me," Rivers said.

"You seeing things, hallucinations and all?" Meeker asked.

"No, I'm *hearing* things. Not imaginary things. I got this idea in my head to tune the Pandora app on my phone to a country music station, and I started humming right along. Only thing is, I *never* listen to country music."

"Charley Pride?" Beemer asked.

The one and only African-American country singer he'd ever heard of.

"Merle damn Haggard," Rivers said. "I couldn't believe it."

"Maybe you were just discovering a new part of yourself," Connie said.

"That's the case, I want all the rest to stay hidden," Rivers replied.

Meeker told him, "Let's go inside and see if we can find someone to arrest."

"Now you're talking," the state cop said with a smile.

Il Corso Restaurant — Midtown Manhattan

McGill, Ellie, and Celsus had a business dinner at a comfortable Midtown Italian restaurant called Il Corso. They ate salad, fish — salmon, sole and sea bass — and freshly baked bread. McGill and Celsus contented themselves with San Pellegrino water; Ellie went with a glass of pinot noir.

McGill saw that Celsus noticed his prospective client imbibed alcohol. He would no doubt take that into his calculations as to how she'd need to be protected. Each successive drink would alter those plans and possibly influence the decision whether to take her on as a client at all.

Celsus's thought process was made easier by the fact that Ellie nursed the one drink throughout the entire meal. No doubt, Celsus also liked the fact that Ellie was all business. She gave him the backstory of the two attempts on her life and what she'd done in Syria.

McGill added the information he'd acquired from Ambassador Fayez Mousa.

Ellie finished up by saying, "Here's what might be the dealbreaker."

She told Celsus of her plan to tell her story on national television, which undoubtedly would be replayed around the world.

Celsus listened carefully and then came up with a scenario neither McGill nor Ellie had considered. "What if the Syrian government issues a warrant for your arrest?"

Ellie was dumbstruck. Finding her voice, she asked, "How

could they?"

Celsus told her, "I don't know exactly what their legal procedure would be, but basically they'd say you killed someone on their soil, as you yourself are planning to admit, and they'd want you brought back to Damascus to stand trial."

"I still can't see what mechanism they could use to get me into one of their courts," Ellie said.

Celsus said, "You've heard of Interpol, of course."

Ellie nodded. "Sure."

"Well, Interpol has partnerships with regional policing bodies. One of them is known as the AIMC, the Arab Interior Ministers' Council. It coordinates the efforts of Arab states in matters of internal security and the prevention of crime. AIMC could go to Interpol and ask for help. Say something like, 'We need help extraditing an American journalist who killed a renowned surgeon who dedicated herself to saving innocent lives in war zones around the world.'"

Celsus took a sip of water while he let that notion sink in. Then he said, "The United States is a member of Interpol. Provided with enough credible evidence, you might well be put on a plane to Damascus. In handcuffs and leg restraints undoubtedly. Conditions would get worse, of course, once you arrived. I can't say absolutely, but I'm pretty sure the judicial process over there doesn't tilt in the direction of a presumption of innocence."

Celsus had done something McGill wouldn't have thought possible.

He'd shocked Ellie Booker.

Gathering her native combativeness, she said, "Yeah, well, the president of that country has murdered his own people by the thousands. That angel-of-mercy doctor cut the head off of a member of the U.S. Congress. And, damnit, I acted in self-defense."

Celsus rebutted her point by point. "You're right. The bastard in charge over there is a soulless butcher, but he runs the show. He has his own military and a chunk of Russia's behind him. Do you have tangible proof that Dr. Hasna Kalil murdered Representative Philip Brock? Yeah, I've heard those rumors, too, but where's the proof? Lastly, is there a single soul in Syria who can and will back up your claim of self-defense?"

Looking as if she'd been afflicted with a case of lockjaw, Ellie said nothing for the moment. She did, however, turn to look at McGill to see if he might throw her a lifeline.

He said, "I'd bet my prospective grandchildren's college funds that Jean Morrissey would never let you or any other American be extradited to that hellhole of a country, but I can't say what might happen after she leaves office. If some joker with a grudge against the media, and your shop in particular, lands in the Oval Office, he might like nothing better than handing you over, eating popcorn while he watches the video of you being roasted on a spit."

"Jesus," Ellie said, sitting back in her chair.

Even Celsus looked just a bit taken aback.

McGill sat forward, extending a hand to Ellie.

She hesitated before taking it.

He said, "You do have some great stories to tell, I'll bet, but this one I think you should save for your memoirs. But first things first: Ride home with Celsus, listen to his plan to keep you safe in the here-and-now, and we'll talk in the morning. Okay?"

Ellie downed the last sip of wine in her glass and said, "Okay."

Central Park — Midtown Manhattan

New York City's premier green space was only a few blocks from the restaurant where McGill had eaten dinner, and he felt like stretching his legs to aid his digestion. He told Leo, "I'm going to take a walk in the park. You can go back to our hotel or catch a bit of nightlife if you like. We'll have breakfast together at 7:30, okay?"

Ordinarily, Leo wouldn't have worried about McGill getting mugged in a park. The man knew how to defend himself like few others did. However, with this current investigation already having a history of a drive-by shooting and an attempt to blow up a yacht, Leo felt a greater degree of caution than was usually required. The last thing he'd ever want to do would be to tell Mrs. McGill that he'd gotten careless and let her second husband fall prey to violence.

"I'll idle along in the car a hundred yards or so back," Leo said. "You won't even hear me, but if need be, I'll be there to pick you up before you can say zip-a-dee-doo-dah."

After urging Ellie to take all reasonable precautions, McGill didn't feel he could make light of someone else's concerns for his safety. "That'll work," he said.

McGill wasn't the only one getting about in Central Park that evening. There were walkers, runners, cyclists, patrons of horse-drawn carriages, and, McGill was pleased to see, a fair number of NYPD patrol cars. Everyone seemed to be at ease, at least in the early hours of the evening.

McGill was always fascinated by Central Park. It seemed to be a huge space even as its perimeter was compressed in by picket fences of large buildings. The trees in the park were all leafless at that time of year. The winter grass was a lifeless gray-green in the lamplight. Still, there was a sense of a natural setting you got nowhere else in Manhattan.

It certainly appealed to all the urbanites sharing the park with him that evening. Everyone seemed to be having a fine time, except for a woman in running gear sitting on the pavement, leaning back against a lamp post with one shoe off and rubbing her ankle. None of the other I-mind-my-own-business New Yorkers seemed to pay her the least bit of attention.

McGill did. He knew her, and he jogged up to a point just short of her.

"Give you a piggy-back ride home, lady?" he asked.

The woman looked up with a glare until she recognized who'd made the offer of help.

Then she said, "You think you can manage to carry me, mister? I may have put on a pound or two since the last time you did that, and you are getting older."

"Yeah, you're right," McGill said, "I wouldn't want to strain a muscle. So I could either leave you where you are or give you a ride in my car."

Blinking away tears, she said, "I am in a bit of pain. How far away did you park?"

McGill said, only half-kidding, "There are open parking spaces in Manhattan?"

Before the woman could respond, Leo pulled up in the Mercedes-Benz S Class, lowered the front passenger-side window and asked, "Everything okay, boss?"

"Just coming to the aid of an old friend," McGill said. "Probably sprained her ankle. Should we give her a lift home?"

"Is she a *good-ol'* friend?" Leo asked.

"One of the best," McGill said.

"Can she pay gas-money?"

"I'll extend credit." McGill turned to Clare and asked, "Should I just help you to your feet or take you in my arms?"

"Your wife might not understand that second choice. Is she still president, by the way?"

"Not for some time now. You remember you were at the farewell party at the White House."

"Oh, so I was. That seems so long ago. You can just sling me over your shoulder if you like. Toss me in the back seat."

McGill helped her to her feet. "It's good to see you again, Clare Tracy."

She kissed his cheek. "You, too, Jim McGill."

Omni Berkshire Hotel — Midtown Manhattan

McGill and Clare Tracy snagged a table in a quiet corner of the hotel bar. Leo, being the discreet soul that he was, declined the invitation to join them and retired to his hotel room, awaiting a call to drive Clare home. The waitress who'd asked what their drinking pleasure might be didn't bat an eyelash when McGill asked for an ice bucket to relieve the swelling in Clare's injured ankle.

She'd brought one with ice cubes floating in already chilled water. Acting on her own initiative, she'd also brought a clean white towel for Clare to wrap her foot in once she'd had enough cryotherapy. Then she'd served Clare a Courvoisier brandy and McGill a Grolsch beer.

They touched glasses and McGill said, "To enduring friendships."

Clare added, "To the one who got away."

McGill bit his lip but only for a second. "The way I remember things, you were the one who … withdrew."

Clare took a sip of her brandy and nodded. "You're right, I did. Silly me. Damn stupid me, to be more honest about it."

McGill knew there was more on Clare's mind than a romantic relationship that had ended decades ago and had been renewed as a warm but platonic friendship far more recently. He said, "If you want to talk about something, pretty much anything, really, I'm willing to listen."

She took a longer pull of the brandy and said, "I got married recently and divorced before the ink on the marriage license was dry."

McGill repressed the impulse to make a wisecrack about the guy's pea brain rolling out of an ear and only said, "I'm sorry, Clare. That had to be awful."

She said, "More like stunning. Didn't last long enough to be more than that. On the plus side, I got the apartment we bought and what had to be a world-record settlement for so short a wifeship. Part of that, though, was because I'd quit a very well-paying job to become a constant companion."

"So you're looking for something to do?" McGill asked.

"Not at all. Once my money from the SOB was locked in, I went back to my old job. Only my judgment and sense of self-worth remained at sea. I'd lost all faith in humanity, which was unfair to the female half of the population. I promised myself I'd never take so much as a cup of coffee from another man. Then you come along right after I trip on a stone in the road, and what do I do?"

"Exercise good sense," McGill said. "Besides, I'm buying you French brandy, not coffee."

"Could've been Kool-Aid coming from you, and I'd have taken it. You are still happily married to the most famous woman in the world, aren't you?"

McGill nodded.

"Good for you," Clare said. "The two of you deserve your happiness. Something I can say about damn few people, including me."

"Would you like me to call Leo to see you safely home?" McGill asked.

She put a hand on one of McGill's. "No, please. Buy me three or four more drinks, and I promise to save any further self-pity until I wake up hungover in the morning."

McGill frowned and that was enough for Clare to withdraw her hand and say, "I'm sorry. You think I should pull myself together and act like a grownup?"

"That would be a start." A thought occurred to McGill. "You think you could put that good mind of yours to use for a few minutes, maybe help save someone's life."

"Someone I like?" Clare asked. Then she grinned and gave McGill's hand a light slap. "Go ahead. See if you can make me think I'm a useful human being again."

Without mentioning Ellie Booker specifically, McGill told Clare of someone being threatened by certain people wearing a specific type of tattoo. The problem was some of the people with the tattoo were good guys and others were bad. How could you distinguish one from the other?

Clare put the brandy glass down. She plucked an ice cube from the bucket and popped it into her mouth. McGill kept a straight face, not wanting to steer the conversation off course.

"Who had the tattoo first," Clare asked, "the good guys or the bad?"

"The good guys."

"Is there a specific individual?"

McGill thought back to his discussion with Jordanian Ambassador Fayez Mousa. "I didn't hear a name, but I have a context and a specific time."

"That should be a good start," Clare said.

"A start leading where?"

"Well, once you know where the tattoo originated, then you find out who that person's friends and/or co-workers are. Would they be entitled to wear such a tattoo? You then use those people to branch out to others, making sure they also had the right to wear the tattoo. As you continue the process, you also ask the legitimate tattoo-bearers if they know or have heard of others using it illegitimately. Chances are the two groups are not using the same tattoo artists. There might be visible distinctions in the quality of the work from one group to the other. You know, maybe like a counterfeiter who doesn't get a hundred-dollar bill exactly right."

McGill smiled and took a hit of his beer. "I like all that."

Clare added a nuance. "Could be the bad guy's tattoos even deliberately vary from the original in some small way, a subtle *'screw you'* to the guys with the original idea."

McGill beamed. "I love those ideas, Clare. I'm going to pass them along to a friend who has enough people to pursue them. How did you come up with all that?"

She smiled with a tinge of sadness. "There are two ways to raise funds for people running for political office. I'm surprised you of all people don't know that."

"I always stayed far away from that end of things," McGill said.

"Okay, so you can raise money from the top down or the bottom up. If you start from the top, my preferred way, you look for the fattest, most sympathetic cat you can. You not only try to get the most money you can from him or her, you also ask for the names of all their closest, richest, most like-minded friends. You keep branching out from there. It's just like your problem: you've got to know where to start."

Clare finished her drink, took her foot out of the ice bucket and dried it.

Didn't bother to put her sock or running shoe back on.

McGill left a large tip for the waitress and called Leo. The former NASCAR driver pulled the Mercedes-Benz S Class up in front of the hotel with the quickness a pit-crew would have admired.

Clare bussed McGill's cheek once again, and he returned the favor.

"Come see Patti and me the next time you're in DC," he said.

McGill went to his room, called Patti at home, and asked, "Did you lower the portcullis since I'm not around to slay any dragons that might be poking their noses where they don't belong?"

She laughed and said, "Too late. The Secret Service doesn't do dragons, but I've already lanced the biggest one, and the kitchen staff is making steaks of him."

"I thought we were cutting back on our meat consumption," McGill said.

"I'm selling the steaks to Chicago sports teams, hoping to boost their places in the standings."

One of the things McGill loved best about Patti was that she never shied away from a wisecracking contest, and more often than not topped him.

"How are things going in New York?" she asked.

McGill brought her up to date on his dinner with Ellie and Celsus.

"I'm a bit surprised Celsus sat down with Ms. Booker," Patti said. "After dealing with you, I thought he'd left government service so he could be more selective about his clientele."

McGill told Patti about the cautionary tale Celsus had spun for Ellie.

"That ought to make her think twice," Patti said.

"You'd think so, but I think Ellie is almost as incorrigible as me. I wouldn't be surprised if she came up with some new rationale for doing exactly what she wants."

After a moment of silence, Patti told McGill, "In the event Ellie Booker does wind up in some Middle East hell-hole of a prison, I would *not* want anyone near and dear to me to attempt a rescue."

McGill laughed mirthlessly, "I'll confess to possessing a certain amount of derring-do, but commando raids definitely lie outside my repertoire."

"I'll sleep well," Patti said.

"Did I mention that I bumped into Clare Tracy tonight?"

"Not until just now."

McGill supplied the details.

"Ouch," Patti said, referring to the quicksilver nuptials and divorce. "On the other hand, Clare's suggestion for ferreting out the bad guys' tattoos seems like a good idea to me."

McGill said, "I'm going to hand it off to Welborn in the morning. Seems like a good job for the FBI."

"Absolutely."

"Anything new on the home-front?" McGill asked.

Patti said, "Well …"

"I'm not sure I like that pause."

"Good news first then," Patti said. "Cale tells me he doesn't have things pinned down quite yet, but he says he's closing in on the hacker who rigged the lottery."

"That's terrific. Some kind of high-tech criminal whiz?"

"Yes, but not one entirely motivated by personal gain."

McGill said, "What else is there?" And then he caught up with what his wife was implicitly suggesting. "There's a political angle to stealing millions of dollars? Why can't things be simple anymore?"

"It's the world we live in," Patti told him.

McGill wasn't going to argue that. Instead, he asked, "What's the less-than-good news?"

"It's not necessarily bad news, but I had a dinner out tonight, too, with Abbie."

"What could be bad about that?" McGill asked.

"The topic of conversation: She asked me how a woman can know when a man is the right one for her. Someone who's more than just a momentary infatuation."

For a second, McGill wondered why Abbie hadn't directed the question to her biological mother, McGill's first wife, Carolyn. Didn't take long to figure that out. Abbie had judged correctly that Patti was more worldly-wise.

That and the guy in question worked for only one of Abbie's moms.

"Cale," McGill said.

"Yes. I know it hasn't been long, and so does Abbie, but I think things are getting serious."

"Long?" McGill said. "It's been less than a week."

"Could mean they're exactly right for each other, Jim."

"Tell me you believe that," McGill said.

Patti replied, "I'm working on it."

CHAPTER 5

Tuesday, February 5, 2019
Welborn Yates' House — Washington, DC

Two little fists knocked on the door while Welborn Yates was shaving in the bathroom reserved for Mom and Dad. His offspring, Aria and Callista, had been taught, and respected, a sense of privacy. Welborn had a bath towel wrapped around his waist and wouldn't have been embarrassed if his daughters saw him thus attired.

Even so, he said nothing in response for a moment. He was enjoying the musicality of the percussion provided by his girls. They seemed to have an intuitive sense of keeping a beat, point and counterpoint. But when they called out, "Daaaad!" it was time to respond.

"Is that someone tapping on my door?" he asked.

"It's us," the girls said as a single voice.

"My little angels?"

"Daaaad!"

"Okay, how may I be of help?"

"There's a lady downstairs who wants to meet with you," one of the girls said.

It was often hard to distinguish which one of them was speaking.

"A nice lady?"

"Yeah." That was the chorus again.

"Nelda."

"Reed."

It took a moment for the name to register: the meter maid he'd encountered last Saturday. How did she know where he lived? Duh. She wrote him a parking ticket. Saw where his car called home … and remembered he had offered her the chance of a new job.

"Okay," he told the girls. "Tell Mom and Ms. Reed that I'll come downstairs in just a few minutes."

Welborn heard four little feet scurry down the stairs and instinctively thought: *Don't trip.*

He finished his shave, jumped into jeans and an Air Force sweatshirt. Eased into a pair of slippers, thinking a prospective boss shouldn't appear barefoot, and went down to meet Ms. Reed. Kira and the girls were already dressed for the outside world. Preschool, Welborn remembered belatedly. He shouldn't have dawdled with the girls.

Welborn kissed his family goodbye, all of them saying it was nice to meet Ms. Reed.

He invited Nelda into the kitchen for coffee. After setting a saucer and cup out for each of them, he asked, "I didn't park somewhere I shouldn't have again, did I?"

Looking more than a little sheepish, she said, "I was just going to drop off my résumé, leave it in your mailbox. Only—"

"My twins were peeking out the living room window trying to see if any of their friends were going to beat them to school. When they saw you, they opened the front door and said hello. Maybe asked if they could be of help."

Nelda nodded. "That's exactly what they did. You've got two little angels there, General."

"The lights of my life, along with their mom. So what can I do for you, Ms. Reed? I haven't quite started my new job yet."

Looking just a bit embarrassed, Nelda said, "I remember what you said, sir, about not starting with the FBI right away, but when

I told my husband and my mother about meeting you they both said I better get my résumé to you as fast as I can. Truth is, I didn't have one. I had to write one up. And I included a copy of my army record showing my commendations and honorable discharge."

"May I take a look right now?" Welborn asked.

Nelda nodded.

Welborn read the documentation closely. When he finished, he said, "Your commanding officers gave you excellent reviews, and your supervisor at your current job does the same."

"I always try to work both hard and smart, sir."

Welborn thought about that for a moment. He was about to say something, but he thought twice about it.

"Something wrong?" Nelda asked.

"I had an idea regarding you, but I'm not sure it's a good one."

"Not good in what way, sir?"

"You know where you found me wool-gathering? That was just around the corner and down the block from where a shooting occurred."

Nelda nodded. "My husband showed me a newspaper we had in our house. You saved a woman's life. Made me feel bad about ticketing you."

"No, no," Welborn told her, "you did the right thing. My idea was to have you be on the lookout for any more … well, bad guys who might be driving by or parked in that same area. You do work a given location, don't you?"

"I do, yes. But you're concerned I might put myself in danger?"

"That's right."

"Sir, I might have directed traffic in the army, but in my heart I was a military cop the whole time."

Welborn smiled. "Good for you. So, you think you could keep an eye out for anyone parked in the area of the shooting who looks wrong to you? Do so without giving possible bad guys any idea you have anything in mind except writing parking citations."

Nelda smiled. "Yes, sir. I think I can do that."

Welborn gave her a phone number, asked her to write it on

her palm.

She did so without questioning him.

He told her, "Memorize that number. Wash it away when you've got it committed to memory. Call me if you see anyone in your working area who looks wrong to you. Don't give yourself away, but as soon as you safely can, write down a description of the car, its passengers, and its license plate numbers."

Nelda Reed smiled as if Welborn had just given her a birthday present.

He cautioned her: "Do not do anything to endanger yourself. I don't want to apologize to your husband and your mother for something bad happening to you."

That dampened Nelda's enthusiasm a bit, which was just what he wanted.

They shook hands, and Welborn walked her to the door.

For the first time since he'd graduated from high school and headed off to the Air Force Academy, Welborn Yates was at a loss as to what to do with himself. He was still employed by the military and posted to the White House, but he'd taken a paid leave of absence. If the girls weren't in school, albeit preschool, the family could have taken a vacation in any number of splendid warm-weather destinations. Only Kira had vetoed in advance any trips that didn't coincide with or exceeded a school vacation period.

She wanted Aria and Callista to feel grounded and in sync with their classmates.

Welborn wasn't about to argue with that idea. He also knew that geographic distance wouldn't relieve him of the need to do something useful. Just before he might have begun to gnash his teeth in frustration, his phone rang. The caller ID read: J. McGill.

Relieved that his informal mentor truly held no grudge against him, Welborn sprinted to his home office. The seldom-used space that now seemed a more appropriate site to take the call. He answered before the phone could ring a third time.

"Welborn Yates."

Had he instinctively omitted his military rank?

"Got something for you to look into if you're interested, Welborn," McGill said.

The seeming answer to an unsaid prayer, Welborn nonetheless asked, "Is this something for one of your cases, sir?"

"Why don't we move on to you calling me Jim? I no longer have any political standing by marriage, and you're leaving the military, right?"

"I am, and I will. You'll understand that there might be some reflexive backsliding, Jim."

McGill laughed. "Nice timing on that. Anyway, yes, this suggestion began with the Ellie Booker investigation, but it's grown into something that has become governmental in scale."

"As judged by whom?" Welborn asked.

"Fayez Mousa, the Jordanian ambassador to the U.S. I have an idea to suggest to the incoming deputy director of the FBI. Even if it's not something you'd handle personally, you could speak with Director Benjamin and see it reaches the right person."

Just what Welborn had been yearning for: something to keep him busy.

Maybe something he could work personally. He'd heard that Byron DeWitt had been directly involved in several cases as deputy director. Of course, DeWitt had almost worked himself into an early grave, too, and was now definitely out of the game. At least as far as Welborn knew.

"I'd like to hear what's on your mind, Jim."

McGill reminded him of both good guys and bad guys wearing the roundels of their countries' armed forces, and that the designs used by the bad guys might have been tweaked to thumb their noses figuratively at the other side. He also mentioned Clare Tracy's suggestion for starting the hunt.

McGill suggested to Welborn, "Find the first pilot, most likely Jordanian, who wore the tattoo. Besides your new standing with the FBI, my thinking is the military men and women in that part of the world would be more willing to talk with a brother combat pilot than just about anyone else."

Hearing the words *brother combat pilot* made Welborn's heart swell with pride.

As McGill unquestionably had figured out in advance, Welborn thought.

The man obviously still had many lessons he could teach.

"I'll be happy to take your suggestion to Director Benjamin, Jim. I'll give her a call as soon as we're done here."

McGill said, "Thanks, Welborn. The only thing I ask in return is a threat evaluation on Ellie Booker. I don't need to know any big national secrets, but I'd like to be able to tell her how many and what kind of precautions she should take. You know, once the strength and intent of the bad guys can be estimated."

"That's reasonable. Anything else?"

"That should do it," McGill said.

After a moment's hesitation, Welborn said, "I really am sorry I acted like a jerk, Jim."

McGill responded, "Can't say I haven't had a bad day or two myself."

Mayor Rockelle Bullard's Office — Washington, DC

Detective Aidan Behan's guts were in a twist as Chief of Police Harriet Wortham stepped into the mayor's office just ahead of him. Behan was tempted to pull the door shut behind the chief and run for the exit. He'd been informed that a decision had been reached on whether he was justified in shooting the guy in Miz Smith's right through his brainpan.

Having had time to reflect on his action, Behan didn't think he could have done anything else. The asshole was holding the store manager in front of him as both a potential murder victim and a shield. The other asshole was demanding that the cops who were already on hand surrender their weapons. That was *never* going to happen.

So, in the blink of an eye, Behan decided to shoot the guy who otherwise might have broken the store manager's neck. Made a helluva good snap shot, too, as he'd already told the shooting incident investigating team. Only you never knew how these things might turn out.

The hulk he'd killed might've been some clown who wrestled professionally and never had any intention of going through with the threat to kill the woman. Hadn't Behan ever seen the guy doing his act on TV? Poor SOB had never really hurt anyone in his life.

That scenario was just the detective's imagination getting the better of him, he knew, but some very strange judgments had been made against cops. Usually by people who'd never found themselves involved in anything more dangerous than a shouting match.

With the mayor's secretary standing directly behind him, though, the detective couldn't make a break for it without knocking the woman down. He didn't think that would help his case any. He stepped into Mayor Bullard's inner sanctum and heard the door shut behind him.

He couldn't imagine the sound a casket closing on him being any worse.

Mayor Bullard locked eyes with him and smiled, gave him a thumbs-up.

Behan felt a wave of relief flood through him. Felt like someone was filling him with warm water. His bones were liquifying as the tide rose.

"Sit down before you fall down, Detective," Rockelle told him.

Behan followed orders, smiled briefly, and asked the mayor, "My job's good?"

Rockelle gestured to the chief of police, who told Behan, "We don't bring cops to the mayor's office to get fired. We keep that kind of thing in house."

Now you tell me, Behan thought.

He only said, "Yes, Chief. That'd be only right."

"We would like you to handle something that would normally fall to other personnel, Detective Behan," Rockelle said.

"Ma'am?"

"The other guy in Miz Smith's that night, the one who was actually yelling the threats when you made your dramatic entrance —"

"The Belarussian, ma'am?"

The mayor and the chief looked at each other.

"You could identify the man's nationality by his voice in the time it took you to punch his partner's ticket?" Rockelle asked.

Behan took a moment to recollect. "I realize now that I actually heard him yelling before I entered the store. He was quite loud. Menacing."

Chief Wortham said, "Okay, even if you heard him, how did you recognize his accent? I'd be hard put to find that country you just mentioned on a map. What'd you say its name is?"

"Belarus, Chief. The capital is Minsk. It's just east of Poland. South of Lithuania and Latvia. North of Ukraine."

The chief laughed. She asked the mayor, "Is this copper ready to go on *Jeopardy* or what?"

Rockelle was grinning, too. "You want to answer Chief Wortham's question, Detective? How'd you know his accent?"

Behan said, "My parents were diplomats at the U.S. embassy in Dublin. Once Poland became a member of the European Union, a lot of Poles came to Ireland and the UK looking for work, as they were free to do under EU law. Belarus isn't part of the EU, but more than a few people from there tried to pass themselves off as Poles so they could travel through Western Europe freely and look for work. They had some great counterfeiters churning out documents for them, but their accents, the way they spoke Polish with Russian inflections, gave them away if you knew what to listen for. I heard enough of both languages to recognize the tonalities."

The mayor and the chief looked at each other.

Rockelle asked Behan, "You don't actually speak Polish or Russian, do you?"

"No, ma'am. English, Gaelic, French, and Spanish only. I might be able to fake things after a fashion, though."

"How would you do that?" the chief asked.

"Well, I have the impression you'd like me to have a chat with the guy who survived the incident at Miz Smith's."

Rockelle nodded. "That's right. He refuses to talk to us so far, and that's his right. But I'd really like to know what his involvement is in this lottery scam former Detectives Meeker and Walker are working on."

Behan nodded. "I'd need the help of a Russian speaker who either has or can credibly fake a Belarussian accent. We'd whisper back and forth to each other. Let the prisoner think I'm speaking English with a Russian accent, maybe even let the bad guy hear me speak a Russian curse word or two. I'm pretty good at picking up accents quickly. The other person would speak directly to the creep. I'd look on as if I were listening closely and also able to understand. If the bad guy is smart, he'll know I'm faking it, and he'll try to cut some kind of special deal with the interpreter."

"You want some sexy babe playing that role, Detective?" the chief asked.

"No, ma'am. I'd like an older guy who looks half-a-crook himself. Someone the creep in the cage thinks he can buy off somehow. The Russian-speaker should also be someone alert enough to improvise if or when I give him a cue."

"So you're going to try to fake out our prisoner somehow, get him to spill his guts," Rockelle said. "Admit that his name is really not Ed Kingsley at a minimum."

"I think we'll get most if not everything the dude knows," Behan said.

"Why are you so sure about that, Detective?" the chief asked. "I don't think it'd go over well if we let you point your gun at him, much less shoot him."

Behan said, "No need to go that far, Chief. We all know that the guy's a crook, and he's looking at maybe life in prison here. But there's an even bigger threat we can use on him."

The mayor understood where Behan was going. "We can say

we'll send him back to whatever killers are waiting for him at home."

"Exactly," Behan said.

Seventeenth Street McDonald's — Washington, DC

Nelda Reed gathered with six of her coworkers, all female, all sisters in writing parking citations for the city, at their preferred breakfast stop. Nelda was buying coffee and McCafé breakfast pastries. So she'd had no trouble recruiting the ladies, all of whom worked beats close to hers.

"What you got cooking, Nelda?" Martisse Jackson asked. "You're a good-hearted lady, but treating us to coffee and sweet cakes, you've got something in mind."

Martisse was also ex-military. The other ladies looked up to the two veterans in their group.

Nelda told them how she'd met General Yates and the favor he asked of her. That and how he'd said he would find her a job with the FBI.

Just the idea set all the other ladies to giggling.

Martisse asked, "You think maybe the man just wanted a little brown sugar?"

Nelda glared at her colleague. "I went to his house, met his wife and little girls. Everybody was real nice. When the missus and her babies left for school, the general gave me a cup of coffee and was a perfect gentleman. Then he asked me to keep an eye out for any bad dudes I might spot while I'm doing my job. He told me to be real careful if I do spot anyone."

One of the other ladies asked, "If we turn in some crooks, do we get FBI jobs, too?"

That drew another chorus of laughs, some of them braying.

Nelda got to her feet. "I'm sorry I bothered y'all. Enjoy your breakfasts."

Martisse caught Nelda's arm, gently, before she could leave.

"Hold on now. That was just a little fun. You gotta admit, going from our jobs to the FBI is a pretty damn big jump. But let's say that's exactly how it works out for you. Well, congratulations. On the other hand, if one of us comes up with something important, we oughta get something more than a treat at Mickey D's, right?"

Martisse let go of Nelda. Gave the woman room to make her own decision.

"Okay," Nelda said. "One of you ladies comes up with something that turns out to be big, I'll personally give you one hundred dollars."

"Doesn't seem like a lot for someone going to work at the FBI," another citation writer said with a smirk.

Martisse held up a hand. "Don't start up again. Which one of you can tell me you wouldn't be happy to get a C-note for making a phone call to Nelda?"

Nobody's hand went up.

Nelda sat back down.

She leaned forward and told the others, "Let me remind you ladies, two of these dudes already came out shooting with an automatic weapon. Then they got drilled themselves. So, like the general already told me, let's not anybody do anything stupid. Be *real* careful, okay?"

With a change of mood that was unanimous, everyone nodded.

Midtown Manhattan

The day was clear and relatively mild, so McGill decided to hoof it to the WorldWide News Building six blocks distant. He hadn't gotten in as much of a walk as he'd hoped last night before bumping into Clare Tracy. Being honest with himself, he knew he'd reached a point in his life where he wouldn't be able to go more than a few days without exercise and not see a drop-off in physical fitness.

More than muscle was involved. On the few occasions when

he'd let his physical discipline slip, he also got cranky. The next thing he knew, he'd be forgetting where he left his car keys — if and when he no longer had a driver to ferry him around, that was.

Today, he'd even gone so far as to have Leo walk with him.

"You kidding, boss?" Leo had asked.

"Not at all," McGill told him.

Leo said, "I think walking's against union regulations."

McGill replied, "Show me your union card."

Leo muttered something about damn Yankees and fell in alongside McGill as they exited the hotel. As they matched the brisk median pace of other New York pedestrians, McGill noticed that Leo's attention was still on the adjacent 52nd Street automotive traffic. No doubt he was analyzing the volume, speed, and lane-changing patterns of the vehicles he saw and imagining how he'd maneuver smoothly through that automotive crowd.

McGill was fine with that. He could nudge Leo to prevent him from bumping into another wayfarer. McGill kept his eyes on the tidal flow of pedestrians ahead of Leo and himself. He also listened for anyone coming up from behind at a faster than average clip.

For all he knew, there were bad guys with guns looking for the chance opportunity to put Ellie Booker down whenever she set foot outside. The assassins' watchfulness might even extend to keeping an eye on people who'd been seen with her. If that were the case, McGill would certainly be one of them.

After all, the first attempt on Ellie's life had come outside of his office building.

McGill was pleased to see there was a strong, visible presence of uniformed cops in Manhattan. The city had learned a hard lesson in the 2001 terrorist attacks, and years later vigilance was still the watchword. McGill and Leo got to the WorldWide News building on Fifth Avenue without being so much as jostled by a fellow walker.

Before entering the building where Ellie Booker reigned, McGill told Leo he could go back to their hotel now.

"Do I have to walk?" Leo asked.

McGill shook his head. "You can take a Citi Bike."

Leo's mouth fell halfway open before he caught on to McGill's joke.

"Yeah, me on a bicycle, that'll be the day," Leo said.

"Hail a limo, if you like," McGill said. "Pay extra to get behind the wheel if you like."

"I just might."

McGill entered the WWN Building before he saw how Leo chose to travel.

Ellie Booker's Office — Midtown Manhattan

A secretary nearly as stunning as Esme Thrice was on duty that morning, and she showed McGill into Ellie's office.

As soon as McGill was alone with Ellie, he asked, "Your choice of hired help out there?"

She laughed. "Are you kidding? I'd have a Joan Jett lookalike, but now that Zara has been gifted to me I'll see how she works out."

"Only fair," McGill agreed. He looked around and noticed the change in décor that had been made. Now there were *two* folding chairs placed in front of Ellie's minimalist desk. Taking a seat, he said, "Your office looks so much better today."

Ellie offered a dry laugh. "I wasn't sure if you'd bring someone with you again. Thought I better be ready, within limits."

"Very considerate of you."

Ellie said, "Celsus Crogher called ten minutes ago. He politely declined the opportunity to keep me upright and breathing. Said he felt sure my ability to follow his precautions wouldn't last even one day. That being the case, he couldn't jeopardize the lives of his people pointlessly."

"Was he right in his opinion?" McGill asked.

"I think I could have made it through the first day; the second would have been where things came apart. You probably doubted me, too, didn't you?"

McGill said, "I thought you might make it a week, and that

could be enough."

Ellie opened the single drawer in her desk and took out a sheet of paper. She placed it flat on her desk and pushed it over to McGill. He took it in hand, studied the image he saw, and said, "This is the guy who sold you that motorcycle over in Syria?"

She nodded. "I sat down with a staff artist here first thing this morning."

"Someone who's definitely skilled," McGill said. "This is close to photo-realism, but how closely does it resemble the man you remember?"

"It's him down to the lopsided smile and bad teeth. Anyone who sees this drawing will recognize the guy on the street if he's here. Turn it over."

McGill did and saw Ellie had included the guy's height and weight in both English and metric measurements.

"Thorough," he said. "If you like, I can give this to Deke. He can pass it along to his NYPD contact, and she'll see it gets to the Joint Terrorism Task Force. You have more copies?"

"Zara's got 500 waiting for you when you leave. But you know what else seeing this guy's face made me think of?"

"What?"

"Celsus Crogher asked if there's a single soul in Syria who could and would back up my claim of self-defense for what I did to Hasna Kalil."

McGill frowned. "I don't recall you saying this guy was on hand when you killed her."

"He wasn't, but I'd bet my new job that he and Dr. Kalil were in on setting up the ambush on Sergeant Jones and me. We catch Motorcycle Man and get him to admit that Dr. Kalil was a party to an attempt to kill two Americans —"

McGill said, "It would make your claim that you acted in self-defense against Dr. Kalil entirely credible. If she had killed you, she could have killed Sergeant Jones, too. The door would be slammed against any court or president ever extraditing you to Syria or any other country."

"Right," Ellie said. "Even better than that, it would give me license not only to tell my story of what happened over there but also to investigate Hasna Kalil's entire history. See what kind of shit she pulled under the guise of being an angel of mercy."

"Probably make the case for Dr. Kalil killing Representative Philip Brock, too," McGill said.

Ellie gave a terse laugh. "The gift that keeps on giving. Now, I only have to stay alive, hope that Motorcycle Man is here in town, and the cops or feds catch him."

McGill said, "Regarding that staying alive part, now that Celsus has said no thanks."

"Yeah?" Ellie asked.

"Maybe you could give Sergeant Jones a call, see how he's recuperating, and you might ask if he has any Special Forces friends who have left the military and might be interested in doing some protection work."

Ellie smiled and nodded. She liked McGill's idea.

Jiminy Johnson Law Offices — Towson, Maryland

Meeker, Beemer, Detective Sergeant Dalton Rivers, and Constance Parker showed up at the law offices of Jiminy Johnson, Esquire without an appointment. The lawyer had the entire top floor of a ten-story building. Connie had called the man while she and the others were still fifteen minutes out from the Baltimore suburb.

Sergeant Rivers had wanted to take his official car and do all the driving. The other three voted to take Meeker's BMW, but they'd let Rivers drive if he wanted. He did. Loved the experience. He glanced at Meeker and said, "I'm gonna have to save up for one of these."

Meeker replied, "I'm just waiting to see what one of your staties does when he stops you for driving 15 miles per hour over the speed limit."

Rivers glanced at the speedometer and slowed down. "Didn't seem like I was going that fast." Nonetheless, his speed climbed up again.

When Connie called Johnson, she said she'd be in town shortly. Would he have a few minutes he could spare for her?

The call was on speaker, and the lawyer asked, "You have some of those fine new pills of yours, girl? I'd surely love to have some."

"Thirty caps do it for you?" Connie asked.

"That'll get me through the week anyway. You come right on up."

So that's what Connie — and her friends — did. Even got their parking validated.

When Jiminy Johnson came out to greet her, though, he frowned upon seeing who had accompanied her. Even though all three men wore suits, the lawyer, who did criminal defense work, among other things, recognized them immediately for what they were: cops.

He turned his attention to Connie and asked, "What's going on here?"

She said, "Something has come up, J.J., I thought you should hear. In your office would be better."

Johnson's eyes flicked past Meeker to Beemer and Sergeant Rivers. Beemer, he saw, was an inch or two taller than him; Rivers had about the same edge at the shoulders. He wasn't going to intimidate either of them into turning on their heels and taking a hike. And the little dude looked like he'd be quick with a gun and come out shooting if you tried to muscle him.

Before anything unfortunate could happen, Connie stepped forward. She pressed a bottle of Clarity capsules into Johnson's hand. Then she took his arm and said, "Let's talk in private J.J. That's all we're here to do."

The lawyer said to the three men staring at him. "I'm not being entrapped here, am I? Just holding the bottle Connie gave me, I mean."

Beemer smiled, pointed at Rivers, and told Johnson, "My

friend and I tried some last night. So we'd get locked up, too."

Rivers nodded. "Yeah, I tried it, too."

Johnson looked at Meeker. "What about you?"

"I like a fine scotch, neat," he said.

"So do I," Johnson said, "when I can't get some of these. Come on in. I'll talk to you as far as my legal judgment allows. If we can't agree on how far that is, you'll have to get an arrest warrant if you want to take me into custody."

He directed his last remark at Rivers, having nicely sorted out just who was who.

Welborn Yates' House — Washington, DC

FBI Director Abra Benjamin hadn't been able to take Welborn's phone call because she was at the White House speaking with the president. The director's secretary suggested to Welborn that he might want to come in and wait for the director's return. She likely wouldn't be gone more than an hour.

Welborn said, "I'll be happy to do that."

Since he had a bit of time to kill, Welborn decided to make a phone call first.

He called Ambassador Fayez Mousa at the Jordanian Embassy. The diplomat took the call but expressed his regrets at being unfamiliar with Welborn and his role in the U.S. government.

Welborn explained his role in the Grant and Morrissey administrations, and without going into specifics said he'd soon be working for the FBI. He also mentioned his first position in government service, "I was a fighter pilot for the USAF, Mr. Ambassador."

The tone of the Jordanian diplomat's voice became noticeably warmer. "I salute your service, sir. May I assume you've met James J. McGill?"

"I know him well. After my flying career ended, I was trained as an investigator at the federal training center in Glynco, Georgia, but I learned a good deal more from Mr. McGill."

"How may I be of assistance, General Yates?"

"Mr. McGill suggested that I find out, as a brother combat pilot, who the first Royal Jordanian Air Force officer was to wear the roundel tattoo of your country's flag."

A note of caution entered the diplomat's voice. "What would the purpose of that be?"

Welborn explained the idea that both patriots and terrorists were now using that tattoo but the designs might be slightly different.

"Mr. McGill and I think it might be helpful to know how to visibly distinguish the good guys from the bad."

Ambassador Mousa said, "I believe my memory has become refreshed. You were the heroic gentleman who saved the woman in front of Mr. McGill's offices, were you not? I have seen that video many times."

Welborn switched his phone to FaceTime and said, "That's me."

The diplomat looked at the caller's image, nodded and said, "I salute you again, sir."

"And I understand your caution, Mr. Ambassador. You're being careful not to divulge sensitive information to just anyone."

"Just so," Mousa replied.

"Would you be able to speak more freely to the director of the FBI?"

"That would be most helpful."

"I'll be in her office soon. Would you prefer to call Director Benjamin or have her call you?"

"I will make the call."

Mousa was being careful again. Welborn assumed the ambassador had the FBI director's phone number or could find it on his own. "As you like, sir."

Mousa asked, "General Yates, may I ask how it is that you went from being a combat pilot to your current duties?"

Without going into detail, Welborn said, "An automobile accident took away my ability to cope with the physical stresses of high-G flying."

"My sympathy, sir. I will call Director Benjamin within the hour."

Jiminy Johnson Law Offices — Towson, Maryland

The XXL-sized lawyer sat back in his desk chair and made its springs creak. "You say there were *two* big winners in last week's Grand Slam lottery? Your name was the only one I saw in the news: TV, print newspaper, and online."

"There was another," Connie said. "Mr. Meeker and Mr. Walker are working for him. Detective Sergeant Rivers works for the state police."

"I figured out that much," Johnson said.

Rivers leaned forward. "You want to tell us who it was figured out how to fix the Grand Slam game? If it was you, that's *real* bad. If you just know who did it, that's still bad enough."

J.J. also leaned in, resting his arms on his desk. "I neither committed a crime nor know of anyone who did."

Meeker said, "You mean in this case anyway, huh?"

Beemer added, "Or are *all* your clients innocent?"

Feeling outnumbered and not about to comment in any way on his clients, J.J. sat back and said, "Will you tell these guys how I do business, Connie?"

She said, "As far as I know, and I met J.J. when we were undergrads at Hopkins, he's always been honest."

Beemer asked her, "Did you come to him asking for monetary help or did he bring an offer to you?"

"It wasn't quite like either of those things," Connie said.

J.J. said, "We were at Duda's Tavern in Fells Point, having some crab cakes and beers."

Meeker and Beemer knew the place, could see it as a place where people could talk about anything and everything. Have a good time while doing it, too.

"Who else was with you at the table that night besides Mr. Johnson?" Rivers asked Connie.

She replied, "Terry Simonton, an investment banker, Annie Clarke who teaches English at UMD, and Nell Rogers, DVM."

The two ex-cops and the current statie all looked at each other.

"Wait a minute, now," Meeker said. "Unless I'm forgetting something here, DVM stands for doctor of veterinary medicine."

"It does," Connie said.

Beemer picked up the thread. "So you had access to animals and you tried out your drug on people?"

"Including you and Detective Sergeant Rivers," Connie pointed out. "Besides, Nell's patients weren't lab animals. They were pets, members of people's families."

"Big Mike has a wife," Meeker informed Connie.

"So do I," Rivers added, "and two sons, too."

"But you gentlemen have the ability to make rational decisions."

Meeker wasn't so sure about that, but he didn't want to get off point.

"We'll leave all that for later," he said. "Tell us about Mr. Johnson here and how he hooked you up with this lottery deal."

Connie looked at the lawyer and said, "J.J.?"

Johnson sighed and gave in. "We were all sitting there at Duda's enjoying our food, maybe getting a little tipsy and Connie told us about this great new drug she came up with and it was going to change the world and make her the world's richest woman. Everybody thought that'd be a good friend to have. All she needed was several million dollars to get started. I said I knew someone who might help her get rolling. She said she needed $10-20 million to get started and attract other investors, ones who wouldn't try to take the whole pie for themselves."

"That's why you wouldn't agree to pay Sammy more than one million," Beemer said to Connie. "You couldn't afford a bigger payout."

She nodded.

Johnson asked, "Who's Sammy?"

"We'll get to that later, maybe," Meeker said. "Keep going with your own story."

Johnson looked like he might dig in his heels, but Connie steepled her hands in a prayerful manner.

The lawyer sighed and said, "I've got this client, a math prodigy. The first time he came to me — and I won't say for what — he said he couldn't pay me cash, but he could teach me how to count cards and not get caught. Not only that, he could tell me what the tolerance was for each casino that had Twenty-One games. How much they'd tolerate someone winning."

"And you laughed and said, 'Yeah, sure,'" Meeker said.

"No, I gave him a small stake and sat next to him while he showed me how it's done. Then, yeah, I had him teach me how to do it. Now, I've got something to do after I retire from courtroom work."

"Let me guess," Beemer said. "This card-sharp came to you not long before Ms. Parker had dinner with you at Duda's."

Johnson nodded. "He did. I hadn't mentioned Connie to anyone. Hell, I didn't even know she needed any money, much less big money. But once she told us how she needed some serious cash to get her new drug off the ground, I took a chance and told her. It wasn't right away, but pretty soon after that, I heard she won the lottery. She's rich."

Meeker, Beemer and Rivers all looked at each other.

The unspoken question was, "You see any crime here?"

Rivers asked Connie, "You put any opiates in that capsule you gave us?"

She shook her head. "None."

"*Any* Schedule One drugs?" Those with high potential for abuse and dependence.

"No."

Meeker asked, "You just came up with a happy combination all on your own?"

"After ten years of study and experimentation, yes."

That left only two questions for Beemer to ask, "Okay, Jiminy, what's the name of this client who's so damn good with numbers, and did you get a cut for bringing in Connie?"

The lawyer shook his head. "Not a dime … and his name is Max Bernecker."

DC Central Detention Facility — Washington, DC

"I want a lawyer," the man calling himself Ed Kingsley said.

The prisoner had been charged with attempted robbery and first-degree murder — causing the death of his own partner-in-crime. He wore handcuffs, a belly chain, and ankle shackles. A corrections officer forcibly sat him down on a chair bolted to the cement floor. Sitting on the opposite side of a metal table with a vinyl top were Detective Behan and a dark-haired young woman wearing reading glasses on the end of her nose.

With his mouth still at liberty, Kingsley yelled, "Lawyer, lawyer, lawyer."

Ignoring the prisoner, Behan said, "Thank you, officer. We'll call you when we're done here."

The corrections officer nodded and stepped out of the interrogation room.

Kingsley thrust his face forward and with a sneer in his voice repeated, "Lawyer."

Both Behan and his companion appeared to listen closely.

Then Behan turned to the woman and said in a vocal tone that might have originated in Eastern Europe, "Belarus?"

Still looking at Kingsley, she replied in a similar inflection, "*Da.*"

Her affirmative answer and perfect Muscovite accent made the prisoner sit back and stare at the woman.

She told him in flawless Russian, "I am not a great beauty, but take a good look at me. I might be the last woman you ever see."

Hearing that sat Kingsley back in his chair. He looked like he wanted to flee, if only back to his cell.

Those lines had been scripted by Behan. He nodded, giving the impression he'd understood what his companion had just voiced.

Then Behan said to the woman in English, using his normal inflections, "If this jerk knew what was in store for him, he'd probably beg me to shoot him. One to the skull and good night."

Kingsley, now angry as well as fearful, slipped and responded in a torrent of Russian. Then, to Behan's ear, he seemed to stop in midstream, having realized his mistake in using that language. With his freedom of movement so limited, the best Kingsley could do now was to hang his head, obscuring the expression of regret and embarrassment on his face.

He didn't notice Behan's companion tap him once on his thigh. A sign for one of the curse words Kingsley had used.

Behan said, "You called me a motherfucker? You'll come up with worse than that when you hear what I'm going to do to you."

The prisoner couldn't stop himself from looking up, perhaps hoping the threat would be an idle one.

"I asked my boss if I could shoot you a few times," Behan told Kingsley. "You know, start with your knees, go to your shoulders, and then put a final round right below your belt buckle. See what killed you first, the shock, the blood loss, or the shame."

The graphic threat drained the blood from Kingsley's face.

Behan, meanwhile, kept up the pressure. "I mean, why not hit you with every awful thing I can think of? You were the bastard in that store screaming your steroid-eating, junkie friend was going to kill that poor woman. You don't think *she's* going to have nightmares for years? Not that a shit like you would give a second thought about someone else."

Kingsley blurted, "I …" But that was as far he could get. What could he say, that he hadn't meant the threat? He'd meant it. Any attempt at denial might make things even worse. The madman who'd killed Vassily might, in fact, start shooting him to pieces then and there.

As if he'd just forecast his own gruesome death, the American bastard said to the woman in passable Russian, "Perhaps you should leave now."

Worse yet, the woman answered in her perfect Muscovite voice, "I will stay. I might learn a thing or two I can use in the future."

From the way Kingsley paid attention, and the terror now on his face, both Behan and his companion knew without a doubt that the prisoner had understood every word they had said.

The woman took off her glasses and asked the prisoner, "And where did you learn to speak the mother tongue, comrade?"

Feeling completely trapped and desperate now, Kingsley replied, "This is not what I was told an American arrest would be like."

He said that in Russian, with an accent straight out of Belarus.

The woman laughed, gave Behan a gentle nudge with her elbow.

He brought up one of the canned Russian phrases he'd memorized and directed it at the prisoner. "Life's the shits, isn't it?"

Unable to restrain himself, Kingsley nodded.

In English, Behan continued, "The really bad part is that it only gets worse. Unless you start to cooperate. So tell me, Ed, what's your real name?"

There was no question at that point about whether the prisoner would cooperate, but he still asked, "I will get leniency for my cooperation?"

"You'll get exactly what you deserve," Behan assured him.

Mayor Bullard and Chief of Police Wortham, after observing a closed-circuit view of the interrogation and confession, looked at each other with dazed smiles. The prisoner had revealed in great detail as to just what he and his now-deceased friend had been doing in the United States, starting with their illegal entry into the country via Canada.

The chief said, "Madam Mayor, this is big, monstrous big, too damn big for any municipal police department to handle on its own. We need to call the FBI, maybe the CIA, and God knows who else."

"You raise a good point, Chief. We're going to need some advice on how to proceed."

"Advice from who?"

"I'm thinking James J. McGill."

FBI Headquarters — Washington, DC

Welborn needed to wait only five minutes for his soon-to-be boss to return from the White House. Director Benjamin's expression, at first, was distant as if she were lost in thought. Welborn knew firsthand that distraction from the mundane duties of life was something a one-to-one discussion with a president could cause with the greatest of ease. He also knew better than to inquire what had transpired in the Oval Office.

He stood crisply as the director drew near, almost saluting but managing to hold back on that. He wore the navy blue Burberry suit Kira had given him for his most recent birthday, along with the caveat that he'd better be able to wear the same size for the next ten years or she might have to look for a younger boyfriend.

When Abra Benjamin finally took notice of who was waiting for her, she smiled.

"General Yates, you certainly know how to dress up; you look quite good in civilian garb."

"Thank you, ma'am."

Welborn knew better than to return the compliment.

"Evelyn sent word that you have some news for me," Benjamin said, referring to her secretary who was pointedly not looking at her boss and guest. No doubt, however, she was listening closely.

Benjamin said, "Let's go into my office and see what new labor awaits us."

Welborn opened the door for the director and stood aside as she entered the room. As he was closing the door behind them, he saw Evelyn sketch the Sign of the Cross in the air with her right hand. He hoped the gesture was made in humor.

The director sat behind her desk and motioned Welborn into a visitor's chair.

"So what new devil has poked its head out of hell this fine day?" Benjamin asked.

Trying to dismiss that image from his mind, Welborn related his phone conversations that morning with Jim McGill and Ambassador Fayez Mousa, adding that Mousa should be calling her office shortly.

"Interesting," the director said.

"Ma'am?"

"I find it interesting that Mr. McGill called you instead of me. That and Ambassador Mousa taking your call."

Welborn felt he hadn't done anything amiss, and while he wanted to get off to a good start with his soon-to-be new boss, he wasn't about to snivel. Not at all. He'd worked well with two commanders-in-chief; he wasn't about to be intimidated by a lesser light.

If the job at the FBI didn't work out, he'd find something else to do.

Welborn said, "I've known Mr. McGill for ten years now, ma'am. Ambassador Mousa said he saw the video of me saving Ms. Booker's life."

Benjamin nodded. "As I mentioned to you when we met in the Oval Office, that was impressive, General. Heedless personal risk and damn quick reflexes."

"You need both to fly combat jets, ma'am."

"I'll have to take your word for that, and I'm sorry if I just came off grumpy."

"We all have those moments, as I know all too well."

Hearing that made Benjamin smile. "Really? Thank you for saying that. My one reservation about you was that you might be one of those seemingly perfect people who make the rest of us feel like *schlimazels*."

"Ma'am?"

"That's Yiddish for a clumsy and luckless person."

"You'll have to speak with my wife sometime, ma'am."

The FBI director laughed. "By all means. So give me a summary of your two phone calls this morning."

Welborn told her about the idea of variations in design on the roundel tattoos and looking for the first pilot who wore one, and how he, Welborn, might be the right person to speak with that man. He added that the ambassador said he would look into the matter, but he would be more comfortable speaking to the director about the results of his inquiries.

Benjamin said, "I think Mr. McGill is right about you being the right man to speak with your Jordanian counterpart. I can't think of any FBI special agent who also has your military background as a combat pilot, so you're the guy if you'd like to get a jump on your job."

"I would." After a brief pause, Welborn asked, "Does my job come with a secretary?"

Benjamin grinned. "It does, but you can't have mine."

"No, ma'am."

"You have someone in mind?"

"I do. Someone with a military police background. She has glowing commendations and an honorable discharge."

"Sounds fine. Where'd you meet her? The White House?"

Welborn knew it was a crime to lie to a federal officer, especially the director of the FBI. So he said, "No, ma'am. She wrote me a parking ticket."

The director blinked twice and was about to respond when her intercom buzzed. Her secretary told her that the ambassador of the Hashemite Kingdom of Jordan was on the line. She took the call immediately and had a brief, cordial conversation. She thanked the ambassador and said goodbye.

She gave Welborn a close look, saying nothing.

"Ma'am?" he asked.

"You are definitely not a schlimazel, General. The ambassador found the man you're looking for, the first pilot to wear that roundel tattoo. His name is Ibrahim Boutros. He's now a major general in Jordan's air force, and he's currently posted to his country's UN delegation in New York City. He'll be happy to meet with you."

Welborn said, "Sometimes I do get lucky, ma'am."

Benjamin told him, "The FBI can always use people like that."

Committed Capital — Washington, DC

Patti Grant McGill picked up the phone in her office, having been told her husband was calling, and asked, "You're home?"

McGill told her, "I needed a change of socks, and you know how expensive everything is in Manhattan."

"You may have noticed we're rather well off."

"Yeah, the private jet was a giveaway. Another ten years of living with all our goodies and I might get spoiled."

"Hard to imagine," Patti said.

"Yeah, I'll try not to let that happen, but I was wondering if I might have a little time with Cale Tucker."

Patti sighed. "You only love me for my office staff."

McGill laughed. "I'll go through the alphabet, A-to-Z, of my reasons for loving you at my earliest convenience."

"Oh, yeah? Give me something starting with Q."

McGill didn't hesitate. "Quicksilver shivers that run down my spine when you …"

He dropped his voice and hoped Patti was alone in her office.

That and she didn't have the call on speaker.

"Okay, okay," she said, already sounding a bit excited. "Neither of us will get any work done if we keep this up."

"Right. So may I speak with Cale?"

"You may, provided you do so on his lunch hour, which starts in 45 minutes, and you don't drag things out all afternoon."

"Wouldn't dream of it," McGill said.

"Would you consider speaking to him in my building's

dining facility, in case he needs to be pulled away for some chore for which I'm actually paying him?"

"I'll bow to any condition you think necessary."

Patti asked, "Have I ever told you, Jim McGill, that there are times when I think there's no end to your charm?"

"Not so much while you're awake. Quite frequently when you talk in your sleep."

"I do *not* talk in my sleep."

"Okay, I learned all those state secrets from someone else."

Patti laughed. "All right, you're pretty funny, too, but if you did overhear anything you shouldn't have, please keep it to yourself."

"Not even my confessor will know."

"Stop by my office and give me a kiss if you can find the time."

McGill said, "Sure. I'd interrupt a board meeting for that."

Before McGill got around to seeing his wife, he stood outside the Committed Capital Building waiting for Meeker and Beemer to join him. He was content to enjoy the pale winter sunlight and the relatively mild DC temperature. If Chicago had had this kind of winter weather when he was a kid, people would be wearing T-shirts and shorts. Softball games would be breaking out in Lincoln Park. Somebody might even start grilling hot dogs.

His reverie was interrupted by the arrival of a current cop, not two retired ones.

Detective Aidan Behan turned the corner of the block and headed McGill's way. He waved when McGill looked in his direction. Son of a gun if Behan wasn't eating a hot dog cloaked in a tissue-paper wrapper. When the detective drew within ten feet, McGill could smell the last bite he popped into his mouth.

He closed his eyes and smiled.

Being a trained observer, Behan asked McGill, "Would you have liked me to bring you a frank?"

McGill opened his eyes and asked, "Is that what you call a hot dog where you're from?"

"Mom and Dad always called them Fenway Franks when they went to the ballpark. There's a place around the corner and a block over where I got mine. I can show you when we get done talking."

"Did I miss an appointment?" McGill asked.

Behan shook his head. "Mayor Bullard sent me out to find you. I tried your office. Esme told me to look over here."

"Something big has come up?" McGill asked.

Before Behan could respond, Meeker and Beemer pulled up to the curb in Meeker's BMW. Beemer lowered his window and asked, "Where's a good place to park? Marvin's fussy about where he leaves his car."

McGill said, "I've got a spot in the building's garage. Leo dropped me off so you can use it." He walked over to the entrance and tapped in his code. Behan followed behind, and they all entered the building by using the underground elevator.

McGill was surprised to see Patti waiting for him when the doors opened.

She saw her husband along with three unexpected companions. "I hope this isn't a hostile takeover," she said.

McGill introduced Meeker, Beemer, and Behan to Patti. Everybody shook her hand, said it was their pleasure and called her Madam President. She waved off the use of that title.

"We have only one president at a time, and she's Jean Morrissey. Ms. McGill will do nicely for now." Then without any worry about embarrassment, she gave her husband a kiss and explained to the others. "I just wanted to say welcome home to my husband."

She turned to him. "Cale's waiting for you in the dining room. I had the staff pull the chairs from the tables immediately adjacent to yours so you'd have privacy. Now, I'll ask them to bring three more chairs back. Tell them you know the boss if you need anything else."

Patti said to the others, "Nice to meet all of you."

Then she left. All three men gave McGill the same look.

"I know, I know," he said. "We should all be so lucky."

Beemer told him, “I love my wife just like that, only I don’t think she’ll ever be president.”

“Count your blessings,” McGill told him.

They used another elevator to go to the top-floor dining room. Cale Tucker and the right number of chairs were waiting for them when they arrived. Cale had a glass of what looked like golden ginger ale in front of him. He stood as the others joined him and introductions were made.

McGill asked Cale, “Do you have enough time for us to have lunch or should we just order drinks and leave it at that?”

Cale looked at his phone to check the time. “I have at least 45 minutes. After that, if the phone rings, I have to leave.”

“Fair enough. We can order some food, and we’ll talk about your end of things first. I have the feeling there are other things the guys and I can talk about after you leave.”

Meeker, Beemer, and Behan all nodded.

Cale grinned. “Heck, let’s get going. I’d hate to miss anything good.”

He tapped his phone and a waitress came. Meeker and Beemer went with burgers and the same ginger ale Cale had. All Behan wanted was a cup of clover tea. McGill ordered two hot dogs, fries and a Coke.

With their orders placed, McGill said, “Okay, Cale, the last I heard, you thought you had a lead on some hacker who might have been in on fixing the Grand Slam lotto game. Without giving away any secrets that might damage national security, what can you tell us?”

The young cyber whiz took a moment to consider what he might say.

“I’m going to give you an alias for the hacker I think is behind all the lottery problems, only it won’t be the same monicker he uses. At least, I think this person is a male. I’ll call him Wendigo, if you know the reference.”

Behan said, “A monster-slash-demon out of Native American folklore.”

"A spirit associated with murder," Meeker said.

"And non-stop greed," Beemer added.

Cale said, "All of that's right. So, anyway, I'm pretty sure Wendigo hacked the lottery's computer system, put in the fix for a chosen person to win the jackpot."

"How would somebody do that?" McGill asked. "It seems impossible that anyone could manipulate televised ping-pong balls."

Cale nodded. "I agree, but far more often than not nobody gets all six numbers right. So the computer keeping track of all the combinations of numbers on tickets that have been sold reports that there's no big winner. So if you can't control all the numbered balls you can see on television —"

McGill said, "You gimmick the computer software that nobody can see."

"And?" Cale asked.

Meeker said, "You put the number you want to win into the computer."

"Doing that so quickly nobody notices," Behan added.

Beemer came up with a logical conclusion. "Once that stuff's done, you counterfeit the winning ticket. If crooks can make phony hundred-dollar bills that pass for the real thing, a lotto ticket would be easy."

"Yeah, that's pretty much the outline," Cale said. "If the computer reports a legitimate winner, the bad guys wait for the next big jackpot in which there's no honest winner and take that pile of cash. From what I've seen of hackers like this, they don't like to share."

McGill said, "They're sharing with Constance Parker."

"She's the front person," Cale said, "a cost of doing business and a way of distancing Wendigo from being caught."

"So how come my brother-in-law Sammy also got a winning ticket if this con game was set up as slick as you said?" Beemer asked.

Cale looked at McGill and got a small nod.

So the young tech wizard said, "Word in the darkest of dark places on the Web is that the people who set up this hack on the lottery didn't honor their agreement with Wendigo. At the last minute, they cut his promised fee in half."

Behan chuckled and said, "Dumbasses."

Meeker added, "If the money-men cheated him, he'd cheat them right back."

Beemer summarized, "So old Wendigo stuck a second winning ticket into the stream, the one Sammy bought."

"Wait a minute," McGill said. "If the fix was put in a split-second after the ping-pong balls showed the winning numbers, how did Sammy buy a winner beforehand?"

Cale said, "I wondered about that, too. Let me ask you, Mr. Walker, did your brother-in-law mention if he bought his ticket at the very last moment?"

"That's exactly what he told everyone," Beemer replied. "Sammy said that was another sign of just how lucky he was."

Cale said, "He was right about that. My educated guess is that Wendigo hacked the terminal that produced the second winning ticket, pushed back its clock just far enough to accept the purchase and print the ticket, even though the drawing had just been completed."

McGill looked for a hole in Cale's reasoning but couldn't find one.

Meeker asked Cale, "Would it help you to find out who this ticked-off hacker is if you had a name for him?"

"Hell, yes," Cale said, beaming.

Beemer said, "It's probably an alias, but we got it from the lawyer who introduced the guy to Connie Parker. That dude set her up to be his front person. His name's Max Bernecker."

Beemer spelled the last name for Cale.

Behan seemed to take a particular interest in that name and said, "I've got another name for you."

"Who's that?" McGill asked.

"Ed Kingsley, the guy whose partner got shot in Miz Smith's?

Also the guy who won $2 million in that same lottery drawing. His real name, probably, is Pavel Morozov. He comes from Minsk, Belarus."

"Probably his real name?" McGill asked.

"He was all but wetting himself at the time he coughed that up," Behan said. "Could be he was still lying, but I don't think so. Mayor Bullard asked me to stop by and ask you how you think we should hand him over to the feds? After the way I interrogated him, using psychological pressure and all, it's not likely a local prosecution would hold up. Maybe not even a federal one. He might have to get sent to Guantanamo or something, but my opinion is the thing he fears most is being sent back home."

"Hey, I'd like to talk to him first," Cale said. "You think he'd speak to me?"

Behan smiled. "If I were in the room with you, probably, yeah."

Meeker told Behan, "You sparked on Max Bernecker's name. I saw it in your eyes."

"Me, too," Beemer said.

McGill and Cale also nodded.

Behan explained, "It wasn't the name itself so much; it was the nationality: German."

The MPD detective explained how Morozov had sneaked into Poland and obtained a forged European Union identification card as a Polish national. From there, he'd moved on to the U.K., established residence, and legally changed his name to Edward Kingsley. Then he crossed the Atlantic to his ultimate goal, the U.S.A.

Beemer chuckled. "Being a white guy with a name like Kingsley, he probably had an easier time getting a green card than most folks."

"That was pretty much what he said. You know, after a bit of persuasion."

McGill asked, "You didn't get physical with him, did you?"

Behan shook his head. "We just led him through some of his darkest nightmares. He's really afraid of being sent home."

"Who's we?" McGill asked.

"My Russian translator, Katerina Orlov, and me. She's an old friend, another State Department brat who traveled the world with Mom and Dad. Anyway, what struck me about the name Max Bernecker is that not everybody ran to the West when the Soviet Bloc crumbled. More than a few of the Communist elite in East Germany beat feet for Russia. Maybe one of their offspring is over here plying a family trade, too."

Cale nodded. "I wouldn't be surprised at all."

Working things through his mind, McGill said, "So there's a chance the Kremlin is ripping off American lottery games … and maybe this Pavel Morozov has been skimming money he's supposed to kick back to Moscow?"

"I can see that," Behan said. "It would explain why he's so afraid of going home. Stealing from us Americans is good, clean fun. Swiping cash from the bosses in Moscow, well, that'll get you killed."

Cale said, "It's more than just larceny. The propaganda value would be enormous if the secret ever got out: 'The hapless Americans can't even protect their foolish games of chance. We can take anything we want from them.'"

"The SOBs," Meeker said.

McGill came up with an even darker scenario. "What if the oligarchs are doing more than just lining their own pockets?"

"Like what?" Beemer asked.

McGill said, "Like using the money to fund foreign agents working in our country, either their own people or, say, guys who wear circular tattoos on the right hands."

Cale Tucker let out a soft whistle.

McGill told Detective Behan, "Suggest to Mayor Bullard that you give Pavel Morozov to the CIA. Maybe they can swap him for one of our people the Russians are holding."

"Good thought," Behan said, "only I'm fresh out of CIA contacts."

"I can help," Cale said.

"Who's looking for Max Bernecker?" McGill asked Meeker and Beemer.

Meeker said, "We thought that was best left to the Maryland

State Police."

Beemer added. "Of course, if he shows up here in town, we just might grab him."

"With the MPD being available to help," Behan added.

McGill asked Behan, "You all right after that Miz Smith's shooting, killing that guy?"

Behan said, "Yeah, I'm fine. That dude looked like he could change a truck tire without using a jack. If he'd sneezed, he would have broken the woman's neck. I didn't lose *any* sleep."

McGill said, "Okay then. Lunch is on me, everybody."

He took his own lunch to Patti's office. He wanted to update her. Let her forward whatever she thought was relevant to her successor in the White House.

The missus wasn't overly fond of tube-steak, McGill knew. She'd politely down one in several delicate bites if a family or political occasion called for it, but she never partook of one on her own. That being the case, McGill put the platter holding his lunch and the cup of Coke at the mini conference table in her office, a distance of ten feet from the chairlady's desk.

As McGill approached Patti, she asked, "Have you already had one of those things or even a small bite thereof?"

McGill shook his head.

"Very well. Kiss me quickly before the aroma drifts this way. I don't want to associate your lips with steamed beef."

McGill laughed, kissed her, and retreated to his meal, saying, "I hope the steamy part is still all right." He sat and began to eat.

Watching from a distance, Patti asked, "Has Cale gone back to his job?"

"It's fair to assume he has, though I can't say for sure since I can't see him from here."

"And you have something to tell me or you would have kissed and run."

"I'd never do such a thing, and I do have some news to share."

McGill filled Patti in on all the facts, surmises and suggestions that arose during his conversation with his comrades.

"How do you know the Russians are holding any of our people?" she asked.

McGill realized he'd made a slip-up on that point. Trying to cover, he said, "I must have heard Galia muttering something when she came out of the Oval Office."

"The two of you haven't been together in the vicinity of that room for over two years," Patti reminded him.

McGill looked upward as if hoping for divine intervention. Then coming clean he said, "You do talk in your sleep a little bit, not at length, or very often, and I've never noticed anyone in our bedroom who might have overheard."

Patti sighed. "Thank you for softening the blow as much as you could. You're right, I'll have to give President Morrissey a call. She needs to know about these possible situations."

McGill said, "Or you could leave a message for Galia and let her carry the water."

"You're right," Patti said with a smile, "let Galia do it. Maybe I'll make that my motto."

"Not for everything, I hope."

McGill wolfed down his dogs and chased them with the Coke.

"I'll be on my way now. No need to kiss me again. I'll stop for a dental cleaning before I go home."

Patti interdicted his exit with a raised hand.

"Wait a minute. On a personal matter, did Cale change your feelings for good or ill regarding Abbie's interest in him?"

McGill said, "I like him. He's smart as a whip and polite for the most part. I just don't like to see kids — young people — rush into things."

"So let them live together for a few years before they make any commitments?"

McGill thought about that for a moment. "Right, just so long as they feel no need to share any complaints in fine detail."

Patti said, "From what little I saw and what you've told me, this Detective Behan sounds like an interesting fellow."

McGill stepped over to the office door and opened it. "Yeah," he said, "but he's way too old for Abbie."

Café Un Deux Trois — Manhattan

Welborn Yates entered the Midtown restaurant shortly before 1:30 p.m. He was wearing his USAF service dress uniform. He took off his hat as he stepped indoors, per protocol. He had two changes of civilian clothes at his hotel room. He was prepared to spend a week or longer in New York City. He'd cleared that with FBI Director Benjamin. It felt both odd and exhilarating to be on duty away from home — albeit only 204 miles by air.

Most military officers and their families would have had a number of foreign and domestic postings over a ten-year period. He'd lived a 15-minute drive from the White House during that same time. That situation had made things much easier on his married life, and he saw far more of his twin girls and participated in their school and other activities more often than most military officers.

The price for all that convenience was the intermittently nagging feeling that he hadn't paid nearly as much of his dues as most of his colleagues. Any time he started to belittle his service, though, Kira gave him a good verbal smack to the chops.

She'd tell him, "You just remember who helped to avenge the deaths of Keith Quinn, Joe Eddy, and Tommy Bauer. You think about that and how much it eased the suffering of their families. There might not be much justice in the world, but you helped to bring some to them."

There were times when Welborn felt sure that his wife could have been a cold-blooded assassin for some government spook shop if her life had taken a different turn.

Welborn had the feeling that Major General Ibrahim Boutros

of the Royal Jordanian Air Force would also be in uniform, but he spotted a lean fellow with closely cropped salt-and-pepper hair and a neatly trimmed goatee wearing what looked like a Pierre Cardin suit sitting at the bar and waving to him.

He walked over to the man and said, "General Boutros?"

The man nodded, stood, and extended a hand in greeting. He took a quick look at the medals on Welborn's uniform as if he were reading a résumé. There weren't many decorations, but there was one of the best.

Shaking Welborn's hand, the Jordanian said with a hint of an English accent, "It is an honor to meet you, General Yates. We have a table waiting."

A waiter joined them and led the men to a table at the rear of the restaurant. The lunch hour crowd, for the most part, had gone back to their offices and shopping. The waiter took their drink orders. He offered suggestions for meals and they were accepted.

Once they were alone, Boutros said, "They know me here. We will have the privacy to speak freely, provided we do not have occasion to raise our voices."

Welborn told him, "My mother taught me how to behave in public, and my wife reinforces those lessons as needed."

The waiter brought Boutros a Virgin Mary and Welborn a bottle of Perrier.

The Jordanian raised his glass, "To new friends and lasting alliances."

Welborn touched his glass to the one Boutros held. "Amen."

They sipped their drinks, and Boutros said, "The video of you saving the life of the woman in Washington was brought to my attention. You behaved as I hope I would have, and now I see you wear your country's Air Force Cross. May I hear how you earned that honor?"

Welborn hesitated just a second, but said, "Sure."

He told his fellow officer about the car crash that killed his three friends in Las Vegas and how he never gave up looking for Linley Boland, the car thief who'd taken their lives and ended his career as a combat pilot.

"I didn't capture the guy," Welborn said, "nor did I kill him. But I put enough pressure on him to flush him out of hiding. That gave other criminals who were also looking for Boland the opportunity to ram his small boat with their much bigger boat. The police found only pieces of Boland in the water, one of which was his head, making a positive identification."

General Boutros nodded at the outcome. "This is a very good story. It has an appropriate ending, one collision begetting another."

Welborn said, "It provided some satisfaction for all of the people Boland had wronged, including me. I wasn't expecting a medal, but the Air Force decided I was instrumental in bringing justice to a man who had killed three of our officers."

Boutros nodded. "I think your superiors acted correctly. I commend them and you."

Welborn nodded. "I've also gotten congratulations from members of other branches of our armed forces: the Army, the Navy, and especially the Marines."

"Ah, yes," Boutros said, "Marines would appreciate such an outcome."

The waiter brought their lunch orders: grilled chicken for Welborn and farfalle pasta for Boutros. Bidding the diners to enjoy their meals, the waiter left them alone. Each man sampled his fare and said it was good. Then they got down to business.

Welborn said, "Had you heard your tattoo design had been misused before I brought the idea to you, General?"

"Please call me Ibrahim, and may I call you Welborn? A lovely name by the way."

"Thank you, and you may."

"To answer your question, yes, I'd heard of others using my idea. At first, it was only said to be worn by other combat pilots, and I was flattered. Then I heard its use had caught on with certain civilians. I wasn't entirely happy about that, but then my wife suggested it might be a proud sign of patriotism, and how could

I criticize that? In truth, I couldn't. So I mostly forgot about the matter."

"Until I brought it up?" Welborn asked.

"Actually, it came to my attention by way of a special agent from your State Department's Diplomatic Security Service. His name is Lonnie Tompkins. He told me he was working with an NYPD Detective Lily Kealoha. A very pretty name, I must say. The detective was doing a favor for a fellow named Deke Ky, whom I have learned works for James J. McGill, your former president's husband."

Welborn had to smile at the length of the informational chain. "Yes, I went to see Mr. McGill on the day I pulled Ms. Booker out of harm's way. He's also the person who gave me your name."

"The USAF has assigned you to this investigation?"

"No, I'll be resigning from the military in the near future and going to work for the FBI."

Boutros took that in and nodded. "Still working in service to your country."

"Yes."

"So, how do you propose I tell the difference between the people who are honoring my tattoo design and those who are profaning it?" Boutros asked.

Welborn said, "I wondered about that on the flight to New York. By the time I landed, I thought I had an answer. I called the medical examiner's office in Washington. I'd heard they'd taken photos of the tattoos on the hands of the two men their police killed. I asked if they could enlarge the images without losing too much resolution. They did and texted me the results."

Welborn took out his phone and pulled up an enlarged photo.

He handed the phone to Boutros and said, "Tell me what you see."

At a glance, he said, "This is my design and well rendered." Then he noticed a discrepancy. "There is something more here. It looks like a teardrop only …" He looked up at Welborn. "It's a drop of blood. That was not my idea."

"You think it might just be a mistake, a slip of the hand by the tattoo artist?" Welborn asked.

Boutros took another look and shook his head. "The rest of the work is meticulously done."

"Swipe up on the image and look at the next tattoo," Welborn said. "It's the second assassin's tattoo."

Boutros spotted the drop of blood immediately and also its difference. "This desecration is just a bit bigger."

"I noticed that, too," Welborn said. "So I called the medical examiner and asked if she could tell if there was a noticeable age difference between the two dead men. She said the difference was obvious. The bigger blood drop was on the younger man. Does that suggest anything to you, Ibrahim?"

The Jordanian closed his eyes momentarily as if a headache were coming on.

"It tells me, Welborn, that these people and their recruits are growing bolder. Less afraid of openly declaring who they are. The consequences of that … well, we've already seen examples in your country."

Welborn said, "Yes. So, Ibrahim, as you go about your rounds at the UN maybe you can spot some individuals wearing a roundel tattoo, and if any of those tattoos has a blood drop that's noticeable to the naked eye something very bad might happen quite soon."

"I have lost my appetite," Boutros said.

"Me, too, but please allow me to pick up the check. I'm the guy who's asking you to call the FBI director if you spot a bad guy. Or several of them for that matter."

"She will take my call?"

"Yes, I've already made that arrangement."

Boutros got to his feet and extended a hand.

Welborn rose and shook it.

"I am very angry and more than a little saddened by all this," Boutros said.

Welborn told him, "If it makes you feel any better, I thought of getting a roundel tattoo of the U.S. flag. In fact, I still might."

Boutros said, "Do so before you leave your Air Force."

Welborn returned to his hotel room. He called FBI Director Abra Benjamin and shared the news about the blood-drop addition to the roundel tattoos. Then he briefed her on his conversation with General Ibrahim Boutros.

"You're convinced he'll help us?" Benjamin asked.

Welborn told her, "My greater concern is he might strangle anybody he sees at the UN with the bad-guy version of his design."

Benjamin produced a humorless laugh. "Let him do a few of those and it might have a salutary effect."

Welborn gave a polite chuckle and said, "The general is also career military. I'm all but certain he will take our discussion up the chain-of-command, probably all the way to the top."

"Jordan's king, you mean."

"Yes, ma'am. Having had the opportunity to watch two presidents work, may I suggest you call President Morrissey and ask that she call the king of Jordan? Get his majesty prepped before he hears General Boutros' request to help us."

After a pause long enough to make Welborn wonder if his connection had been dropped, Director Benjamin said, "Very savvy move, General. It almost scares me how politically astute you are. I'll call the White House right away, and if the president doesn't take my call promptly maybe she'll take yours."

M & W Private Investigations — Washington, DC

Marvin Meeker opened the door at his and Beemer's place of business. Detective Sergeant Dalton Rivers of the Maryland State Police had come calling. Just looking at the man, Meeker knew that Rivers felt uneasy being in someone else's jurisdiction. Meeker couldn't resist twitting the man.

"You bring your gun with you?" he asked.

Rivers face tightened. "I was told I could. I have your mayor's word. She was also the one who told me to come down here."

Meeker answered noncommittally. "Well, then."

He gestured to Rivers to step inside.

Doing so, the Maryland cop asked, "You think she'd go back on her word?"

"Mayor Bullard? Never." Meeker shook his head for emphasis. "Still, you never know. She's a busy woman, getting the word out to the police department might take a day or two, and there are thirty-eight hundred cops in the MPD. Might take a while for the word about you carrying your gun to circulate to every last one of them. You probably want to be on your best behavior."

Rivers' frown deepened as Beemer, who'd overheard everything, stepped out of his office and said, "Marvin's just messing with you. Returning the warm welcome you gave us the first time we met. Come on in and have a seat. You want something to drink, I'll get it for you."

Moving to Beemer's office, Rivers asked, "You got sparkling water?"

"Sure, you want a glass?"

"A can or bottle will do."

"I'll be right back. Don't let Marvin get under your skin too much."

Playing along with Beemer's lead, Meeker gestured to a guest chair. "Have a seat."

Rivers sat, and Meeker took the chair next to him.

"Is he the good cop and you're the bad one?" Rivers asked.

Meeker nodded. "Yeah, most times. That's our natures. We knew each other in college but never said much beyond 'Hi.' We were both at the MPD training academy together, too. By then, we'd ask each other how things were going. We worked different areas on patrol, but when we both made detective at the same time, we got put together. By that time, we'd gotten to know each other and had become friends. We each knew our role and liked it."

Stepping back into the room, Beemer had caught that last bit. "We *usually* play the same roles, but there are times we improvise."

He handed a chilled bottle of San Pellegrino sparkling water to Rivers, gave one to Meeker, and kept one for himself. Beemer sat behind his desk, raised his bottle and said, "*È meglio essere temuti che amati.*"

Meeker looked at Rivers and asked, "You dig Italian?"

Rivers shook his head.

"My man just said, 'It's better to be feared than loved.'"

Rivers smiled. "Oh, yeah, Machiavelli. You want all of what he said, it was, 'It is better to be feared than loved, *if you cannot be both.*'"

Meeker looked at Beemer and they both laughed.

Beemer said, "The man knows his Machiavelli."

"Just never heard it in the original tongue," Rivers said.

He took a hit of his San P. and his hosts did the same.

"The man must've have gone to college," Meeker told Beemer.

"University of Maryland, Baltimore County," Rivers said. "Made my mama and daddy proud."

"Good for you," Beemer said. "Now, tell us if you've had any luck finding Max Bernecker."

Every sign of good humor departed Rivers' face. "I can't find that SOB anywhere. For all I know, he went back to wherever the hell it was his ancestors came from."

"My guess on that one would be Germany," Meeker said.

"Maybe Austria, possibly Switzerland," Beemer added.

Rivers got the feeling his hosts were showing off, making fun of him.

The sense of camaraderie began to dissipate.

Until Beemer told Rivers, "It's okay. We found him, more or less."

"How'd you do that," Rivers asked, "and what does more or less mean?"

Meeker said, "Jiminy Johnson invited Connie Parker and us to have dinner with him. Don't let it hurt your feelings, but he likes us better than you."

Beemer added, "What he did was give us Max's phone number and told us he'd back our play if we called him and told him we could use some money to take our business big time."

"So that's what we did," Meeker said. "We called the man, said we needed money, and he could call Jiminy as a reference. Which he did and called us back. Said we should talk."

"When and where are you meeting him?" Rivers asked.

Beemer looked at his watch and said, "Right here, any minute now."

Rivers asked, "You don't think he'll get just a bit suspicious when he sees the sign on your building here, the one that says 'Private Investigations?'"

Meeker said, "The man would have to be a fool not to turn heel and run."

Beemer added, "Only there'll be some MPD cops close by to keep him from getting too far."

As if it had been cued by a film director, the doorbell rang.

Meeker, Beemer and Rivers went to the front door.

Detective Aidan Behan was there. Four uniformed cops were behind him. Behan had a hand on the collar of a slim, blonde-haired fellow who needed a shave.

Meeker asked, "Is that you, Max?"

McGill Investigations International — Washington, DC

After having a fast-food lunch, Margaret Sweeney and her husband Putnam Shady were on the roof of the McGill building looking out at the city's skyline. The day that had started mildly warm was taking on a cool if not chilly note. Putnam felt the change in the weather more acutely than Sweetie because he was nursing a chocolate milkshake he'd carried out of Mickey D's.

"Remind me," he said, "what are we doing up here?"

"Checking out the rooftop hardware and the view. Jim said "I never took you for a techie, Margaret."

"I'm not, but it is useful to know what resources you have."

She moved to the parapet and looked down at the street to see whatever passersby, pedestrian or vehicular, were within view. Putnam approached his wife cautiously, pleading a tendency to vertigo and the desire to see their daughter grow up and start her own adult life.

Sweetie told him, "Stand next to me. I'll put my arm around you."

Putnam crept forward and Sweetie slipped her arm around his waist.

He said, "Guess we know what my choice is given the alternatives of mortality or proximity to the love of my life."

"You made the right move," she told him. "We're not going to fall, and if God wants us, we're not making things easier being up here. His reach extends all the way to the ground."

Putnam grinned. "I know that line. You got it from Bishop Sheen."

Sweetie smiled. "Yeah, I did, and why not? How many priests these days get recognized for doing something positive? Back in the day, the bishop won two Emmys for being the year's outstanding TV personality."

Putnam took a sip of his milkshake and said, "Now, that's something I didn't know."

Still looking down at the world below, Sweetie said, "I'm starting to worry, more than I usually do, about the world Maxi is growing up in. Seems like almost every day there's a new crisis of some kind, and, overall, the seams of civilization appear to be shredding."

Putnam sighed and replied, "Before I met you, that came across as the natural order of things to me. These days, I have to admit my outlook is more optimistic."

"Great," Sweetie said, "we're switching roles."

"That or you're ready to go to law school."

Sweetie laughed and kissed Putnam's cheek. Then she said,

"I've been thinking: I'd like Maxi to start taking some lessons in Dark Alley."

"What, you mean from Jim McGill?"

"Ideally, I'd like Caitie to teach her. She's the closest in age to Maxi. Caitie would also rip the beating heart out of anyone who seriously threatened her."

"Margaret?" Putnam said, as if unsure of what he'd just heard.

"You know what I mean," she said. "Caitie will do whatever's necessary to protect herself."

"That's pretty much what you just said without the graphic detail."

"Well, would you want our girl to do anything less, if she had to rely on herself?"

Putnam's answer came without delay. "No, I wouldn't."

"It's just too bad Caitie's in Paris, but I think Abbie could show Maxi the fundamentals."

Sweetie might've said more about the subject only a black SUV on the street below stopped directly opposite the front pedestrian entrance to the McGill building, and Sweetie got a very bad vibe from it. So did Putnam judging by the way he reacted. He hurled the capped cup, holding the remaining half of a large chocolate milkshake, in the vehicle's direction.

Sweetie had to pull Putnam back from a follow-through that would have carried him off the roof.

No pitcher in the entire history of Major League Baseball had ever thrown a more perfect strike. The moment a man holding a compact automatic weapon stuck his head out of the SUV's driver-seat window Putnam's missile impacted the crown of his skull. The lid flew off and the contents poured out.

The physical damage done was slight at best, but the psychological effect had to be stunning. The would-be shooter's head and eyes were drenched in a wave of sweet, opaque, viscous liquid, as if delivered by the hand of God. The gunman wouldn't be able to see where he wanted to shoot.

Not that he didn't try to clear his eyes with the back of a hand.

That was when Putnam screamed at him with a ferocity Sweetie would have thought impossible for her husband or any other human being. Someone else inside the SUV pulled the would-be shooter back into the vehicle. A moment later, it shot forward, speeding toward heavily trafficked Wisconsin Avenue and broadsided the cargo box of a fully-loaded city garbage truck.

The impact was fatal to the two passengers inside the SUV.

Neither of whom was belted in place, as was determined later.

Both of whom wore roundel tattoos.

Sweetie and Putnam took in the whole sequence, as did the security cameras on the McGill building.

Sweetie hugged her husband tight enough to make his ribs hurt.

Then she kissed him with a passion he'd remember until his dying day.

Which left Putnam with only one thing to say: "I was aiming for the windshield. I thought if I gummed that up, they might split."

Sweetie laughed and kissed Putnam again.

Then she said, "Don't forget about your scream."

Putnam said, "That one went right where I wanted it."

DC Central Detention Facility — Washington, DC

Detective Aidan Behan had Max Bernecker decked out in all the same restraints Pavel Morozov, aka Ed Kingsley, had worn. Max was led into the same interrogation room by the same corrections officer. The C.O. sat Max down with a hard shove and locked him into place. Then he was left alone to stew for a while. Let his imagination go to work on him.

Get him to wonder if all the legal niceties might not be observed.

Unlike the previous interrogation, Mayor Rockelle Bullard and Chief of Police Harriet Wortham were watching from behind a two-way mirror. Max suspected that someone was looking at him and began screaming the lyrics of the tune of "I Got Rights."

Behan let him rant until he grew hoarse and emotionally exhausted.

Then he and Cale Tucker stepped into the room.

Max tried to shrink away from Behan, but the restraints and the fixed-position chair left him no room for retreat. So he tried to escape by closing his eyes. He even began to hum loudly, a ragged, buzzy melody line unfamiliar to Behan.

"Is that supposed to be music," Behan asked Cale, "or is he just generating noise?"

Cale responded, "It's an old death-metal single circa the turn of the century."

Max opened one eye and focused it on Cale.

Who also added, "Can't remember if the group was anarchist or neo-Nazi."

"Not Nazi," Max snarled.

"That right?" Behan asked, taking a seat. "You prefer commie tyrant music? You grow up singing the State Anthem of the Soviet Union? You know, along with the Red Army Choir? Come on, you know the lyrics: *An unbreakable union of free republics. Great Russia has welded forever to stand.* Where else can you find lyrics like that?"

To the amazement of both Cale and Max, Behan started to hum the anthem's melody, which glorifying Communism or not still sounded better than death metal.

Breaking Behan's spell, Max yelled, "I'm American!"

The detective shook his head. "No, you're not. I saw it in your eyes. You recognized the melody of the old hammer-and-sickle song. Not one American in 100,000 would know it."

Max wasn't ready to give in. "Yeah? How'd you know it so well then? You a commie?"

"State Department brat. I can hum the anthems of ten different nations. Know a handful of lyrics from each of them, too. But you, you're what, a *Stasi* brat?"

Behan thought Cale would understand what he meant by that term.

For the benefit of the mayor and the chief of police, he elaborated. "The *Stasi,* the secret police, were very powerful in East Germany, and then they weren't. Some of their top scumbags had the grace to commit suicide. Others nipped at the heels of the Russians when they fled Germany, and some even became rich by sucking up to their old Kremlin masters."

Behan grinned and continued, "My guess is your family did okay in Russia. You were good with computers, got into the FSB and, lucky you, even got posted as an illegal to the United States. You could enjoy the good life here and then, wonder of wonders, you came up with the idea of looting American lotteries."

Max remained silent but the guilt in his eyes was clear.

Then Behan made an intuitive leap. "Hell, the U.S. isn't the only nation with lottery games. Just about every country that has electricity and running water has at least one big game. There's the EuroMillions, OZ lotto in Australia, and even Union Lotto in China. Did you get into all those games, too? Was *all* of this your idea?"

Max still didn't speak, but an assortment of muscles in his brows, cheeks, lips and chin began to spasm. It looked as if his face might fly apart at any minute. Behan held up a hand.

"Don't go to pieces now," he said. "I've got something to show you, and I'll be honest in saying it's horrible to look at, but you need to see it."

The detective took an iPad out of a suit pocket and started a video playing.

He turned it to face Max at just the right moment.

It was the exact point in time when Behan's shot hit the guy in Miz Smith's.

Max began to weep.

In a quiet voice, Behan said, "Now, *I'm* not going to shoot you. Nobody in U.S. law enforcement is going to shoot you. But your pals back in Russia, once the global lottery scam is revealed, they'll have to get rid of you one way or another, and I'm sure it won't be pretty. You're the only one who can connect the Kremlin with stealing huge sums of money from countries around the world."

Max finally spoke in a weak voice. "I'm not the only one."

The ghost of a smile crossed Behan's face. "See, you've already got something to trade. We'll get some federal officers to take custody of you, make sure you're tucked away somewhere safe, but in the meantime you can talk to my friend here about the computer end of things. He'll know what you're talking about. Are you good with that?"

Max nodded.

Behan stood up. He slid the iPad over to Cale.

"I'm going to leave that video here," Behan said. "In case you get forgetful."

Before Behan left, Cale had a whispered exchange with him.

"You think this guy is really Wendigo?" he asked.

Behan gave a minute shrug. "You're the high-tech guy. You tell me."

Washington Executive Airport — Clinton, Maryland

Leo had just pulled into one of Committed Capital's parking spaces at the airport, the first step on McGill's return to New York City when McGill got the call from Sweetie. Hearing her message, it was all he could do not to curse. Even with Sweetie on the line and knowing her distaste for profanity, he had to struggle. The battle between restraint and rage produced a low growling sound deep in McGill's throat.

The rumble, unlike anything he'd ever heard, alarmed Leo. "You okay, boss?"

McGill only shook his head.

Sweetie overheard Leo's note of concern and said, "Go ahead, Jim, let it out."

McGill limited himself to saying, "This shit has to stop."

"What shit is that, boss?" Leo asked.

McGill relayed what Sweetie had told him about a second

aborted attack on his office building. Without being asked, Leo pulled out of the parking lot and headed for highway I-495 and Washington, DC.

Sweetie told McGill about Putnam's improvised heroics and primal scream.

"God bless him," McGill said. "So two more of these bastards are dead?"

Sweetie said, "Yes. The way things are going, though, we might have to ask the city to close this block to vehicular traffic."

McGill gave a humorless laugh. "That or the city might ask us to move our headquarters to the North Slope of Alaska."

"Not while Rockelle Bullard is mayor," Sweetie said.

"Yeah, I suppose. Leo and I are on our way back. How far out is the security perimeter?"

"Two-block radius," Sweetie said. "You have anyplace special for us to meet?"

McGill thought for a moment. "Is Dikki still holding our old digs on P Street vacant?"

"The last I heard, yeah. He says it's going to hold historical significance someday."

"Not that any of us will live that long," McGill said. Then he sighed and added, "I suppose I shouldn't even joke about that at a time like this. Anyway, see if you can get the keys from Dikki and let's meet there. Are the phone lines still working?"

"I'll find out. Who are you thinking of calling?"

"We have offices around the country. Who knows how far these bastards will go?"

Sweetie said, "As far as they can probably. You think all this is because we're working with Ellie Booker?"

"Can't think of any other reason," McGill said. "Has to be spite and a warning to anyone else who might think of engaging with someone on their blacklist."

"We can't have that," Sweetie said.

"Yeah, we'll all have to keep our milkshakes at the ready."

***

McGill said goodbye to Sweetie and called Welborn Yates, hoping he was still in Manhattan. Welborn answered and said he was, noting the urgency in McGill's voice.

"What happened, and how bad is it?" Welborn asked.

McGill told him about the foiled drive-by attack and said, "I imagine FBI Director Benjamin has been alerted as to what happened already, but maybe she should contact Ambassador Mousa and get the Jordanians into high gear. See if they can put their hands on some of these creeps back home."

"I'll do that right away," Welborn said, "and with her permission, I'll see if I can get in touch with General Boutros again."

"We'll take all the help we can get," McGill said.

"What about Ellie Booker?"

McGill sighed. "I'll do whatever I can for her. If her yacht is safe to use, maybe she should head out to sea."

"Ironic, but not a bad idea," Welborn said. "I'll get cracking."

McGill called Patti next and said, "I'm okay."

"Thank God for that," Patti replied. "Edwina just brought me the news, and she was shaking like a leaf."

"I imagine," McGill said. "Can you spare the time to call the kids? I'll call Carolyn."

"Of course. I'll get right on it."

"Great. I know I'm probably wrecking your schedule, but after reassuring the kids, and suggesting strongly that Ken and Caitie stay right where they are in California and Paris, do you think you can get through to Jean Morrissey?"

"I think so, yes. The president has been very good about taking my calls. What do you want me to say?"

McGill said, "I was just asking myself, 'Why would these guys want to hit us twice?' If they have anybody in the country who can read English, they have to know by now that Ellie Booker is in New

York and running WWN. Even if the terrorists are still pissed at her, and I'm sure they are, more than ever for losing three of their people in attempts to kill her, going after us seems to be overkill. Their resources can't be infinite."

"There must be some reason they find compelling," Patti said.

"Yeah, there must be, and I just had an idea of what it might be. Ellie told me that when she confronted Dr. Hasna Kalil there were three men in the medical tent recovering from their own surgeries. Ellie also said Dr. Kalil seemed more interested in protecting them than saving her own life."

Patti intuited what McGill had in mind. "Terrorist leaders. Not just battlefield officers but command staff. At least one of them."

"Maybe *all* of them," McGill said. "Could be a drone strike got lucky and almost took out their joint chiefs. But maybe our military and civilian intelligence have yet to identify and understand how important these guys are."

Patti saw where McGill's reasoning led. "But the other side probably assumes we know. So they're lashing out in vengeance. Trying to show us they're still a viable enemy. That would explain a second attempt to shoot up your building and possibly kill as many people inside of it as they could."

"If you can't hope for victory, get all the vengeance you can," McGill said. "I don't know where our military took these guys or if they're all still alive, but if they are still breathing and in-country over in Syria or, say, at a military hospital in Germany, the soldiers working security had better be on high alert."

"I'll call the president immediately," Patti said.

McGill said, "Right. I'll take care of calling the kids."

"And Carolyn."

"Yeah. We have to make sure everyone stays safe."

Shortly before he arrived in Washington, and at the speed Leo was managing that wouldn't be long, McGill made one more call before reaching out to family. This one was to Ellie Booker. She made him wait for no more than ten seconds before picking up, but that was almost long enough to make him start shouting into his phone.

"What's up?" Ellie said by way of answering.

McGill provided a terse summary of the aborted attack on his building, including his speculation about the significance of the three post-op patients in the medical tent.

A silence almost as long as the wait for his call to be answered ensued.

"I never gave those guys a second thought," Ellie finally said. "You get into a war zone over there, it's not just military-age men getting shot or blown to pieces. It's everyone, kids to geezers."

"Only you said these individuals seemed particularly important to the doctor," McGill reminded her.

"No doubt about that," Ellie agreed. "I guess I thought it was just a medical concern. Wanting to make sure the local guys didn't suffer a set-back."

"How old were they?" McGill asked. "Was there anything about their appearances that set them apart from the crowd?"

"As far as I could tell, none of them was clothed, which makes sense for surgical patients. They were all covered toe to chin with sheets that might have once been white. Their eyes were closed. Two had beards, one dark, and the other gray. The third looked too young to shave."

"Was there anything about their features that suggested a family resemblance?" McGill asked.

That question occasioned another pause. Then Ellie said, "Their noses were all about the same size and shape. There were differences for sun exposure and other wear and tear, but, yeah, I'd bet they were three generations of the same family."

"So if one of them was important …" McGill said.

"Most likely, they all were."

"Call in that staff artist of yours," McGill said, "the one who did the likeness of the guy who sold you the motorcycle. Describe the post-op patients in the tent as best you can. Let's see what we come up with."

"You're thinking we should turn the sketches over to who? The military has the guys themselves."

"If they haven't been zipped into body bags already. Maybe they were photographed, they probably were, but why take chances?"

Ellie said, "You're right."

"Text me copies of the sketches. I'll see they get to the right people in government."

Ellie laughed. "Yeah, you're probably the only P.I. in the world who can do that. Did you ever distribute those pencil portraits of Motorcycle Man that I gave you?"

McGill said, "Sure did. Now, I have to call my kids and tell them to be careful, but I have one more suggestion."

"What?"

"That special forces soldier whose life you saved, Sergeant Desmond Jones?"

"Yeah?"

"Give him a call. Ask him if he has any top-end military friends who can keep you safe for the time being."

After a brief pause, Ellie asked, "How many and for how long?"

"As many as you can get for as long as necessary," McGill said. Then he added, "Double the security on your office building and home, too. The way I see it, these guys will be coming for you."

33rd Street Northwest — Washington, DC

Nelda Reed was doing her job writing parking tickets, but she was way behind. Not that there was a daily quota to reach. There was, however, an algorithm the city used to generate the *expectation* of how many people ignored the necessity of plugging their parking meters or overstayed the time limit for which they had paid. The math whizzes even had adjusted the expected number of violators by the months of the year, the time of day, and weather conditions.

That day, however, the motoring public seemed to be observing its civic duties with unusually high regard. Nelda had written only two tickets when the geniuses said she should have written twenty. If the city lost 90% of the revenue it expected from parking violations, well … Nelda had to think the first budget cut would be to the number of meter maids gainfully employed.

That notion made her wonder if General Welborn Yates — and wasn't that the fanciest name she'd ever heard — would really come through with a job for her. An FBI job at that. Yes, she had her military police experience and an associate degree certificate in law enforcement from UDC Community College, but would that impress anyone at the FBI?

Maybe with the general speaking for her. Otherwise, no way in the world.

Nelda was wondering what her future might truly be when she saw something out of the ordinary. Right there, parked two cars up, a fancy new Audi sedan, as sleek as a black cat, but somehow it still looked wrong to her. Okay, there was still time on the meter, so there was no call to write a citation, but the driver's door was slightly ajar.

In Washington, even in daylight in Georgetown, that was almost as obvious an invitation to car theft as a sign on the windshield saying: *Please steal me.*

Not having been born yesterday, Nelda approached the vehicle with caution. She left the driver's door just the way it was and peered through the window. The car had a push-button ignition … and the key-fob was right there on the console.

The whole thing smelled like bad fish to Nelda. She supposed it was possible someone could be so distracted as to leave the fob behind and the door open, but she wasn't buying it. Not for a minute. She looked behind her to make sure there was no approaching traffic. The street was clear for the moment.

She dropped down, proned out on her palms and toes, and looked at the underside of the vehicle, and there it was. Something that sure as hell wasn't standard equipment. The object was about the size of an 8.5x11 sheet of paper. Only it was about two inches thick and looked like it was made out of gray putty. Two wires ran from the gummy slab up into the engine compartment.

Nelda couldn't help but think the wires ran to the car's battery.

Using the physical fitness she'd acquired in Basic Training and hadn't let slip since, she popped up to her feet. She took out her phone and made a call. Not to the police, fire department or any other emergency agency. First things came first.

She called Martisse Jackson, her friend, fellow meter maid, and former comrade-in-arms, and told her to pass the word as fast as she could to all the other ticket-writers they knew not to open any car doors that were left ajar. She told Martisse about finding the bomb.

"Are you serious?" Martisse asked.

"I am. Don't let anybody open or close any car doors."

"What're you going to do?" Martisse asked.

"Call the police. Let them figure things out."

"Right. Good. I'll call all the ladies. Have them pass the word along."

"Say a prayer, too."

"Yeah."

Nelda called 911 and told the police operator where and when she found the bomb, how she suspected it might be triggered. Then she added the rhetorical question, "Who knows how many other of these things there are in the city?"

The emergency operator didn't speculate. She told Nelda to stay at a safe distance and wait for help to arrive. Nelda said she would. But she stayed close enough to shoo away any fool who might come along and either tried to steal the car or just politely closed the door.

Then she called General Yates. She'd memorized his number after writing it on her hand.

Part of the reason for that was to reassure herself she hadn't been imagining things.

The other part was it never hurt to have a friend in the FBI.

42nd Street — Manhattan

NYPD Detective Lily Kealoha and Special Agent Lonnie Tompkins of the State Department's Diplomatic Security Service introduced themselves to General Welborn Yates on the sidewalk outside the UN Building. Given that Welborn was still in uniform and had three stars on each shoulder, they knew he should be accorded a measure of deference. Still, they thought his tradecraft could use a little work.

The guy was clearly looking for someone, but he was being way too obvious about it.

"You want to be a little more subtle," Lily told him.

"About what?" Welborn asked.

"You're waiting to corner someone, right?" Tompkins said. "Maybe even make an arrest."

"Wait a minute." Lily said. She asked Welborn, "Do you even have the power to make an arrest, General?"

"I do. I'm with the Air Force Office of Special Investigations."

Lily nodded. "Another fed."

"I'm based in the White House."

"Uh-oh," Lily said. "Forget that crack about needing to be subtle."

"Local cops," Tompkins said with a sigh. "What're you going to do?"

The wisecrack earned him a gentle elbow to the ribs.

Stepping back, Tompkins added, "They can be touchy, too."

Welborn told both of them, "I'm not trying to be inconspicuous. I know how to do that. I'm waiting for General Ibrahim Boutros of the Royal Jordanian Air Force. I want to be seen so I don't inconvenience my fellow airman."

Tompkins asked, "You were a combat pilot, General?"

"For too short a time, but yes." Welborn raised his eyes. "There's

General Boutros now."

Welborn saluted his approaching counterpart.

Before Boutros arrived, Welborn asked Lily, "Who did you think I was looking for?"

She hesitated only a second. "A Syrian national we know only as the Motorcycle Man."

Welborn said, "I have the poster with the illustrated likeness of him. It's in my inside jacket pocket. I have the likeness memorized." After a moment's hesitation, he added, "In case the two of you haven't been alerted yet, there was another attempt of an attack on the McGill Building in DC just a little while ago."

That was news to the New York detective and the State Department man.

"How many dead?" Tompkins asked.

"Just the two attackers," Welborn said. "I don't have any more details just yet, but you, Detective, had better check in with your people about raising the threat level for this city."

"Right away," she said.

By that time, General Boutros arrived. He asked, "Am I interrupting something, General Yates?"

"Nothing we can't share with you, General." Welborn told his counterpart about the second attempted attack in Washington. "It might be a big help if we can get our hands on the Motorcycle Man."

Boutros formed a thin smile. "We have him."

"You do?" Welborn replied.

"He tried to seek asylum in the consulate of a neighboring country. They owed his majesty a favor and handed him over in light of the request we made."

Welborn asked, "Will he be made available to U.S. authorities for questioning?"

Boutros gestured with open hands. "That very matter is being discussed right now between your government and mine at a level far above our poor heads."

Welborn was wondering if FBI Director Abra Benjamin was

in on that powwow when his phone rang. He took a look at it only because it might be Kira calling, but he saw the caller was Nelda Reed. He was tempted to let voice mail handle it, but on impulse he told the others, "Pardon me," and took the call.

Nelda gave him the latest news from the nation's capital.

She'd found a car-bomb in Georgetown, and four others had been found by her meter maid colleagues so far.

One of which had exploded and had been audible to everyone in the White House.

In a mournful voice, Nelda told Welborn, "We lost Louise in that one."

Georgetown — Washington, DC

McGill had seen for years that traffic in town was growing progressively worse, but he'd never known a surface street to come to a complete and prolonged stop, barring a horrendous multi-vehicle collision that turned a major intersection into a spur of the moment junkyard.

The thing about auto wrecks, though, they were inevitably accompanied by the blare of sirens from emergency vehicles. Neither McGill nor Leo had heard anything more than the occasional frustrated bray of a car horn. So where were the fire department trucks and ambulances?

If they weren't needed, what the heck was the problem?

Leo swung the driver's door open and stood on the door sill for a better view. From that vantage point, he had just about an NBA center's point of view. "Don't look good, boss. Nobody's going anywhere."

"I'll get out and walk," McGill said.

They were only a few blocks from his office building. He wanted to get a look there before heading over to the old place on P Street where he'd meet Sweetie.

"Won't do any good," Leo told him. "The cops have got the

sidewalks barricaded up ahead, too."

"Maybe they'll let me through," McGill suggested.

"Whoa!" Leo exclaimed.

"What?" McGill asked.

"Just saw a guy in a bomb-squad suit come around the corner of our block. Maybe we both better stay put."

McGill shook his head and said, "Yeah."

He knew the warning about bombs: Even if the shrapnel didn't get you, the shock wave might. Then his thoughts turned even gloomier. Hell, he imagined, might be getting stuck in traffic for eternity.

Only in that case, there would be both horns and sirens creating an ear-splitting din.

It was only a gentle tap on the window to McGill's left, however, that gave him a start.

Then Leo said, "It's Abdul-Malik, boss. The driver for the Jordanian ambassador."

McGill asked, "You know him?"

"We spoke a couple times when you and Ms. McGill met with the ambassador."

McGill lowered the window and Abdul-Malik told him, "His excellency would like to speak with you, sir, if you can spare the time."

McGill had to smile. "I think I can."

Leo told him, "I'll stay close if traffic ever starts moving again."

McGill nodded. He followed the Jordanian driver two cars to the rear where a Mercedes limo with diplomatic plates was stuck like every other vehicle on the street. Abdul-Malik opened a rear door, and McGill slid inside. He noticed the partition between the driver and the rear seat was raised. Ambassador Mousa extended a hand and the two men greeted one another.

Mousa explained, "My man saw your man when he stepped out of your car. I hoped you might be able to speak with me, sir."

McGill said, "I thought our informal discussions had ended."

"As had I. That surely shows how little we know of our futures."

"I'll go along with that," McGill said, "but maybe you know more than I do about what's going on down the street. Leo said he saw a man in a protective bomb-suit."

Mousa asked, "You have heard about the car bombs?"

McGill winced and shook his head.

"Your police and other agents have found eight so far. Only one has detonated, killing one of the women the city employs to issue fines for parking infractions."

"Oh, hell," McGill said, shaking his head.

"I'm told the alarm was sounded by another such woman. She has certainly saved many lives. However, your police officers and others will be extremely busy for some time."

McGill said, "Checking the whole city for other possible bombs. Starting with the ones they know about and working their way out from there."

"Just so. There have been announcements made online and by radio and television."

"All things I generally ignore," McGill said. "I'll have to start doing better."

Mousa nodded. "Such is the world, but I am glad to have found you. Given the situation, I would like to ask if you might deliver a message for me in confidence. I think you might be able to reach the appropriate authorities more quickly than I would."

McGill said, "As you pointed out, I am just a private citizen these days, Mr. Ambassador."

"I know. You are also the husband of the former president, who is close to your current president, but if you don't wish to act in that capacity, I will understand."

McGill needed no time to ponder, given the current circumstances.

"I'll help."

"Thank you." The ambassador took a moment to gather himself and said, "When the male tattoo artist was compelled to confess, he gave our intelligence people the name of a special forces soldier not a pilot who had betrayed his king and country.

"The tattooist and his late wife also had produced counterfeit roundel tattoos for other traitors we have identified. As a Jordanian, the tattooist will meet such justice as his king decrees."

Mousa paused for a moment. "There is something I must tell you now that wasn't mentioned before. The tattooist's late wife was not an Arab. She was a westerner. What we have determined only recently … she was a Russian."

"And he still killed her?" McGill asked.

"We think he may have been following orders, possibly from the wife herself."

"God help us all," McGill said.

"Would that it were so. From my government's point of view, however, we have to be both merciless and very careful. With a large Russian military force in neighboring Syria, we are facing a challenge unlike any we've known since making peace with Israel. If need be, we will defend our country against any foe, and we'll also hope for support from our friends, of course. But it would be much better if …"

The ambassador paused to search for the right turn of phrase.

"If everyone holds their fire," McGill said.

"Exactly."

McGill said, "You'll also be busy continuing to find people in your ranks with the wrong kind of tattoos."

Mousa said in a flat voice, "We will do our best to see they never harm us or our friends."

"Good to know," McGill told him. "I'll make sure your message reaches the White House."

"Thank you. You will be a less obvious messenger."

"Yeah. Assuming we ever get out this traffic jam. Then again, I think I have a pair of running shoes in my car."

The White House — Washington, DC

Patricia Grant McGill shook President Jean Morrissey's hand.

The two women met in the Oval Office. With them was Chief of Staff Galia Mindel. Chairman of the Joint Chiefs of Staff Marine General Robert Drummond, the country's highest-ranking uniformed military officer, was en route to the meeting. Having been warned of the city's traffic gridlock, the general was choppering to the White House grounds. He was expected to land shortly.

Mayor Rockelle Bullard was also on the way to the White House.

Her mode of transportation had two wheels instead of two rotors.

She was coming on a bicycle.

"Please take a seat, ladies," the president said, taking her own.

Patti and Galia sat.

The president said to Patti, "Please tell me what you've learned about —"

She was interrupted by her secretary buzzing in on the intercom. "Madam President, General Drummond and Mayor Bullard are here."

"Send them in, Marie," she said. "Ladies, let's rearrange our seating."

The president welcomed the newcomers, shaking their hands. She positioned Galia, Drummond, and Rockelle on a sofa. She and Patti took a facing loveseat.

The president said, "Let's start with—"

Her secretary interrupted again. "I'm sorry, ma'am, but Mr. DeWitt is here, and he brought Mr. McGill with him. Mr. McGill says he has a message for you from the Jordanian ambassador."

The president looked at Patti. She could only shrug.

"Please send both of them in, Marie."

McGill and DeWitt entered. Being familiar with the setting, each of them felt at ease taking a guest chair from in front of the president's desk and sitting next to their wives.

"Make yourselves at home, gents," the president said in a lightly mocking tone.

She told her husband, "The Jordanian ambassador sent Mr.

McGill. Who sent you?"

"FBI Director Abra Benjamin," DeWitt said. "She's stuck in traffic. Also a bit annoyed that she doesn't have her own helicopter."

The president turned to McGill. "How did you get here, Jim?"

"Jogged, while calling my kids and my ex."

"Nice multi-tasking." Turning to DeWitt, she said, "Madam Director will have to get a pair of sensible shoes. All right, let's look at this mess chronologically. As I've heard things, today's first terrorist act was the assault on Mr. McGill's place of business. Please take it from there, Jim."

McGill related the story as he'd heard it from Sweetie.

Everybody in the room smiled upon hearing the details and laughed when the president said, "The milkshake throw heard around the world."

They nodded when the president turned serious and added, "I'll have to see what presidential commendation I should award Mr. Shady. Alright, what's next?"

DeWitt told the president, "Chronologically, I think it was the call from City Parking Officer Nelda Reed finding the first car bomb in Georgetown and being alert and suspicious enough not to set it off."

"That was damn fine work," General Drummond said. "Word I've received is she's former army, military police. She's in line for some sort of recognition, too."

"From the city as well as the armed forces," Rockelle added.

DeWitt resumed his narrative. "Ms. Reed called General Welborn Yates, whom she met in the course of her official duties. She told him what she'd found. He called Director Benjamin. She called me, and here I am. Oh, one more thing. Ms. Reed also called a colleague and warned her not to touch any cars with slightly open doors. The friend passed on the warning down the line of her coworkers. It's fair to assume that she saved a number of lives with her warnings."

The president said, "I've heard that there was one car explosion. Someone didn't get the warning in time?"

Rockelle answered. "Madam President, the MPD has received word that some of the booby-trapped cars had cash left on the driver's seat as an enticement. We suspect that was the case in the car that was detonated."

Jean Morrissey shook her head. "This is just horrible. We have to make somebody pay for all this. I take it the person who set off the bomb has yet to be identified."

Rockelle said, "My people tell me the parking violation officer who worked the area of the explosion is Louise Kearny. She's missing and is the suspected victim, but physical analysis will not be possible. The bomb blast was so powerful that no identifiable remains were found."

Moving on with a pained sigh, the president asked, "What's next?"

DeWitt said, "General Yates also told Director Benjamin that he heard from Jordanian Air Force General Ibrahim Boutros that his country has taken custody of a fellow called The Motorcycle Man, possible real name Salih Wasem."

"What's his relevance?" the president asked.

McGill explained the man's sale of a motorcycle to Ellie Booker and how Ellie suspected him of setting up the ambush of Sergeant Desmond Jones and her.

McGill added, "It recently occurred to me, Madam President, that Salih Wasem might also know the true identities of the other three men on whom the late Dr. Hasna Kalil performed surgery that day."

"Why is knowing that important, Jim?" the president asked.

"If three of the terrorists' most important people fell into our hands by happenstance, that would explain the scale of this reprisal. The way I see things, this has to be more than just getting back at Ellie Booker. Dr. Kalil may have been important to our enemies, but she couldn't have been *that* important."

Patti added, "Allowing for the possibility that there are other facts Jim doesn't know."

McGill nodded. "Right."

The president turned to General Drummond. “Your opinion, Bob?”

“It could go either way, Madam President, but I’d be inclined to agree with Mr. McGill on this one. The last report I’ve had on the three men we took out of that tent is the oldest guy died and the other two are expected to recover.”

“You and I will discuss their disposition later. Does anybody have anything else?”

Rockelle said, “I’ve got something. I mention it only because it involves another foreign individual.”

“How’s that, Madam Mayor?”

“A man calling himself Ed Kingsley, who was involved in an attempted robbery of a Miz Smith’s convenience store here in town, was the winner of a $2 million lottery prize.”

“Why would someone who won that kind of money commit a small-time stick-up?” Galia asked.

Before Rockelle could respond, McGill held up a hand. He didn’t speak at first. He looked to everyone else in the room as if he were having a religious experience, an epiphany.

Then he said, “Madam Mayor, was this the same store where Samuel J. MacCray bought his winning lottery ticket?”

Rockelle nodded. “Yes, it was.”

“Maybe Kingsley came into the store to steal the video file of that transaction, not petty cash,” McGill said.

“What’s this all about?” the president asked.

Rockelle began to sense where McGill was going and said, “It might be about a foreign connection, ma’am. Under interrogation by Detective Aidan Behan, Edward Kingsley admitted that his real name is Pavel Morozov. ”

“Russian?” the president asked.

“Said he’s Belorussian from Minsk,” Rockelle said.

“Owned and operated by Moscow,” General Drummond explained.

McGill said, “Madam President, that brings me to the last thing I learned today, courtesy of the ambassador of the Hashemite

Kingdom of Jordan, Fayez Mousa. He said the kingdom's security people have found a husband-and-wife team of tattoo artists who do work for terrorists in that part of the world. The man is a local person; the woman was a Russian."

"Was?" the president asked.

"The husband killed his wife as the king's security people were closing in. So we have a Russian and the next-best-thing-to-a-Russian involved in terrorism and a plot to loot the lottery system. You put those two things together and what do you get?"

President Jean Morrissey's jaw tightened. "You have the American people, via a lottery game and Russian hacking, financing a terrorist effort to destroy their own country." She looked around the room, focusing on Patti, McGill and Rockelle.

"Thank you all for coming. Your help has been critically important."

All three of the people who'd been complimented understood they'd also been dismissed. Galia, General Drummond, and Byron DeWitt would be staying. Upon leaving the building, Mayor Bullard retrieved her bicycle and said goodbye. Jim and Patti were about to leave the White House grounds on foot when Patti's personal Secret Service agent, Daphna Levy, caught up with them.

She asked McGill, "Are you armed, sir?"

McGill shook his head, and Daphna handed him her Sig Sauer P229. She kept her H&K MP5 submachine gun. Then she asked McGill, "Would you rather I walk point or drag?"

The streets were still gridlocked.

"Whichever you think is called for at the moment," McGill said.

"Point," Daphna said, "but please listen closely for anyone coming up from behind. Especially anyone who's running. Give me a yell before you open fire — if you have the time."

"Will do," McGill said, tucking the Sig Sauer into a jacket pocket.

Daphna moved a dozen paces ahead of the former First Couple.

Patti quietly asked McGill, "If things are really as bad as they seem, shouldn't you have that gun in your hand?"

McGill shook his head. "I can get to it quickly. Also, you can bet, as crazy as things are right now, that the cops, the FBI, and maybe even National Park Service Rangers have snipers on rooftops throughout the city. They'll all be on edge, too. Maybe one of the younger recruits sees the former president standing next to a guy with a gun in his hand, and the kid doesn't remember me or recognize who I am."

A shudder passed through Patti. She pulled McGill closer and said, "Okay, maybe I should have the gun."

M & W Private Investigations — Washington, DC

Meeker, Beemer, Sammy MacCray, his wife Francine, and Dexter Wiles, Esquire, were at the private investigators' office building discussing their position vis-a-vis that of Constance Parker as to how the lottery jackpot for which they both held tickets should be divided.

The suggested starting point, naturally enough, had been a fifty-fifty split. Francine, however, had pushed for seventy-five twenty-five division in Sammy's and her favor. After all, she said, shouldn't they get additional consideration for pain and suffering in securing funds that were rightfully theirs?

Dexter Wiles said, "There is precedent for recompense owing to emotional distress."

"Yeah, that," Francine said.

"But asking for such consideration sets up another hurdle for us to clear," Wiles said. "If the judge were to think we were being greedy, he might *lower* our award to less than an even split."

"A judge can do that?" Sammy asked.

"Judges can do just about anything they want, as long as they don't fear having their decisions reversed by a higher court or step so far out of bounds they lose their jobs."

"Doesn't seem right," Francine said.

Meeker laughed. "At least half the people in *any* court case will think the decision was wrong."

Beemer added, "If a judge is really at the top of his game, both sides will walk away shaking their heads."

"Unless one of them, of course, is on his way to prison," Meeker added. "There's no walking away from that."

Before things could go any further, Mayor Rockelle Bullard, recently back at her office, called with bad news. She got right to the point, in her usual fashion, "Marvin, Big Mike, I've got bad news for your clients."

With the call on speaker, the clients heard that. Before either Sammy or Francine could object, Wiles asked, "What sort of bad news, Mayor?"

"Our local prosecutors, after interviewing the robber who survived the incident at Miz Smith's and talking with computer experts who've looked into the matter of the two tickets with the winning numbers, have decided that both of those tickets were the products of illegal contrivance."

Meeker translated, "The fix was in."

"I know that," Wiles said angrily. "So, Mayor, are you saying my client's ticket is worthless?"

Francine began to cry. Sammy looked like he'd been sucker-punched.

Rockelle said, "No, it has value as evidence in a criminal case. Once the streets are cleared, I'll send Detective Behan to take custody of it."

Meeker and Beemer looked at one another and sighed.

Dexter Wiles, though, wasn't having any of what the mayor said.

He told her, "No."

Silence held sway for maybe five seconds before the mayor said, "What do you mean 'no'?"

Everybody at M&W Private Investigations other than Wiles was also waiting for an answer to that.

The attorney said, "My client purchased that ticket legally.

Whether there was an intent to defraud by any other party is immaterial. He bought the ticket: he owns it. It may not be seized by any outside party."

Meeker and Beemer smiled at each other, enjoying Dexter Wiles' show of bravado.

Mayor Rockelle Bullard, however, wasn't amused. "You have heard of subpoenas, haven't you, Counselor?"

"Do your worst," Wiles said.

Rockelle said, "No, no, Dexter. I'm going to do my *best,* and I'll make your head spin."

The mayor broke the connection. For a moment, there was silence in the room.

Then Francine said, "If the damn thing isn't worth a nickel, why are we gonna fight the mayor? She'll win in the end anyway."

Meeker and Beemer were beginning to see where Dexter Wiles was going.

They were even thinking their old boss might be in on the gag.

Sammy and Francine didn't have a clue.

Dexter Wiles explained to his clients: "Your lottery ticket might not award you several millions of dollars, but it could be worth, maybe, up to one million dollars."

"How?" Sammy asked.

Dexter Wiles turned to the investigators, curious as to just how intuitive they were.

Beemer said to Sammy and Francine, "You ever hear of the word collectible?"

Meeker added, "People will pay all sorts of money for a historic piece of paper."

Beemer took the next step. "Old Dexter here just made sure your lotto ticket is about to become famous, what with starting a court fight with the mayor over it. Social media will be all over the story."

Meeker said, "Which will only make it more valuable. Of course, being a lawyer, Dexter isn't doing all this out of the goodness of his heart. We'll all be taking our cuts of whatever that ticket sells for."

Sammy sighed and nodded. "That's only fair."

Francine looked like she didn't think so.

Dumbarton Oaks — Washington, DC

Patti's feet were sore by the time she and McGill approached home. Traffic had begun to clear, but Leo was still stuck on a gridlocked block. McGill had offered to personally transport the missus the final quarter-mile, honeymoon style or fireman's carry, whichever she preferred.

She passed on both choices with small thanks.

"Let me know when you can arrange for travel on the wings of angels," she said.

"You'll know that time has come when I get my halo," McGill replied. "Meanwhile, how about I give you an arm to lighten your way?"

Patti took McGill up on that offer and asked, "I won't slow you down if you have to make a quick grab for your gun, will I?"

"Nah, I practice distracted quick-draws all the time."

With whom, Patti was about to ask when both she and McGill saw Daphna Levy sprint toward their house. McGill told Patti, "I'm going to run now. Stay as close behind me as you can."

He had the gun in hand now, and for the life of her, Patti couldn't see how he'd done that. McGill took off, racing to support Daphna in whatever danger she might face. There was no such thing as competition sprinting in high heels, so Patti kicked off her new Christian Louboutins and began to run.

Even pounding the pavement in nylons, her feet began to feel better. Still, she was unable to stop as quickly as McGill just had. She feared that she would slam into him, maybe knock him down or more likely bounce off her husband like a rubber ball. Neither thing happened. McGill turned, extended an arm and wrapped it around her.

He gathered her to him as if he'd just stepped through their front door and was providing a welcome-home hug. Only he still had the gun he'd magically produced in hand. Patti was somewhat reassured when she saw him stick it back in his jacket pocket.

"False alarm," McGill said. He nodded toward their house and its circular driveway.

Special Agent Daphna Levy was barking at Detective Aidan Behan. He stood outside a silver Subaru Outback and had his badge in hand. He and Daphna weren't quite conversing at a shout, but the back-and-forth was intense enough to hear fragments at a distance.

McGill suggested to Patti, "Why don't you do the peacemaker thing?"

"Who's the plainclothes cop?" she asked.

"Detective Aidan Behan, the guy you said sounded interesting."

"Okay, and what will you be doing?"

McGill looked down at his wife's unshod feet. "Fetching your shoes."

When McGill made it home with Patti's shoes in hand, he found his front door open. He was nearly tempted to pull the Sig Sauer out of his pocket again, but the vibe wasn't at all menacing. Especially after he stepped inside and he heard Patti speaking French in a genial tone and a man replying in the same language and manner.

He found them both in the kitchen sipping drinks: Patti a chablis, Behan a ginger ale.

"All's well?" he asked.

"Must've been a temporary power outage," Patti told him. "Daphna's checking with Potomac Electric."

Behan said, "The gate was open when I arrived. That didn't look right. So I drove in, parked, and checked the exterior of the house. Everything was locked up and looked okay, but I decided to stay on the grounds and hope you weren't out for the night. The special agent thought I was some sort of miscreant. I showed her my badge and we talked things out."

Patti told McGill, "The detective came to see you, Jim. Police business, he said."

"No signs anybody tried to get in even if he didn't succeed?" McGill asked.

"Not a scratch," Behan replied. "The special agent said she has people en route to do a top-to-bottom check."

"Good," McGill said.

Patti said, "Aren't you going to ask just what the detective wants, Jim?"

McGill looked at his wife. "Remember how I said at the White House there might be a connection between the Russians scamming the lottery and the terrorists with the tattoos?"

"Yes."

"And Mayor Bullard told us Detective Behan interrogated a man named Pavel Morozov."

Patti said, "I remember that, too. The detective and I were just discussing the matter."

"In French yet," McGill said. "Well, if my guess was right that the Russians are using lotto loot to finance bad guys in our country, who should we talk to first about that?"

"Pavel Morozov," Patti said.

"Before the feds jump in and spoil the fun for all us local cops," Behan said.

Behan was playing on McGill's history in municipal law enforcement for sympathy.

McGill knew that, but he didn't mind.

He only asked, "You want me to play the good cop or the bad cop?"

DC Central Detention Facility — Washington, DC

As it turned out, Detective Behan wanted McGill to play both roles, good cop and bad cop. Even more than that, he wanted to see if McGill could both impress and scare the foreign agent with his status as the husband of a former president. McGill wasn't sure he'd been all that notable, but was willing to give it a try.

It had been a long time since he'd interrogated anyone, but as Detective Behan had said once you'd done it, you never forgot how. McGill understood the implicit challenge Behan had handed him: *Show me what you've got, old man.*

Okay, he wasn't ancient. Even so, he still wanted to measure up.

Morozov was already locked in place when McGill entered the interrogation room.

He sat down and said, "You're way past the point of asking for a lawyer, right?"

"*Da.*"

"I don't speak Russian. You could curse me in your native language if you want, but if you do, I'll recognize your tone. Being profane won't help you. I'll just leave and send Detective Behan in to continue the questioning."

Morozov leaned forward and said in a quiet voice. "That man murdered Vassily."

"Murder is a legal term in this country. No American court would ever apply it to what the detective did. It would be accurate, however, to say he killed your companion. That should tell you something important about his character."

"What about you?" Morozov asked. "Have you ever killed anyone?"

McGill didn't dodge the question. "I once shoved a man through a window."

"Killing him?"

"Well, he was trying to detonate a bomb at the time. He succeeded but only after he'd started to fall. It's impossible to say whether he was blown to pieces in mid-air or after he'd hit the ground. Either way, he didn't suffer for long."

Morozov drew the appropriate inference. "You're saying I might suffer for a long time."

"Depends on what bothers you. From what I've heard, you're

going to be locked up for the rest of your life. It's only the conditions of your incarceration that are up for discussion."

The prisoner was about to reply when he caught himself, stared at McGill for a moment, and took another direction. "I recognize you now. I've seen photos. You were even mentioned in one of my briefings. You are приспешник. *Prispeshnik.* The Henchman."

McGill shrugged. "That's me."

"Why is someone of your rank interrogating me?"

"To show you how seriously the American government is taking this situation. If you help us, you might have books to read, decent food, maybe even a bottle of good vodka on New Year's Day."

Morozov began to think about that, taking too long for McGill's liking.

The guy was trying to figure out all the angles he might play.

McGill got up. "Then again, if you're of no further help, well, nobody on this side of the world is going to miss you when you're gone. I'll send Detective Behan in. He's just outside."

McGill's hand made it to the doorknob before Morozov called out, "Wait!"

With his back still turned to the man, McGill asked, "For what?"

"What is it you want to know? I may not have anything you want."

Turning to look at the prisoner, McGill said, "We want to know how long you've been running your lottery frauds, how much money you've stolen, which games are involved, how many countries have been touched by this kind of theft, and most of all a complete list of the terrorist organizations you are funding with this money, and how you make the money transfers to them.

"All that and any other questions that may arise," McGill added.

McGill knew that intelligence professionals would have more questions for Morozov, ones that he would never think to ask.

The man's mouth formed a bleak smile. "You would have to keep me in a cell forever if I told you all that. If I were even able to do so."

"Like I said," McGill told him, "all we're talking about here is how miserable you want to be for the rest of your life. Oh, yeah, there is one more thing. If we get the answers we want from other sources before you decide to talk, you're going to be in a very bad way. More than a few prisoners in our super-max prisons … well, you can guess what happens to them."

He stepped out of the room and left Morozov to ponder the horrors.

Dumbarton Oaks — Washington, DC

When McGill got home, he found his daughter Abbie waiting for him in his living room. It wasn't unusual for her to drop by once or twice a week, but never this late. A grad-student at Georgetown University, she had an apartment of her own near the campus. She also continued to have around-the-clock protection from the Secret Service, as did her siblings Ken and Caitie. That measure of top-notch protection helped McGill to sleep well at night.

Still, seeing Abbie sitting alone now, even within the confines of his own home, raised a sense of alarm in McGill. Something must have gone wrong somewhere. But with whom, and how bad was it?

McGill sat next to his eldest child, took one of her hands, and only said, "Tell me."

Something must have happened to Carolyn, he thought, and that was why Patti wasn't sitting there with Abbie. The inner cluster of the McGill clan needed to work out their feelings before Patti lent whatever comfort she could.

McGill's intuition missed by a mile.

"I'm in love," Abbie told her father with a beatific smile.

Now he really wished Patti was in the room with him.

"Anybody I know?" he asked.

"Of course, you do. Patti's already told me that."

"Cale Tucker," McGill said. "I have heard his name mentioned, and I think you've come to an awfully quick conclusion."

To McGill's surprise, Abbie nodded, "I've been wondering about that myself. I don't consider myself impulsive."

"Nor do I," McGill said.

"But, Dad, my heart says this is the right guy."

"I'm all for heart health," McGill said, "but I favor giving your mind a vote, too."

Abbie took McGill's free hand in hers. "I've already told Cale about my Dark Alley training, and I said if he breaks my heart, I'll turn him into tapioca."

McGill smiled. "That's my girl. How'd he take that threat?"

"He said he'd give me a head-start by beating himself up if he ever disappoints me."

"Did he look like he meant that?"

"Yes. Then I even went a step further and called my baby sister in Paris."

That one caught McGill by surprise. "You talked to Caitie about romance?"

"Only because she's made calls to me on the same subject."

McGill noted the use of a plural — calls — and all he could think was, "God help me."

"And what words of wisdom did the young *auteure* provide?"

"She just cheered the news and said to tell Cale that if he ever broke my heart, she'd beat him up, too. And, of course, he knows implicitly you'd do the same. All that and he didn't even flinch."

"For a slim guy, he sounds pretty stalwart, and if you love him, how could I object?"

Abbie kissed McGill on both cheeks. "Good. That makes it unanimous."

"Patti and me?" McGill said.

"And Mom and Lars."

McGill laughed. "You thought I'd be the holdout and the others would gang up on me?"

"Dark Alley of the heart," Abbie said. "You fight to win."

McGill hugged his daughter, and the two of them stood up. "Your special agent is lurking nearby to take you home?"

"Cale's waiting two minutes out."

"Ready to make a quick getaway if the occasion arose?"

"I told him I could get a ride with the Secret Service, but he insisted."

"Good for him. Another gold star on his potential son-in-law score sheet."

"Oh, yeah, Dad, one more thing. Cale gave me a message for you."

"What's that?"

"He said he's getting very close to whoever had that second winning lotto ticket printed."

"That's great," McGill said.

"Only he also said it looked like it's going to be someone really scary."

McGill hugged Abbie and told her, "Start teaching your boyfriend Dark Alley, and give me a call the minute you need any kind of help."

CHAPTER 6

Dumbarton Oaks — Washington, DC
Wednesday, February 6, 2019

McGill sat up in bed so suddenly he startled Patti awake, too. "What is it?" she said, eyes wide and putting a hand on her husband's arm. "A family emergency? I didn't hear the phone ring."

McGill kissed her cheek and shook his head.

"I had an idea … in a dream, I think."

"An idea?" Patti said. "I hope it's a world-beater after almost making my heart stop."

McGill put an arm around Patti's shoulders and drew her close. "Sorry about that, but it was pretty much a reflex on my part."

"So what is this bed-shaking idea? Tell me before it slips away from you and you have to go sleep on the sofa in your hideaway."

McGill withdrew his arm from Patti and steepled his hands in front of his face. "Okay, what I was thinking is … we have to grab or more likely deport all of the terrorists who were involved in setting up the car-bombs here in Washington yesterday."

Patti blinked and stifled a yawn. "Okay. You figured out how to do that?"

"Yeah," he said. "We put Ellie Booker and General Ibrahim Boutros on television first thing in the morning." He glanced at the bedside clock and saw it was 3:18 a.m. "Well, the next thing in the morning anyway. Let's say 7:30."

"Why General Boutros?" Patti asked.

"He's the Jordanian Air Force pilot I mentioned at the White House, the first man to wear his nation's flag roundel tattoo. General Boutros is well and truly pissed that terrorists have misappropriated and defiled his idea."

"Ambassador Mousa didn't tell you that last part."

"No, Welborn did. He sent me a lengthy text updating the situation shortly before I came up to bed. My mind must've been working on things since my eyes closed."

Patti sat up, adjusted a few pillows, and leaned back against the headboard.

"Go on," she said.

Working things out in his mind, McGill said, "Basically, we have to sort out which guys with the roundel tattoos are the good guys and which are the bad guys. That seems like it could be a difficult problem at first. There's a slight difference in the designs, but getting guys with diplomatic immunity to sit down for a close examination seems iffy at best."

"Even so, you've thought of a solution?" Patti asked.

"Two," McGill said. "I'd bet General Boutros could identify suspicious tattoo wearers intuitively, the way an honest cop knows who the crooked cops in his station house are. Not to say people are bloodhounds, but in certain situations, you can almost *smell* who the bad guys in blue are."

Patti donned a mirthless grin. "The same thing applies to corrupt politicians."

"Anyway, that's the first step," McGill said. "Have Ellie interview General Boutros on national television. Put the word out that he and some trusted colleagues will be looking for people who have no right to wear the tattoo and who will be prosecuted when they return home."

Patti chuckled. "That should produce a long line of characters with diplomatic privilege heading for the airports. Here in Washington, in New York, and in consulates throughout the country.

But you said you had *two* solutions. What's the other one?"

McGill said, "I told you about Ambassador Mousa informing me that his government had arrested a tattooist in Jordan who inked a lot of the bad guys. We have Ellie say that guy is talking, giving up the names of all his clients. Which is probably not a bad guess. Not only is the guy squealing about the locals, he's also providing the names of other tattooists in neighboring countries, and they'll soon be ratting out their clients, too."

Patti chuckled. "You can be devilish at times, James J. McGill."

"All in all, it's not a bad plan," he conceded. "Just one thing worries me."

"That being?"

"Some of the die-hards might take a pass on making a getaway and try to go out in a blaze of … well, mass murder."

"So go call the FBI," Patti told him. "I'll wake up the president."

McGill said, "I will, but I need to talk to Ellie first. She's the one with the WorldWide megaphone."

"Holy shit!" Ellie Booker said, after answering McGill's call and hearing what he had to say. "This is the best story idea I've ever heard. This will be the biggest news story of the year, and it'll be all mine. In terms of being the on-camera reporter anyway. How'd you like to become my executive producer, Jim McGill?"

He laughed. "Not my thing in any way, shape, or form."

"Okay, but I don't think I could get that Jordanian general on-set all on my own."

"I'm going to call General Yates to help out there," McGill said. "He's my next call. What time will you need him?"

"If we go on air at eight, I'll want to see him and General Boutros by seven. We can script the questions I'll ask him. He can tell me if there are questions he can't answer. I'll ask the questions anyway, of course, I just won't push things."

"Make sure you don't lose the man before the cameras go on,"

McGill said.

"You sound like a producer already."

"Give me a heads-up once things are set, okay?"

"You bet. Hey, you know, you never sent me a bill for your services."

McGill told her, "The meter's still running."

Welborn Yates was asleep in his New York hotel room when McGill called. He gave Welborn the details of his plan, including Ellie's phone number in case he needed to reach out to her. "This is a little late in the process," McGill said, "but do you think you can reach General Boutros in the next few minutes and get him to go along with the plan?"

McGill could hear the excitement in Welborn's response. "He's a patriot, and fighter pilots are always ready to scramble at a moment's notice. Nothing gets the adrenaline racing like an unexpected call to duty."

"So that's a yes?" McGill asked.

"Absolutely."

"One more thing," McGill said.

"What?"

"Call FBI Director Benjamin, too. The Bureau should have special agents watching all the right embassies in DC and consulates around the country, not just the UN"

"Right. Anything else?"

"Godspeed, Welborn."

Former Secret Service special agents were less thrilled to be awakened in the depths of the night, but Deke Ky still managed to answer his phone by its third ring.

"This better be good," Deke said by way of hello.

"I need to reach Detective Kealoha," McGill said. "Can you give me her number?"

"I can do better than that," Deke mumbled.

A second later, a woman's sleep-fuzzy voice said, "Hello."

McGill said hello and apologized for calling at such an ungodly hour. Then he said, "I'm putting in motion a plan your department's top brass should know about." He outlined what he had in mind and added, "The NYPD should be on the watch for die-hards, especially after all the bombs that were planted here in DC."

Much more alert now, the detective said, "Yes, sir, we should. Thank you for the heads-up. When's this story going on air?"

"Eight a.m. WorldWide News."

"Right. I'll get on to my commanding officer right away."

"You need me to put any weight behind you?"

"You still have that kind of weight?" she asked.

"Personally, probably not, but my wife's talking to President Morrissey right now."

The detective laughed. "Always good to have friends in high places. I'll call you if I need any help. Grumpy here can give me your number."

Patti had just gotten off the phone with Jean Morrissey when McGill walked into her home office. He asked, "Just wanted to be sure. You got through to the president herself?"

"Yes. She's putting all the wheels in motion. The nation will be as prepared as it can be for any attacks."

"Good," McGill said. "I'm sorry to ask you this, but may I borrow your plane again? I think I should be in New York today."

Patti said, "You keep this up and I'm going to embarrass you … I'll buy you a plane of your own."

The White House — Washington, DC

Byron DeWitt walked into the Oval Office in tennis shorts and a Cornell University t-shirt. He didn't bother to wear socks or shoes. In that bloodshot hour of a still-dark morning, there was nobody around to criticize him. The Secret Service special agent watching the main door to the president's lair only grinned at him. Then he nodded in appreciation when DeWitt gave him one of the three cups of coffee he was carrying.

He took the other two cups into the Oval Office and sat down on the visitor's side of the Theodore Roosevelt Desk. He set a cup of coffee down in front of Jean Morrissey.

"Caffeine the way you like it," he said.

She replied, "You went to Cal, not Cornell."

"Huey gave me this shirt. He went to Cornell."

"Huey who?"

"Huey Lewis. His music still wears well for me."

The president nodded and took a hit of her coffee. "You know old rockers, do you?"

"Yeah. I can introduce you to some if you promise not to giggle girlishly."

Tired as she was, the president laughed. "I'll do my best."

"Patti McGill lit a fire under you?"

Jean told her husband the news.

He said, "Car bombs here in DC, and now undercover terrorists with diplomatic immunity. I'd ask what's next only I don't want to know."

Jean Morrissey sighed and stared at her coffee.

"You're reconsidering, aren't you?" DeWitt asked.

They both knew what he meant: whether to forsake a second term.

"Only if you agree and only if I don't see someone I can trust to do this job well."

"The first one's a given if that's what you want. The second one's ..."

"A real crapshoot," the president said.

30,000 feet over New Jersey

Jetting high above the Garden State, McGill took the risk of waking his wife again, but she answered on the first ring and was feeling more snarky than sleepy. "Miss me already, do you?"

"Always," McGill said. "Now that I'm more fully awake, I had another idea."

"The hits just keep on coming."

"This one is pretty good, if Jean Morrissey has her hockey-player game-face on."

"I feel that's a given."

"So what I'm thinking is, if these terrorist creeps are using the cover of foreign missions, let's put their homelands in a bad position. Maybe these countries can be persuaded or coerced into stripping the bad guys of their diplomatic status before they can leave the U.S."

Patti was silent long enough to make McGill wonder if the call had been dropped.

Even so, he waited long enough to hear her say, "You know, of course, that every foreign embassy has its spy contingent. The same goes for many secondary outposts."

"I do know that," McGill said. "I read it in a Daniel Silva novel."

"Yes, well, sometimes saboteurs and even assassins also pass through these environs."

"I'll bet they do, but tell me, please, if things have gotten to the point where out-and-out terrorists have become full-time staffers."

Patti replied. "Not during my administration, but I've been out of office for two years now."

"Would Jean sit still for such a situation?"

"No, not if she were directly confronted with such a reality."

"I'm pretty sure General Ibrahim Boutros will make that situation clear in short order."

"So your suggestion is?" Patti asked.

"Lean on any country that's knowingly sheltering in-house terrorists disguised as everyday personnel. Tell them to strip the creeps of diplomatic status and hand them over to the FBI or face some kind of economic or other reprisals. You know, like shutting down their entire diplomatic and commercial presence in this country. See how they like that."

"Kick them out of the club of nations, at least to some extent," Patti said. "I like that. Only I won't give it directly to Jean. I'll send it through Galia. We don't want to alienate the White House chief of staff. Otherwise, I'll get stonewalled someday when I want to speak directly to the president."

McGill said, "Hard to believe, but I'll take your word for it. You'll let me know what you hear?"

"Certainly. I'll be put on your payroll soon?"

"We'll negotiate your compensation when I get home."

Battery Park — Lower Manhattan

FBI Special Agent in Charge Leonard Wilkes, the top fed in the New York City Joint Terrorism Task Force, told McGill, "You're a civilian. You're owed a measure of respect as the husband of a former president, but you have no operational presence in anything that goes on in this city, today, tomorrow, or ever. You understand that?"

McGill hadn't been looking at Wilkes. The Statue of Liberty stood just across a narrow stretch of Upper New York Bay. Lady Liberty rose tall and awe-inspiring in the glow of the lights focused on her. McGill never tired of looking at this great symbol of the nation.

Leo, standing next to McGill, felt the same way.

As did Deke and Detective Lily Kealoha who were also present.

"Did you hear me, sir?" Wilkes asked.

Without looking at the man, McGill said, "I did."

"Good. Then I —"

McGill raised a hand, turned to look at the man, and asked him, "Do you know who the Bureau's next deputy director is going to be?"

"I beg your pardon." Then Wilkes understood he'd better answer the question. "No, I don't know."

McGill said, "I do. I was the guy who gave him his practical education as an investigator. Do you understand the subtext here, SAC Wilkes? I won't get in your way or that of Captain McKinney, but don't try to muscle me. You have more important things to do, and you'd be fighting way above your weight class."

Wilkes pointed a finger at McGill and was working out a rebuttal when he saw his NYPD counterpart, Captain Thomas McKinney, shake his head. Letting the fed know he wouldn't be getting any support from him. Wilkes let his hand fall.

He managed to find some words for McGill, though not the ones he'd been grasping for just a moment ago. "Please stay safe, sir. It'd be a shame to lose someone as *important* as you."

Wilkes left, figuratively and literally getting out of McGill's way.

Captain McKinney stepped forward and extended a hand to McGill. "I'm pretty sure the SAC just said 'fuck you very much.' Reading between the lines, that is."

"I think you're right, Captain. Detective Kealoha gave me your name. Good to meet you."

"So who's going to be the next deputy director of the FBI?" McKinney asked.

McGill knew the man was testing him, seeing if he'd just been bluffing.

"You saw the video of the man who saved Ellie Booker from the shooters in DC?"

McKinney nodded. "That's the guy?"

"It's his if he wants it."

"Good to see someone like that get a big job. He'll understand how things can be for the rest of us. Just between you and me, you're not armed, sir?"

McGill shook his head. "Left my firearms at home."

"Glad to hear that. You're not inclined to any foolhardy

impulses, are you?"

"Not as much as I once was. I can no longer leap tall buildings in a single bound."

The captain grinned and then turned to Lily. "Detective, you ride with Mr. McGill. Try to restrain any sense of heroics that might overcome him."

McGill told the captain, "Just so you know, I'm the guy responsible for getting everybody out of bed early today. I wouldn't want to see anybody … well, any of the good guys get hurt because I had a couple of bright ideas."

Captain McKinney nodded and said to Leo and Deke, "You two guys work for Mr. McGill, right? You help Detective Kealoha, okay? Mr. McGill might not think he's Superman these days, but this is Gotham City and he might still have a little Batman left in him."

McGill grinned. Then he turned to look back at Lady Liberty. The sun was just coming up, a minute or so after seven a.m., and the statue took on a new kind of glow. Less than an hour to go before Ellie Booker went on air with General Ibrahim Boutros and told the world …

A radio call came in over Lily Kealoha's police radio.

A gun battle had just erupted on the Brooklyn Bridge.

FDR Drive South — Manhattan

McGill told Leo, "We need a catbird seat view of the Brooklyn Bridge."

"Just give me an address and I'll plug it in," Leo replied. "Make sure y'all are buckled in, too."

They'd rented another Mercedes S-class sedan. The speedometer topped out at 160 mph. Unlike many other cars, this one came close to the boast. Still, triple-digit speeds were for the race track. Making time in the most densely populated urban area in the country during the morning traffic rush was another matter entirely.

Nonetheless, Lily Kealoha gave Leo an address, he entered it in the navigation system, and they were off. *Tout de suite.* Deke was up front with Leo, just like the old days. Deke had been through variations of this drill before and had learned to have complete faith in Leo. McGill, seated in the rear with Lily, had also been there and back.

For Detective Kealoha, however, it was a whole new world. Likely without conscious awareness, she reached out and took McGill's hand. He only returned a bit of pressure. When Leo was in the zone, you didn't want to distract him.

The former winner of three NASCAR races threaded all that German metal through spaces that seemed too small for a Moped. Inevitably, Leo needed to vary the speed. Even so, he left every other driver on the road sucking his fumes, and he never caught a single red light.

Arriving at the address Detective Kealoha had given him in what seemed like no more time than you'd need to boogie across a dance floor, Leo pulled into the building's driveway. He looked at the others and said, "Damn, that was the most fun I've had since Mama made me stop racing."

Deke socked Leo on the shoulder, and the three passengers exited the vehicle.

McGill asked Lily, "You think we can find a good Democrat in this place?"

She laughed. "Are you kidding? The last Republican in town left with Rudy Giuliani. What are you looking for?"

"A place on, say, the tenth floor of a high-rise with a great view of the bridge. That and a telescope, if anyone here has one."

"No problem." Lily showed her badge to the guy at the front desk, who turned out to be a retired NYPD cop. He knew just the woman they needed. Then he asked, "This have anything to do with the trouble on the bridge?"

McGill nodded. "It occurred to me that the NYPD down there might need a spotter."

"Damn good idea."

With nearly the same efficiency Leo had displayed, the doorman got them set up. The only thing that was asked of them was that the apartment owner, a silver-haired woman, wanted to stay and watch the proceedings.

McGill told her, "This might be the stuff of nightmares."

The woman was not dissuaded. "I used to be an ER nurse."

"Okay."

Thanks to the doorman's scrounging, McGill and Deke each were given a pair of binoculars, a Nikon and a Bushnell; Lily had the use of a tripod-mounted Celestron telescope. Luckily for the three of them, high-rise Manhattanites had a fascination with high-end optics.

All three of the observers at the view window saw the same thing. The cops and the feds had both ends of the bridge blocked, as far as letting vehicles enter the span. They were letting cars and trucks off the bridge one at a time, making the drivers step out. Two or more of the people with badges and automatic weapons checked the interiors, and then each vehicle was allowed to leave.

In the middle of the span sat a cube formed by eight white cargo vans. The Mercedes Sprinter Worker models, ironically. In the central open space was a cluster of men in dark blue coveralls. Some of them were armed with what looked like M4 automatic rifles. At least two of the weapons were mounted with grenade launchers.

The men with the weapons were watching the bridge and gazing up at the sky.

The others were on their knees cutting into the bridge surface with power tools.

The former ER nurse who owned the apartment edged close to the window and looking on with bare eyes asked, "Why attack the Brooklyn Bridge for Christ's sake?"

"It's a national historic landmark," Lily said. "There's symbolism at work here."

"And you can't drive a truck to Liberty Island," Deke added.

"Thank God for that," the woman said. "Why don't the cops just shoot right through those vans? They must have weapons that can do that."

"Could be the vehicles are packed with explosives," McGill said. "Setting off detonations is the last thing they want. It might take at least part of the bridge down."

The apartment owner pressed her nose against the window and started cursing a blue streak at the terrorists. "You lousy bastards!" she yelled.

Lily took her into her bedroom to calm her down.

There was work to do, and they didn't need any distraction.

"Okay, here we go," Deke said.

"Where?" McGill asked.

"Coming in from your left, maybe a hundred feet above the bridge."

Two police helicopters were approaching. Lily returned to the room, saw the aircraft, and said, "Aviation Unit coppers. They'll be armed to the teeth. They can do fast rope deployment but, Jesus …"

The two aircraft diverged as they flew over the white van blockade, one toward Manhattan and the other toward Brooklyn. Both choppers drew fire without being hit. Neither aircraft returned fire.

"Man, those guys in the choppers were lucky," Deke said.

Lily nodded. "They can't count on that again, if they make another pass."

Without looking away from the scene on the bridge, McGill told Lily, "Please get me the highest ranking officer you can reach down there."

Lily was going to ask what McGill had in mind, but Deke signaled to her, tapping his index finger against his opposite palm. *Make the call.* Then he steepled his hands prayerfully. *Please.*

"Try not to get that FBI jerk," McGill added.

Lily managed to reach Captain Thomas McKinney. McGill took the call and explained to the NYPD commander where he was. High enough to monitor the scene without having to worry about drawing fire.

"I'll get someone over there to join you right now," McKinney said.

McGill told him, "That's fine, but I have an idea that might help, and the sooner the better. Those guys behind the vans have just opened a hole in the bridge. I wouldn't be surprised if packing it with explosives comes next."

"Jesus, okay, we'll hurry up with something. What's *your* idea?"

"We need the Air Force and then some kind of gas that incapacitates people."

"The Air Force?"

"Yeah," McGill explained and added he'd heard the strategy had worked once before.

He also told everyone at bridge level to cover their ears as tightly as they could.

The cops, God bless them, didn't waste time debating the idea. The Air Force, praise to them too, also moved like lightning. Four F-15s out of the Stewart Air National Guard Base, only 60 miles north of the city, swiftly arrived in single file like a band of avenging angels.

Flying only 100 feet above the bridge, each plane laid down what was called a sonic boom carpet. A boom's intensity was greatest directly below the aircraft's flight path. The force had been known to shatter glass and dislodge roofing tiles. The physical consequences for human beings included fear, anxiety, distraction, headache, hearing loss, muscle impairment and loss of balance.

That was what could happen from a single sonic boom.

The bastards on the bridge got hit with four in close succession.

The men inside the barricade on the bridge went down like bowling pins. Things only got worse for them when canisters of tear gas landed in their midst. An NYPD lieutenant, a man named Mike Burke who'd been sent by Captain McKinney, arrived in the high-rise apartment with the perfect view just in time to see all the terrorists on the bridge writhing in agony like bugs on a hot griddle.

McGill handed the binoculars he'd been using to Lieutenant Burke.

He took a better look, smiled, and said, "Hell, yes!"

McGill left Deke to stand in for him with Lily and the rest of the NYPD.

He and Leo had to get to the WorldWide News Building.

WorldWide News Building — Midtown Manhattan

Leo worked his behind-the-wheel magic once again and got McGill to Ellie Booker's office building like the finish line at Daytona was in sight and he was making his move on Richard Petty. Going for the win by a photo finish.

All that and he pulled to a feather-soft stop directly in front of his destination.

"I really like doing this, Boss," Leo said. "I think competitions between top-end drivers using big city streets with all sorts of obstacles for their courses could make a real interesting TV show."

McGill had been ready to bolt from the car, but he paused.

"You're going to leave me, Leo?"

"Well, eventually, I suppose. All things must pass, right? But for the moment I'm just thinking of this TV idea as a sideline. During vacations, holidays, and like that."

"Uh-huh," McGill said.

"It occurred to me that Ms. Booker has her own TV network. Maybe you could put in a good word."

And McGill thought, why not? If he couldn't help Leo after all the time they'd been together, what kind of a self-centered wretch would that make him? He said, "I'll see what I can do, Leo."

He ran into the building, stopped at the security desk, and identified himself.

Ellie's producer, a young guy named Erskine Zenn, took the call from the security guy, and said McGill was on the all-access list. Even so, another security person, this one a female person, took him up to Studio 3-A and handed him off to Erskine Zenn just outside the studio control room.

The guy struck McGill as being no older than his daughter Abbie. Or Cale Tucker for that matter. He thought that a new generation was about to seize control of the country, not inch by inch but in leaps and bounds. McGill was old enough to take the rite of passage with some equanimity, but he wondered how the cohort looking at an upcoming 40th birthday was feeling.

Probably that the geezers who'd preceded them had held on to the reins of power too long, and the youngsters behind them were pushing ahead too fast.

The other thing McGill noticed right off was there were three guys of that in-between generation watching the show from the wings. They all had closely cut hairstyles and the type of lean fast-twitch musculature most commonly seen on racehorses. One of them had turned to spot McGill's arrival. The other two kept watch on more distant points of access to the studio.

Ellie had taken McGill's suggestion and brought in Special Forces people to help keep her safe.

Erskine gave a gentle tug on McGill's sleeve and led him into the control room. Closing the door behind him, he said, "We can talk now. Ellie just started her interview with General Boutros. So I'll have to keep one ear cocked that way."

"Understandable," McGill said.

"Did you hear anything about the attack on the Brooklyn Bridge?" Zenn asked.

"Can you keep your ears cocked in different directions at the same time?"

"Sure. Can't everyone?"

McGill thought no doubt about it: The generation caught in the middle was in big trouble.

But that was someone else's worry. He told Zenn about the part he played in the confrontation at the bridge. The young producer's ears might have been tuned to different stations, but both eyes were focused on McGill.

"You called in the Air Force?"

"I didn't. I suggested it to the police, and they made the call.

The idea wasn't even mine. I just remembered something a colleague came up with some years back."

"Resource mining," Zenn said. "That's almost as cool as original thinking."

McGill knew the comment was intended as a compliment, but it still made him feel old.

Nonetheless, the kid producer told him, "We've got to get you on at the next commercial break. I'm sure Ellie will want to hear from you."

"Ask the general if it's okay with him, too."

Zenn blinked as if that had never occurred to him, but he said, "Of course."

The producer excused himself to advise his staffers about the unexpected guest who'd be joining Ellie. As if by magic, a young female makeup artist appeared at McGill's elbow. He knew better than to argue about going on camera without makeup. He followed her to the chair where she worked her magic. Made him look ten years younger.

Too bad that effect hadn't been put in a pill yet, he thought.

When McGill stepped into the green room to await his summons to the stage, he found both Welborn and Detective Behan there. He shook hands with Behan, but Welborn just gave him a wave.

"The general got himself some new ink this morning," Behan explained. "He wouldn't shake my hand, either."

"That being said," Welborn told McGill, "here's what my tattooist did for me this morning."

He extended his right hand to display a roundel of the U.S. flag between his thumb and index finger.

McGill smiled and said, "Looks good."

Behan said, "Next thing you know, uniformed cops will have little badges tattooed on their hands."

"Not the plainclothes or undercover guys, huh?" McGill asked.

"Nah. We've got to be inconspicuous. It's hard enough not looking like a cop as it is. Some of the guys I know, if they got a tattoo that said who they really are, it'd be about halfway up their large intestine."

That rang true for McGill, too. He'd known cops like that. The brotherhood in blue could be highly secretive about their private lives … and now that McGill thought about it many air forces around the world also used blue as their predominant color.

He'd heard about the military diplomats at the UN who wore roundel tattoos on their hands, and there were probably more of them in the embassies in Washington and at consulates around the country. How many of those guys who had out-in-the-open tattoos that said one thing had another inconspicuous one that said something else?

If that were the case, might even General Boutros be among them?

Most military men and women didn't change sides, McGill knew, but treason had to be as old as warfare. He thought it would be a good idea to have American doctors go over every inch of Salih Wasem, the Motorcycle Man whom Ellie suspected had set up the ambush for her and Sergeant Desmond Jones. Mr. Wasem might have some informative body art on him.

Of course, the Jordanians might not hand Wasem over to the FBI.

Even so, General Drummond had said that the military was holding the two living big shots who had been recovering from their wounds in Syria when Ellie had barged into their tent. No doubt the military also knew where the body of the guy who died from his wounds was buried, too. All three of them could be closely examined for discreetly placed ink.

He'd have to talk with Patti about all this. If she thought his notions were worthwhile, she could take them to President Jean Morrissey. Or at least to Chief of Staff Galia Mindel.

Erskine Zenn opened the green room door and told McGill, "You're on."

He stepped onstage, shook hands with General Boutros and Ellie and told the world of his small part in the drama on the Brooklyn Bridge. He deflected credit to Leo, the building's doorman, the apartment owner, the NYPD, the U.S. Air Force, and General Welborn Yates, who'd introduced him to the idea of sonic boom carpet bombing.

Ellie laughed off McGill's self-effacement.

"So you were just along for the ride?" she asked.

"Maybe I stirred the soup a little," McGill allowed.

Ellie Booker's Office — WorldWide News Building

McGill took a seat in one of Ellie's visitors' chairs. The folding aluminum models had been replaced with sleek black leather chairs complete with armrests. McGill was about to comment on the upscale furnishings, but Ellie beat him to the punch.

"Zara dragged those chairs in here," she said, referring to her stunning new secretary.

"And you didn't object?" McGill asked.

"I got the feeling she'd have cried if I said anything critical. If she tries to lug in a matching sofa or even a small boardroom table, though, I'm going to fire her."

"Maybe you should give her advance notice on that last part," McGill said.

Ellie grinned. "Maybe I should call her in after you leave and give her a list of do's and don'ts. Only I'm not sure she takes dictation."

"Speaking of new hires, how are the special forces guys working out?" McGill asked.

"Now, them I like. Low key and deadly as pit vipers. What more could a girl want?"

"A DC cop," McGill suggested, referring to Detective Behan.

Ellie came as close to blushing as McGill had ever seen. "Yeah, him. I suggested we should have a drink, if you'll remember, and now he's holding me to it."

"He seems like a good guy: interesting, well-rounded, multilingual, and a damn smart cop."

"I'd ask you if he paid you to say that, only I know better. Anyway, he took the time and money to come back here, so, yeah, we'll have a drink and maybe even dinner."

McGill just nodded. He knew Ellie had a history of failed relationships, and he wasn't a matchmaker. All that being the case, he changed the subject.

"What'd you think of General Boutros?" he asked.

"The man's damn near as modest as you. I checked his public history before I asked him to come on. He's a genuine hero over there. There aren't many aerial dogfights these days, but the few he was in he won. He also blasted a bunch of enemy ground targets while avoiding anti-aircraft fire. Except for one time. He barely made it home on whatever the equivalent of a wing and a prayer is these days."

"So, all in all, he's one of the good guys?" McGill asked.

Ellie's eyes narrowed. "As far as I've found out. You have reason to think otherwise?"

McGill said, "Detective Behan made a comment about some cops being highly secretive about their personal lives. That resonated with my own experience. It all made me wonder if these tattoos worn by various nations' pilots aren't a little too obvious a sign about where their loyalties lie — except for General Yates who just had a U.S. flag roundel inked on his hand."

"He did?" Ellie stopped to think about McGill's point. "I agree with you about General Yates, and not just because he saved my life. Otherwise, I think it's possible you're right, even in General Boutros' case. The guy you'd least suspect always makes the best spy."

McGill said, "It's not really my line of work, but maybe you or some other interested party could take a look at the general's family history. Even if he's clean as a whistle, maybe his father was also in the military over there and didn't do too well in the wars with Israel back when Jordan was still one of their combatants."

Ellie took a pen and a pad of paper from her spartan desk. She quickly scribbled several lines of notes. McGill didn't think she was making a grocery list.

When she looked up, she said to McGill, "So you're just the guy who stirs the soup, huh?"

"Occasionally, I have a few ideas relevant to the task at hand. Once in a great while, I even have to throw a punch in anger. But I think I'm mellowing with age."

Ellie laughed. "You really crack me up. You once set fire to a giant thug in Paris, and I bet you'd do the same thing again if the need arose."

"Possibly," McGill allowed.

Ellie took a long moment to ponder another thought.

McGill didn't interrupt.

Then she said, "You've really helped me. I could have been blown to bits out there on my boat. Right now, I don't think those guys with the hand tattoos are half the threat they were to me a few days ago, and with the ex-special forces guys looking out for me, I'm not much worried at all. Again thanks to you. So I want to ask you one last thing."

"Go ahead," McGill said.

She told him of Hugh Collier's dying declaration that he'd killed Sir Edbert Bickford.

"What do you think that means for me?" Ellie asked.

Keeping a straight face, McGill told her, "You know what it means, Ellie. The proceeds of a murder can't be considered a legal inheritance. If what Hugh Collier said is true, he took possession of WWN illegally. So there's no way you could inherit the company from him legally, especially since you knew in advance what had happened."

Ellie said, "How about if I thought Hugh was BS-ing me about killing his uncle?"

McGill shrugged. "I'm not a lawyer. That kind of claim might insulate you from a criminal charge, but I'm guessing a shoe is about to drop, and some other party interested in running the company is going to tie you up in legal knots for years. Was Hugh the kind of guy who'd put you in that kind of fix?"

Ellie sighed. "There were times when we were the best of

friends and others when a knife-fight might have broken out."

McGill could understand both ends of that equation. He stood up to leave.

"How much do I owe you?" Ellie asked.

"What can you afford that won't be drawn on a WWN account?"

Ellie named a five-figure sum.

"That'll do," McGill told her.

Then he pitched Leo's urban race car idea to her. Ellie liked the idea — in concept — but she said it could encourage too many loons to imitate the pros and wind up killing lots of innocent people. The lawyers would never allow it.

Another showbiz dream shot to hell, McGill thought, but at least he'd tried.

As he was leaving, McGill heard Ellie buzz her secretary and said, "Send the cute cop in, will you, Zara?"

McGill's Original P Street Office — Washington, DC

Having been awake since the wee hours of that morning, McGill napped on the flight home, but in the Gulfstream G6 the flying time between New York City and suburban Washington, DC was 20 minutes. Adding in taxiing time, he caught another 40 minutes of shuteye. He trudged between the plane and his car.

As he climbed into the backseat of the Chevy, Leo suggested maybe they could trade in the good old Chevy for a Mercedes. Thinking that might soothe Leo's feelings, dispirited as he was to learn his showbiz dream wasn't going to come true, McGill said, "Sure, get something nice."

Knowing he was still valued, Leo took it easy getting to Georgetown, giving the boss another half-hour of rest. Waking up in front of the old building, McGill had a moment of temporal dislocation. He wondered if the last two years at the new site were all a dream. Climbing the stairs to his old third-floor office, he decided they weren't.

Former work sites looked impossibly quaint and cramped only after you'd moved on to bigger and better things. Nonetheless, there was a sense of homecoming when he stepped inside. Sweetie and Dikki were there. So were Meeker and Beemer, and even Her Honor Mayor Rockelle Bullard.

"Don't everybody inhale at once," McGill said. "We'll suck up all the oxygen."

Sweetie gestured him into his old office chair and said, "We did a lot of good work here. If it seems humble now, maybe that's good for us."

"Yeah," Meeker added, "but once you've had better, going back is not easy."

"Nobody ever launched a terrorist attack on us here," McGill said.

Rockelle said, "If you want to sell the new building to the city for a really good price, we'll buy it."

McGill shook his head. "No, thank you. Good memories are comforting, but it's better to make new ones than dwell on the old ones. Is there anything we can do to make the new building a less attractive target, Madam Mayor?"

"I've got some traffic engineers working on that," Rockelle said.

McGill said, "Good. Now, let's hope some software techies can make our lottery games harder to hack. It occurred to me that those thieves could have run the jackpot up to a billion dollars and then cashed in, putting the money to all sorts of malicious uses."

"That or just sticking it in one of those see-no-evil foreign banks," Beemer said.

"You guys and your clients are going to come out okay after the dust settles?" McGill asked.

Meeker said, "Dexter Wiles has a plan. Nobody will get rich, but our bank accounts will still look better than before. You still want your share, right?"

"I was thinking you could give it to the Howard University scholarship fund," McGill said.

Meeker and Beemer looked at each other and grinned.

"The man is slick," Meeker said.

"Knows we're not going to short our own college," Beemer agreed.

Sweetie said, "Deke called us, Jim. Gave us the lowdown. Explained that your contribution to the happy outcome in New York involved a bit more than you let on to Ellie Booker and her TV audience."

McGill shrugged. "There are too many people tooting their own horns already, especially in this town. We're not losing any clients, are we?"

"No. Esme's quite busy answering calls, in fact."

"At the new place? Is she safe?"

Rockelle said, "After what happened here and on the Brooklyn Bridge, just about every cop with a badge is out keeping watch. Same thing is going on all over the country. Big cities, small towns, everybody. The most amazing thing is how little politics is involved."

"A common enemy can do that," McGill said. "If we're all safe for the moment, I'm going home to sleep. I'll call my wife and see if she can leave work early."

Sweetie said, "She's waiting for you at home. We talked a little while ago."

McGill shook hands all around, went downstairs, and told Leo to do his no-red-lights-allowed trick.

Dumbarton Oaks — Washington, DC

Secret Service Special Agent Daphna Levy met McGill's Chevy at the front gate to his house's grounds. Leo stopped the car, lowered his window, and said, "How you doin', cuz?"

Sharing a surname, the two of them kidded about kinship but neither had gone to the trouble of ascertaining one.

Daphna peered into the car and saw McGill was asleep in the rear, his chin resting on his chest. She told Leo, "I know you're good at your job, but I thought that was more high drama stuff like you must've done in New York. Didn't think it included the easy-does-it rides."

"Like the champ often said, 'Float like a butterfly, sting like a bee.' You and me, we've got to be versatile. Everything okay around here?"

"All buttoned down. We have extra help for the time being."

Leo glanced through the windshield, "The inconspicuous sort."

"Yes, per Mrs. McGill's request."

"Well, let's get the boss inside."

McGill woke up groggy but felt the little charge he always did when he saw Patti.

He smiled and said, "Hey, good looking, can you put an old copper up for a while?"

She threw her arms around him, gave him a kiss and said, "Thank you."

He kissed her back and asked, "For what?"

Patti didn't tell him immediately. She closed the front door to the house and led McGill to the room that had been configured and furnished to resemble his White House hideaway. Had he been better rested, McGill might have taken that as a sign. As it was, he simply enjoyed the comfort of his old leather sofa and Patti holding his hand.

She said, "I am very grateful that you were able to help out in New York … from a distance."

"Deke gave you the lowdown, too?" he asked.

"He did. Who else got a report?"

"Sweetie."

"Of course."

"The FBI boss on the scene made a stink about asserting his authority."

"Good for him."

"I liked the NYPD people much better."

"As one might expect. What else have you heard?"

A shiver ran through McGill, pushing aside his fatigue for the moment.

"What else is there to hear?" he asked.

"Quite a bit, I'm afraid. Some of it is public knowledge via mass and social media. Other parts came from family and the White House."

"Family first, always," McGill said.

"Abbie called to say that Cale told her he was asked to return to the NSA, based on work he did independently of both the government and Committed Capital. Cale discovered that the second winning lottery ticket, the one Marvin Meeker and Michael Walker brought to your attention, was not the work of a disgruntled hacker after all."

McGill asked, "Who was responsible then?"

"In a word, China. They found out what the Russians were up to and threw a monkey-wrench into the works in the hope they could take over the scam at a later date."

"God help us," McGill said. "So the global cyber-war is definitely on."

"It is."

"And that's why Cale is going back to the NSA."

Patti shook her head. "He's not, at least not full time. He said he can't do work that he would never be allowed to share with Abbie."

McGill beamed. "God love that kid. I'm liking him more all the time."

"Me, too. Cale is, however, making himself available to consult with the NSA. Work out bugs in systems. Improve our cyber defenses. Even develop large scale strategies. Things he can talk about in general terms with his sweetheart."

"Always good to have topics for dinner conversations," McGill said.

"I also had a call from Mayor Bullard," Patti said.

"Regarding?"

"Constance Parker's new pharmaceutical. Michael Walker sampled it and told the mayor he thinks it could be a useful medicine, not just a feel-good high. Committed Capital tends mostly to look at computer science breakthroughs, but now I think maybe our portfolio should be broader. Some of my people are going to talk with Ms. Parker. We'll see if anything comes of that."

McGill nodded.

And Patti sighed. "And then there were the other events, as related to me by the White House."

"Yeah?" McGill asked.

"The military and our intelligence people have confirmed that the three men found in that medical tent in Syria are, or in one case, were members of the same family and among the top strategists for continuing terrorist activities in the event that their current plans fail."

"Well, I'm glad they're off the board anyway," McGill said.

"That is good, but we still don't know who their subordinates are or how capable the second tier is of putting any new plans into effect. We can already see some new diplomatic movements taking place."

"Like what," McGill asked, "if I'm allowed to know."

"We have no firm ideas of eventual consequences, but what's easy to see is that high-ranking personnel from embassies, consulates, and other offices around the country are being recalled, sent home. Many of them have already left the country. More than a few have roundel tattoos. Within a matter of days, the number could be in the hundreds. There's even talk at the State Department of severing all relations with a number of countries. With what we're learning from Pavel Morozov, it's likely even our relationship with Russia will be scaled back."

McGill whistled softly. "Wow."

"Indeed … and then there's the news that hits much closer to home. Not family but someone who's almost as close."

"Who's that?" McGill asked, his neck muscles tensing.

"Galia suffered a heart attack."

"She *died?*" McGill asked.

"No, thank God, but she won't be returning to work anytime soon."

McGill made the intuitive leap. "So what's Jean Morrissey going to do? Bring back her brother, Frank, to be the White House chief of staff?"

Patti shook her head. "Jean asked him, but Frank is still angry at her for being fired. He turned her down."

"So who else is there?" McGill asked.

Patti took both of McGill's hands in hers and, looking him in the eye, said, "Me."

ABOUT THE AUTHOR

Joseph Flynn has been published both traditionally — Signet Books, Bantam Books and Variance Publishing — and through his own imprint, Stray Dog Press, Inc. Both major media reviews and reader reviews have praised his work. Booklist said, "Flynn is an excellent storyteller." The Chicago Tribune said, "Flynn [is] a master of high-octane plotting." The most repeated reader comment is: Write faster, we want more.

You may read free excerpts of Joe's books, or drop him a line, by visiting his website at: *www.josephflynn.com.*

All of Joe's books are available for the Kindle or free Kindle app through www.amazon.com.

The Jim McGill Series

The President's Henchman, A Jim McGill Novel [#1]
The Hangman's Companion, A Jim McGill Novel [#2]
The K Street Killer, A Jim McGill Novel [#3]
Part 1: The Last Ballot Cast, A Jim McGill Novel [#4 Part 1]
Part 2: The Last Ballot Cast, A Jim McGill Novel [#5 Part 2]
The Devil on the Doorstep, A Jim McGill Novel [#6]
The Good Guy with a Gun, A Jim McGill Novel [#7]
The Echo of the Whip, A Jim McGill Novel [#8]

[continued ...]

The Daddy's Girl Decoy, A Jim McGill Novel [#9]
The Last Chopper Out, A Jim McGill Novel [#10]
The King of Mirth, A Jim McGill Novel [#11]
The Big Fix, A Jim McGill Novel [#12]

The Ron Ketchum Mystery Series
Nailed, A Ron Ketchum Mystery [#1]
Defiled, A Ron Ketchum Mystery Featuring John Tall Wolf [#2]
Impaled, A Ron Ketchum Mystery [#3]

The John Tall Wolf Series
Tall Man in Ray-Bans, A John Tall Wolf Novel [#1]
War Party, A John Tall Wolf Novel [#2]
Super Chief, A John Tall Wolf Novel [#3]
Smoke Signals, A John Tall Wolf Novel [#4]
Big Medicine, A John Tall Wolf Novel [#5]
Powwow in Paris, A John Tall Wolf Novel [#6]

The Zeke Edison Series
Kill Me Twice [#1]

Stand Alone Titles
The Concrete Inquisition
Digger
The Next President
Hot Type
Farewell Performance
Gasoline, Texas
Round Robin, A Love Story of Epic Proportions
One False Step
Blood Street Punx
Still Coming
Still Coming Expanded Edition
Hangman — A Western Novella
Pointy Teeth: Twelve Bite-Sized Stories